STRANGE
TUNNELS
DISAPPEARING

gary
ley

STRANGE TUNNELS
DISAPPEARING

seren

seren is the book imprint of
Poetry Wales Press Ltd
Nolton Street, Bridgend, CF31 1EF, Wales
www.seren-books.com

ISBN 1-85411-302-x

A CIP record for this title is available from
the British Library

*The publisher works with the financial assistance of the
Arts Council of Wales*

Printed in Plantin by Bell & Bain, Glasgow

part one

JOSE

1

I could still remember the dead dog hanging from the lamppost. It hung limply in the heavy Lima air; its shadow like a puddle on the sidewalk, large and rounded, darkening the already poorly lit street. I viewed it from a doorway, standing still for a second, taking it in; then, gathering myself, I walked towards it, stopping once to view the footprints along my path. They were coming towards me, becoming clearer. Like a detective I bent down and investigated them. Blood, I thought, unsurprised, knowing they couldn't have been water: in Lima it never rains. I looked up. I found myself staring at the last look on the dead dog's face. It was a snarling sort of look, the top lip curled up, the teeth clear. It was the perfect expression to greet the police.

It was a strange image to hold onto. Why that, of all things, why that? Is that where my crisis came from? What it grew out of? I'm not sure. All I know is that I was delving into the past, blurring through all the happy times, the easy times. It was as though my life experience was on a tape, which my mind was playing: fast forwarding, rewinding, stopping, starting, searching, sometimes stumbling on something that had rich possibilities. My first trip to Lima, perhaps. My first lecture at La Contute, the teacher training college. The evening walk up Calle Union. The discovery of the dead dog. The crowd. The police.

I know now that such recall is part of the crisis. Like the feeling of nausea and the panic and the way you indulge yourself, giving yourself time, deluding yourself until you see it as it is: a melee of trial and error, an array of leads and clues that draws you on and leaves you switching back and fore. The present. The past. The present. The past. There's always something there, something to empathise with. After all, you want to be distracted. You need that. So you consider the strangest things. The police, for example. The police at the scene of the dead dog. They had arrived the following day. Three policemen with a step ladder. I saw them from my hotel window. They joined the Church of San Francisco and the large colonial square and El Agustino, the shanty town climbing up the hill, and the drug dealers waiting for the tourists and the tourists marching away. The policemen made me attentive. I knew what they would see. I waited for them to clear the small crowd that had gathered by the lamppost. While they shouted, "Go on you. Get home! There's nothing for you here", I thought how I wasn't in favour of violence, how I wasn't in favour of killing, not even of killing dogs. Even so, looking at the scene and thinking of the dog made me realise how death and the threat of death could be used. It made me realise what a weapon it could be.

And the empathy? Well you almost become one of the policemen. You think how the task is new to them, how they can't work out their roles. How many up the ladder? Who should go up? Who should stay down? How should they handle the dog? Then you're away, breaking the scene down into symbols. Perhaps you start with the dog. To the police it must have seemed an unredeemingly wicked figure. It was more difficult assessing what it meant to the people. For it to have an effect it needed to be seen. If it wasn't seen first hand, it needed to be reported. Was a journalist nearby? There was no-one there after the police had dispersed the crowd apart from an old woman with her mouth open, shouting. Her words were enough to draw one of the policemen to her. She shook a fist and moved away. As venomous as the dog, I thought, suddenly seeing the dead animal as a portent, conveying the idea that killing people was a short step away. An overture, I thought, remembering there had been other dogs. I had read of them: all strung from lamp-posts; all with messages tied around their necks. "Follow the line" and "Looking for a myth" were the most common ones. Sometimes there would be a one-off message prompted by a current event: a sex scandal involving a government minister had brought the response the next day of a dead mongrel and the message, "You can't teach an old dog new tricks." I laughed at that. It seemed so light compared to the message on the card I had seen. "Except for power, all is illusion," was the message I had read. It was on a torn up piece of cardboard, scrawled in scarlet, underlined.

Illusion, power. I ran over the message. And there was the power, the policemen shouting at each other, still not sure how to deal with the corpse. I could see they would have preferred it to be human. They would know how to carry a human, how to move it with some dignity. Suddenly the smallest of the policemen seemed to lose patience. He took charge, climbing to the top of the ladder. He called to one of his fellow officers, positioning him under the dog. A wail of protest followed. It was disregarded. The policeman up the ladder began to cut at the rope. He suddenly seemed quite serene, as though he had made an assessment and calculated that by cutting the rope with his left hand and grabbing it below the cut with his right hand he would be able to cut free and hold the dog. His colleague was positioned beneath him just in case. "Right," he said as he began the final cut through the rope. It brought a cry as he held the dog firmly and grabbed at the ladder with his knife-holding hand. He nearly fell. The weight of the dog lurched him to his side, but he just managed to hit his hand against the rail of the ladder and grip. The knife fell. It bounced off his colleague. And for a second, power seemed in disarray.

Most leads and clues are like that. They go nowhere, but you relish them. And the relish is heightened by isolation, by having no-one around whom you know and can play off. I had the stars and the fishermen and the water. I had Lake Titicaca in the late spring, after the worst winds, after the flamingos had settled for the night and the tourist boats had glided back to Puno. So I clung to identity. To ideas. To photographs. To memories. To things before the problem, before the intervention, before any threat of disturbance. Something before Lima, before the dead dog, before the policemen. My childhood, perhaps?

I was born in Chuschi, a village in the hills near the towns of Cangallo and Ayacucho, a couple of hundred miles from Lima, which was a day's bus journey away. We lived in a hut by the river, a mud hut with a thatched roof and a smell of wood, burning wood. By rights I should have stayed, I should have followed my father. He was a steady man, a caring man. He showed little, but kept his calm and direction, reading the Bible daily, believing its tales: God is good, God is kind, God will look after you, if you do this He will do that. My father was sold on the deal and I was part of it. I was to be cared for, considered, delivered almost to the land and God. He would give me soil and sun. I would give Him my soul. But when I was ten something intervened. It happened in school. In a language class. I wrote an account of our home, a simple account of structure and relationships that became complicated. I saw things, things I shouldn't have seen: tenderness, tensions, conflicts, idiosyncrasies, manipulations. Somehow all of that came through. I don't know how. I no longer have the essay, but I remember my teacher reading it and pulling away. I remember the moment so well, the way he pulled off his glasses and scratched his chin saying, "José! José!" He exclaimed it in a way that said what are you doing, why are you mixing it with reality, why are you seeing through it, saying we are poor?

But we were poor. And it was alright for God to say yes you can cope, you can get through anything, but anything included a mud slide that swathed away our best crops like a knife stripping bark. It left the land white, the rocks exposed, glistening. Beautiful in a way. I actually enjoyed it. A vivifying moment, our teacher said as the exfoliation drew us to the window. At that moment I could not believe that everything would just continue. That's it, I thought, knowing instantly why my father needed God, some being that would stop the thoughts that at that point seemed essential. Why? Why now? Why here? Why us? The questions poured. They drenched my teacher who stopped and stared again. His look said there is a tomorrow, there will be a dusk, there will be a dawn. All those questions, it said. I knew what he meant. He meant most children accept. They accept God. They accept Chuschi. They accept the way their father lives. "But you José, you wonder why he spends five hours on Christmas Day reading the Bible, why he thanks God for bread. You need to take your time José. Let's see where you go."

Where I went was secondary school. My teacher got me in. It was where he was educated, a couple of villages away, a long walk on a river bank where I would take in the look of the land and the people and think how easy it is to understand. I was grateful every day.

"He has a fine mind, Mr. Perez," I heard my teacher say. He had come to our house to convince my father that I would benefit from more education. I was outside, getting water, fetching it from the stream. Getting water was my job until my sister was old enough to carry the orange plastic buckets that dredged the shallow stream. I did the job well. I was choosy. I knew the little hollows where the water was sufficiently deep to avoid scooping up gravel, though I could do little about the water's grey colour and the interest of our neighbours' dogs. They played by my side. Dogs, people: the stream was so polluted. Sometimes I could see the excrement. Others couldn't. Or didn't want to. They chose to ignore it. It's the stream our grandparents and great-grandparents used, they'd say, knowing the field above the river was frequently used as a toilet.

"Cholera?" I'd say, "you heard of cholera? You know what it is, how it develops?" The lack of hygiene made me cringe, but I obeyed. Before school. After school. It was my job. To go out, fill up the buckets twice and bring them in. The first load went into pots and pans, the cooking utensils that my mother was working with. "Here son, here," she'd say, holding out a pan, indicating where she wanted the water. I always enjoyed looking into the pans. The contents intrigued me. I particularly liked it when they were filled with beans. I loved the colour of beans. So unnecessary, I'd think, considering why food needed such colour, how it was important to identity, to the trigger of taste. An absurdity, I thought. One of God's ruses my father would have said, one of His little games. "Beans," my mother'd say, missing the issue, never understanding my intrigue. "Hey!" she'd shout, kicking away a guinea pig. They were everywhere. All over the hut, playing and chasing, searching for a morsel of misplaced food. I'd kick them away too. I never liked them. I always wondered why we tolerated them, why they made my mother smile. "Hey you, off!" I'd shout, flinging out an arm. "Sorry, sorry," I'd add, seeing my mother's look. "I'll get the rest of the water." I wouldn't wait. I'd learnt that. Never wait, just correct yourself and go. I knew how to behave and, before my mother could react, I'd be out over the high step running down to the stream.

"Mr. Perez, I have sixty students. Ten will go to high school, four will go to university prep school and only one will get a place at university. If you allow it, José will be the one. I wouldn't normally say that Mr. Perez. I mean it's not easy, coming here, because I know what you want. You want your son to stay on the land. You want him to follow you. I can understand that. He can too. I've spoken to him. He wants to help you. And he wants to go to school. It's difficult for him. All I can say is if you could do without him for a while, let him go to school. Give him a chance. I know the secondary school. It's good. It's a fine school. I know the staff. Mr. Chavez is a good man. You know Mr. Chavez? You'll have seen him. He preaches. He comes to our church occasionally. He was here a few months ago. Remember? He told a story about the man who saved the soil from the landslide across the valley, how it was such good soil, how his crop grew and grew in record time. You'd like him Mr. Perez. He takes care. He is concerned...."

Somehow it worked. All those words. Words, words, words. They were like the landslide, pouring down. Only they were more targeted, burying my father who pouted and puffed and, as always, said little. Why? How? His usual questions surfaced, demanding occasional checks and prompting expressions other than the deadpan that, to me, always seemed so bleak. Like the landscape, I'd think, the landscape with its bare soil and occasional caches of potatoes drying in the wind, the serious landscape. It suited him. I thought of his hatred of moral laxity, his circumspection. It was the link with religion that had helped me. A fortuitous link, it zigzagged through the conversation, always returning, binding it.

"God would want him to do what is best for us. I believe that. I believe in family, in links. The land is a link. An important link, you agree?"

Castro, my teacher agreed. He sat on the mud ledge just inside the door watching my father who was in his normal position to the left of the straw bed he shared with my mother. He squatted for hours there reading the Bible slowly or carving with his one good knife. He carved faces out of strips of wood. Righteous faces, sacred faces. My mother would come in occasionally and sweep up the offcuts and say, "It would be easier outside." He would nod in agreement and carry on delicately turning the blade, pressing out the pupil of an eye or smoothing around the cavity of a chin. His movements were flamboyant. He knew his skill. He wanted it to be admired. Like it was now. By my teacher, Mr Castro. Castro was always good with words. He found them easily, yet I sensed my father's absorption distracted him. It made him nervous, his broad shoulders shaking slightly, his arms moving with his words. He folded and refolded them as he listened to my father.

"But he could do good. Do what God wants. We must all do what God wants. We must all try to do good. You believe that?" my father asked. He was into questions. They were reassurances really. Little prods that pushed for a nod or a smile or a touch of warmth that somehow hung on a look. It was a simple technique. It worked. "Could he become a priest? I mean is that possible? Can school do that? There can be nothing finer. To be the voice of God. The voice of God. Imagine that. Instructing. Sorting out."

School and religion converged then, convincing my father, satisfying my teacher who played on it, grateful for the way it allowed him to breach my father's defenses.

"It is a strong link, don't you think, Mr. Perez, religion and education? It is understanding. It is seeing the truth."

"Ah."

I knew that sound well. The gasp. The exclamation. It was like a first breath, a breakthrough; and, although I was several yards away from the doorway, I knew my father would have put down the wood and the knife, that for the first time he would be eye to eye with Castro. I also knew that that was a confirmation of the existence of something deep within that had an energy. It was something my father couldn't disguise. The sound was warm, the look was warm. It was so different to his normal wizened frown. Yet it came upon him so infrequently and without any apparent warning or signal. It just occurred. At least it seemed that way. But gradually I learnt it was all about enlightenment, about someone pointing out something that my father had known and understood and believed in. God, religion, the spiritual was at the core of the look. It was that that shook the sigh out of him.

But all those thoughts of childhood come and go. They are always there, good times and bad. They give way more easily during difficult times, during times of crisis. They allow the immediate past to barge in. It always seems rude, the immediate past. It always seems ill mannered, yobbish even. It talks over, it imposes. It always seems crucial, which it is because it normally

13

holds the key. It holds the event that changed things, which in my case had to do with Lima. I knew that. Not the Lima of the dead dog and the first lecture at La Cantute, but the Lima of my seventh annual lecture, the Lima of 1989, the Lima of a few days ago when the lecture went well and I stayed on just for a day or two to buy some oil paints and see some football. Refreshed, I took the bus south to Arequipa, a full day's journey, and, from there, the train to Puno, where I teach. Nothing extraordinary happened on the journey. We were five hours late; a failed locomotive at Arequipa had delayed us, but I was happy enough, arriving home, feeling the freshness of the Puno air, smelling the lake. I was breathing that in, taking deep breaths, when the intervention occurred. Someone in the wrong place at the wrong time. Someone out of context. A man. His voice calling softly, "José! José! Here."

I turned and saw a colleague, Jorge Prado. He was standing in the doorway of the railway station's ticket office; a finger to his lips urged quietness then wagged and beckoned. I followed him into the room. It was there he told me it wasn't safe to go home, that the police had called at my house not once, but twice.

"At my house?" I said, clearing the chewing gum from my mouth. I chewed gum to flavour my breath. I used mouthwashes too, the mouthwashes you can buy from street stalls at two sols a bottle, the mouthwashes that taste of alcohol and burn away any soreness on your gums. I did that out of habit. Because I had done it for years. Of course the rottenness that had caused me to start chewing gum had long gone. I had earned money and paid for treatment, I managed that at the end of my first year of teaching. A couple of sols a week. For my teeth. To stop that liquid oozing out of my gums, the liquid with the dreadful taste. Sometimes in the mornings it would have accumulated in the well of whichever cheek was against my pillow and my tongue would chase it, probing the teeth that I knew to be bad. The ones on the lower right. And the two top left. Or I'd press with a finger and the tooth would make a noise as if it were releasing a bubble of liquid that was trapped just beneath it, like a spring. My mouth would swell too. I'd have an abscess once or twice a year. I had one just before I sought treatment. The dentist didn't recognise it and when he pulled a tooth that was thoroughly rotten, pus erupted in my mouth. Poverty, a voice in my head said when that happened. Poverty. It was like a mark, like a deformed leg or a swollen belly or thinning hair. It marked me out. Poor, it said.

"So when were they at my house?" I asked, coming out of thought.

"Two days ago. I thought they'd be here tonight. I mean the normal ones are, but these guys, the ones that called, they were special. They were mean."

"Julia? What about Julia?" I added quickly, thinking of my sister who lived with me. "Is she alright? Where is she?" My concern was immediate. To Jorge it must have been understandable. He knew everyone in Peru was under pressure, that it didn't take much to disturb anybody's calm. He also must have realised the conclusion I had drawn, that once targeted it was easy to join the statistics and be disappeared.

"Julia wasn't in."

"Thank God."

Jorge sat down. He was a large man, built for slow movement and even slower gestures, but he lived on his nerves. They flicked expressions across his face and gave his limbs lives of their own, contorting him into strange positions. He wanted me to join him now. He pointed, brushing a seat, taking my bag from me and placing it on the floor. "Come on," he said in a whisper. "We're safe here. Allippio knows. He's with us." Allippio was the station master. I could hear him whistling outside, shutting the gate that the passengers went through. "Let the crowd disappear. We'll go through the market. Allippio's left the bottom gate open. Leave it a while. He knows the drill."

As though they were tiny, the giant orange-coloured double doors of the waiting room clicked shut behind us. I leant back against them causing them to click once more and stared up at the ceiling and then slid my gaze down across the grille of the desk at the front of the room. Light through the window fell on the signs *Tarifas* and *Horarios* and then moved on to search amongst the sweet papers and the morsels of stale bread strewn across the floor. Finally it touched the double-sided seat that occupied the centre of the room. I stayed on my feet knowing the pew-like seat had been heavily chiselled by wear and tear and that jagged pieces of wood snagged clothes. I could see the potential splinters flanking Jorge and smiled. "So where is she?" I finally asked.

"Julia? She's safe. We got her out."

"Out? What do you mean out?"

"La Paz."

"La Paz!"

"She's in La Paz," he emphasised, his head nodding, encouraging his words. "She's quite safe. No more questions now eh? You have my word."

"Jorge, she's my sister. I need to know."

"OK, OK." He moved his legs extravagantly, placing them back underneath the chair, before stretching out. The movement seemed to elongate his whole body. "But listen, at this moment, she's safer than we are. So come on. You know we'll look after her. We'll find her a home, get her a job. You know how we work. Hey she's already Bolivian."

I knew what that meant. A new name. New papers. A new identity.

"When she's settled, I'll tell you where she is. We'll get you there. Alright?"

"Does that mean a visit?"

"Yes, of course it means a visit. You know it means a visit. That's easy. You know that."

I nodded my head. I knew the northern side of the lake was fairly unprotected, that with a little knowledge it was easy to pass into Bolivia without being questioned. "OK, OK," I said slowly. "You sure now?"

"Course I'm sure."

I thought of the numerous occasions when Jorge had been economical with the truth. I smiled. Jorge smiled too. "Hey, this is serious."

Jorge dismissed it, stopping for a second as the light from the window above the other double door that led out onto the street smeared across us. We stayed perfectly still. "What we really need to know is why they called."

"Why?"

"Yeh. What's up? Why you? Why did they target you? And why now?" Jorge shook his head and looked up. He scratched his chin with his left hand and took a long look out at the empty platform and the disused railway sidings. He shook his head again. "I mean why now? OK they're suspicious of you. We know that. You've worked at Ayacucho for christsake. Everyone who has worked at Ayacucho is watched like a hawk. But why move in on you? And why now? Why not two years ago?"

"A crackdown?"

"What? Now? Oh you mean on the way?"

"It's happened before."

He shrugged. I half smiled. It was a baleful sort of look. I used it when something nice was being said about me. It seemed out of place here, but I was trying to deflect attention. That was why the look was normally employed. I needed time, time to consider what had happened and what I should do next. Why, I thought. Why? The speech. The speech in Lima. The speech about the future. It replayed in my mind. I didn't mention it because, before I had set off, I had gone through it with Jorge, checking its contents were acceptable. And they were. The trouble was I had drifted from the text and spoken off the cuff. I wondered what I had said. All I knew was the speech was well received. "Your best yet," Juan Rivera the politics professor of the college had said. "So adventurous. Almost visionary," he added with a wink that intimated I had risen in his esteem. It said courage was valued in Peru, that speaking out in a time of fear was courageous. But courage has repercussions, I thought: the police, my home, Julia. The list almost made me cry.

"Your speech was fine," said Jorge, clearing the look of doubt on my face.

"You don't know."

"Juan phoned."

"Juan?" I said dismissing the significance of Juan.

"What do you mean, Juan?" Jorge imitated my voice.

"Juan doesn't matter. What he thinks is not imperative. Look what I'm saying is it's some little spy who took against me, some secret policeman in the back row who didn't like my jokes or my eyes."

"Best yet, Juan said." Jorge's half smile returned. It mixed with a nod. The usual protests designed to play down compliments were withheld. Instead my mind concentrated on the tangents and sidelines, on the images and nuances that Jorge didn't know of. In particular it concentrated on the way I had let myself drift. Stick to the text was always Jorge's advice. It says enough, I remembered Jorge saying before I had left. "And she's in La Paz?" I found myself muttering, talking over my thoughts.

"Julia? Yes. La Paz. Hey you know how we do it. You know how easy it is. Remember Cifuentes? And Degas, remember Degas?" He laughed in a way that said there was no way I could ever overlook Degas. "Degas. With the beard."

I nodded. Of course I remembered Degas.

"There's no border. No real border. And no checkpoints. And no police, well none to speak of. So it's easy. Alright? Now we must let her settle. Hey come on, you know this. We'll have news soon. A week or two and you can go and see her." Jorge smiled. For all his nerves, he had a reassuring manner. Avuncular, I thought, feeling satisfied. But Jorge expected more. His right foot began to tap nervously, pumping his leg as he looked my way expectantly, wanting me to be demonstrative, to show how happy I was with what he had offered. When, in return, I offered nothing, he looked even more anxious, frowning and sighing. I knew he was waiting for the follow-up question. But the question never came. Instead I turned my attention away and missed the further small show of anxiety that left Jorge fumbling with a cigarette and cursing himself. This was neither the place nor the time for such an indiscretion. I leant back. Jorge rubbed his face. I noticed that, but I was more taken by my own lack of control. I thought how the crisis stopped ideas developing, the way it rushed them through, interrupting them with this and that, with some trivial thoughts like who would look after my house and who would take my classes.

"Talk about perspective. You know what I'm thinking? I'm thinking who's going to take my classes. I mean my sister's disappeared, the police are after me and I'm hiding in a railway ticket office. This is surreal. And all I really want to know is who will give my Monday morning lecture. Can you believe that?" I shrugged.

"That's teaching for you."

"So come on, tell me, who's going to be giving my Monday morning class?"

"Bordes," said Jorge, quite dispassionately.

"Bordes! You're joking. You are joking?"

"No. Bordes. He was the only one with any time."

"But he's verging on the functionalist. He'll be gone within a year."

"He'll be gone within six weeks. He'll make such a mess of your classes." Jorge laughed quite loudly, forgetting himself.

"Oh great. And what happens then? What you like on Gramsci?"

"Gramsci? Who the hell's Gramsci?" joked Jorge, shaking his head, unable to deal with the reaction. He rubbed his thighs and folded his hands. The movements made me think how a colleague had once said that Jorge was like a conjurer, all hands and exaggeration, that he always looked as though he was about to produce a rabbit from a sleeve in some wild dramatic movement.

"You'll be alright." Jorge was tapping his feet again.

"OK. Come on then. What happens next?"

"Next? Oh we look after you. We hide you away."

"Bolivia?" I asked, sensing I was about to follow Julia.

"Taquile," said Jorge.

The journey across Lake Titicaca to the island of Taquile took four hours. A long four hours. We slipped into a small boat pinned between the quayside and *Ollanta*, the old ferry that used to run to Bolivia. Jorge whispered a goodbye, saying he would be in touch, then we sailed. I quickly learnt I hated boats. I put them on par with vaccinations and meetings. It was the inactivity that really got to me. No pen. No paper. I had a book, so I tried to use a torch, but I found the rhythm of the boat disturbed my concentration. Somehow I couldn't stay with a line. As the boat rode the waves, my eyes rose too. When the wave passed, my eyes fell to a different place on the page. It was because I kept looking up. I knew that. I kept anticipating the wave – its size, its length – and I stayed with it for a second after it had passed considering the physics that kept us afloat.

It was when we turned around a promontory and the lights of Puno disappeared that I relaxed. I considered how two hours previously I had been on a train, sitting in a carriage day-dreaming about a forthcoming trip to New York to deliver a paper. By now I should be home, safe. That drew a smile. Jorge had promised to look after my house for me. He said he'd move his brother in. It was important to have somebody there. I knew that. I knew too that I couldn't stay on the island forever. A change of government would help. A revolution would be better.

I laughed at that. Out loud. The man steering the boat laughed too. It made me edgy. I expected words and they came.

"So you're a cousin of Ramon's?" said the man, sitting at the back of the boat, his hand on the tiller. He was a small broad man with a baritone voice. He kept looking my way. I sensed the gaze. I sensed the inspection. He sighed occasionally. I wondered if the sighs were connected to the looks he gave me or to the visceral sounds of the engine, with which he seemed in tune, pulling faces at any strange splutter or boom.

"Yes," I said, a deft movement of my hand again sweeping away the gum from my mouth. I was sure that in the poor light the boatman saw nothing but a gesture that went with my mood or thoughts. "Yes," I repeated, remembering the story that Jorge had drilled into me, how Ramon, a year two student at my college had suddenly become a cousin, a cousin by marriage and how I was visiting. I looked away, trying to kill the conversation with a show of indifference. I was playing the role well. Ramon a cousin? I could accept that. More importantly, I could carry it off, make it believable. It was being married that worried me. But now Julia is my wife, I thought. It was a wise choice: Julia was the only woman I knew well.

"Strange time to travel," remarked the boatman.

"Missed the last boat."

"Couldn't wait till tomorrow?"

"It's a long story." I tried to dismiss his questions, to emphasise my indifference.

"And you're related to Sebastian?" Sebastian was Ramon's father.

"No."

"So to Flores?"

"Yes."

"She's an incomer. There's not many incomers on Taquile."

"No?"

"He's a good boy, Ramon."

"Yes. Yes he is," I agreed.

I listened as the man inquired about Ramon's college work, asking whether it would take him away from the island, but the words failed to gather momentum and like an old engine they soon spluttered and stopped. In the silence I shook myself. All this seemed too cloak and dagger for an academic from a provincial university. And Jorge was an unlikely hero. He was made more for slapstick, I decided, replaying the walk from the station in my mind. It emphasised that neither Jorge nor I was suitable for the clandestine, the stealthy. Yet it had been effective. We had strolled through the market, blending with the crowd and then taken the less used roads to the east of the stadium to get to the port. All the way I had kept my head down, knowing I mustn't be seen, that to be seen would mean more extensive searches, that the island wouldn't be big enough or far enough away. I kept thinking of Jorge's speculation. "They think you're in Lima," he kept saying, surprised at the lack of police presence. "They must think you're in some safe house, hiding away, that you've stayed on, that you're staying with a friend or that you're having a couple of days by the sea. After all it's summer in Lima, so why not." Jorge's laughter allowed a less serious look to come over his face. "Got it wrong again, haven't they? Bloody police."

And while he spoke, I kept asking, "Where are we?", the back streets being unfamiliar to me. They all looked the same with the concrete slabbed road surface and the unattractive wires that fell like blow-away hair, loping across the space between buildings.

"The stadium's there." Jorge would point, fixing our position. The stadium replaced the railway station, which we had quickly left behind, though, for a time, while following the railway track, we were able to look back and see the green-painted metal gates that would be opened for trains to trundle down to the port and the large circular orange-coloured water tower that stood by the gates. That was a good landmark. It did the job so much better than the stadium, which we saw only occasionally.

"OK," Jorge said when we turned a corner and found ourselves in a small well lit open square. The square was filled by a long, rectangular turquoise-coloured tented building. "*Teatro Cine Video Escorpio*," I said, reading the white sign above its entrance. *Attracion universal* the sign bragged. Drawings of van Damme, Stallone, Schwarzenegger and Bruce Lee, who was featured twice, welcomed the public. A blackboard listed the night's showings.

"This is it," smiled Jorge. "You wait here. One minute." I was left outside with my suitcase, trying not to look at the array of coke bottles and chocolate being offered by a vendor. I couldn't buy anything. I couldn't put down my case to pay: there were puddles everywhere, puddles and mud and pot-holes that were sliced through by the steel blades of an old railway track.

"It's OK. Your boat awaits," laughed Jorge as he reappeared. "Right, Taquile here you come," he said marching away.

The fisherman broke my concentration. He was talking again. "You know the island?" he asked. I didn't reply. "You're preparing yourself, that's it, preparing yourself for the steps."

"Steps?"

"The steps up from the harbour. You climb up a cliffside. Oh you know. You're playing with me."

"Oh the steps. Yes Ramon mentioned them."

"All six hundred of them knowing Ramon. He hates them. They're so lazy this generation."

I nodded in agreement.

"Hey what is your name? Come on we've four hours on this boat."

"Three hours twenty minutes," I said, correcting him. I had been counting the minutes.

"Under normal circumstances, but there are strong waters tonight. And this is an old boat. It will be another four hours. Perhaps four hours five minutes. You wait and see."

"You're very precise."

"I know these waters. I've been sailing them all my life. And I've had a very long life."

"José."

"What?"

"I'm called José. You asked me my name."

"José," he said with relish. "José. A noble name."

"And you?"

"Hernando."

"Another noble name."

"Hernando? Her...nan...do," he emphasised. "No. Too many syllables."

"One more."

"One is enough," laughed the man. "José is like a first breath. It is so sweet."

I smiled. "So what's the island like?"

"The island? The island is sweet too. Everything is sweet on the island. The mornings, the nights, the women, the food."

"The food? What will I eat?"

"What will you eat?" He smiled again. A broad smile, a full smile, as though warm thoughts were seeping from his mind through his skin. A strange osmosis, I thought trying to take in the roll of his expressions. "*Pejerrey*. King fish."

"Is that a good fish?"

"Yes."

"I've never had *pejerrey*. I've had *trucha*, trout."

"*Pejerrey* is similar. Only its meat is white and it tastes a little less sweet. Trout is too sweet. We prefer *pejerrey*."

"Any cereals?"

"Barley, wheat, *quinoa*. Lots of *quinoa*. And potatoes. Even more potatoes."

"So I can have chips?"

"Yes José you will have chips, lots of chips." Again he smiled. He seemed such a jovial man. A good advert for the island, I thought, considering how for many visitors he would be their first point of contact. "And corn. You can have lots of corn. Only the corn here is small. Not like the corn in Cuzco, eh José? You been to Cuzco?"

I nodded.

He sat down, taking up the tiller once again, perching himself on the back rail of the boat, his feet on the bench that ran around the back of the boat. The exaggerated movements as he stretched up to see ahead suggested an elasticity and a looseness that he should have lost long ago. "You seen the corn?" he asked, pulling a face. "The corn in Cuzco? It's smaller and sweeter on the island. Much sweeter."

"Sounds good."

"Good? Oh yes, it is. It's very good. Hasn't Ramon told you all this? Oh you'll enjoy it. The island is unique. It keeps the system of the Incas. You understand? Today for you, tomorrow for me. That is Taquile. We share. We share everything, even chips, eh José? Even chips!"

It should have been a comfortable night. In my American bed. With Brahms on the stereo. The Violin Concerto. My mail to read and the newspapers to catch up on. And Julia would have brought some apple pastries from the bakers opposite the cinema. Rosaria, the shopgirl there, called me Mr. Apple Eyes and made faces in the pastry to entertain me. And if Julia had forgotten to do the shopping it would have been a pizza from Gringo Bill's on the High Street. A big pizza, a *doble glutano*, a double fattie.

But all that was exchanged for a wave from Hernando who, after cutting the engine and drifting the boat expertly on a wave flush against the harbour wall, tied up and set about sorting out his sleeping arrangements.

"So you're not coming with me?" I asked, seeing Hernando produce a thin, single mattress from a cupboard under a seat. Something about the way he handled it indicated it wasn't for me. The care wasn't there. I remembered the precision he had shown at the docks in Puno, wiping down my leather case and brushing down the deck before finding a secluded appropriate spot and rushing off to find some clean tarpaulin to cover it.

"Come with you," mocked Hernando. He laughed loudly. "How can I come with you, eh José? I am the nine o'clock ferry from Puno this morning. Let's see, it's one o'clock now, so that means I must leave here at three to get back to the mainland in time. I have two hours sleep, eh José. Two hours sleep." He clutched the mattress and smiled more warmly. "Alejandro will take you to your bed."

"Alejandro?"

"Sebastian's son."

"Alejandro? Ramon is Sebastian's son."

"His other son."

"Oh Alejandro," I gushed.

There was a knowing look in Hernando's eye. I ignored it, shuffling and checking I had all I needed. I moved to get my suitcase which was to the front of the boat.

"Hey José, it's too heavy. Leave it with me. Go on. Leave it," he urged. "Take what you need. Your toothpaste. Your chewing gum."

"I think I've got all I need in my day sack." I tried to think of the contents of the bag that was slung over my shoulder. Toiletries, oil paints, a few rolled up canvasses, sun-glasses, a pen, paper, a hat. "Will they have towels on the island?"

"Towels!" For some reason Hernando laughed. "And this afternoon, when you're having your chips at Sebastian's, your bag will appear, eh José? Special delivery eh? Hernando's deliveries."

Though I wasn't happy with the arrangement, my slight paunch and the large suitcase dictated that six hundred steps would be at least five hundred and fifty too many. "OK," I agreed stepping up onto the jetty as Hernando held the boat as tightly as possible to the sea wall. "I'll see you and my possessions tomorrow then."

"Today," corrected a smiling Hernando. "This afternoon, yes? I'll be there. Hernando will be there. Oh and take this." He seemed flustered as he fumbled under a seat, grumbling as he located whatever it was he was looking for. "Go on. You'll need it." He handed me a towel.

As I moved away I wondered if the strong moonlight highlighted my pale, ghostly gabardine overcoat. I was dressed for Lima not Taquile. I knew that. I wondered what Alejandro would make of me. I would probably scare him away. But I saw almost immediately that Alejandro wasn't easily scared. He appeared from behind a small square hut that looked new and out of place half way along the harbour wall. An abrupt "Hello. Follow..." was all the thin, teenaged boy managed when I approached. It made me long to be reacquainted with Hernando's sociability and curiosity.

"Can we have a break?" I asked plaintively after seventy or eighty steps. We were contouring up the hillside, occasionally twisting back on ourselves, zigzagging. "You see, unlike you young man, I am no athlete. I need to think myself up these steps, you understand?" There was no reply. I turned and looked back towards the lake. "What a night! Isn't the moonlight lovely?" I gasped. Light from the full moon was catching the tops of waves, scrambling the surface of the lake with white lines, shading it, making the lake lighter than the sky; the mainland was a black intervening mystery. I stared into it, wondering about the textures of the darkness and the speckle of lights that were like animal markings. Rafters of roads underpinned it. Roads and houses. I looked for towns too, towns like Puno, but Puno was hidden behind a promontory and I could see no others. That made it all more of a mystery, a dark rural mystery.

"OK," said Alejandro, moving again. Focus, I thought. Pick on something. His hat. I kept my gaze on Alejandro's hat. I couldn't make out its colour as I followed him up the steps, but it was remarkably tight fitting to the sides and the top of his head, stretching to its contours perfectly until it fell away at the back of the temples into a wonderfully loose bobble. There was something larva like about it as it shook in front of me as though some great insect, a huge butterfly perhaps, was about to emerge from it. Its activity became more electric while I rested and Alejandro scrambled about on the steps in front of me looking for something. I watched him move forwards and run back, bending down eventually to pick up something in front of me. A terse "Ah" suggested he had found whatever it was he was seeking.

"Sniff," he said. He was offering me a bunch of herbs, a bunch of four or five different herbs tied together by what looked like a piece of root. I smiled and stood up.

"Sniff," repeated Alejandro. One very deliberate, slow nod urged me to comply.

I was still sniffing the herbs when Alejandro cried, "Good night," and left me in one of the huts in Sebastian's compound. It was the last one at the end of the lower of two courtyards to the right of the main path. Two steep steps cut out of stone led to the hut. I sat on them. The door was open. I looked around the room. I felt surprisingly at home. Chuschi, I thought sensing a glow of recognition. Mum, dad, Julia. The hut reminded me so much of the family home. The steps down into it did that. As did the bareness. The only furniture was a bed, a brown painted, iron framed bed. I stood up and tiptoed across the floor onto the tarpaulin which covered the stones and earth around the edge of the bed. I sat on the bed and took off my shoes. "Ah," I gasped, leaning back, finding the bed a little small, but quite comfortable. I pulled one of the two blankets that lay on it over my legs and smiled.

"I'll need candles or an oil lamp," I remarked to myself, realising the torch in my day sack wasn't adequate. I took it out and shone its light across the floor towards the steps and the door. It was a thin, light door: mud and straw plastered onto a wooden frame; one, two, three, four, five pieces of wood ran horizontally across it. Then I moved the torch to illuminate a ledge that ran around the periphery of the room. It comprised three planks of wood, three planks supported by intermittent stones. And finally the torch's light touched the window behind my bed. Its frame was set into the only adobe wall - the other three walls were made of stone. An "Alps Ski" sticker was fixed to the top right corner of the frame.

"Fine," I said, settling and closing my eyes. I found the one pillow, which was perched on the right side of the bed. I sighed. I felt calm, surprisingly calm given the excitement of the evening, calm and tired. I would sleep. That surprised me. But it was a good sign. It meant I might be able to relax a little. It meant I might actually grow to like the island. "Like, like, like," I mumbled under my breath. The word seemed so important. I needed to dwell on it, to pick on what was good for me, on what offered me solace or happiness, on what offered me relief. The island's role in that was crucial. It had to exist around me and let me consider La Paz and Julia and what Jorge had said. If I could find such a focus I knew for the first time in years I would have time for reflection. And that would be so beneficial. It would be like providing my mind with a warm room and a glass of *pisco* and saying you have time. Time. That was the real luxury. I had to use it well.

part two

HUGO

1

You can't tell much from portrait photos. They are too framed, too composed. They cry out for the formality to be de-emphasised or removed. That was certainly true of the first photo I saw of Henry Meiggs. He was sitting stiffly, back straight, shoulders turning, allowing his eyes to peer over the photographer's gaze. Up one side of his head a signature ran. Something Meiggs. It looked like 'Ho', but was probably just H dot. The Meiggs was clear. M.E.I.G.G.S. The script had great loops, curving the 'm' and the two 'g's. It told me a lot. Flamboyant, carefree, it suggested. Wild, direct, dramatic. It gave me insight, even though, to me, the name Meiggs, in itself, had great sonority. I had met it before, some two years earlier in a geography class. But the photo gave the name Meiggs a greater resonance. A photo on a cover. A book cover. In the library.

I knew at the time, when the English teacher said choose the biography of anyone with a name beginning with the letter 'm', that most boys would choose MacMillan or McCartney or even Arthur Miller. No-one would choose Meiggs. Except me. *Henry Meiggs, Yankee Pizarro*, was the title on the cover. I liked that. I knew what it meant. Henry Meiggs, awkward bastard. That's what it meant. Appropriate, I thought, considering what I knew of Meiggs, reminding myself of the geography class. We had been learning the mechanics of cross sections and had been given a transect through Peru to draw for homework. Suggest what the difficulties might be in constructing a railway across Peru and outline ways in which the difficulties may be overcome, was the question. In passing the teacher mentioned Meiggs. "An American built the railway," he said. "A man called Meiggs. Henry Meiggs. His family originally came from Cornwall."

I thought little of that at the time. Cornwall. A man called Meiggs. So what? After all it was the cross section that had grabbed me, the astonishing cross section. It was full of steep slopes, precipices almost. The sight of the contours directed my thoughts. How could a railway be built through such terrain? I sat staring at the transect, at first thinking no, impossible, a railway couldn't be built. Then I went home and asked my father. He was a train driver, a man who loved his job, who loved railways. He knew about transport. "Oh come on son it's simple, isn't it? Why do you need transport?" he asked, laughing. "I mean it must be the same for Peru, mustn't it?"

Must it? Really? I took my time taking in what he was saying, but then I realised that if there was a good enough reason for construction, then, whatever the difficulties, it would be built.

There seemed to be a lesson there. Something about motivation. Reason, motivation, action, I repeated. Reason, motivation, action. It became a sort of model for behaviour. I applied it to Peru, thinking there were resources that needed to be carried to the coast, that there were people who wanted to holiday in the hills, that there were troops that needed to be mobilised quickly to some vulnerable location. Something had to cry out. Something had to say build, build a railway and build it quickly. A profit or a strategy seemed the bottom line, some reason that bit politicians or entrepreneurs and forced them to act, to move in.

It was then I thought of tunnels. They seemed to provide the answers. Mountains, slopes, railways. Difficult, my mind kept saying until it recognised the potential of tunnels. They gripped my imagination, turning me momentarily into an engineer, an engineer in Nineteenth Century Peru, an engineer acting for the politicians. That was Meigg's role. I didn't realise that until I opened the biography and saw Peru. Peru – the first railway, it said. I empathised with that. After all, in my mind, I had played the role. I had designed tunnels, tunnels through the hills. I had drawn them on my cross section. A dashed line equals a tunnel, I had written, adding a key. So I had strange tunnels, the longest ever seen, going for mile after mile at different altitudes and in different geologies through the hills.

Now, in Peru, some ten years on from my first sight of the book in the library, I sit on the bed of a hotel room in Puno, a small city on the banks of Lake Titicaca. And I am cursing Meiggs. "Bloody Meiggs and those bloody Brazilians." They are to blame too. They are to blame for bringing me here. They are the people I have been negotiating with. Varig Airlines. I have been trying to sell planes to them. Airbuses. I work for Airbus. Airbus Industrie. Varig Airlines of Brazil had expressed an interest in buying two Airbus 300s, so I was sent with our chief negotiator, a German called Helmut. I had no intention of visiting Peru. It was just a simple business trip. Go to Sao Paulo, do the business and get out. But the deal broke down: Varig wanted time to think over our best price and service arrangements. "Give us three weeks" they said.

It was December 17th. Three weeks meant returning after Christmas. I hate Christmas. It holds no attraction, so this was my chance, my chance to understand Meiggs, my chance to go to Peru. So I put Helmut on a plane to Europe and I left for Peru. I had three weeks, three weeks to search out all the railways Meiggs had built, three weeks to try to understand what made Honest Henry tick.

Honest Henry! It is difficult understanding how someone I had learnt of all those years ago could exert such influence. But the answer is simple. Meiggs had been with me since childhood. He had been my hero, my childhood hero. And boys need heroes. And heroes stick, they endure, they hold a fascination, perhaps it is not always as strong as Meiggs' grip on me. That is unusual. I'll concede that. I won't even attempt to explain it. But most men will know, most men will understand. OK mine was a strange choice. It was like Richard, a school friend adopting Oldham Athletic as the football team he supported or Kenny choosing Fairport Convention as his favourite band. The choice smacked of the maverick, it was certainly very individual and that was to become a major strand of my life. Being individual. Self, self, self. I'm not ashamed of that. Self, self, self. Be different. Be successful. Like Meiggs. Meiggs building railways in Peru. In Peru! An American from the Catskill Mountains. How did he get to Peru? Why did he go? In the 1860s for heaven's sake. Why not England or France or Wales? Why Peru?

I ask him that in my mind. I talk to him. I talked to him when I was a boy. I talk to him now. Perhaps not quite as often, but now and then I still sense he is there, in my mind. He was always there when I was a boy, because boys get close to their heroes. They picture them. For me that was easy: the portrait at the beginning of the biography showed me what he was like. He was like Gene Hackman. What am I saying! He was the image of Gene Hackman. The likeness lay in his pale eyes that were narrow and long and intense with just a suggestion of an eyebrow. "He must have been fair," I thought, when I first took in the likeness. A straight nose, quite a long nose, ran between the strong bones that set his cheeks. Fine features, I thought, but sagging, ageing, the jowls settling over his collar. Late middle age had well and truly set in. "Fuckin' jowels. I'm like a fuckin' Great Dane, you hear me?"

I heard him. I had a name for him too. I called him Popeye after Hackman's character in the *French Connection*. Popeye. I heard him in the bedroom at night, on my way to school; I heard him in lessons; I heard him on the bus home. He became a best friend. He interpreted things for me. He provided an insight, a way to view homework and politics and girlfriends. He liberated me. He did things I wasn't allowed to do. Like swear. He did that the first time I saw him on the front of the biography. Popeye, I thought. Popeye swears. So Meiggs did too.

"Fuckin' ridiculous," he was saying to the photographer when he was having his portrait taken. "It's green that screen. Hey you listening? What have you seen in Lima that's green? I mean people will look at me and say where the hell have you been?"

"But it's in black and white," I retorted, playing the part of the photographer.

"I don't give a shit. It's green. You can tell by the shade. Green is sort of half way. So they'll be saying where the hell were you? The jungle? The fuckin' jungle. Oh yeh that's where I was. A sort of walk away yeh? Saturday with the scorpions, yeh."

"They have scorpions in the jungle?"

"Hey how the hell should I know?"

"I think they do. I think someone's told me."

"Oh they have, have they?"

"Yes I think so."

"Well this is Lima. The only green thing here is wee, you hear me, god damn wee. So what am I doing eh? Will somebody please tell me? What am I doing in the photo? Having a good whizz?"

Meiggs concentrates my mind. He makes my early years so vivid. Even the years before the English class. I can remember my first day at school, my seventh birthday party, the day my local football team, Swansea City, was promoted to the first division. I can remember the years and events so clearly. They are like pinches or cuts or bruises. I can see them and feel them. And they convince me that I was so sensitive. That shocks me now. I consider a situation and wonder how that could have been me, how could I have noticed or cared about something that I would now pass by? Like the smell of cigarettes, the smell on my white shirt when I was in school. I hated that smell. I hated my parents for smoking and letting it settle on me. Hate, hate, hate, I'd think, sitting in my junior school class next to Jamie Owen. He always sat by me and every morning he made a habit of sniffing my shirt. "Persil," I'd say, covering up, knowing what the face he had pulled meant. He was from the private estate, the estate that provided the school with Jeromes and Annabels. I was part of the Susans and Garys who walked in from the council estate. And that was the beauty of the edge of Swansea, the mix, the social melting pot of Jeromes and Garys. You could tell who was from where by the clothes, by our hair styles and complexions, but manners and voices were similar: they mixed and matched, they copied and wore down the edges that separated classes.

Such assimilation produced well balanced eleven year olds, like Mark, my best friend who was the son of a politics lecturer at the local university, and Philip, the son of a council plasterer, and Jamie, the son of the head of the local office of the Land Registry. Philip and Mark and I were inseparable. Jamie was in and out of our group. He coveted our friendship and we let him into the gang because we knew his father played the most amazing table tennis. Jamie would have us around to his house and we would take on his father, all the time watching the movement of his father's hands, marvelling at the understated beauty of his defence and the explosion of his attack.

"You coming round?"

"To see Dag?"

Dag was Jamie's father. D.A.G. Owen. He was so respected that we all began to call each other by our initials. Philip became Pod, Mark became Mew, Jamie became Jo. I was the difficult one. Hugo Vaughan Young. So I became plain old HVY. I liked that. I liked it more than Pod or Mew. I liked it because it didn't blur or canter through the significance of the letters. It dwelt. I liked the idea of dwelling. It was what I did. It was what I did in my friends' houses. I lingered learning how others ate and talked and listened. I assimilated. So, by Oxford, I came from outer Swansea, from the suburbs, from the rural fringe as some were calling it. Outer equals middle, I learnt. Outer made me middle class. And my father had an office job, which was true at the end of his career when, for the final years of his working life, he became a wages clerk. I never mentioned detail. He just worked in an office. That was adequate: it made him middle class. School worked too. I owned up to a grammar school education, which was actually true, though I drew back from mentioning the school's conversion to the comprehensive ideal when I was in form one. "There's no private sector in Wales," I'd say, pre-empting an inquiry. "Well none to speak of. In Wales everyone goes to the grammar school."

No-one argued. No-one knew what made up middle class Wales. Why should they? Why should it bother them? To them Wales was a little province full of coal mines and misty valleys and smelly steel towns and rugby clubs and pigeons. And now they were learning that amongst all of that there was a middle class and it was made up of boys like them, boys who made nicknames up out of initials, boys who prowled in packs, boys who read Biggles and Jennings books. Somehow that reassured them. It relaxed them. It was what they had wanted to hear. And it let me in. It allowed me to be accepted, to become one of them.

Meiggs was so much part of that. He was like a friend from the posh estate. He was a Dag or a Mew. And he was so right for the time, the late 1970s and the 1980s, the Thatcher years, because he seldom did things in a small way. It wasn't his style. "Big, big, big. Think BIG," he'd say. Big made a statement. It frightened, it intimidated, it impressed. It repulsed some people too. Those who were jealous, those who knew they couldn't dig in and find the courage to take on the difficult contracts that Meiggs encountered. Because that was what it was like. It was gladiatorial, daring, so different from the disappointingly vapid lives that others led. And it was also a shield. I felt that. He could hide behind it, coming out whenever he felt like impressing, when he had learnt his lines, when he was word perfect and confident and ready to perform. All of that was like a film that surrounded him, a layer that came out of the house and protected him. There's so much covered, I thought. There's so much I can't get to. The cultural context for instance. First generation American. The family from Cornwall. That much I knew. But what of politics? What of religion? I could only guess.

I learnt from him though. I learnt how to hide and how to leave clues, how to play the tactician and dangle the bonus. I enjoyed that. "A big house son," Popeye would say. "Something big. And clever. Something that would take their breath away. *Quinta Meiggs* son. *Quinta Meiggs*." That was his dream palace in Santiago, Chile. There was a photo of it in the book. It was 300,000 pesos worth of house, four wings around a central tower with a marble exterior. Grand enough. And clever. Clever because the something that would take their breath away was a central heating system. A warm house in the Santiago winter. Central heating ahead of the United States. Live extravagantly the whole thing was saying. Be first. "*Soy yo quieren tiene la sarten por el mango*. Because I'm the one who's holding the frying pan by the handle. That's what the Spanish say."

Quinta Meiggs. So different to Blenheim Avenue, where I was brought up. Blenheim Avenue with its standard council house look, the fifties estate with a tree in every garden and the narrow roads. My mother had wanted to buy. She had wanted something bigger and better. She had wanted to climb social ladders, but circumstances held her back and, when she said, "Let's buy", my father replied, "No I think we should wait love. Prices will come down. You mark my words." With that their chance had gone and my parents eventually moved out of the rooms they were renting in a Gower farmhouse and into a Swansea council house.

"They got it wrong son. Listen," Popeye would say, sitting me down at night. "They're fucked. They're gonna be pushed around for the rest of their lives. You see that? Course you do, you're not stupid son, so listen. You want freedom? You want to make something of yourself? You can't do that here son. You hear me? You get away. You make out. OK have a conscience. I had a conscience. Oh yeh I did. A big conscience. Sometimes now, looking back I think I had too big a conscience. The South Americans said I was benevolent. Benevolent! Now I'll tell you what that means son. It means making sure you have the money to have a conscience. You gotta have the money son. So you look after number one, then be benevolent, yeh? Hey you got it son. You fuckin' got it in one."

The book confirmed what Popeye said. Meiggs had a conscience. For me, for a time, that was more important than all his triflings with the workers and the manipulation of management. The connections and coincidences such relationships triggered seemed shallow compared to the depth of Meigg's conscience, of the way he remembered others. The book said he realised money was being made at the expense of someone else. That was crucial. It said there was no getting away from the mechanics of the market. Winners and losers, Popeye would say. "As long as I'm the winner, great. Fuckin' great." But the effort of being a winner turned him into a desperado, drifting, saying little, thinking money, only money. After that it was easy. Money made, he could indulge his interests. Such expenditure on civil matters was like a tax on success. It told him he was on top. It reminded him of whom he had defeated and of who was working for him. His philanthropy was like a wager then. He was betting on himself, promoting himself and, in a way, paying them back. It was a calculated charity, but it was a charity that worked well for Meiggs. It gave him a dividend because he understood drama and, in particular, he understood how he could dramatise himself. He was good at that. And it was just as well because, if he was to be the philanthropist, then he would have to play the part, anticipating where and when it would work and, scripting it, telling himself where he should enter and how, down to what he should say and when he should say it. So, for instance, in December 1863 when the the Temple of Company in Santiago was destroyed by fire he listened to the outcry of emotion. Give us a fire service, it was saying. Meiggs obliged. He went to Boston, bought a fire engine and paid for its carriage to Chile. He also bought a bell that would announce future Santiago fires. Whenever it rang people thought of Henry Meiggs. Good old Don Enrique, its peal seemed to say. It seemed to colour Meiggs, to say he was a man who matched endeavour with generosity.

2

I go out. Puno is cold, grey, uninviting. It is one of those bare after-noons that the guidebook has warned me of. For a while I sit in a park but someone tries to talk to me. I have a coffee. Another person sidles up to me. I look away. I don't want conversations. Can't they tell? I walk out, back past my hotel and on towards the cinema opposite the bakery, a block away from the railway station.

"What you doin' son? Hey Hugo you can't go in there. I mean what d'you wanna spend time in there for? You want to see a movie? Do it at home. Do it in Toulouse, in Dolby stereo, on velvet seats. What is it with you? You like slumming it? Who the hell likes slumming it?" Popeye pauses, checking what I am reading. "Oh I get it. Yeh I see. You want anarchy. That's what you want, is it? Well hell Hugo there's enough of that out here. Those guys back there. Gee." He shakes his head.

"The topiarists?"

"The what?"

"In the main square. Where I sat down."

"That was the main square? What sort of shit town is this?"

"Puno's renowned for its topiary. The guidebook says so."

"Oh the guidebook says so, yeh?" He mocks my words. I know exaggeration will follow. "OK Pittsburgh, yeh we'll allow you to link yourself with steel and you New York, yeh you've got Wall Street, that's OK. And what about you Puno – Puno, Peru? What's your speciality? Topiary! Oh that's cool man, real cool."

"The bird was alright." I picture the head of the open-beaked bird that a team of five men in dungarees had been working on.

"The bird was alright! Hell Hugo did you see its head? That bird was shit out of luck. It looked like an elephant for chrissakes."

I smile. It is all I can manage. My attention stays with the poster in the dark wood display cabinet that is fixed to a white stone wall. A tube feeds into it providing power for the thin strip light at its base.

"*Los Hermanos Marx,*" I say to myself. "The Marx brothers." I wonder if I should go in. I sense I need to be alone, that I need to stop looking suspiciously at every passing face, that I need to dis-engage the city and take my mind off the guidebook's warnings. Don't go out after dark, it says, beware of curfews, it says, don't go here, don't go there, don't accept sweets or drinks from strangers, avoid guided tours by friendly English speaking students. Beware, take care, avoid, don't, don't, don't. I hate such words. Perhaps the cinema, even without Dolby sound and velvet seats, may relieve me of the smells and sounds of Peru and the grind of Spanish.

"...*este affiche es una locura pero estos tres locos hacen mas locuras en una noche a Casablanca....*" I read the words on the poster. *Una noche a Casablanca.* A Night in Casablanca. The title is partly obscured by a black strip of tape. White letters on the tape announce: "Matinee 16.00."

Four o'clock. I check my watch. It is three forty. "*Sala con cali-faccion*" boasts a further streak of white words on another piece of black tape. It underlines the names of the supporting cast: Charles Dance; Lois Collier.

"Hey senor, chocolate?"

I glance at the woman by the cinema's entrance. The pop corn girl. She sits, arms folded. The black trilby perched on top of her head is much too small for her. It disturbs her image and makes me notice that her grey-patterned dress clashes with the brown check of the scarf she is wearing and that her bright pink apron has slid around her waist to drape down her back. She offers me a drink from the two white pails that stand on blue wooden stools in front of her; a selection of chocolate bars line a tray that sits on her lap. I move past her.

"Hey, Hugo, at least get some candy. Jees you're on vacation for chrissake. You're supposed to be enjoying yourself."

"So it's just for the one night, is it?" Groucho, a hotel manager in the film, asks an elegant young couple at reception. "You'll be telling me next your name's Smith." The subtitles substitute Gonzalez for Smith. The slight, warm laughter in the auditorium acknowledges the name's significance. My laughter follows. But I soon realise that Gonzalez may be the name to use for dirty weekends in Madrid as well as Lima. A gaffe indicates that, a big gaffe. It tells me the translation has probably been carried out in Europe rather than South America. It happens when Chico and Harpo covet Groucho's hotel lunch. "We should sample it boss," insists

Chico who illustrates the danger of what the meal may hold by saying, "Hey boss, you could be eating guinea pig." The subtitles keep with the script. Guinea pig becomes *cuy*, which is the correct translation. But guinea pig is a delicacy in Peru. "*Cuy? Cuy!*" the audience cries. The Peruvians struggle to comprehend. Some work it out and boo and hiss. Some walk out.

"*Perdon, perdon....*"

"What you doin'?"

"I'm going too."

"Why, for chrissakes? Hugo why?"

I like the foyer of the cinema. I like its quietness. I am the only person there, sitting on the stairs. Groucho whispers. I can sense the punchlines from his tone. Sometimes a laugh confirms my suspicions. It makes me smile. I like being right. I look around. The decor of the cinema is very Art Deco with symmetrical spiralling staircases that feed the foyer from the raised entrance. It is grand, elegant. It is red and gold, warm and magnificent and empty but for the drapes that cover both the double doorway that leads to the auditorium and the grille of the ticket booth that sits in the well of the entrance. I recall being by the booth earlier, being given a pink twirl of tissue paper. I had assumed my seat number was printed on the paper and walked away to find the paper was only my entry ticket. "*Asiento?*" asked the usherette at the double doorway. I should have noted the number of the hole on the seating plan from which the girl in the ticket booth had pulled my tissue paper. "Forty four," said a voice over my shoulder when I looked confused. They had experienced gauche Westerners before.

Gauche! Since when have I been gauche? I am into the analysis of my behaviour now. Recent events have prompted that. Why? What should I have done? How could my behaviour have been more calculated or appropriate? I should have plumped for concealment. I should have acted dumb. But I am too up front, too eager to take control, to be connected with the norm. But what is the norm? How can I come to South America and expect to approximate the norm? I am Welsh, British, European.

"Hell there you are son. What you doin'?" asks Popeye, catching up with me. "Why'd you walk out? I mean there I was thinking, great he's relaxing, he's forgetting about all the shit we've been through. It seemed sort of recuperative in there, you know?"

I plan my answer. The noise. That's it. It surprised me. The conversations. The detachment. And the echo of the audience reading the subtitles, the peel of translation turning Groucho's one liners into long paragraphs. That would do. I wouldn't tell the truth; I wouldn't reveal how I felt fear when a stranger had stumbled out of the darkness and sat alongside me, how the figure in the dark had peeled off a coat, coughing, before reaching into a pocket and fidgeting in his seat. His movements were too much for me.

"Hey even the seats were OK. You notice? Mine sort of dipped down beyond the ninety degrees and I kept sliding. Jees I kept sliding. Had to sort of get my legs underneath it to prop it up. But it was OK. At least there was material on it."

"The seat was fine."

"So what was it?"

"Oh you know.... The noise. I mean they can't keep quiet. They have to have their conversations. They have to talk and talk..... There's no respect."

"Respect? What d'you mean respect? Respect for what?"

"For art I suppose."

"Art? Oh you mean the film. That dumb guy blasting his horn and the little Italian schmuck and the smart arse guy with the ridiculous moustache. That was art? You could have fooled me. But hey how can art be important to a Peruvian? I mean right now they're barely alive. You've got to get beyond the struggle of life to enjoy art. Art's a middle class thing. Hey Hugo you should know that."

I stifle what I feel. I know events have turned me against Peru. I shake my head and fall into silence. I look down at the tiled floor and then up at the one poster that is framed and on the wall. I take it in. "You were right about the anarchy," I remark.

"Eh?" Popeye looks up too. The poster sits between the two windows on the wall to the left, the wall that looks out over the street. The windows are set back. They are deep and metal framed. Green shutters lie against the red wall. Sunlight emphasises the depth of the window. And between the windows is the poster of a huge round faced man with a black coat and hat. His face is like a snowman's, white and round. It stares out at us. Red button eyes shine above two black dots that hint at a nose; a dusting of rouge suggests a little health. The man's right hand is raised so an index finger can touch a small sensitive lip. The gesture says, 'Quiet'. White words across the man's dark chest say, "*Ley del cine. Ya! Decimos.*"

"Hell that's a dumb rule. I mean they can't keep that rule. Not here. I mean, well that's just stupid."

"Why? ...." I bite my lip. I should have given myself time to think it through. I have missed something, something that is peculiar to Peru, something that is painful for Peru, that it isn't proud of, that it is hiding from me or I am missing because of my concern at present for nothing but myself.

"You don't see it, do you Hugo? Oh gee. They're illiterate for chrissake, god damn illiterate. Most of the people in this cinema can't read or write. Why do you think they bring a son with them? Because he can tell his father what's going on. You get it now? You understand? All those conversations. Shit Hugo that's just necessary. It has to be. The law of the cinema. Huh! *Decimos*! Oh yeh."

The dull yellow light in the glass over the door of my hotel room is a warning. I stare at it. I know I didn't leave it on. I don't do such things. I am in control. I am aware. I am never distracted. So I open the door slowly. I stare in. I smell another body. The smell of a traveller. It haunts me, having turned my stomach on buses and planes and in squares and parks and cathedrals. It has accompanied me. It has made me short with many people. I will be short again. I sense it.

I breathe out heavily as the body on the bed breathes in. It is a long body, male and young in a lime green tee shirt that has been dragged by the activity of sleep around the man's midriff. The man's back is brown with a scuff of white where skin is peeling. Jeans give way to socks. One trainer is on the floor; the other is half on the right foot. There is no movement. I shut the door.

"I'm not having another person in my room. Hey listen!" The middle aged man at reception irritates me. He smirks, keeping one eye on a television that is fixed to the wall. I move forward. I place both my hands on his desk. There is a bell on the desk, a small hand bell that is half hidden by a newspaper. I pick it up and ring it.

"OK," the man says sharply. "OK."

"I paid for a double room."

"Which room is that?"

I glare at him. He knows which room. "Room seven," I tell him.

"Then you have a double room."

"I know I have a double room."

"So?" He reaches down and picks up a plate. Rice and grizzled meat are played with. He forks up a piece of onion.

"I paid for the other bed to be empty."

"You paid for the room."

"Yes."

"So did the other guy." He pauses, looking into his plate, smiling to himself. "These things happen," he says slowly. "How long have you been in Peru? Because in Peru it's normal. It's how it is. OK?"

"No it's not OK." I'm not sure where to take the conversation now, how to lead it.

"Hey you should come back next year. Next year we'll be more First World. Next year we'll be more modern. The new hotel will be ready by then."

"What new hotel?"

"The new hotel down by the university. A hundred dollars a night. You'll like it. It will be more you, yes?"

I refuse to follow his words. "You have another room?"

"We're full."

"Well that's too bad."

The man pulls a face. He sits up, delving for language. "Too bad?" he asks. "Too bad for who?"

"For the guy who's asleep on my bed. One rucksack, one trainer," I announce, moving his plate to make space for the items which I have brought from the room. I bend down and pick them up off the floor. "Oh and one pen and a diary." I take the book and pen from my inside pocket and push the plate further to the left to make more space. "I'll send him down when he wakes which will be soon, in about half a minute I reckon. You ready for him?"

"Oh mister come on. It's been a bad day."

"I'm sure it has."

"You see it is Tuesday."

"So?"

"Tuesday is a train day, an arrivals day. Beds are scarce. We have to make use of what resources we have."

"My bed you mean."

"Not only your bed. Sometimes I let travellers have my bed. Sometimes I sleep in the corridor or on the floor by here, behind the desk." A hand points down and sweeps over the space. I do not react. I look at the diary. Paul Yeats is written in black ink in the top right corner of the cover. "Right I'll go and get him. He's called Paul. Be nice to him will you? I will."

"Where you goin' now? Hey hold on," begs Popeye. "Christ Hugo."

I walk past the reception desk and down the corridor towards the road. The corridor smells, a fetid smell. Dots that are small insects swarm. I duck and weave to avoid them. A Peruvian is slouched on the stairs, drunk; he mumbles and finds a smile as I step over him. A poster of the lake and the floating reed islands of the Uros indians is threatening to fall on him. A pin in one corner holds it. A pulse of wind up the stairs ripples it. It settles again, as does the drunk who laughs to himself and shouts, "Hello" when the stairs begin to creak. I make my descent, stepping upon hundreds of pieces of paper that are scattered over the stairs. Business cards. Names and addresses of other hotels. I bend. The headroom is low. It's made for South Americans. Some of the cheap blue paint of the wall flakes onto my jacket as I brush by.

I rub the arm of my jacket and stand in the doorway. I look left and then right. I don't want to go out. The inclination is not really there. It's a matter of energy. And a matter of confidence. I check my watch. One wrong smell would send me back upstairs. One wrong word. One wrong look. One wrong thought.

"So where you goin', son? Sure is a strange time to go out. I mean it's gonna be dark soon. You know how it is here. No twilight. It's as though ol' God just turns out the lights. He never forgets. Ten past six. Click."

I look straight ahead, at the building opposite, at the wires that are everywhere, at the houses that look unfinished with their flat roofs and the vertical metal rods that await more concrete. The rods sway in the strong evening wind that blows off the lake. I look at them and think how the ambition seems to be to build and build, to go ever skyward.

"You should have gone to a *hospedaje*."

"A what?" I ask.

"A *hospedaje*. You know sort of family homes. They let you in. Then they shut the door behind you. You know what I mean? They sort of take it upon themselves to entertain you."

There is a hint of entrapment about what he suggests. It strikes a chord. Everything suddenly seems alluring: the colour of women's clothes, the look of the lake, the smell of a dinner. I trust nothing.

"Hugo, there's no time. You can't go far."

"I'm just going up the hill."

"The hill?"

"The one by the cathedral. You know by the topiary. There's a viewpoint up there, by a sculpture."

"Oh yeh? How do you know? Don't tell me. The guidebook says so, yeh? The fuckin' guidebook says so."

I ignore the gibe. I stride out, left, down to the square where the students were massing earlier. Old men have replaced them now. They sit on the ornate iron seats, their arms folded, their heads dipping with sleep. A council worker is scrubbing the one wall that surrounds the park's centre-piece fountain. '*Aplastar las tres malditas*' someone has written, in black. The writing slants to the right. A small girl, well dressed in a red and white cardigan and blue trousers and black sandals stands alongside the words crying. Her mother is saying, "Oh dear."

"So why the sculpture? Why go there? I mean you sorted out Paul Yeats. Oh boy did you sort him out. Mind you he was so bushed he didn't know what had hit him. All that shit. Hey where did he go? What happened to him?"

I shrug. "I don't know."

"You don't know!"

"I don't know and what's more I don't care. And neither do you."

"I don't?"

"No you don't."

"But Tuesday is a train day. An' a train day is a strain day. You heard that guy."

"Paul Yeats got off lightly."

"Oh yeh, I'd say so too. I mean ol' Paul he pays for a bed and gets put in with you. Because beds are scarce and it's a Tuesday and we have to use all our resources, yeh? An' because you're sort of a bit difficult at the moment."

"Difficult?"

"Well, you know, a bit shaken."

"Look, let's forget Paul Yeats."

There is a moment of thought, a welcome moment. I view the backs of a group of men who are looking into '*Video Club Audiovisual Ariel*'. A football game is on the television that is in the shop's window. The men all have their hands in their pockets. There are no words. There are no intimacies until one man taps another on the shoulder and drifts away. I move too, passing the cathedral and the new town hall and the topiary and the police departments and the museum that is never open. The road goes straight up the hillside before it sweeps to the right towards a small car park. From there a path runs through the outcrops of rock. It leads to the sculpture.

"Manco Capac," announces Popeye.

"This is?" I say looking up at the sculpture.

"Yeh. Mind you he wouldn't thank the artist. I mean he looks more like some ol' market trader than a warrior. Jees look at his limbs. They're way too short. An' he's knock-kneed for chrissake. I mean how can a warrior be knock-kneed. Jees!"

I laugh. The white stone sculpture is a of a cloaked man holding a mace in his left hand; his right hand points towards the lake. The plinth is covered with graffiti. Names mostly. A hammer and sickle. A CND sign. 'Coco '76' is clear, as is 'Keops' which is stained in yellow on the black painted edge of the plinth's base.

"Hey perhaps he's got something."

"Who?"

"Ol' Manco there. Why don't you take his advice? You want a little solitude, a little silence, yeh? Is that right? You want to sort yourself out. I mean that's why you're here, isn't it? I mean in Puno. Well why not give it a try?" Popeye points in the same direction as Manco Capac.

Go out on the lake, that's what he's saying. Find an island, somewhere less frenetic. Somewhere without railways and armies and students wanting to try out their English. Somewhere without strangers sharing my room. Somewhere without Paul Yeats.

This is unplanned. It isn't part of my itinerary. It is as surprising as the temperature of the Puno morning that wraps me in the fog of my breath. I am cold. I shiver.

"Told you to bring a hat," says Popeye.

I pull up my collar to protect my neck.

"You need a scarf."

"I have a scarf."

"Oh yeh that beige thing. Hey Hugo that's too thin. Listen you can get an alpaca scarf here for a dollar. A dollar! Shit that's the cheapest warmth you can buy. Pure alpaca for chrissake."

I ignore him. I move slowly. It is six in the morning. It will be a bright, windy morning once the sun gets up. I decide to wait for it by a window and contemplate breakfast. What will it be? Banana pancake? Porridge? Toast? All three perhaps. And where? *Troubadours*. I like *Troubadours*. It reminds me of the tapas bar in Toulouse where I go most evenings after work, the tapas bar run by Luigi, an Italian. I love my evenings in Toulouse. They are so flexible. They form out of whims, whims to go here and do that and see so and so. One phone call and the evening falls into line. Life in Toulouse is so easy to organise.

Troubadours is closed. I half expected it to be. It is a late opening rather than an early opening sort of place. I shrug and move on, knowing something will be open. It has to be. One restaurant will cater for the early morning trade.

One does. A small entrance invites me to stroll through the kitchen on my way to the dining room. It is a spacious room. I glance at the high ceiling and nod at the man at the small table in the corner. He is the only other customer. His face looks white and lined. Lacking sleep, I think, sensing torpor. I smile as my bread and fried egg arrive and the volume of the music, issued by speakers either side of the kitchen door, increases. "European level," says a smiling waiter as he passes. I recognise the guitar. Joni Mitchell. I tap my foot along to the rhythm of "Big Yellow Taxi"; the pace slackens when the following song develops into "Unchained Melody".

Never heard her sing this before, I think. I laugh to myself recalling my mother's Sonny and Cher record. They sang this. "Oh my love..." I hum along with the tune, stopping to laugh occasionally as I think of my father's hatred of Sonny, how something about Sonny Bono grated. His untidiness, perhaps. His cheek. I remember his flat, scratchy voice. My father saying, "Bloody hell, it wouldn't be so bad if he could sing...."

"So you're gonna go....." Popeye interrupts me. "Gee Hugo sometimes I wish I'd keep quiet."

"You like it here?"

"Puno? Hell no. But Christmas is coming an' I just sort of guess that it has a little more to offer than a dull ol' island. Not that I've ever been on an island. I've been on a boat and I think that's sort of the same. You know?"

"Surrounded by sea?"

"Yeh. An' you better believe there's not much comfort on a boat."

"So it's all about comfort is it?"

"When you're travelling? Oh yeh. I mean it's sort of grim if you're not comfortable. I guess that's why you kicked out Paul Yeats."

"You've experienced this?" I question his exposure to hard travel.

"Oh yeh. It was sure cold in seventy two. Hey I nearly fuckin' froze out on that railroad. Hell you got to be warm. An' you've got to have good food. That's essential, real essential. An' you need a good bed too. Sleeping under the stars ain't so hot. That's just plain dumb, particularly in Puno. I mean in July it can go down to minus twenty. Boy that's cold, real cold."

"So how did you rate last night?"

"In the hotel? Oh that was fine. It must have been. I mean look at me this morning. I'm all snappy and green. Yeh I'm fine. Now what do you say we take the boat that goes to both islands, the one that calls in on Amanthingy on the way to Tranquillee or whatever it's called. That a good idea?"

The boat that takes in both the islands is full. A man tells me, a sort of harbourmaster. He sits in the middle of the large roundabout that is at the end of the carriageway that leads to the port. He looks comfortable. The grass around him is like a camomile lawn. It mats and interweaves and leaves small blotches of red earth. I stare at the blotches, at the inquisitive ants that seem drawn to them and then I look up at the faraway birds. They are singing. A radio is playing.

"Just the one? Just you? No friends, no wife? That's no problem. You'll get on the Taquile boat. I'll see to it." He stands up and dusts himself down and marches away. I take his place. Around me a circle of pebbles borders an area of thicker grass that surrounds a plinth and sculpture. I look up at the sculpture. Another pointing man. "An admiral," shouts the harbourmaster as he walks away. "A famous admiral." Stumpy legs and fat hands convince me that the admiral is as badly proportioned as Manco Capac. The Peruvians have a capacity for that. I recall the topiary in the main square.

"That our boat?" I ask, my peripheral vision takes in a white barge that is filling up with Peruvians. Two three wheeler bikes with storage areas across their front two wheels arrive as I look. Colourful bags are unloaded and thrown onto the boat. A woman stands on a large stone that is positioned to allow passengers to embark without wetting their feet. She cries to one of the cyclists. He moves another bag. This seems to unsettle a man on the barge who tugs at a bicycle that is at the back of the boat. He lifts it up and drapes one of its wheels over the boat's side so clearing sufficient space to allow another bag to be thrown on board.

"It's the one next to it. It's got to be." The adjacent boat is larger with a canopy and a Peruvian flag at its stern.

"You seen the water?" Popeye asks.

"The water?"

"The colour."

At its edge the lake is green, full of algae. Further out, some fifty yards away, a reflection of the hills to our right indicates where the water clears. The algae surrounds the small barges and the much larger, black and white painted, disused ferry, "*Ollanta*", that sits against the far harbour wall. It seems part of a museum like sector that includes old cranes and railway stock and beached dinghies.

"Great boat," I remark, casting a glance along the lines of the old ferry. It looks recently painted, but its shape gives its age away. It is bulky and square, nothing is streamlined.

"Must have been in operation when that ol' admiral there was

50

settling scores with the Chileans."

"The Chileans?"

"Yeh, the great war of the seventies. Around the time we were building the railroad to Arequipa. And the central railway. Yeh it was a pain in the butt. Had to send the Chilean workers home. Had to get a special agreement with the Peruvian government that they would have safe passage. Oh it was a hell of a pain."

A mural confirms the war with Chile. A painting of a sea battle. It separates the carriageways just before the final roundabout. The Chilean ship in the mural is black and white with heavy-looking masts. It looks ponderous alongside the shark-like Peruvian vessel that is grey and slick and is firing a broadside. Two gaping chasms in the Chilean boat's hull emphasise the Peruvian success.

"You see the name of the battle?" Popeye inquires. "*Combate naval de Angamos*, yeh? *Angamos*."

"Where? It says that?"

"Underneath. It's in black an' that's kind of daft because this place is so grimey. You see it now?"

Yes I see it. There is a date too. Eight. Ten. Eighteen seventy-one.

"Yeh that's about right. Eighteen seventy-one. Yeh, good year that son. Eighteen seventy-one."

On the boat I lean back and let the sun warm my face. It is a quiet morning and even with a spluttering engine and a fussy navigator the journey seems serene. We go out through an area of reeds following markers in the water. The navigator sits beside me at the back of the boat, perching on the back rail, standing up occasionally to see the markers. "Normally it is busier," he remarks.

I wonder what he means, whether he is referring to the traffic on the waterway which is quiet but for the waves we drive against the reedy banks surrounding us. "It's Christmas," adds the navigator. "No-one comes to Taquile at Christmas. It's too quiet. You westerners prefer Puno. Puno they say when I ask them where they are going to spend their Christmas. But you are staying on Taquile."

I wonder how he knows that and realise my bag is a give away. Most of the other passengers are visiting Taquile for a few hours and have no bag or just a day sack.

"So what is wrong with a quiet Christmas? Perhaps you can tell me, eh? Can you do that?"

I do not answer.

"Ah you want to be quiet too." The navigator smiles, sensing the irony. He stands up again. I learn that is a signal that another marker is coming into view. I take a deep breath.

"You smell the lake," he says, the wind catching his loose white shirt. He tucks it in. "It is like the sea, eh? The birds , the fish, the water." He breathes in. "A good smell, eh? And what do you see? Can you tell me that my friend?"

I hate the over familiarity. It makes me wonder about the island. Will all the islanders be as friendly? It isn't what I want. I want anonymity. Just for a few days. Just until I sort myself out.

"Eh? What do you see?"

I ignore him. I stare forward. My eyes fix on the canopy, on a tarpaulin that for some reason is spread out over a black, leather suitcase, a new looking suitcase. As I look I see the vibration of the boat is causing the tarpaulin to slip slowly away. The suitcase is black with a zip and handles. A combination lock sits between the handles. The case intrigues me. I try to link it with its owner, but nobody fits. A growl from the engine and the tarpaulin slips further away. Embroidered initials are revealed. Gold letters. An old fashioned scroll.

"*Perdon.*" I stand up and move forward. One yard, two yards. I look around, to my left, to my right. It is as though I am taking the navigator's question seriously. I see him smile and, as I turn one last time, I move another yard closer to the case. I see the initials. JNP, I read. The case is clean and modern. It isn't South American. I can sense that. The design tells me. It is sleek. It deserves a smart shirt and a good suit and a casual pair of trousers.

I return to my seat. JNP. I reflect upon the initials. They don't belong to the navigator. I am sure of that. I have heard someone on the boat call him Hernando. No, the suitcase isn't his. I look his way to check my instincts.

"Hey mister," he says, catching my eye. "You have a paper, a newspaper? If you finish with it, could I have it? I like papers. You see I am nosey. I like to know what's going on in the world. What do you say? You have a paper?"

I say nothing. I close my eyes. I turn away.

part three

JOSE

1

I'm not sure how I became a member of Sendero Luminoso. It just happened. I suppose it was membership by association, by where I first taught – the philosophy department at Ayacucho University. It was a new university and it was probably its youth that made it need to be radical – more radical than I would have advocated – but I was in it, part of it and I was swept along. Membership by association I always thought, considering it rather loose and luke warm.

It became warmer one day when I was called out of a lecture. I remember the lecture. It was on the Frankfurt School. A first year class. I had been talking about Bader-Meinhof when I saw the deputy director of the college enter and stand at the side of the room. I couldn't have missed him: the room had windows all the way along the side that faced the quadrangle and the wooden walkway outside the room had creaked in a way that indicated somebody was there. The door clicked and in he came. He moved to the far side of the room and leant against an old radiator. He appeared to be reading the latest graffiti on the wall. "*Aqui se queda la clara la entrariable transparencia de querida presencia Commandte Che Guevara.*" In red. Previous bits of graffiti lay underneath poking through looking like bruises or bad veins. I looked at the graffiti and felt the stiff breeze that was blowing in through a broken window adjacent to the door. The breeze ruffled my notes on the lectern. That was enough to unsettle me, but then the slightest thing could do that. I was a nervous lecturer. I felt pressure and frequently displayed my unease, so when I could I controlled it. "Excuse me a minute," I told the class, deciding to pull away.

"Just a word," the deputy director said. He was a tall man who held himself well. His head slightly arched back so protruding his chest. Good stature for a man in his fifties. His hair was very black, jet black. Probably dyed, I thought, because he possessed an obvious vanity, one attribute of which was a warm impudence that suggested he could allow himself the freedom to intervene or interrupt anything. "Could you call in after your class? Nothing to worry about," he said continuing. "Just a quick chat."

"Something's come up," he said later when I entered his study. "I know you normally deal with Jorge and this may seem strange. But please don't worry." His charm made as much of an impression on me as his office with its mahogany chairs and coffee machine and carpets. All cobbled together. I could tell that. Nothing matched, but some effort had been made which certainly wasn't true of the windswept lecture theatre and my own office which was little more than a cupboard, pink painted with a dangling light bulb, a filing cabinet that refused to close, a desk and a calendar donated by Wagner's glue factory in Lima.

"Take a seat. Coffee?" He tried to relax me. A smile accompanied his offer.

"Please." I watched him leave his desk and move to the coffee percolator. "Black," I said anticipating the question.

"Now this is good coffee," said the deputy director while pouring. "You know I can never understand why it is that countries that have the coffee bean can't make coffee. Have you ever.thought about it? I mean you're a thinker aren't you Mr. Perez?"

"I teach philosophy."

"That's not the same."

"No, no it isn't," I agreed, edgy now, wondering why the preliminaries were enduring. I accepted the coffee. The deputy director smiled. His was a controlled smile, his mouth not opening, his nostrils widening slightly. "No sugar, yes?"

I nodded.

"See. That's intuition. You approve of that?"

"Of intuition. To a degree,"

"To a degree," he laughed. "You're hedging your bets. You weren't doing that earlier."

"Earlier?"

"In your lecture."

"I don't in my lectures. I tell the students how I see it. They can read then and decide for themselves. They like it that way."

"So I've heard."

"It's not my method. I learnt it from Arnez." Arnez had been my tutor at undergraduate level. He had retired now.

"We all learnt something from Arnez," responded the deputy director. "Still, it's effective. That's what counts." A bell rang. An alarm clock bell. It rang in his briefcase. The warm impudence returned in a cheeky grin. "Sorry," he said, not in the slightest bit embarrassed as he opened up the briefcase. The volume of the alarm suddenly increased as he flicked back the clasps of the case and pulled out a box of pills. "Noon. I take zinc at noon," he explained. "It's good for the sex drive. You understand Mr Perez?"

Was that a slur? I couldn't work it out. I couldn't put together his expression and the words and how they gelled. And he didn't give me time. "Now how can I put it?" he said, pausing to swallow the pills. He put away the briefcase and sat back holding his hands out in front of him. He pressed his thumbs together. It seemed an awkward gesture. It allowed me to smile, to congratulate myself. I was reading the tactics well. I knew I couldn't win, yet I also knew that I shouldn't let the deputy director have an easy ride. I wondered what I should say next. Stay quiet, I thought, let the deputy director draw it out, whatever it was. I wanted to know. Why was I suddenly important? I sensed I was. The whole situation said so: the office, the delay, the protractedness.

I tasted the coffee. It was strong, rich, gritty. Its aroma mixed with a flowery smell from a source I couldn't locate. My gaze scrutinised his desk. A blotter, a pen, an open book, two upright framed photographs, one of his wife and himself standing by a lake, one of himself with a visiting delegation.

"I did enjoy it," said the deputy director, breaking back in before I could study the faces on the photograph.

"What?"

"Your lecture."

"You listened to it?" I said, slightly off balance again.

"Mm, I sort of hovered." The deputy director smiled. Something about the look said it was his prerogative, that he was exercising his authority. "It sort of grabbed me. Critical theory eh?" The deputy director waited. It was an attempt at engaging, but it didn't draw me. "So what do you think? Do you agree with it?"

"With critical theory? I'm not sure." I wanted to laugh at that. Being compromised, I allowed a smile to move to the edge of my lips. As always my mind searched through the literature, trying to find something appropriate for my situation. Marx, Gramsci, Althusser. Marcuse. My mind refused to settle.

"Come on. If I were a student you'd have to give me more."

"If you were a student you wouldn't ask such questions."

"Why?" The deputy director seemed intrigued now.

"Because I'd have told you by now that the trouble with any ideology is we never perfectly understand it, that ideologies are never perfectly worked out. So reality provides surprises. It's a bit like a butterfly in a collection pinned to polystyrene, wings open, in a glass case. It looks perfect. But it's when its alive that's important, when it's on the wing.... We need to see how it survives. The most beautiful things can be vulnerable or ill equipped." I stopped myself. I wanted to move things on. I hated games. I wanted to know what the interview was about. I hoped my answer and my change of tone told the deputy director that I wanted to get to the point. I wanted him to see that yes I knew the department was gaining an ideological rigidity, a strict Marxist orthodoxy. I wanted him to see that I had understood the university had become a laboratory. I both agreed and disagreed with such a move, though that was an irrelevance. All that mattered was that I had toed the line. I had been given a course and was expected to teach it. Sometimes I managed to do that without becoming too involved. As long as it reflected what I felt, which it did most of the time, fine, I was happy, though I still wanted to take liberties, to draw things out.

"You're from Chuschi?" the deputy director said with a start, edging forwards.

"Yes." The reference to my home village surprised me. Chuschi, my mind repeated. What's the relevance of that?

"Tell me about it." He moved back in his chair and allowed it to carry him to his right and then to his left. The movement was meant to indicate a degree of relaxation, but somehow it fell short. It couldn't hide the fact that this was the crux of the conversation.

"Chuschi?" I struggled to find words. To me the consideration seemed futile. I didn't expect it to lead anywhere. Another waste of time, I thought. "It's small... but for a village I suppose it's large. It's more like a small town I suppose."

"Population?"

"Five, six thousand."

"Good."

I wondered what else to say. The brief was so unfocused. Should

I talk about the landscape or the people? Or the farming problems? Or the weather? Or religion? Yes, what about religion? Or traditions? There was so much. "Why?" I finally said, maintaining a graveness.

"Oh it's just that we're looking for some villages. Not any old villages mark you. A group of villages. And Chuschi's in the group we're considering. We want to carry out a little experiment there."

I understood the logic. I told the deputy director that. I understood the idea of the war of little wars, that individual revolts could and would spread and grow together. That meant responding to differences in class and economics and ethnicity and age in the various regions of Peru, though I wondered how that fitted Chuschi and I laughed when the deputy director started talking about depeasantised youth. How I hated jargon. Depeasantised youth indeed. What nonsense. There was no alternative. Peasants or what?

"Of course there's an alternative," the deputy director argued. "You took the alternative. There must be many like you."

But there wasn't. I used a pause to check that, to try to think of others in the village like me. No one, apart from Julia, my sister, came to mind. The others had all stayed. They had remained firmly in the peasantry. But I couldn't tell the deputy director that, so I let him win the point and then moved to other issues. "But it already has strong communal structures. What I'm saying is why destroy those to create them again? It doesn't make sense."

The deputy director listened and thought. He nodded once and smiled. I had impressed him. He admired the spirit and vigour of my mind. "I can see you care about this," he said, seeming a little moved for once. "But it's not just Chuschi. We want to take over eight or nine villages. Some small, some large. Some reformed, some feudal. Mostly Catholic, but one Protestant. And we want to change the social structures," he admitted. "It's just a little experiment. You know, just to see if the people react in the same way. Interesting, don't you think?"

I nodded. I thought of my own lectures on Peru, how I'd say that it was special, how I'd talk about reality and fiction and use the analogy of how in fiction when a man beats his wife there'd be a reaction, that the conflict has to come to a head, that the man would go to jail or his wife would kill him, that there'd be drama. But in the real world, nine times out of ten, the man would go on beating the wife and the wife would come to accept it. It would become part of her life. "Peru is like the fiction," I'd say, tidying up the analogy. "Things happen here. There is always drama. It's becoming unreal." I thought over that view. I wondered where it left the deputy director's experiment. I shook my head.

"You disagree?" he asked.

"No –"

"Well?" The deputy director seemed a little lost.

"I just think you need to educate the people first. You can't just move in and say this is what's going to happen. You can't dictate. You have to get them on your side. You need to explain things to them. If you move in and say all of you will get on well with each other, they'll laugh. They're all different. They don't trust. There's always been conflict. Understand? You ask them. Conflict between the landowners and the peasants, the Church and the peasants. There's always been conflict. And it goes on," I added thoughtfully.

"You still have contacts in Chuschi?"

"Contacts," I laughed. "My father lives there. My best friend lives there. I go back at least twice a year."

The deputy director nodded. "You were saying it continues."

"Conflict? Oh yes. There's conflict now with the next village. Chuschi is Catholic, Quispillaqta is Protestant. Some sect or other moved in. They don't get on. Peasant versus peasant." I shook my hands as though indicating the organisation would have its work cut out.

The deputy director laughed softly. I was disappointed. I expected a more elevated response, something that respected the impact of my words. The laugh was saying you underestimate us. It gave way to a sharper, sterner look, a penetrating look. A look of thought, deep thought. It was checking what was being said and reasserting that they, the organisation, would be in control, that they would be the scientists of the experiment. And I knew I was very much included in that experiment. Part of the team, I thought, respecting my position. After all, all I wanted was to keep my teaching; that more than anything is what I lived for. It was what the deputy director might ask me to do beyond that that worried me.

"We would favour committees," he said, slipping ahead of my

thoughts. He was watching me carefully. "Committees made up of people from the village."

"And one or two of us?" I suggested.

"Just to nudge them along. You know open their eyes, let them see what's possible."

I shook my head. I laughed again, not sure if I was arguing in the general or the specific, but that seemed irrelevant as I realised what was coming. He's going to ask me. The local man. Yes, me. I realised I fitted in. Committees. Meetings. I hate meetings. But I'd be there. Me the local man, me pushing people along. I didn't like the sound of that.

2

The island did its job well. I was pleased with it, like a teacher is pleased with a student or a fisherman is pleased with a river or a football fan is pleased with a player. It performed. It stuck to its task. And that meant that in my first days I hardly noticed it, though that is deceptive because it provided me with moments when I would wonder at its diversity, at how a stark wall of rock, which was how it appeared from the mainland, could curve and carve and reveal a succinctness of bays and coves and hidden valleys. I would sit for hours on top of the cliff and try to unravel the geography of the slight slopes and rolling coastline which was like lacy, fleeting skirts, revealing shadows and rocks as I moved on and upwards. The great beauty of the island was that I knew each of the bays and coves was accessible, that I could walk around its periphery in a day. I liked that. I liked its size. I liked its serenity too, the way you could escape from the limpid gaze of its two thousand smiling inhabitants and find your own rock or hollow and hide yourself away.

It was a fine mix, the mix of landscape and solitude. And people. I shouldn't forget people. They were part of the mix too. They helped me each day when I would settle with the oils and pieces of canvas I had bought in Lima. I painted. People mostly; Hernando, the fisherman whom I had become acquainted with on the boat, in particular. Some days when I couldn't find him I was forced to return to previous paintings and reassess them. The light of the day would change them. My thoughts would change them too. I didn't find that unsatisfactory, though I preferred it when he was with me and I could draw the cuts on his fingers, the perspiration on his nose, the bruise on his arm. I wanted to elicit his carefulness, his eye for detail. My subject, I called him. "José's subject," he boasted proudly.

And while I painted, I thought of Lima, of my talk at La Contute, I thought how I went there every year to talk to its economics society about the state of Peru's political structures. It was a difficult topic. I knew it would draw in outsiders now that the political situation had become acute, that in the audience there would be eyes watching and minds assessing the message. So I camouflaged things: I criticised in allegories. Being clever again I thought, remembering some of my words and the way my nose would twitch to throw back my glasses so I could gauge reactions. I also recalled how going out afterwards relieved the stress of performance. I love going out. I love city streets. I love the hustle and the bustle. And normally they lead me to a cinema. This time, after my talk and walk, I found myself in a cinema in Calle Union. I saw a poor film. All action and nothing else. American. Cops and robbers. I gave up on the film annoyed by its vacuity and the antics of the Peruvian public who, reading the subtitles, felt no need to concentrate on the sound. It left them free to talk. About politics. About football. When the couple next to me began a conversation about starting a family, I found myself listening and wanting to offer advice. I had always been like that. Interested. Wanting to help. Though I would never impose myself and proffer an opinion, it did allow me to become philosophical and analytical. So it was almost inevitable that by the time the couple were silenced by an impasse – the boy for, the girl against – the film was two murders on and I was out in the street.

So much freedom, I thought. But why wasn't I picked up? Why weren't there plainclothes policemen in the foyer and by the street stall near the Church of La Merced where I stopped for a *churro*? I spoke about the film to the girl behind the counter. "Don't bother," I said when she remarked she had thought about going to see it. "Stay in. Write."

"Write?" she laughed. "I never write."

"Start. Here, I've a pen and paper." I reached inside my jacket and produced a notebook and biro. "Go on. Take them," I urged, passing the notebook and pen to her. "You'll pick it up. It's easy. You stay in tomorrow. Write. Forget about the film."

"What should I write?" she asked, accepting the pad uneasily, exchanging it for the *churro*.

I gave her the money and took a bite of the *churro*. I nodded my head, tasting it. "Good," I said, licking my lips. "Now what should you write? Try cops and robbers. Set it in New York. A couple of murders. A shoot-out. A car chase. Easy. Give the cop a drink problem. Or drugs. Or girls. Or better still all three." The girl laughed. "Hey you like that. There. And make him a Catholic. A good Catholic. Make him understand guilt. You'll get it," I added.

But why wasn't she an agent? Why didn't she handcuff me when I closed my eyes to take in the succulence of the *churro*? So many opportunities, I thought. My mind moved to another plane and began to treat my dealings with the *churro* vendor as a snapshot of my life. It focused on the way I treated people, on the way I worked a slant on everything. Like the film. And the girl, the poor girl. What did she think of me? "Too clever," I cursed, my mind also considering occasions – too few occasions – when I had been witty. It made me see I wasn't renowned for it. It wasn't that I was incapable of humour or wit, but rather that I buried it beneath an intensity that was unrelieved and dominant. Sometimes, though, very occasionally, a remark came to me and, as though it surprised me as much as the person I was conversing with, I would laugh too.

Like I was laughing now. I had noticed the fisherman had put down the net. "You're miming," I said in an accusing way.

"Miming?" Hernando seemed lost. The laughter upset him a little. After all he was being polite. He didn't want to move until the sketch was finished, but the net was repaired so he kept his hand moving, sewing up air, tidying imaginary edges.

"Look at you," I laughed.

Hernando considered his hands. He let them work on, his fingers going over and through, tieing something up. "José, look. I am like a machine," he said, suddenly seeming gaunt and fidgety. Worn down, I thought. The old man stopped his hands and placed them behind his back as though he were putting them away. "Too old to fish," he said, laughing again. "Too old for the ferry run. Too old for the fields. I don't know. Machines are better than men. You know that José?"

"Rubbish."

"Of course they are. If I was a machine you could oil me. Put a new part in. Charge me up. I'd be as good as new, eh José? Instead we just wear out. That's what we do." He edged towards me. "Can I look?"

I was still finding lines, adding shadows. I held my head back like a real artist. "Tomorrow," I said, knowing I was protecting the old man, that I had painted in all his years at sea.

"Oh come on José, I can take it. I know what age is. I can feel it. Listen, I can hear it." He moved his knee. It clicked. "See?" Another laugh came to him. I knew that it was at this point that he normally gathered up his things and marched away up the stone steps to the arch where we would stop and talk politics. He made his move. I stayed.

"You not coming? I'll buy you a drink. Eh José? A drink?" He stopped when he reached me. He put down the net at his side, trying to glimpse the sketch as he bent down. "Come on," he urged, "you can tell me how we're doing."

"How we're doing," I repeated in an admiring way, as though I was analysing all the subtlety of Hernando's speech. "You know something? You're different. You're not like the others."

"Me? Oh I am. José I am," protested Hernando.

I shook my head. I had been with Hernando long enough to scrape away all the trappings of the island and reveal something exclusive, something the other islanders didn't seem to be near to possessing. "You look further," I suddenly said.

"No, no, no, I just admit to it José. The others they think like me. They're shy."

"No." I shook my hands to emphasise a point. "You're different. I didn't think you'd be different, but you are. You're what I expected. You understand?" I explored the fisherman's face for recognition, but found only surprise and bewilderment. I offered more words of explanation. "I mean I didn't think there'd be a difference, you see?" I paused. I couldn't find the words I needed. I tried harder. I took a step back. "I used to look across from the mainland and think it's the same. Because it's so close. I mean it's there, the island is there. I used to see it every Tuesday on my way to Juliaca. I run a course there on Tuesdays. I used to see the island like I saw my students."

"And I see my fish," laughed Hernando.

"What I'm saying is I thought everywhere's the same. The whole of Peru. You understand?" I kept checking. I wanted to believe my words made sense. I was pleased when Hernando nodded. "Rural is rural, that's what I believed. Forget places." I stopped to think of the view across the plain, past the llama herds and the mud huts, out into the lake and the gap in the peninsulas that presented Taquile on clear days. It was like a shop sign. Framed, dominant. Striking too. It worked in the way it promoted itself. "You think about Peru. You're different."

"Peru? Hey I'm global José," laughed the fisherman. "But this is Taquile not Peru. You have to remember that to understand this place José. You know we pick fights with Peru. Over the boats, over the hotel, over the school."

The list surprised me. I sought clarification. "The school?" I asked.

"Didn't you hear about that? Oh what goes on on the mainland? Doesn't news get across to Puno José? Only good news I expect, news that the state wants to tell." He stopped, sensing my impatience or my desire to hear what had happened in relation to the school. "Well in 1981 they tried to get our children to wear the standard Peruvian school wear. You know grey and white , a shirt and trousers, but we said no, we said we have our own clothes, the clothes of Taquile. And we won. We wouldn't have it. We always win. They want to build hotels. We say no. They want to run their own boats back and fore to Puno. We say no. You see José it's different here. That sort of thinking makes us float away. It cuts us loose. You understand?"

I understood. I thought of Puno. I considered the differences. Puno with the police pressure, the trucks around the cathedral, the gun squad, the explosives squad, the Sunday procession relayed through loudspeakers to the whole of the city with the local division of the army parading, carrying flags. Puno with the national anthem, with the mayor crying, "*Viva! Viva* Peru! *Viva!*" and with the crowd responding. There was none of that on Taquile. No army, no procession, no police, no roads. Tranquillity, I thought.

"So come on José. How are we doing?"

"We" was Izquierda Unida, the United Left party, the coalition of left of centre groups who joined together to fight elections. It was 1989. A general election was due. Izquierda Unida had been fancied. Hernando was a supporter. "We've a chance, haven't we?"

"You think they can win?" I asked still working away, though now on another sketch of another man I had seen the previous day.

"Izquierda? Of course they can. People get fed up. At present there's too much blood and too much hardship. People want change."

I understood what he meant. The blood was the revolutionary left, the hardship the government. I wondered which the old man considered the worse.

It was my moments with Hernando that settled me. For the first few days on the island I found myself thinking, "I should have stayed. I should have given myself up in Puno. What was Jorge thinking of?" But thoughts of the way terrorists were dealt with quickly dropped the charges against Jorge. I knew if I were caught I would be deemed a subversive or a traitor. Whatever they called me would bracket me with the terrorists and I knew the legal system didn't tolerate them, that they were dealt with outside of the law. That frightened me. I thought how military judges were used, how defence lawyers weren't allowed to question witnesses or have access to evidence. Such a system would have incarcerated or killed me.

"So Jorge was right," I'd say, thinking of cells and doors and staring at the door to my hut. Hardly a prison door. I'd laugh, considering the locking mechanism which was a piece of wood shaped like a mallet that could be pushed in towards a loop of metal on the door's frame. Four cuts were made into the handle part of the mallet shape. The metal loop could be pressed into one of these cuts to secure the door. Such a lock was only functional from the inside, so during the day the door remained open. Open, close, open. I'd play with the mechanism, gripping the fat handle part of the mallet shape and pushing it, sliding it in and out of the metal loop. It seemed such a simple function. Use it, use it, I'd think, saying to myself, "Cliffs today. Binoculars, binoculars. Where are they?" I moved over to my bag and began to search through it, wondering all the time why I had brought binoculars. Why had I taken them to Lima? I couldn't work it out. What was there in Lima to see? Why? Then I realised I had misplaced them. I always misplaced things. Julia called it a disease. "That's a disease," she'd say when I double checked that I'd picked up my chewing gum. Going back to the house for the gum meant double checking that the power was off and the taps were turned off. I could never remember such things. My mind was always elsewhere, always with Gramsci or Althusser, or my morning lecture. It was never with taps or kettles or, in this case, binoculars.

"José?" A voice. Hernando's voice. "*Hola!* Any news, any happenings, any developments, any events?" That was Hernando's standard opening, his greeting. He issued it and then seemed to regret it when he sensed I was painting. "You're working," he said, coming into the room and seeing a sketchpad on the bed. "I'll call back. I'll see you later. I won't stop. I'm on my way to the port to have a look at the arrivals, to see if I can sniff a paper. You know that Frenchman, the one who arrived the other day? He had nothing with him. Can you believe that, eh José? I mean most of them buy a paper to read on the boat. But him? Nothing. Absolutely nothing."

"So how do you know he didn't have a paper?"

"How do I know? I asked him." Hernando was smiling now, leaning back against the adobe wall. "I do that now. Now that I've got someone to read to me, eh José?" The smile told me just how much Hernando enjoyed our time together. It made me recall how yesterday I had read out loud a paper he had brought and Hernando had gasped and moaned and laughed. He had enjoyed the detail. He had seemed almost to participate in the stories. A family disturbance. A train crash. A broken water main. And a murder. It was that that had really excited him. A murder. I linked that to his disappointment now.

"So you don't know any more about the murder?"

"What murder?" he said cheekily. A glint in his eyes giving his interest away.

"Oh come on."

"OK, OK. Yes of course I wanted to learn a bit more. I mean there were so many unanswered questions."

"You still think Sendero did it?"

"Of course Sendero did it. Who else would have done it? That's why it's so frustrating. I mean that Frenchman. Hey José I could have killed him, you know that?"

"For not having a paper?"

"Yes. For not having a paper." Hernando laughed to himself. "Shot in a restaurant," he said slowly.

"The man in Puno? Drinking his soup." A top ranking government official visiting Puno for the day to look at the plans for a new town hall had been shot in a restaurant.

"Drinking his soup. Is that what it said José? You didn't say. Drinking his soup." Hernando chuckled. He was pleased now. He knew how difficult it was to interrupt me, to get me to put down my paintbrush and talk. "So we'll have to see what they trawl today. You know what? I feel lucky. I feel that we're due a break. I think we're due a radical. A *La Republica* reader. That Frenchman was a reactionary. He would have been an *El Commercio* reader."

"Really?"

"I can tell."

"Can you now?" I picked up the brushes off the pillow and inspected them. Clean, clean, clean, my mind said.

"Yes, I can tell by the way they look. You know. Clean trousers, clean shoes. And a shirt. That's the giveaway. A shirt. And he had glasses too."

"Sounds like me."

"You?" Hernando laughed. "He's nothing like you José."

"What do you mean?" I stood upright and presented myself. I flicked my glasses back up my nose. "Glasses."

"Yes."

"A shirt. And flannels."

"I didn't mention flannels."

"You were about to."

"Perhaps I was. OK Flannels."

"See."

Again the old man laughed. "But your hair José. It should be more styled. An *El Commercio* reader is more fussy. You just have it short. And you chew gum José. No *El Commercio* reader would chew gum. You're more of a *La Republica* reader José. You're looser. You're more passionate. You're no *El Commercio* reader José."

Hernando left then. He did that when I lapsed into thought. Something would stir him to move quickly, sometimes without a word. This time it was the prospect of the cliff. I knew he didn't like climbing, that it wasn't an activity that he relished. I had learnt that when I arrived on the island, when he had told me of the cliff-side path.

"I'll see you," he said, holding up a hand to indicate his departure.

Two minutes later I moved out of my hut, my hands touching pockets establishing where I had put the binoculars and the notepad and the camera, my small auto focus camera. "And film," I said, touching a pocket of my jacket. I moved quickly through the first courtyard looking straight ahead, minimising the risk of being side-tracked. I was disappointed when, climbing the steps leading to the upper courtyard, I became aware of Sebastian, Ramon's father.

I knew I would have to stop and talk because Sebastian, a farmer and a *charango* player and a staunch traditionalist, had already flummoxed and intrigued me, opening up whenever he saw me about the history of the island and its way of life. A little rueful, he seemed to speculate that all the tradition and history in the world couldn't equip one for the vagaries of modern life. Yet he praised modernity too, saying "Thank God for tourists" whenever he saw a westerner.

"Sebastian," I said lightly, feigning some sort of joy. He was sitting in one of the plastic chairs, holding a hammer in his right hand. On his lap was a sandal and some tacks. He was one of those incredibly practical men that, given the resources, could mend or construct anything. And because he was so connected to the old skills, he had an exaggerated idea of loss and the need to transfuse his understanding of tradition into others.

"So what you do today? You look for duck?" he asked, looking up.

I sighed. I hadn't understood the question. It related to some myth Sebastian had tried to demystify the previous day. I struggled to recall it. He had told me so much. I couldn't believe such a small island could generate such a quantity of folklore. Duck, duck, duck.

Nothing. Birds, yes. I remembered that birds were associated with predictions. I ran over the species in my mind. The flamingo. The thrush. I recalled them. They had a significance relating to the quantity of crops that would be harvested. But the duck? Nothing. I had no recall.

"You no remember," accused the old man. He shook his head; his face ever smiling. "Remember what Sebastian say? How flight direction important? East to west is best, yes?"

"Yes," I said, grabbing some recall. "Yes, of course. East to west is best." I smiled. But I didn't understand it. It didn't make sense.

"So now you know, yes?"

I took a second or two to articulate the difficulties in my mind. Duck, duck, duck, flight direction, east to west is best. The concepts formulated and ordered themselves. Somehow they cohered. "You said no-one knows what it looks like. I mean this duck. Is that right?" I waited for a response from Sebastian. His poor Spanish meant there was always a slight delay. I imagined his mind translating Quechua, his language, into Spanish. Then came the smile like a bolt of realisation, then the yes, yes.

"Yes, yes," he said obligingly.

"Well if you don't know what it looks like, how do you know which way it flies?"

"Ah...." Sebastian smiled. He enjoyed the point. He enjoyed the superiority it gave him, the way he saw that I hadn't thought hard enough, the way the obvious had been missed. He pointed to the side of his head. "You use."

"You listen," I said.

"Yes." He touched his left ear again. " Listen. See?... Birds."

I could hear birdsong. I wouldn't have noticed it normally, but it was undeniably there, somehow on top of all the other island sounds which were mainly natural: the beating of bushes in the wind, the scamper of animals. There were some interferences. A radio. The moans of man's constructions as tin roofs vibrated and walls absorbed and reflected the wind.

"You......." He struggled for the word. "You follow, no? You track, yes?"

"Oh you track the sound," I said, concentrating hard on his words.

"Yes, but this duck no go quack, quack."

"No go quack, quack?" I laughed as I found my Spanish deteriorating to his level.

"No, the night time duck, it go tic, tic, tic, tic, tic." He almost spat the sound out through the gap in his front teeth. It was a sibilant sound, a little louder than a hiss, a little sharper too.

"Tic, tic, tic, tic. No duck goes tic, tic, tic, tic."

"This duck, the night time duck, it go tic, tic, tic. All night. All through the night. Tic, tic, tic, tic."

"So you've heard it?"

"Me!" Sebastian pulled a sharp face. It said shock, horror. He had the face of a silent actor. It somehow made up for his lack of Spanish vocabulary. Many of his adjectives were creased in his jowls or rolled out of his eyes. "No, no, no. I no want see. Me see night time duck? Oh no. You keep fingers cross you no see. It no good to see. It kill."

"If you see it?"

"It bad luck. It big bad luck."

"To see it?"

"No, not see it. See it OK. But hear it." He sliced a finger across his throat to indicate what hearing it would mean.

"If you hear it you die?"

"Yes. Anyone hearing it will die. Within three day." He half closed his eyes and started nodding his head as if to indicate that here was another old wives' tale that should be treated with cautious disdain.

"Right," I laughed enjoying the actions and expressions that somehow ran over the words. They seemed somehow clear but hidden. Like polished pebbles at the base of a clear pool. You could keep them in view. You could appreciate them, but you couldn't fully comprehend them.

"Some believe it," said Sebastian, turning away, tapping the hammer against the heel of the sandal. "Sometimes I believe it. Perhaps you should too. While you here, yes? You believe it for me. For Sebastian Marca Yucra, yes?"

3

May 1980 was my first official visit to Chuschi. I wondered what Nico, my best friend in the village, would have said if he'd have known the visit was sanctioned by Sendero. He knew something was up. I sensed that immediately. He knew how out of character it was, how we had a routine: Christmas and the first week of July, that's when I visited. But this was May, early May and all I had as an excuse was a letter he had sent me, a letter that told me how a group of migrants to the village had set up a cooperative, how they had bought large numbers of cattle and sheep and had taken over thirteen of the villagers' cornfields. The locals felt threatened. Nico described it as being like an earthquake. It had shaken the community's spirit, it had introduced new ways, it had instituted a new class that was close to the government. A visit by a state administrator seemed to substantiate that. His appearance was seen as interference. "We're waiting for the aftershock," said Nico.

He reiterated that when I sat and listened in the chair by the window in Nico's lounge above his shop. "You're aware," I kept saying. "You've become political. You have become political."

"Hey what's so surprising? Anyway it's not that. It's not like that," replied Nico insistently. It made me smile. I thought how a year or two previously Nico had disregarded the locals' confrontation with the church. He wanted none of that. He washed his hands of it. "You shouldn't dabble with the church," he had said as though he viewed it as a superior being, something that was there to be obeyed. He had been equally non-committal when the villagers felt threatened by a sergeant from the civil guard who owned land adjacent to Chuschi. The sergeant wanted more land. He threatened some of the villagers, saying pay up or else. Even though they knew what 'or else' meant, the Chuschi villagers showed him where he stood. They invaded his farm, destroying his crops.

"Taking the law into your own hands," Nico had said. "You can't do that. You have to have law. You have to have order. It gives some sort of structure and we need that." Law was another of Nico's superior beings, but the cooperative was different. It wasn't superior. The mestizos who ran it were flesh and blood. "So is that why you're here, my letter? Hey come on, it's so unlike you. You never just arrive. You're meticulous. You plan things. My God, it's a woman," he said suddenly, startled by the possibility. "You're getting married. That's it, isn't it?"

"Hey hold on," I objected. I laughed at the way Nico's thoughts were advancing in all directions.

"But we're not prepared."

I knew what Nico meant. I knew how he came to live by our routine and how Tania, his daughter, pencilled the dates of my visit in on the calendar in the shop and how near the date of my visit she would go to Cangallo and buy in treats. Chocolates for me. Pisco for Nico.

"Ah sit down, sit down." His arm directed me to a chair by the window. He poured me a drink. "So," he said, putting the bottle away. He clicked his fingers and pointed at me. " You're voting here." He had remembered there was to be an election the following day. His words offered me a way out, but it came as I was about to utter the excuse I had rehearsed. I decided to keep to my plan.

"Your letter intrigued me."

"But that isn't the real reason."

"My father isn't well," I said, rushing my words. "Nothing serious. Just a strain. Thought I'd come home and help out for a few days –"

"Hey that's nice of you," Nico sounded surprised.

"It's a busy time. Gives him a chance to rest up, get better."

"I saw him the other day." The memory had made Nico raise his tone. "Carrying something. A big box. He was in the square. He was talking. He's always talking. He said you'd been to Lima."

"I have. My yearly visit."

Nico pulled a face. It was meant to say that he still found towns unappealing. I wondered why, knowing Nico had never been to a town larger than Chuschi. Such subjectivity bewildered me. I wondered how somebody so intelligent could apply such loose logic. I could only think it was the Peruvian way.

"I couldn't do it." Nico was off again, pontificating about experiences he had never had, making them elegantly gruesome because something told him that is how they should be. He sat down and pulled another face. "Tania's cooking. You'll join us?" He waited for me to nod a reply. "Now come on. I want to know.

What's it like?"

"Lima?" I asked, thinking how well Nico used his face, how he could contort it into shapes like mirrors at a fair. They exaggerated his words, laying emphasis where others would use sound. A fine instrument I thought, considering how useful it would be to a lecturer.

"No, not Lima. Lima," he groaned, "I don't want to hear about Lima. I'm not interested in Lima. You know that. You know I hate Lima. I hate all towns."

"You've never been to a town."

"Lecturing. I want to hear about lecturing. I want to know how you do it."

I smiled at my friend. I used the pisco like I used a glass of water in my lectures. It gave me time to think. It calmed me: the picking up, the drinking, the putting down. I thought how, when I was lecturing, I used other tricks too, how I kept my shirt out of my trousers around my back. That let in air. It cooled me. Another trick was speaking slowly, taking deep breaths. I thought how my thin voice sometimes shook and broke, how I sometimes needed to gulp in air. I thought of my fears too: that someone would ask a question I could not answer, that someone would object to something that I said. I thought, too, of the way a thin knowledge of some topics sometimes made me like a salesman, how on such days I relied on technique. "I shock," I said slowly. "Sometimes it is the only way to get through, to communicate. Understand?"

While I spoke, I was aware of movement in the square. I turned and looked out through the open window. A gang of boys were sitting on a bench. I could hear them. I couldn't make out any words: they were speaking too quietly. There was no elation or vitriol. There was a level. One tone. One pitch. It was conspiratorial. Too reserved for boys on a night out, I thought, trying to turn and see them more fully.

"I'd better check," said Nico, pulling another face. I missed the look of concern, though I imagined it. I knew Nico was responding to a slight smell, a hint of burning that was rising up the stairs. "Tania is the worst cook in the world," Nico whispered. "Don't tell her I said so. Do what you normally do." That meant praise Tania. I always made her smile by saying her rice was the best in Chuschi. Though a slight exaggeration, it was the one thing Tania cooked satisfactorily. "You always say that," Tania would say. "Then it must be true," I would counter. I was thinking about this when Nico left the room. His absence allowed me the opportunity to stare more openly outside. I counted the shapes that were moving. One. Two. Three. Four. In the time taken glancing at my watch, the four shapes disappeared. Again I looked at my watch. I studied the seconds hand.

"Be with you soon," Nico shouted up the stairs.

"OK. Don't worry. Can I do anything?"

"You could buy us a meal," laughed Nico.

I laughed too. I looked again at my watch. Half a minute had passed. A long half minute. "Come on, come on," I said trying to find a distraction. I looked around the room, thinking how it changed little. Always Spartan, I thought. Two chairs and a radio. A bookcase. I read the titles of the books. "The Idea of Politics". "The Home of Man". Books for a thinker. With the thought came a sharp burst of light from outside. It flared like a firework, throwing shadows momentarily onto the far wall. It turned me towards the window. Three of the four boys were visible now, illuminated by the flames that were rising from a bonfire of paper. The wind was blowing some of the burning paper away. The paper glided, ducking and darting, amusing the boys. There was laughter. Some shouting. And a whelping sort of noise, followed by a triumphant, "Yes, yes, yes." As though it was synchronised, the richest glow came from the fire at that point. It seemed to reflect on something two of the boys were holding. Something long and thin was being held in the air, pointing skyward. Like a man starting a race. I realised I had seen such a pose before. "Guns," I said aloud, sounding shocked. "Oh no. Guns," I repeated edging closer to the window. The appearance of the fourth boy calmed me. He came out of one of the town hall windows carrying a box. I watched him tip the box's contents onto the fire. That seemed to be a signal. The boys ran. One went north of the plaza, two went south, one put his gun away and calmly strode towards Nico's house. As he passed beneath the window, he seemed to wave up at me.

"What's going on?" asked Nico, standing at the top of the stairs with a bowl of food in his hand.

"I'm not sure," I replied. I smiled as I turned round to face Nico.

I thought of the dead dogs, of the warnings, of the way the press had predicted the guerrilla movement would expire quickly.

"What do you mean? Hey come on, you can see what's going on. What is it?"

Again Nico's face said it all, his eyes looking squeamish, lined now; his mouth staying ever so slightly open. Like a baby being sick, I thought staring at the mouth. I took my time answering, turning once more to look at the fire. "I'd say there will be no election tomorrow."

"No election?"

"See the fire?"

Nico moved to the window and looked out. "Oh my God," he said slowly.

"That's democracy burning," I said, viewing the scene with Nico. "See the box?" In the corner of my eye I saw Nico nod. "That is a government box. The sort they send out and collect the ballot papers in."

"And the papers, the burning papers-"

"I would guess they're the ballot papers."

Nico shook his head slowly. "What is the point of that? I mean, what is the point? And who would do it? Here. In Chuschi." Nico made it clear the action didn't ring true. "Oh," he shouted with an air of frustration. "What should we do?"

"I think we should eat. There's nothing we can do. Nothing at all." I turned and smiled at Nico. "Now where's the best rice in Chuschi?"

I told the deputy director about the boys. Reporting back was necessary. It was part of my brief. So I did it well. Succinct and clear, though the rehearsed words covered a torment. It came to the surface when the appropriate point in the story was reached. "They did their job well," I said.

"Well trained."

"Professional." I used the word without knowing what professional in the terrorist context implied. Thorough, perhaps. Stealthy.

"So no complaints," said the deputy director, summing up. He looked precious as though he was eager now to move on and wish me good day.

"No.... No complaints. Except...." I paused. I thought of the boys laughing, the boys dispersing, "... well there was one thing."

"Yes?"

"It bothered me a bit..." Again I struggled to find the words. Another pause seemed to establish itself. It threatened to drain my eloquence. I finally blurted the words. "They had guns. I couldn't understand that. Why was it necessary to arm them with guns? I mean they're boys, boys who are easily impressed, boys who might let it get to their heads. I mean they didn't need guns... Look, what I'm saying is it seemed so unnecessary."

"Unnecessary?" There was a tone of disbelief in the deputy director's voice.

"Yes ..." My lips parted, but no words came out. I could see the deputy director smiling.

"Really Mr. Perez. Don't you think we should arm our *cadres*?"

"In Chuschi? Of course not. There's no need. Why on earth should they need guns in Chuschi?"

"Confidence." The deputy director shrugged away my questions. He reached forward and dipped his fingers into a bowl of peanuts that he kept on his desk. "Want one?" he asked pushing the bowl my way. "No? Terrible habit I know but it's better than the alternative."

"Which is?"

"Another cigarette." He fingered another nut. He ate them one at a time. He picked at them and I looked at his hair wondering whether, if it wasn't dyed, it would be silver with a slight yellow nicotine stain at the front. I took a nut.

"Planning helps confidence," I remarked. " And it was well planned. We knew where everyone was. We knew routines, what happened."

"And what if the civil guard had arrived? They have guns."

"Why should the civil guard arrive?"

"A tip off. A surprise patrol. Who knows. It's a possibility."

"It's unlikely," I scoffed. "Extremely unlikely."

"But a possibility, yes? And you know we take no chances. We plan for possibilities, for all eventualities. That's why we're so good."

"It just seems to me that for something so straightforward,

something that was hardly important."

"Hardly important!" gasped the deputy director. "Everything we do is important."

"But it didn't make the papers."

The deputy director paused and considered my words. I was surprised at that, never before had he afforded me such time. Let him think, his face seemed to say. It was still superior, still looking down. But it didn't intimidate me and I used the time too, thinking of the ballot papers, of how they had made only a paragraph at the most beneath all the analysis of the election results. Yet I saw their symbolism. I knew they were an announcement, that they were like the dead dog, that they started a process. I could see that. I didn't need to hear it from the Deputy Director. So they were significant, I thought, momentarily feeling a sudden need to apologise. Stop that, a voice in my head was saying. It mediated. Smile, it said, smile at him, make him feel edgy too. So I smiled and waited to hear from the Deputy Director what the ballot papers were announcing, what process they were starting.

"Right," he said, beginning to tell me.

The process developed over the following months. And I was at the core of it. I was involved in a committee. My local knowledge had involved me. "Give me something else," I kept telling the deputy director. "Philosophy. Development of ideas, that's my line. Not operations." The deputy director laughed at that. "There is no difference," he said, remaining formal. He kept as calm as ever. "You've heard what we've said. For the moment we preach ideas."

The reality was somewhat different. I heard of infiltration, of notes being sent to schools and teachers. Demands were made. They were like seeds being sown. The committee sat back and waited, knowing the position of strength it was in. For them it seemed simple. The teachers had been groomed at the college in Ayacucho. They knew of revolution. They would comply. Faith told the committee so. But it left me doubting. So it was with some surprise that I heard of the turn out of teachers at a meeting in Chuschi. It was high, very high, almost one hundred per cent. I was surprised, given the success, to be summoned to see the deputy director again.

"You haven't heard," exclaimed the deputy director rather softly, still applying his normal restraint. "No word from your parents or friends? Well, well."

"When? Today?" I stopped. Under my breath I cursed him. He made me feel so uncomfortable. I analysed the feeling, realising it was like an itch. It made me move in the chair and want to find the spot and rub the irritation away. It made me wish it was as easy as that.

"A complete success. You heard that?"

"Yes," I said in a rather doubtful way.

"Of course you did. Well there's been a development. Can't say I'm surprised. I mean something had to happen if you know what I mean. Some sort of retaliation."

"Retaliation?"

"Yes. The police have arrested four schoolteachers."

"They've done what?"

"Someone talked."

I bit my tongue. I saw the deputy director was still smiling. It was as though he was relishing the challenge.

"They've been tortured."

"How do you know?"

"Our sources. Our people on the ground." There was little warmth in his words or in his expression. It was an indulgent look. It responded only to his thoughts. I had no influence over it. I watched, sensing when a thought arrived and went. There, I thought, something arriving. It broadened the deputy director's smile.

"Are they alright?" I asked.

"Two were killed. Beaten to death."

"Beaten to death?"

"They're making a point. It's the way they work, frightening people, scaring them into submission. I would have expected retaliation. You can't go quiet in this game."

"Game!" I found some control. "What are their names? Do I know them, the men who were killed? Are they from Chuschi?" They must be secondary teachers. They must be. My mind was racing now, filling with the names of teachers from the village where I went to secondary school: Cervantes or Rivera, Costas or Gimenez. Not Castro, my mind said. Not the man with the words that charmed my father. Not the man who educated me.

I watched the deputy director fumble through the papers on the desk. "Where is it? Where is it? Ah...." He read through the information. "One from Chuschi. A teacher at the primary school. Augusto Castro. Castro, a good name eh?" He removed his glasses and pushed the paper to one side. "Paper," he tutted, searching for the pad that he scribbled notes on. "I think we need to get closer to the truth. Do you know what I mean?"

I said nothing. The words barely registered. They barely touched the pain. I held back tears. I clenched my teeth. I folded my arms across my chest. I held myself like I had seen fellow villagers hold themselves at the death of a child. That brittle abstraction, that smother of comfort. I thought of the way God would help. The way the spiritual covered up emotion. But none of that could touch me, none of it could clear away what I thought of Castro. He was so influential. He was so perfect and clear and beautiful. And now some idiot with a gun had swept him away. I grimaced and crunched my teeth and I fought and managed a half smile so that the deputy director would suspect nothing. He picked up a pen and began to write. Like a doctor writing a prescription. I waited for his words.

"I hear your father's not been so good," he eventually said still looking down at the pad he was writing on. "Sounds as though they could use you on the farm. You know, while he's ill. I tell you what, why don't we give you some time off? You could go home then, help on the farm. What do you think?"

5

"You're quiet."

"What?"

"Quiet. You thinking or dreaming José? Hey you know what? That's it José, you're becoming one of us. A dreamer. A real islander, eh?"

"Like you?"

"Yes. We're quiet. Haven't you noticed José? Haven't you noticed?" Hernando laughed. He shook his head and looked away from me, out towards the small boy I was sketching. We were sitting on the quayside. The small boy was swimming in the protected harbour area. The water was calmer there. It seemed clearer too. The harbour wall did that. It provided a backdrop that picked up the stroke of the boy. An easy stroke. It fitted in with the afternoon. Like a windmill turning. As if connected with the motion, a gentle breeze blew into my face. A wave came with it. It came in through the entrance to the harbour. We watched the boy duck into it.

"José the islander." The old man became contemplative. He edged closer to me and sat on the harbour wall. I watched him pull his legs forward. They dangled over the wall. The movement finished, he suddenly laughed. "So you like it here, eh José? Is it better than Puno?"

"You been there?" A daft question. A going-through-the-motions question. I censured myself immediately, biting my tongue and waiting for Hernando's smart reply.

"Puno? Oh yes, once or twice a week to pick things up. Things like you, eh José. Remember? Things they call consignments." He winked indicating the secrecy and significance of such work.

"I mean have you stayed there? Have you been ashore?"

"Oh yes. Sometimes I have to stay overnight. Sometimes I just pull a blanket over myself and sleep on the boat on my little mattress. In July, August it is too cold. I go ashore, get a room. It's OK."

The last words were a give away. The old man harboured a desire to move on or visit other places. It was a young man's dream, yet, somehow, it fitted his personality well. Such vitality. I considered how it suited him. More than anything it set him apart. It made him interesting. I often wondered why he was different. His appearance was similar to the other islanders. Like most peasants of his age, many of his teeth had gone and he garbled his words, but it was the meaning of his words rather than their sound that mattered. Their curiosity, I thought, defining their difference.

"Hey José, why don't we go out? Take an afternoon off. Take your paints. What do you think José? We should be in a boat on a day like today, eh José?"

As he spoke, I thought how there was also something about him that didn't ring true. It wasn't the words. They were simple and clear. The skein of his thoughts seemed reasonable too, particularly when he was authoritative, when he spoke of sea conditions and the wind and what the catch would be and what the islanders thought. I was always impressed by that. I had told him so. But something didn't fit. It made me take another look. And there it was. His appearance. Not his face. That was as craggy and as rough and as dirty and as lined as any of the other men on the island of his age. It was his clothes. I could see that now. The fraying trousers, baggy and loose, the old white shirt with the wind blowing up the sleeves, the Indian cap pulled down over his ears. The fraying and the dirt seemed out of place. The fishermen never appeared like that. They rubbed against nothing but water and blood, their skin normally only suffered from dryness, from exposure to the wind.

"Hey have you heard?" I asked , smiling now, thinking of the importance of what I was about to say. "Your party, they've split up. I forgot to tell you. They've been divided."

"Izquierda? Izquierda Unida have split?"

I thought of what I should say about the implications of the change.

"Ah it was bound to happen." he sighed. "We were saying that the other night, weren't we José? Remember? You said the terrorists should lie low. Forget the targets. Forget the need for positive action. Let them live, you said. You said they would do more good alive."

"I said the system would destroy itself."

"So you don't think the terrorists should help it on?"

"The terrorists?" I shook my head. I wondered what this had to do with Izquierda. "The terrorists? Why should they? So they kill some underminister."

"You mean the man in Puno the other day."

"Yes, the man in Puno. An irrelevance," I said sharply.

"But then the democratic left falls apart. That's what has happened, eh José? Izquierda splitting up."

"I suppose it is."

"So that makes the terrorists more important. I mean perhaps that's the only way." Hernando shook his head in a slow way, a way that said he had seen it all before, that such coalitions had come and gone in the past, that ambition and power had always divided the most well-meaning of groups. "Ah the leaders fouled up, eh José? It's always the same. A good thing always comes to a bad end."

"In Peru it seems to."

"Yes," agreed Hernando thoughtfully.

"It's like a film," I said, falling back on my old analogy.

Hernando smiled. "I know what you mean. Still..." He used that word casually. Still. As though he were dismissing the conversation, as though it were lost for good. Something so delicate, I thought, a little surprised at how low politics was in Hernando's esteem, how it wasn't crucial or significant. It was more like possessing a vague level of support for some football team, a level which made you take note of a score if the radio happened to be on and it was time for the results. You wouldn't search for the score. It was something that was invasive only if the circumstances allowed. Oh well, I thought, imitating the attitude and wanting to laugh.

"By the way José, Sebastian will be coming to see you today." The verve returned. I admired it. "He said I should warn you. You mustn't worry."

"Me?" By contrast my tone was grim. I wondered if Hernando picked that up, whether it told him what I thought of Sebastian.

"Yes you."

"Why?"

"Does he need a reason? Oh what's wrong José?" Hernando laughed. The laugh's lightness said he knew how Sebastian could behave, how he could search for people like a dog looking for a toy in a room, how he wouldn't give up no matter how inconvenient a meeting might be. "You've noticed José, how he can go on."

"I've noticed," I said quite definitely.

"But he's OK. Believe me he's a good friend to have. His heart is with you. It is José. And anyway you'll like what he has to say."

"Which is?"

"You'll see. You and the Englishman will see."

"The Englishman? What Englishman? What do you mean the Englishman?"

I had seen the Englishman arrive. I had been painting up by the reception point while I waited for Hernando to deliver my suitcase. It was the afternoon after I had arrived. To me the Englishman was just a European. Blond. Tall. Pretty. With wonderful hair. And deep blue eyes. Shining eyes. Like pools on top of ice. To get his nationality so quickly showed Hernando's need to interact and understand. It emphasised his curiosity. I smiled. "So he's English," I said to myself, returning to the courtyard after an afternoon painting birds, the big yellow thrushes that loved the island. Birds. A strange subject for me. So strange I called it an exercise. I used it to sharpen my precision, to absorb detail.

"Sebastian," I said, approaching the lower courtyard through the gateway from the eating area. Sebastian was standing there, shaking his head, responding to my scrutiny and moving away. I descended the two steps into the lower courtyard and moved onto the spot he had vacated.

"He no in. He go away." Sebastian threw his hands up into the air. They dismissed the Englishman and left me looking into the Englishman's hut, which was on the left side of the lower courtyard opposite Sebastian's hut. It was as bare as my hut. A bed. A small square of tarpaulin on the floor, a smaller square than I had. The bareness emphasised the Englishman's possessions. I took in detail. A towel at the end of the bed, a felt hat. Something he's bought, I assumed: some clothes, a sleeping bag, a suitcase, a pen, some writing paper. And along the ledge laid out in a line were small stacks of printed sheets. I wanted to go in and tidy the stacks, to neaten them and space them apart precisely. But a voice in my mind wouldn't permit me, so I shuffled to my right and began to turn away. It was then I saw a ripped up toothpaste carton, some fruit peelings and a newspaper. A discarded newspaper. I moved forward and took the paper. I would dispose of it. Like room service.

An hour or so later, when I went out to paint, I took the paper with me. I placed it at my side. The sun warmed it. Now and then I placed a hand on it, touching it like skin. I did that more and more because my painting was disappointing. I wondered why. The birds had been easy. So had the boy in the harbour. But now I was working from memory, trying to draw Hernando with his craggy cliff-like face. I'd touch the paper and try again. Hernando with warm light on his stiff lips, lines rippling out from the corners of his mouth as ideas hit his mind. Yes, yes, yes. My mind would react excitedly, recognising it was a good face to draw. Expressive, I thought, touching the brush on the mouth, arching the lips, lending a trace of doubt. I painted more shadow in. A breath perhaps. Something more: a word. Hernando speaking.

"José!"

That's it. The baritone voice.

"José!" Hernando. Behind me. I turned around. He called again. He wouldn't have expected to find me at the top of the island, near the *ruinas*, near a wooden cross that had been pushed into the rubble that once had been a tower. Beneath it there was a boy in the shadows, knitting, his wool wound around his head. A young girl and a small boy came towards him. They passed by, the girl kicking a football, the small boy scampering after a sheep. They ran towards a small peak and a view of the next island. "*Hola*" they said to the knitting boy. He nodded. I laughed. A knitting boy! That seemed so strange, yet it was what the teenage boys of the island did. They knitted for the tourists. Hats. Jackets. Jumpers.

"José! Where are you? *Hola! Hola!* José!" Hernando again. In view now. Climbing the steps. I thought of the newspaper, of moving it, of hiding it away.

"José! You were well away. Any news, any happenings, any....." He broke away, eyeing the paper. "*El Commercio*. The Englishman. You've spoken with him."

"Sort of," I said, picturing the Englishman, the blond svelte Englishman. It was his manner I viewed. The robustness. The arrogance. The way he held himself, swaggering his way around the island.

"What's he like?"

"I'm not sure."

"What do you mean not sure?"

"Well it's sort of strange. I mean he hasn't said anything."

"But he's given us a paper. *El Commercio* too." The old man smiled.

I put down my brush and wiped my hands deliberately, cleaning between my fingers and around my nails. I used the nail of my thumb to scrape out a bit of blue that had caked on my index finger. It flaked into bits. Then, holding my hands out in front of me, I blew the last dust away and picked up the paper. "You know when this is?" I pointed to the date on the newspaper. "You know the significance of this?"

"The significance of what?" asked Hernando.

"December ten."

"December ten?" Hernando shrugged. He was enjoying the intrigue. He liked games. "It is significant, eh José? December ten?" He watched me nod, then, thinking quickly, I imagined he was trying to work with what he knew: anniversaries, saints days, *fiestas.* Nothing came to mind. So he must have tried to make associations with the unknown. "Your birthday, José. Your birthday."

"It's when I arrived."

"When you arrived?"

"Here. When I arrived here."

"The day you landed. Then it's only a couple of days old. That's good José. Oh that's really good."

The realisation made me read more quickly. There were things I had to search out, things that may have been reported. Nothing on page one, I thought, skimming. A controversy over cuts in health care and reactions to rumours of privatisation were discarded quickly, as was an argument between Church and government officials and the destruction caused by a bomb in Pisco. Freak weather in Cuzco was dwelt on, but only because of a photograph of teeming rain. I turned the page.

"Whoa!" objected Hernando, arching his eyebrows. He looked disappointed. Like a child being denied a treat. Hernando's face lined by the sun and the wind exaggerated the feeling. It seemed untidy to me. Ravaged, desolate, I thought, fingering my glasses back up my nose. Expertly I flared my nostrils so that a wave of skin blocked the downward slide of the glasses. In focus, Hernando's expression seemed almost violent: vehemence seemed to fill it. "There's nothing about Izquierda Unida there."

"On page one?"

"Nothing. I'll go back and tell you about the bomb at Pisco."

"The bomb at Pisco," gasped Hernando. "What bomb at Pisco?"

"It's not important," I said dismissing it.

"A bomb is not important?"

"No. But this is."

"What?" The old man could barely contain his curiosity. He

shuffled forward, tried to look over my shoulder, snatching a look at my eyes in order to assess the direction of my gaze.

"Police investigate the assassination of government minister Enrique Valquez."

"Sendero," whispered Hernando in a knowing way.

"Valquez was shot dead in Puno on Thursday evening –"

"Sendero," repeated Hernando. I ignored him.

"Police are studying photographs of the Valquez cavalcade. One photograph is thought to have been taken moments before Valquez was shot alighting from his car."

"Alighting from his car. He was drinking soup," shouted Hernando. "He was drinking soup. Hey alighting from his car. What do they mean alighting from his car? Bah!" He shook his head. His eyes, fully open and straining, showed his annoyance. "I mean.... Reporters. They make it up. Soup. In a restaurant." A calm shake of his hand set the scene. Like a waiter directing a couple to a table. "And we believe it. We take it in."

"I know, I know. We invest emotion."

"Yes," shrieked Hernando. "That's what we do. We invest belief in it. Yes."

"You do. You're too free with them."

"With them? What do you mean with them, eh José? What do you mean?"

"With your emotions."

"Ah my emotions. Yes. Yes I am."

I thought of Hernando's speculation when we had read the previous report, of his concern for the chef. Such ridiculous considerations. What a wide range of feelings the report had drawn.

Hernando sighed. "So what's the significance of the photograph? You seem to know."

"What do you mean?"

"You nodded José. When you were reading about it. You nodded."

"Oh the police may see someone," I suggested. "Someone they know. They may even see someone with a gun. It's a big break for them. I mean technically they can do almost anything with it. What I'm saying is they can enhance it, you know, make it bigger, clearer." My words covered my knowledge. It couldn't have been

Sendero. I knew that as soon as I read the report. Certain things said so. Certain words. Certain disclosures. Particularly the fact there was a photo. Sendero would never have allowed that. They wouldn't have been so slapdash. I quickly checked what I knew. Assassination. Assassination. My mind worked like a computer. A key word and then a print out. The order. The system. The way to do it. Employ a series of squads. My mind went through their roles. One squad moves into the area where the assassination is to take place. They blend in. They dress as students, as newspaper sellers, as shoe shine boys, as street cleaners, as traffic policemen. They are on hand if something goes wrong. So it couldn't have been Sendero. I knew that if it was, three quarters of the people in the photo would be *cadres*. The assassination squad would be there too. For someone to be mingling with a camera and to be allowed to take a photograph without the ice cream sellers or the newspaper boys crowding in and sorting the situation out was unthinkable. "No it couldn't have been Sendero," I said, again thinking aloud.

"Oh come on, José. It was Sendero," argued Hernando.

"I don't think so."

"Hey José, you're skimming," accused Hernando, seeing me turn another page.

"Oh I'll go back," I said. The reassurance let me move on silently to page nine. A strange part of the paper, the part after the foreign news and before the sport, the section that allowed a lull to sweep in. A place for the insignificant. And there it was. I read it to myself silently. 'Professor disappears' was the headline. Police in Puno are investigating the disappearance of politics professor, José Norville Perez and his sister, Julia, said the story. It went on: Professor Perez gave a lecture at La Contute College in Lima last Monday evening. He was due to return home on Tuesday. His sister is thought to have been accompanying him. Nothing has been heard of the professor of politics and philosophy since he checked out of his Lima hotel on Thursday morning. Thursday morning, I thought, checking each detail of the story for accuracy. I returned to the words: Professor Perez was due to travel to the United States of America to deliver a paper on neo liberalism at Yale University at the beginning of next month.

I stopped there. I had forgotten about the conference at Yale:

events had overtaken it: I had dismissed it. How could I think of that with the police tracking me? How could I even contemplate going? I sighed. It seemed such a waste. I had the plane ticket. It was in my case. A flight from Lima. The police would have traced it. The computer would have told them who had bought it and when. They would have been in touch with the travel agent and the airline asking them to monitor any changes. No escape route there, I thought. Or was there? I shook my head. The movement was out of place. Hernando, noticing it, sensed the abstraction.

"We'll read the rest later," he said.

"You sure?"

"Yes. I have to meet the boat. The catch will be in soon. I'm helping with gutting. One of my friends is ill. Stomach trouble. You want to come along José? Yes? That's why I came looking for you, to see if you were doing anything." Hernando laughed as he scrutinised my face. The expression he expected was pulled. He knew I hated the late afternoon smell on the beach when the fish were sorted and gutted. I hated the untidiness too. The bits of fish that were left to wash away in the waves. "You keep it for tomorrow, José. The paper," qualified Hernando, reacting to another look on my face. "Sort out the good bits. You do that José?"

6

His sister is thought to be accompanying him. I reconsidered the newspaper report of my disappearance. His sister is thought to be accompanying him. Where did they get that from? I couldn't explain it. After all it was easily checked. Perhaps it was some young reporter cutting corners, drinking in a coffee bar when he should have been tracking facts; perhaps it was the editor spotting an omission: police look for two, only one is mentioned, better tidy it up.

I read the article again. Once more I stopped at the mention of Julia. I had thought her safe; it was I who was under scrutiny. That must be right. After all it was I who stood up and informed young minds what life in Lima would be like in the future. She was persecuted because of that, because she would know things about me. What a crime: knowing me! But what did she know? OK we lived together, yes. But we were separate. I only saw her at breakfast. And then only briefly. She taught. I lectured. And at night, she went out, teaching dance mostly. She was a good dancer, the best in Chuschi by far and one of the best in Puno. And to be the best she practised and practised, always coming home after I had gone to bed. Sometimes we saw each other on Saturday. Ditto Sunday. And twice a year we would go to the cinema together. We both liked cinema. And either in January or July she would accompany me home to Chuschi. It was a distant sort of closeness yet, intellectually, we had much in common: she had tended to take on my views. She agreed with them, I always said, explaining what appeared to be her almost blind faith. They make sense, she'd say, accepting that schools worked for the state, that they inculcated the ideas of the ruling class. Her agreement always surprised me. I wondered when she had converted, because she hadn't always been such a disciple. Certainly back in the early eighties she hadn't been. And I had needed her help then. The deputy director had wanted me to use her, to get her to be Sendero's voice in Chuschi.

"You have to lie low," the deputy director had said. "Lie low and be heard."

I laughed at that. "Oh yes lie low and be heard. And just how do you propose I do that?"

"You get a voice," replied the deputy director.

"A voice! I have a voice."

"You speak through someone else. Someone who will work for you."

It couldn't have been Nico. He would have refused. He was a democrat. Sendero would have been unfathomable to him. Its appeal would have been too. I knew that. So in December 1982 when a popular committee was formed to run the village, I had to turn to Julia. There was nobody else. My parents were too old. My friends weren't committed. So it had to be Julia, Julia who was fifteen. She was bright, beautiful, curious. The power intrigued her. She would represent youth, I thought, she will be my eyes, my ears. "Right, I see," she said. Not once did she ask about the ideology and why this ideology was superior to all the others on offer. She craved experience, nothing else. The committee offered it to her.

"So what happened today?" I'd ask after a meeting.

For the first few meetings she would go through the minutes, saying who said what and who responded and what she said. I would mull over what she had reported and, after consultation with the deputy director, I'd tell her what to say. The system seemed to work well. The vanguard programme was instituted. It made me happy. The deputy director was happy too; as was Julia. It also worked well on the ground: a communal planting programme was introduced; the boundary disputes with Quispillacta were sorted out. And that pleased the villagers. They were happy too.

But two to three months into the committee's work I noticed a change, a change in Julia. She became less communicative. She began to offer me a summary rather than a blow-by-blow account. "Is that all?" I'd ask, sensing a cover up. She would nod. "You sure?" I didn't realise Julia was developing her own voice, that she was for-mulating a programme of her own. "Much to admire, much to enjoy," was her verdict on the committee when I asked her opinion a year into its existence. The answer worried me. It wasn't what I expected. Rather, I had expected her to become reluctant, disin-clined to get deeply involved in its machinations. Thriving on it was exactly what I hadn't expected. And when she confessed to speaking out against blocking the road to stop the weekly market functioning, I was alarmed. "What do you mean no? What do you mean oppos-ing it? You know we want more self-sufficiency. Less laziness. And we can tax these people, tax the traders on their profits. There's all sorts of possible benefits. So what are you trying to do?"

"What am I trying to do? Where would we get our salt? You thought of that? I mean it may not be important to you, but what's the attraction of privation? And what about you?"

"Me?"

"Your chocolate. Where would you get your chocolate?"

"My chocolate!" I exclaimed.

"It's an example. Nico hasn't got everything. Come on. This is about conditions. What's the point of having conditions that are worse. Once a week we get choice. Do we want that? I think we do. What's the point of causing deterioration?"

I hadn't argued with that. I had stood open mouthed, wondering where she had gained such vision. So pragmatic, I thought, smiling at her. I still sensed no danger. I still sensed that I held something over her, that I could claw her back, that I could manipulate her.

Prove it, my mind was saying, prove you could control her. I thought back, right back, back before Sendero and the interest she had developed, back before I had involved Julia, back to being just brother and sister, back to growing up. That always brought the strangest thoughts and considerations, considerations like age. Julia wasn't a good age for me. I mean in terms of us interacting, enjoying each other's company. Our activities were never really linked. She was four when I was fifteen. She was fifteen when I was twenty-six. We should never have connected, but somehow we did.

Early on it was football that did it. She was a tomboy. She'd always want to play. "Pass the ball stupid, pass the ball! Hey come on," she'd shout when, in my late teens, I was out in the strange open space between our house and our neighbours. It was almost a square, a village square, a place for conversation and chance meetings by the stream while washing or collecting water or during group meetings when the primary health care worker came to talk to us about childbirth or hair lice or malnutrition or vitamin C.

It was a place for games too. Simple games to begin with. Home made games. Games with stone and wood and imagination, chasing and catching. Then I was given a ball, a leather ball. Over time it gradually deflated, getting softer and softer. I'd kick it against the two shacks that made up our house or against the bank beyond the stream. Julia would watch.

"Let me, let me," she'd shout, putting down the small teddy bear that she carried everywhere, the teddy bear that had been her only present one Christmas. "Oh come on José. José!" she'd plead and plead; and I would not give way.

"You should be inside."

"With momma? Oh yes, like a little housewife."

"Yes."

"So girls have to be inside, yes? You're like dad. Inside cooking, eh José? You know what we're having today? Beans. Soon I'll be looking like a bean."

"It's July. You know how it is. July is beans. You know that. It's what nature gives us. You know how it works, how we're linked to the land. Climate, soil, land."

"And beans." Julia pulled a long face. "They give me a sore throat. You know that. You know my problem, why I nearly choked as a baby. You know what they said at the hospital in Cangallo?"

"A small oesophagus," I whispered.

"You remember?" She pulled another face, turning up her nose, wrinkling it. "I've hated beans ever since that year when they were like cannon balls."

"What year?"

"You remember? *El nino*. The rain. The size of the beans."

"Most of them rotted."

"OK, OK."

"Go on," I laughed. She always moaned, but the good thing was she told my mother exactly what she was telling me. The beans did hurt her throat. She did dislike them. She did have a small oesophagus. So she would beg and beg for dried potatoes. And my mother would give in. Then I would moan. But I would be told to keep quiet. Me. Not Julia. I wasn't direct enough. I knew that. I was too clever, talking of malnutrition, of deficiencies, of common difficulties in our area because of the starch base of our diet. And of what we could do. How a little help from the government could tell us how to introduce new crops and open up difficult areas to agriculture.

"Oh listen to him," my mother would say.

"No, it's right," I'd protest. "It's right."

"Well why hasn't it been tried?" My father would ask." God tells us what to grow. He puts things in the soil."

"What?"

"God puts things in the soil. Through us. Through nature. We learn from him. He tells us what will grow, how it will grow. He told our forefathers. He tells us."

I didn't argue. I kept my head still and looked across at Julia. Sometimes she would smile; sometimes she would pull a quick face. Sometimes the communication of our looks would break up her discipline and a laugh would emerge. "Oh go on," she'd say quickly before apologising to our father. "Sorry dad, sorry."

"You need to be Julia. You need to try to learn, to understand."

"About God dad?"

"Yes."

"Oh I do dad. I do."

"She goes to Church dad," my mother would say, becoming defensive.

"I know she goes to Church. We all go to Church."

"On Sundays, yes of course we do."

"Mum's trying to say I've started going on Wednesdays too dad."

"On Wednesdays?"

"I clean the Church dad."

"Good girl. That's a very good thing to do."

I would listen and admire the way Julia was so much more adroit than I was at manipulating, at getting her way. She was patient too. She worked out a strategy and kept to it. Sometimes it failed. Like when she had wanted to spend more time with her friend Dolores, dancing.

"Food before dance," my mother said. "Your stomach is above your legs."

She didn't argue with that. Instead she waited for *fiestas* and observed. She would pick on a dancer. And a dance. Just one of each. She'd absorb them, taking in the attitude, poise and rhythms. She would remember every step and practise the movements again and again until she perfected them.

Her dedication impressed me greatly, so I wasn't surprised when my mother caved in and allowed her to start performing at local *fiestas*. She quickly became the best dancer in the village. The star turn, my mother said. Perhaps it was that that gave her confidence, that led her to question me, because we began to argue. Reading also encouraged argument. It infused thoughts. She began to consider issues, to think, to decide where she stood on this and that. I approved. It was important she came to consider, to weigh up and assess processes and paths. I had wanted that. I had craved it in the way she had wanted me to dance. But she had given in. She had succumbed. And I had gloated. "You want to read it? Go on. It's short."

"Really?"

"Yes. Look." I held up Marcuse's *Essay on Liberation*. "See."

"It is."

"I told you it was. Hey don't you believe me?"

"OK."

"You'll read it? Great. It's short and sweet and a stepping stone."

"To where?"

"To some sort of truth."

"Not a God José? Not like dad's God?"

I shrugged. I let her decide for herself. That was important: to get her to consider and to agree with me. And most of the time she did agree, saying, "Yes I see," before qualifying any conclusion. "So you're saying we're too hasty?" she said one day after a consideration of a change in government policy.

"In condemning? Yes. We should consider alternatives. We want action and action tends to need to be up front."

"Of course."

"Yes."

"But you're not sure." She knew my expressions. I tried to stay po faced, not committed, but some trace of emotion or tone was enough. I gave myself away too easily. She had told me that. "So why aren't you sure?"

"Because if things aren't as you want them, they need to be corrected."

"Corrected?"

"What I'm saying is correction in Latin America seems to mean war."

"War?"

"It's the only way." I insisted. "In Peru, it's the only way." I explained my reasons, pointing to the grasp on power of the bureaucracy, of the old guard, the families who had come from Spain and had formed an oligarchy. So much concentration was wrong. Julia agreed with me. But war? She seemed to question such an outcome. "You see nothing here resembles democracy, so nothing peace offers can bring change. It hasn't in the past, so why should it now? One whiff of change and out comes the army."

"A coup?"

"A defence. The army is an internal force here. It's not for us. It's not to defend us. Its for the oligarchy, to defend them from us."

She would nod then, agreeing. I was saving her time. She was jumping levels of argument and truth. She was fixing on my wavelength and understanding where I was coming from and, more importantly, where I was going to. "Yes, yes," she'd say. "But that's easy."

"No. No it isn't. War isn't easy. You've got to be sure."

"Sure of what?"

"You've got to scrutinise the possible outcomes, assess whether it's worthwhile."

"And is it? I mean in relation to this war, Sendero's war." She always did that. She always enjoyed excursions around the hypothetical and then suddenly, unexpectedly more often than not, linked back to reality, to the case in point. Sendero. That was the perspective. That was the application. I thought from scratch. Flaws came to mind. Not the positive side, the side that had some journalists saying that within five years the war would be won. I disregarded that.

"Come on José. Is it worthwhile? I mean on the basis of what you've just said. Possible outcomes and all that."

I said nothing. Momentarily I smiled, then drew back. I wondered what to say.

"You don't know," accused Julia, seeing the look on my face. "You don't know."

"I'm not sure." I sighed. She had cornered me. She had found the essence of all my doubts. "I should be sure, but I'm not."

"Why not? Why aren't you sure?" She seemed to want to press the issue. It made her anxious, edgy to the point that she raised her voice. "Come on," she said, "I want to know."

"OK," I tried to calm her. "It's the violence. I can't stand the violence."

"How can you want change and not stand violence? You said yourself in Peru change means war. Change means war. You know what? You just haven't got the stomach for the real fight. That's the nitty-gritty of it."

"OK" I sighed. "I just don't understand why."

"Why what?"

"Why it has to be that way. Why words and arguments can't convince."

"Because there's an oligarchy. Because they don't listen. Because there's an army. Because people like you and I just don't get serious."

I could sense disgust now. Disgust with me. And I was disgusted too, disgusted that she could attack on such a limited front, such a human front. It worried me. It really worried me. I tried to explain, to subdue her, to make her see what it was that had got to me. "What I really hate is the way revolution turns everybody into an enemy."

"Everybody?"

"Just about."

"Who do you mean, José? Mum, dad, me?"

"Not you."

"Mum then. Mum who's working all day, every day and doesn't have the time to think. Or dad. Dad who believes in God. Or Nico."

"What I mean is they're compliant. Nico's compliant. OK he doesn't point a gun up my nose, but he points capitalism."

"Nico?" she laughed. "Oh you mean his shop. Is that it José? Is that the nearest thing we've got to global capitalism? Nico's shop? Good God José."

"Not his shop, at least not in itself. It's just his acceptance of it."

She shook her head. The movement seemed to point to the way inheritance had woven its way around us all, that we were all bound to a father and an acceptance of what was allowed. That was the Peruvian way. "You really have no leeway, have you? There's no excuse. Not for Nico. Not for me. Not for you."

"Quite. That's it. The combatants are too all embracing. They just hang onto the system. They support it. They're like buttresses on a tree. You seen those trees? In the book on the Peruvian rain-forest, the book in school?"

"But they have to support it."

"Yes, you're right. Of course you're right. What choice do we have? Like father like son. We have to support it."

"Perhaps that's why somebody, some time, has to step in and show the way."

"But war isn't easy. It has to be just."

"Just?"

"Yes. Just. You mustn't abuse power. Power mustn't be abused."

"Or seen to be abused."

There. A thought. And it was moments like that, moments of such clarity, that showed me what she could be capable of.

7

Sebastian broke up my thoughts. Sebastian making a sound that was similar to one my father used to make. "Ah." A knowing sound.

A sound that said, I've found you. "Ah," he repeated. I was standing by the window in my room, looking out, down into the bowl that forms the core of Taquile. I didn't turn around. I let the sound linger. It was long and concealing, hiding a deficiency in language, a lack of words. Ah. It was still there. It warmed me up. Like coming in from the cold. Like standing in front of a fire.

"*Alimpunjay tata*," he said suddenly after waiting for a time. This was Quechua, not Spanish. This was how to greet people properly on the island. This was my lesson. We had played this game twice before.

"*Alimpunjay tata.*" I managed that. And he responded, prompting my next line but I was trembling, faltering, breaking into laughter, a nervous laughter that signalled failure, a laughter his sounds and expressions cut through. "I'm sorry. I'm lost now."

"*Pacharem*," he prompted.

"*Pacharem*," I repeated.

"*Cama.*"

"Of course. *Cama. Pacharem cama.* Yes, *pacharem cama*," I said more assuredly, remembering the words now.

"*Alimpunjay tata....*" He tried again, but the attempt again broke down into laughter. "Oh," he said. Again a long, smooth sound. It brought warmth to the smile he manufactured. "So dark," he said referring to the strength of light in the room. He began to fumble in his pockets. He tutted before finding what he was looking for. A lighter. A cheap looking, transparent lighter. "Ah." The familiar sound greeted its appearance, but that gave way to a huge sigh when he found it didn't work.

"*Finito*," he said in a pathetic way.

"*Finito*," I repeated, looking on.

"Ah..."

I laughed. A flame began to shoot at the instance of a flick. It appeared briefly, beckoned by some magic touch. He tried again. The touch deserted him. A bewildered look spread across his face. "Oh." A croaking sound now, anguished. He plunged the lighter at the candle on the windowsill. It was his movements that pleaded, at first fast, but then much more coolly handled, recognising precision was vital.

One. Two. Three. Four. Five. Six. I counted the flicks. Seven. Eight.

"No possible," he cursed. "*Finito*. You?"

Me? I stopped to consider what he meant. Me? *Finito*? Am I *finito*? There was no sense there. "Me?" I asked.

"You have?"

"Oh have I got a lighter?"

"Good, good."

"No, no I don't," I said sharply, realising the need to respond quickly. "I don't smoke."

"No lighter? Oh."

He went then. He just smiled and backed away. His finger saying wait. His eyes suggesting he had forgotten something, something of significance, something vital. He returned with his usual verve, clutching a waistcoat. "For you," he said shrilly, his high voice so expressive, urging me to accept the coat. I looked at it and then, reaching forward, touched it. It was crudely made. I could see that and the coarse material had a trim that I hadn't seen before. "Yellow," I said, disguising my tone so that my dislike of the colour wasn't obvious. How could I say I liked the cut but not the colour, how could I refuse it? I tried it on, shuffling my shoulders, getting comfortable. I put my hands into the two side pockets. I reached to draw the coat together, but there were no buttons.

"You come?"

"I come?" I asked, trying to understand. "Now?"

"No. Now," he laughed. "It no Christmas."

I laughed too, sensing a fractured moment. What had intervened? The jacket? The need for money? Did I have to pay? It was that more than anything that made me feel uneasy.

"It no Christmas," he said again.

Christmas? What was the significance of that? I thought of Hernando, of his saying that Sebastian will be coming to see me. But he hadn't mentioned anything about a jacket. I decided it must be a present. But why give it to me now? Why not give it to me on Christmas morning or Christmas Eve? I shrugged my shoulders.

"For fiesta," Sebastian said, pulling on the lapel of the jacket.

"The jacket?"

"Yes. For fiesta," he emphasised. "You come? You must dress up. Be like me."

"Oh I see. You want me to wear this, so I'm part of the family so to speak."

"Yes, you family."

A Christmas fiesta. And I was being invited. I was being asked to attend. To go to the family celebrations. That was what Hernando had meant. And I had to go in the clothes of the island, not the shirt and the trousers that I normally wore. I was being asked to show some respect.

"You come? Christmas. Christmas afternoon."

"Christmas Day?"

"Yes. Christmas afternoon."

It was my turn then. I decided to make it long and lingering. "Ah," I said, smiling Sebastian's way.

*

"He's invited me to a fiesta."

"A fiesta?"

"On Christmas Day." I smiled at Hernando. We were in my room. Hernando was sitting on the ledge. I was on the bed, laying out, staring up at the tin roof that dipped from the door to the back of my room. Old rags plugged the areas where the sheeting overlapped. There was a slight rhythm to the roof's movements: light rain was scampering across it, running with the slope and dripping into the animal pens that lay beyond my room.

"Sebastian's invited you? You know being invited is quite an honour." A thoughtful Hernando made it sound like a very bleak privilege.

"But I feel so distant. You know the island, its culture. I'm not part of that."

"But Flores is your cousin."

"But it's not me. I mean anyone can see that."

"So?"

"Well I'm not sure I can fit in."

"Into what? A fiesta? Oh come on José you're not trying."

"The traditions," I countered.

"Tradition's not a bad thing," said Hernando warming to the words. "Being traditional doesn't mean you're backward, eh José?

100

Sometimes a tradition can seem quite modern. You understand José?"

The words clashed. I wondered what underpinned Hernando's idea. "Take marriage. You know about marriage here José? Has Sebastian told you? Has he told you about *sirvinakuy*?"

"About what?"

"*Sirvinakuy*." Hernando smiled. He enjoyed such moments. He enjoyed catching me out. José the clever one. José from the mainland. José with the good job and the sophistication. He enjoyed the supremacy local traditions gave him, the way they allowed a reconsideration of the possibilities of life. Marriage, he must have imagined me thinking. Marriage is marriage. What is different? Come on. "*Sirvinakuy* is a trial marriage," I found Hernando saying over my thoughts. "One year. One whole year, José. You see if you get on."

"That still happens?" I sounded doubtful.

"Oh yes. Hey José, you stay and we'll see what we can do, eh? You like that?"

I thought the comment unnecessary and light. I never coped well with lightness. I never understood it. I shook myself. Remember the story, my mind was saying. You are married. Married to Julia. Remember Julia is your wife. So bluff it or change the subject or tell the truth. I stared at Hernando. I decided to change the subject. "So what have you been doing today?" I asked rather softly.

"Me?" Hernando sought unnecessary qualification. "Me? I've been playing the fool. You know what? You know what I did today?" The old man laughed loudly as he thought over his morning and afternoon. "You know José, this is age." He laughed again. A long laugh.

I listened. I considered. Hernando used names to address people and I didn't. I never use names, not in conversation, not in letters, not in lectures. And I remembered Nico saying that people who played football when they were young got into the habit of using names. You'd call for the ball, he said. Diego, Pietro, Umberto. I imagined the cries. I wondered if Hernando had played football. I had. I had loved football, but I didn't use names. I smiled. I could destroy Nico's logic.

"OK, OK," Hernando controlled his laughter. "So I'm down there, on the beach, sewing a net that had snagged. It had caught on a rock. So I'm sewing and sewing and people are talking. I'm talking too. Talking about crops and weather and *fiestas* and the island. And then it happens." He laughed again, though more quickly and with much more control. "I sew two nets together. Two together," he emphasised. "I mixed them up I suppose."

I waited for the final smile and nodded. "That's being distracted not being old."

"You think?"

I nodded.

"I hope so José. You see? That's being old. Wondering what caused it. Anyhow..." He took his time changing the topic. "...how's your friend?"

"My friend?"

"The Englishman."

I wanted to ridicule the idea, but instead I just pictured the tall, thin Englishman with the chiselled features and the wonderful hair that sat under his brown felt hat.

"He's a gringo," Hernando shrugged. "It's difficult liking a gringo. I know that's tarring them with the same brush, but they're so superior. They know so much. And this one in particular does. Apparently he's been quite rude to Sebastian. I mean who could be rude to Sebastian? He's all smiles and kindness Sebastian."

I frowned. I wished I had interjected earlier. Now I needed to rail against racism, to move away from generalisation and deal with the individual, the Englishman, the rude Englishman. I needed to break into Hernando's words and denounce the Englishman's attitude. *Gringo, gringo, gringo.* The word resonated class. *Gringo.* Superiority. *Gringo.* Dominance. It's all in the sound I thought; it engenders hatred. Green go. Green go. I considered its roots. The green of the uniform. The military. The intruders. The animosity may have been warranted once, but now ordinary people with ordinary lives arrive in Peru and hurt no-one. It seemed wrong to brand them, though I understood the persistence of the prejudice, how the understanding and values and perspective of Peru had been shaped partly by foreign intervention and how recognition of that grated on national pride and dignity. Yet circumstances change and the layering of culture through time isn't laminar. It's roughness can make people angry or contemplative. Like Hernando. Like me. The extremes, I thought, wondering whose reason will succeed, whether the culture will evolve or whether the roughness will create a fiction grinding Peru to a halt, riveting it to its old ways.

8

I thought of Julia after Hernando left. Julia after she had joined Sendero, after I had planted her in the organisation, after she had become my voice on the Chuschi committee. Julia in July 1982 when she had been on the committee six months, six months of arguing, of my coercing her, of conversations with her about the dialectic. She particularly hated that. She found theory difficult. "It's to improve our conditions, right?" she kept asking, shaking her head as I talked her through the semi feudal model of Maoism and the backward steps I thought Sendero were taking. Her objections annoyed me, yet the understanding she gained warmed me. She had grasped the need to take out the power sources in rural areas and so create a vacuum into which Sendero could step. "A sort of liberating force, yes?" she'd ask, smiling her belief in the tenets of social justice and the redistribution of wealth. What she struggled with was the short term, the instability, the destruction, the killing. Like me, I thought, just like me. Good teaching, yes. A protege, perhaps.

But Julia was unpredictable. Some friends of mine on the committee in Chuschi told me that was how they viewed her. Unpredictable. A loose cannon. A maverick. They never knew what she would say, how she'd react or how she would vote. They never knew if she was going to talk quietly or rant and rave. That made them edgy. It made some of them want her off the committee; others thought she was charismatic, that she would draw people in. Julia was unaware of such debate. She ignored the machinations. "Hey you know what? They are pleased with me," she told me, unaware of the truth. "I say what I think. They respect that."

Some did. Others found her erratic. Few gave her unqualified support. Certain instances were talked about, particularly those times when she would emerge in public as a voice in the crowd. That happened first when they captured the governor of Chuschi. "Here he comes," she said, standing next to Nico in the main square. A crowd of between one hundred and and one hundred and fifty had gathered. "Oh look," she laughed, giggling in the way a lot of young women would at the sight of a naked male body.

Nico cringed. "Why do that?" he asked. "So he's human. Big deal."

The governor was standing on the platform that was normally used in July on Independence Day for the village band. He was crying and shivering, trying to avoid looking at people.

"He's a figure-head," Julia suggested. "It's good to show the vulnerability."

"Oh come on we know that. We're not naive. We're not stupid. There's no need for it." Nico sounded indignant. He thought it cheap and undignified. "We should be above it." Nico's criticism was rising in pitch. It penetrated some of the laughter as the governor was forced to stand on a seat. "What now?" said Nico, expecting more theatre.

"They'll kill him," said Julia.

"What? Here?"

"Yes." She seemed definite. It irritated Nico. He hadn't come to the square to see blood, he had come to hear words, to take in reason and assess the best way forward. But it was action that was called for. It came in the form of a young man who stood alongside the governor. He called to the crowd. "Death? Doesn't he deserve it? Don't we deserve something better? Isn't he the symbol? Isn't he the voice of the oligarchy, of the government, of the oppressor, of all the things that keep us poor? I say he deserves to die." The man broke off to allow the crowd to cheer. "I say he deserves to die now."

"No," a voice called out. Its cry was piercing. It shot through the crowd, echoing around the square. Its authority brought a silence. It left everyone looking at each other suspiciously. Everyone that is apart from Nico who knew where the sound came from. He saw the heads around him turn. Once or twice they faced him before moving slowly away. Nico felt numb. It had been so near and so strong. It was as though it had emanated from deep inside him. Somewhere in his imagination. Like a dream. Like living a dream. He heard it again. "No! No! No!" It was Julia. Julia, he thought, watching her begin to move. She strode forward, arms pumping, pressing forward, parting the crowd. "Julia wait," he had shouted, but she had gone. The radical innocent, he thought, expecting the worst. He hadn't thought her capable of holding the crowd, of engaging it. "Out the way, hey *pasar*," she was saying. When a man didn't move, she slapped him. He moved. Nico should have seen there was some support, that it wasn't just he who supported Julia.

"Let's think," Julia said when she reached the platform. "Let's think." She stood still for a second. Pure theatre. The wind could be heard. The wind that would eddy around the square. It seemed trapped now. It shook some leaves, creaked a shutter, went away and came back just as Julia's mouth reopened. She resumed. "Look what we've done, "she said. "We have control. Do we like it? Course we do. We like it. We can do what we want. We can make things better. We can kill the governor." She emphasised the possibility, adding a pause for effect. It lit up the option and she questioned it, shaking her head and peering into every face in the crowd. Some returned the look, shaking their heads slowly. The movement gathered momentum and left them shouting. "Live." Some replied, "Die." "Live...." "Die...." "Live..." "Die..." The cry of "live" was getting stronger. "Yes," replied Julia. "And I'll tell you why. If you kill him...." She stopped and started again. "If we kill him," she emphasised, "we will have troops by the river, in the square, in our homes. We will have troops here tonight. And some of us will be disappeared. And some of us will be tortured. Most of us will be interrogated. And all of us will be in fear. Do we want that? Let him go, that's what I say because we've made our point . We've voiced our dissatisfaction. That's what we wanted to do, yes? To say we're suspicious of what's going on, yes? To say we need support ... And perhaps, just perhaps, after a little bit of time, we can go on as we are. That's what we face. Because troops will come here. For a day. Perhaps a week. If we kill him there will be troops here for good. Forever. Do we want that? You decide."

It was Nico who shouted first. His voice broke the silence that had temporarily returned. All eyes were staring forward, waiting for a little leadership: many were unsure whether to support or oppose. Nico decided to try to direct it. "Let him live," he shouted. Others cried too. "Yes, let him live," he heard them say. "Live!"

"Yes," said Julia, growing on the stage, moving assertively, swaggering almost.

"Aha," said Nico, sensing the plot hadn't been followed, that the pantomime like banter, "Shall we kill him?" was meant to deliver a yes, yes, yes. He knew any dissent would have had to have come from within. And Julia had provided it. Julia, the loose cannon. "Let him go. Let him live!" she was shouting, pushing her hands in the air and thumping with the words. "Life not death! Life not death!" she began to chant, finding a chorus that the crowd could turn into an anthem.

Her intervention worked, the life of the mayor was spared, but there was a crackdown. And as Julia had suggested on the stage, it only lasted a few days, but it was targeted and powerful. It happened six months later in December 1982, just before Christmas. A combined force of police, army and civil guard arrived in Chuschi. The committee fled to the hills. I can recall my parents telling me that Julia said, "I must go." She swam across the river; they saw her duck into a hedge on the opposite bank. It was the last they saw of her for two years. They waved and waved, knowing she was there, that she was looking back. A shot from behind them ended their goodbyes. They rushed into our adobe hut and cried.

I should have foreseen violence. I knew the way Sendero worked, that harassment, intimidation and killing were at the core of their technique, that they had to get the peasants on their side. They did that by obtaining a picture of the community. What do you like? What do you dislike? What's amenable? What can't be tolerated? They tried to understand people. The good guys that emerged were courted; the bad guys turned up dead.

It was simple politics. In Chuschi its application picked on cattle ranchers from the next village. They didn't stand a chance. They were hated without the rustling: Chuschi was Catholic; Quispillacta, the next village, was Protestant. The rustling opened up the wounds: a public execution of two of the rustlers in the main square was welcomed by all except Nico. "What's going on?" he wrote angrily to me. "People are being killed now. The ballot papers have become people — and we smile as though it's right. Have you heard about it? I mean we look at each other now. Who's next, we're thinking. It could be me. The shopkeeper. The capitalist. Is there anything more evil than that?"

I wrote back. I didn't go to Chuschi. It was close to my normal July visit. But beneath my words lay an abhorrence that rode over any radical didacticism that my Marxism wanted to preach. It was alright on paper, I thought, but seeing the blood of people made me wonder even more about its legitimacy. "Let us hope it's quick," was all I managed to say. I often wondered what Nico made of that, whether he interpreted it as an admission of guilt? It was an involvement Nico could never have dreamed of.

Such questioning always put in doubt my commitment to Sendero. The incident seemed so minor. Cattle rustlers in Chuschi. Could the revolution really evolve out of that? I began to doubt its capacity to go on and be effective in a meaningful way. Could it? Should it?, I would think, knowing only alienation and pessimism could come from such a stream of thought. I felt that in the hills to the north of Ayacucho when I was sent on a training exercise with some new recruits. They were given a route and a mission and were told to imagine it was real, that they were on the run, being chased by soldiers or the civil guard, that they needed to regroup and fight back. To me they were running away. I told the deputy director so. "Stand and fight," I said, surprised by my advocacy of violence. "What? And be wiped out?" the deputy director answered. "What sort of revolution's that?"

In regrouping, four of us were left to build a tunnel. It didn't go anywhere. It wasn't meant to. It was just an underground corridor, a sort of shelter. "A tunnel to hide everything that might give away our presence," the orders had said. As I worked, I wondered what that included. "Explosives," I thought, digging down. "Supplies, medicines." I extended the list as we dug down the requisite two metres. Then we worked the horizontal. I worked in the morning with a young student named Raul.

"We'll have to camouflage it," I said inspecting our work.

"They'll fall in," laughed Raul, thinking of Michael and Pablo. They worked in the afternoon until sundown.

"No not now. When we finish it," I said. "That's what you'd do, isn't it?" I asked the others when they arrived to relieve us.

Neither of them seemed sure. We were still debating the point when we started digging the following day. Raul and I worked hard. I puffed and blew. Raul laughed at that but, like me, he was covered in bites. The perspiration stung as it found open sores. The discomfort didn't agree with me. Again I questioned the activity. "Bloody job," I moaned. "Why me? I'm too old for this. Doesn't affect you youngsters."

"You want to bet," retorted Raul.

Michael arrived. "You still here?" he joked.

"So are the insects," responded Raul.

"Bloody insects," I moaned.

"And so is capitalism," said Michael, jumping into the tunnel and peering down its shaft. "Hey you're doing well. You're in four metres."

"Two metres more should do it," I said.

"That's a regulation tunnel, is it?"

"You'll be finished by tonight." I breathed deeply, ignoring Michael's gibe. "We better meet then and discuss how we camouflage it and what we put in."

"I saw branches up there," said Michael referring to a pile of twigs and scrub that Raul had collected. "I guess the cover will cool things down in here as well."

"And keep the weather out," added Raul, who maintained an unflinching expression. "You know what we've got next? Guess. Raft building, that's what. Raft building. Just what you need for a revolution, eh?" But nobody was listening to Raul. The mention of raft building had started a buzz. It excited us. Michael was talking about designs when I left for base. It was the last time I saw Michael alive. The tunnel collapsed two hours later, trapping Michael and, by the time Pablo had run back to base for help and returned with two or three men who dug and dug frantically, Michael was dead.

I frequently think of Michael. He would have been a doctor now, practising perhaps in his home town of Juliaca. What work he would have done there: working with the poor, breaking down all the barriers tradition imposed. Michael would have been good at that. Hunting pigs and building tunnels and becoming the bazooka man seemed such a misuse of talent. I wasn't the only one who had recognised that. Michael had recognised it too. But the cause was too great. It was a leveller. "I shouldn't be here," I remembered him saying. I had agreed, bursting into a diatribe that supported the concept of a vanguard party. Lenin had proposed that, the idea that some form of elite should transmit theory to the proletariat. "I should be treating or educating," Michael had said. Instead he had been sent back for a second week, disciplined for some indiscretion. I had learnt that just before Michael took the spade off me to dig for a final time. "Why am I here? I must be mad. You know that? And all because I fell asleep."

"Fell asleep?" I said passing him the spade. "What do you mean?"

"Didn't you know? I was here a month ago. They found me asleep at my post. I told them my diet is wrong. Too much starch at midday. You drop off if you sit down after too much starch. At least I do. I know my body, my metabolism, but they ordered me. They had me sitting down, guarding the path... So I was given kitchen duty for a week. And when I had finished that I was sent back to this. Digging holes for the hell of it. What training! Anyone can dig holes."

Michael was right about the starch and wrong about the holes. I told the deputy director so. "I don't understand it. I mean we have engineers, people who could look at the soil and rock and say dig there. We just dug. And we got it wrong. All because a lecturer of philosophy and a doctor of medicine were playing engineers. A doctor died digging a hole. Is that right? How can that be right?"

part four

HUGO

1

"What do you want to be Hugo when you grow up?"

"A rabbit."

I must have been a nice child, saying whatever was in my mind, always having a favourite thing to pick on at any time. Rabbits, trains, bicycles, lollipops. I used them all. But it was mainly animals. I loved animals. I used them easily and effectively to bring on sighs and comments like, "Isn't he lovely?" or "Couldn't you eat him?"

"No you can't!" I always protested, genuinely appaled by the prospect. I believed them. I believed they would. After all they were adults. So I had to put them right; I had to point out where they had gone wrong. And I'd tell them in a thorough way, in a way that made me wonder where my later laconicism came from. Because that's how I come across now. Laconic. Uninterested almost. Half scornful sometimes; downright rude others. I suppose I always go to the edge of things and, if pushed, I speak my mind. People dislike that. They find it strange and troubling. They aren't used to it. So they normally become defensive, accusing me of having an overweening ego, or of showing off, or of joking. Joking! That's the worst. I'm always serious. I never joke.

"It's for you." A voice at the side of me. A small voice, a young voice. A child. A little girl in my hut. She is showing me a sketch. And she corrects me. I never joke: did I think that? Except with children. I joke with children. Let's get that right. I tolerate children. I don't like them. I don't want them near me. They have nothing to offer me, but at least they have an excuse: they are children, like I was when I wanted to be a rabbit, like I was when I really believed my aunty was going to eat me.

"Go on Hugo. Hugo, I made it for you."

So I accept what the little girl offers me. It is a piece of graph paper; crayon colours from its reverse are showing through. She smiles. I smile, though I want her to go away now, to retreat, to disappear, to leave me alone.

"The three kings," she says, already capable of much better Spanish than her father, Sebastian. I admire it. I can speak almost perfect Spanish. I can speak French too and German and passable Russian. I'm a graduate linguist. An achiever, some would say. A natural, I say. I have talent. It's as simple as that.

The little girl starts pointing at the paper that I am now holding out in front of me.

"The three kings," I say, qualifying what she has told me.

"Yes. You know the story?"

I nod.

"They bring gifts. To Jesus. Jesus is there."

Jesus is a pink blob. Pink on yellow. Yellow, I think, having to concentrate, to make her think I am taking it in. She will go then.

"You see?"

I nod.

"He's a baby." She smiles. All her senses alive now. She sniffs. My antiperspirant. She flexes her nose. Once, twice. "You know Jesus?"

"Me?" I have to interpret what she really means. You know Jesus? As a child, I would have thought everybody, irrespective of age, would know what I know; I would have thought that I had inherited my knowledge, that there are no obscurities. Is she different?

"He's the son of Mary. That's Mary." She points to another pink blob, a larger less shapely blob. Mary is a little like a soft strawberry, a going off strawberry, the goodness seeping away; Mary is almost squelching. "And Joséph's the father. He's...." She has left Joséph out of the drawing. I sense her discomfort. I see her eyes move to the left, to the right. I smile as I read the words on the graph paper. I do not translate. I keep it in Spanish. "*A mi amigo Hugo.*"

Hugo. She knows my name. And she becomes silent, absorbed in the superimposition of Joséph in a corner. A rather peripheral Joséph, I think, watching her draw, but at least he's a pale brown colour and slightly elongated. She grips the pencil and concentrates. I see the effort on her face. And deep in thought I move my eyes away and look around the room, the bare room. So stark, I think, stretching out on the bed, which is strangely comfortable. Unexpectedly so. So much so that I get up and peel back the blankets and reveal the layer of foam and the wooden struts that underlay the straw mattress. The mattress is on an old iron frame.

The bed is the room's only furniture. It is the room's chair and wardrobe and table. At night I move everything off it and use the ledge that runs along the wall in front of it, the ledge where the little girl now sits and draws. The ledge comprises three planks of wood suspended on several piles of stone. Somehow it is level. I wonder how. I make a mental note. I will investigate it later.

"Oh." She drops her pencil. It is on the floor. On the dried mud. On the caked floor. She is looking for it, scolding herself, saying, "No, no." The pencil must be important, valuable to her. It makes me bend down. I touch the mud and the little rises of shining stone where feet have smoothed the surface. I touch a nail, a bottle top, a coin, a German coin, a pfennig. I lift up the tarpaulin that acts as a mat. It surrounds the bed, keeping my feet warm at night when I take off my shoes.

"Ah." The pencil. It has rolled down the slope towards the bed and slipped under the tarpaulin. She smiles and moves back out of view behind the trunk of a tree that is cut and shaped to rise in the middle of the room. It supports the roof. I stare at it. It has a wizened shape. Its bark is cut here and there like shards of steel. It has a metal look.

And while I observe, the girl, reunited with her pencil, draws. Humming now. Some tune. A tune I have heard on the radio. A pop tune. Peru's number one. And again I consider why I am here. Henry Meiggs. The answer: Henry bloody Meiggs. That is why I'm here. Henry Meiggs, Honest Henry as he was known in Peru. The Yankee Pizarro. The awkward bastard. Henry bloody Meiggs.

"Will you buy? One sol. Little Rebecca, she make. Oh...." The sound says wonderful. Look at that, it says, his fingers pressing on something intricate. He is asking me to admire something: its art? its technique? its strength? I am not interested. He should understand that. He should realise that I am a man. I don't wear bangles, so why should I pay a sol to leave it beside my bed on the day I leave the island? And why should he be allowed to barge in and bother me? "One sol. For education. It do her good. You know Rebecca? You like?"

Like! Huh! I know what I dislike. I know what I hate. I hate Peru.

I want to say that. I want to say it loud and clear. I hate Peru. I hate its lack of hygiene, I hate its toilets, I hate its pavements, I hate its food, I hate its heat, its cold, its dust, its radio, its people, particularly its people. I hate its buses, its cars, its streets, its sheets, its breakfasts, its chocolate, its bread. That's food, I've said food. And I hate Mary and Joséph being followed by a hard sell. How could he? The old duffer. The bloody old duffer. He must sense my contempt. He must see it in my face. But he proceeds undeterred. Even with his language difficulties. Because his Spanish is limited. He struggles for words, stopping and starting, always pausing before a sentence, giving himself time to think, to rehearse in his mind the next probing word.

"Ah my Spanish. It no good. You know, I first."

First? First what?, my mind asks, finding a little energy. Don't be drawn, it tells me, don't be drawn.

"I mean I first speak Spanish. Rebecca, Dina, they speak, they speak good. I no speak until fifteen. I go Arequipa, you know Arequipa? I get work. Arequipa good place. Give me job. Give me home."

I am not interested. Go away, go away you old duffer, my mind begins to urge. Push off! Do you hear? Just sod off! My revulsion graduates through various peals of obscenity, priming abuse, leaving it in my throat, on my tongue. Look, sod off!

"Thank God for tourists, I say. I practise. Thank God for tourists." He smiles. A big smile. He uses his face well. It somehow compensates for his deficiencies. It conveys moods. Joy at present. Even ecstasy. He overcompensates. "I mean Alejandro, my son, he stay. He no go. Because of tourists. Because of you. Thank God for tourists." The old man laughs.

I am not interested. I couldn't care. I really couldn't care whether his son is here or in Timbuktoo. I don't care.

"But me? Arequipa. Oh. And Lima. I guard there. A watcher. How you say?"

That's it. I walk away. No words. No smiles. I have just had enough. I want silence. That is all I demand from this island. Silence. So I can think. Noise disturbs me. Noise distracts me. It is uninvited. So I leave the old duffer by my bed. I leave his smiles and conversation and walk out into the lower courtyard and up the steps to the plastic picnic table and the chairs. There is nobody about. I pass the kitchen where one of the old duffer's daughters is singing along to a tune on the radio. I move out onto the track that leads to the pueblo.

2

Breakfast. Always the same. Me and the other guest, the rather shy guest with the shirt and trousers, the rather tidy shirt and trousers, the loose fitting shirt and the slightly too tight trousers. The fastidious guest who is always brushing himself down, removing a crumb, pinching a hair and lifting it from his shirt as though it repulses him. He frowns. He always frowns. His snivelling nose struggles to control the slide of his glasses. He uses his nose a lot when his head is down, when he is writing, scribbling away and thinking, losing himself in periods of thought that leave him staring out towards the lane. He always faces the lane. Perhaps he wants to be distracted. Perhaps he is waiting to greet someone, someone who will take him away. He doesn't look right here. He looks out of place. He reminds me of an academic. He has that look, as though he would be at home in corduroy, planning pitiful rebellions against the authorities. A little pinko, that's what he looks like.

A little pinko. Perhaps I'll call him that. Little pinko. *El pequeno pinko*. Yes, that'll do. Because I'll have to have a name for him. I mean he's always there. I can't avoid him. I try to. But every morning I hear him washing. He stands outside my door and hangs his shirt on the courtyard wall. He stretches and sighs, trying to hold in his stomach which is large and pouting, displaying an excess no other islander seems near to possessing. "Right," he says. He has a bowl of water. The old duffer's eldest daughter brings him that. "Dina! Dina!" I hear him call. "Any water?" And she comes out smiling. Then he coughs and sighs and splashes the water over himself. He goes then. Back inside. He reappears when I sit down to breakfast. He fidgets as though he wants to talk, but I sit with a file and eat and he sits at the end of the table staring out, drinking a coffee slowly, staring and drinking, saying nothing, staying still. Apart from today, that is. Today he smiled when I called the old duffer over and asked for a mirror. "I need to shave," I said. "I need a mirror. Do you have a mirror?" The old duffer laughed, "Ah," he said, shuffling away. He came back with a pair of tweezers. "No. A mirror. I need to see, I need to see myself. You understand?" His reply was a mime. "One hair. Pull," he said, showing me how he shaved, pulling out hairs with the tweezers whenever they appeared. "Do you have a mirror?" I asked again. "Look, do you have a mirror? Do you understand? I need to see. I have hundreds of hairs." I scratched my chin. The roughness made a sound, a scratching sound.

"Yes. Tweezers. They work good."

"Well. They work well." I stopped then. Too many words I thought. "OK, OK. A bowl."

"A bowl." He nodded, moving off in the direction of the kitchen.

"And water. I must have water."

The pinko nodded. I looked away. "Why am I here?" I cursed. In German. "Why am I here?" In Russian. I didn't want the little pinko joining in. I could sense he was up for some cosy chat about the old duffer and the island and how he fitted in. I didn't want to know. I wanted to shave and to go off down to the beach for a long swim and a sleep.

"Here mister." The old duffer was grinning again.

I watched him approach. "Where is the water?"

"There. Water. Splash, splash. See?" He shook the bowl.

Of course I know what the problem is. There is no tap water. I hear the girls of the family collect water every morning at dawn. They pass my window. Five times back and fore they go, talking and laughing when they leave and puffing and panting when they return. It is hard work. So water is used sparingly. It isn't offered. It has to be asked for. But I need it. "I must have more," I said. "I need to wash properly. You understand?" I thrust the bowl his way, spilling some of the water as it slopped in the bowl.

"More water?"

"Yes. More water."

"Now?"

"Now."

The little pinko turned away. I knew what he was thinking, but I am paying good money. I expect water. Water for Christ's sake,

118

water for me to wash. OK it means the girls will have to make another trip in the morning. So what? I'm paying for that. I expect it. It's as simple as that. I expect it.

3

I know now when to go for my breakfast: any time after nine, it has to be after nine; any time before that draws the risk of interruption by the old duffer. He always seems to be around until then, shuffling about, fussing, moving from task to task. "Checking out," he calls it. I have heard him tell the pinko. I have heard him relate a story of how, when he lived in Lima, he came home from work one evening to find an empty space where his raffia house should have been. "Burglary's something else in Lima," he quipped. It is the only time I have heard him attempt a joke. Other times he is serious, giggling occasionally to make up for his language deficiencies, but that is a nervous laugh, nothing more. It is with him all the time, with him when he is searching for the sole of a shoe that is to become the spring for a gate, with him when he is searching for the old tyre from which he would cut himself a replacement sole, with him when he is counting out the matches in a box the pinko had given him. At least forty it said on the box's side. "*Quarante, quarante y uno*. Forty, forty one," I heard him sigh.

He checks out until nine. By ten past he is in the small plot of land adjacent to the compound. I hear him there, talking to his son. It is then that I slip out and order a vegetable omelette and a *mate de coca* from his daughter in the kitchen.

"Tea? Yertil, the best," she says, emerging from the kitchen.

"Yertil?"

"Yes."

"No *mate de coca*? I'd like *mate de coca*."

"*Mate de coca*." She nods.

"Yertil is *mate de coca*?"

"No. No *mate de coca*. None today. Only Yertil."

"Yertil." I nod now. A glance through the kitchen door at the table that is inside helps. I see the red and green label on a tea bag and the trademark, "Yertil".

"Oh I see," I say as if I know the nature of the tea blend well. The warmth of my recognition makes her smile. A laugh overdoes it, it tells me she doesn't associate me with smiles.

"Here," she says, pouring water into a cup that already has a tea bag in it. "Yertil. It's good."

I take the cup away to the table and begin to dip the bag in and out of the water, then I swirl the water so it laps against the bag: I want it to brew quickly. The girl watches. I stop. Go away, my mind says. Go away. I look at her. She smiles. Sod off. Leave me alone. I sip the tea. I don't want to encourage conversation. I don't want conversation. I just want to read about Meiggs, to understand the source of his strength and consider how he would have dealt with my situation. My situation, I laugh. The sound seems to startle the girl. She smiles and retreats to the kitchen. Good, gone, I think, watching the door close after her.

"Now where was I?" I am on page five. That holds a memory: our teacher saying, "Books will make you think. You'll find yourself stopping and starting, considering." That's exactly what I am doing. Stopping, starting, considering the names of Meiggs' children. Henry Hoyt, Manfred Backus, Fannie Yip. I say the names over and over in my mind. Henry Hoyt, Manfred Backus, Fannie Yip. Like learning a poem, my tone changing their significance, making them seem like great verse one minute and like doggerel the next. But, always, as I roll out the syllables, I wonder how Meiggs came upon such names. Was there a nineteenth century book of names that he had used? Henry Hoyt supports that. The h's. But the others seem too random, too wild. Manfred Backus, Fannie Yip. German and Chinese, I think, wondering where the influences come from.

I think of my name. Hugo Vaughan Young. HVY. And how my father wanted to call me Paul, after Paul Newman. Or Robert, after Robert Redford. And how my mother wanted something middle class. Something like Timothy. She liked Timothy, but she thought it wasn't unusual enough. So she went to the library to find a name. She opened up Shakespeare pledging that the first name she came across that she liked would become my name. She found Hugh. But again she thought it wasn't unusual enough, that it sounded too Welsh. So I became Hugo.

120

But there were no films in the mid-nineteenth Century and Meiggs didn't seem like a Shakespeare buff, so something else must have influenced him. Friends, I think. That seems feasible. Manfred Backus. Fannie Yip. A German accountant, perhaps? A Chinese business woman? Manfred Backus, Fannie Yip. A reward for connection? Or a way to connect? I pull a face, a clown like face that pushes up my mouth and juts out my upper lip and says I don't know. It suggests I am still dissatisfied, because it just doesn't seem enough to me. It is too prosaic. I want more. I want the reason to be strange and lovely, something like an impression gained from touching, from smelling or seeing. Just a sense of something, something fleeting even. The reflection of a moment.

I like that. That's how it should have been, I think, looking up, seeing the pinko is there now. I wonder how long he has been sitting at the end of the table, facing the path, always facing the path and always writing or reading and always in a stiff shirt and trousers. Stiff shirt. I like that. Yes that's much better. I prefer it to pinko. The pinko, the stiff shirt. I watch him. White shirt, brown trousers, a nervous man, always flicking pages with a dangerous impatience, a man who would never finish a book, a man who would pick at pages and words. His nervousness seems to irritate his hair which falls into his eyes and his glasses which slide down his nose. I see him smile at the words he is reading. I see the touch of movement in his eyes that says the writing has fallen flat, that it isn't providing, because that is what I sense it needs to do for him. I sense that this man is attached to words or what they convey. Ideas, that's it, ideas. He is learning from them. Like a son with a father. It is that sort of relationship. He looks up. It is like a challenge. He looks my way. Look away, a voice in my mind says. Disregard. Disengage. Leave him alone. Leave him well alone. Leave him with his words and ideas.

I forget the tea. I forget the stiff shirt. I forget the old duffer's daughter. I just think how I came to the island and why I came to the island. After all the island was never part of my itinerary. It had no railway. It had no connection with Meiggs. But I came because I was seeking refuge, because of something that happened at

Chincheros, a place near Cuzco, a place that interrupted my plans to travel Meigg's railway. Chincheros. A place. A place for some relaxation. A distraction, a something other than Meiggs, a place providing perspective, a lovely place, small and overlooked by snow capped serrated mountain ranges and pastures that lead into its alleyways; Chincheros with its market and the remnants of its Inca ruins and its decaying colonial church. Always the mix, I think. Ruins and churches, somehow when they come together they draw curiosity. Like a palimpsest; layer upon layer of culture rubbing against each other, breaking each other down or building each other up, leaving bits that peep through and catch the eye. It was the church I liked. The art. The hand-painted figures on the wall. The colours like mountain light, penetrative, clear, almost dancing off the walls. "*Se puede...*" I remember imitating the taking of a photograph and a group of locals by the door nodding and laughing. One pointed to a bowl for donations. "*Si, si,*" I smiled, searching for money. It was easy then. Smiles and laughter and handshakes followed. But I had to go back. I wasn't satisfied with just a look. "No film. Shit. I don't believe it. No bloody film."

"Hey mister," the youngest of the locals said softly, reminding me where I was. As a penance, I put more money in the tray. "OK," said the boy, his laughter restored. "Money good. You come back soon yeh? Try Sunday. The market. You like? Jumpers? Ponchos? You like?"

I shouldn't have returned. But the invitation struck a chord. The pleasantness, the warmth. The promise of a good market. I needed to buy jumpers and scarves. Quick, easy presents for Helmut and the Varig negotiators, for my boss back in Toulouse, even for my secretary. And those frescos, those figures with their shy reserve. I liked them. I couldn't explain that. I just liked them. So I returned with a full film in my camera, relaxed and happy. I went straight to the frescos. The flash of my camera excited them. I saw the flower motif, the large leaves like overflowing water. They were so vital. Like a cascade. They filled the viewfinder until I felt a tug shunt me as though I was a big weight, anchored, but shaken, the Spanish words around me gabbling as the sounds coalesced and the people focused on me.

"One minute, one minute."

The words. Clear now.

"Just one minute." The words coming out of a group of people. "You. What do you think you're doing? You seen the sign? Of course you've seen the sign. But you decide to ignore it. Yes? Because you're superior, because you're American or European, because you think you are better than Peru."

"What?" It was all I managed to utter. I stood open mouthed, looking at the man who was confronting me. He was short, powerfully built with a moustache that seemed to cross his face like a water level. It looked as though it should have been indicating something. Fury, anger, belligerence, I thought, taking in the expression on his face. That was set.

"You, you bloody Americans."

"I'm not American."

"You bloody Europeans. You come here, you think you can do anything, yes? So you disregard. You do what you want. And you do this." For once he moved his head.

"Respond," Popeye was saying. " Respond. Hey this gook needs putting in his place. Don't take all this shit. Don't take another word. Turn the fuckin' tables. You hear? Go, go, go. Fight, pay, charm. You hear? Those are your choices. Those are always your choices. Fight, pay, charm."

"I must have your film," insisted the voice continuing. The words stopped all movement in the church. They fixed all eyes on me. Fight, pay, charm, I thought. Fight, pay, charm. Which one? Choose, choose. "I want you to open your camera now. This minute." The man's words were almost frantic, agitated by my lack of response, by the way the shock of the moment had numbed me. This is South America. This is hassle. This is what all the guidebooks warn about. This is mad and dangerous and unpredictable. It needs care. Tender care. "You see the sign? Look. Look!" He dragged me across the Church, pulling on my arm. I didn't resist. I went with the force, closing my eyes, wondering if I should react. Fight, a voice tried to say. Fight. But all the people seemed close and the Church seemed so delicate. I stared at the sign.

I was in the wrong. I couldn't believe it. I was in the wrong. I saw it. I read it. No photographs. I read the sign. Over and over. No photographs, no photographs, no photographs. But it hadn't been there on my last visit, when I had asked the locals, when I had paid. There had been no sign then. I was sure of that. "Charm," said a voice. Popeye's voice. "Charm. *Pero nunca caes de tu burro*. But don't fall from your donkey, eh? Don't admit to any mistakes."

"And you just do as you want? That's a joke, one big joke. You don't care, do you?" The man's anger seemed to be intensifying. "You really just don't care. You come here, you do this. What does it matter?"

"We didn't see the sign." The voice wasn't mine. It belonged to a Swiss man who had followed me into the Church. I had spoken to the man outside in the market, a mindless where-you-from, where-you-been type conversation, the sort travellers have several times a day. We had parted as quickly as we had met and smiled at each other once or twice in the market. Now he was saying what I should have been articulating – a defence, some sort of explanation of my actions. "There's too many people," he said, "there's too many people in the Church. You can't see the sign. You see? They block the view." He pointed at the sign that had been suddenly hidden from view by an encroaching group of locals who were curious. "My friend here, he was like me. He just walked in and turned right. He didn't see the sign. I didn't. There were people in front of it. It's too low."

"The sign?" said my aggressor, shaking his head, seemingly surprised by the accusation.

"Yes. It needs to be higher. It needs to be above the bodies. It needs to be bigger too. You should put it on the door."

The criticism wouldn't be taken. I knew it. I expected words, a wild reaction, vile and ungraceful, its vitriol directed at me, everything somehow merging in fury. But, surprisingly, the man reacted by releasing my arm and walking to the door. The locals stood there. The men who had laughed and smiled on my previous visit. The men I had made my contribution to. "Too many people," my aggressor muttered to himself as he approached them. Their turn, I thought, imagining the look on the man's face. He strutted like a general in the height of battle. These were his lines. "We close up," he said. "No more people in today. We close."

"It's early," someone dared mutter.

"We close."

A conversation followed. It gave me the chance to move away. "You go," said the Swiss man. "You get to the bus. You must get away."

But I wanted to brazen it out, to see the Church, to make the point I had done nothing wrong, nothing that would harm or hurt, nothing premeditated or destructive. I looked at the fresco. I took it in. Every detail, every dab of colour, every fleck of dirt. Then I moved away. Slowly, elegantly, smiling at the locals, I slipped by my aggressor and out into the darkness. Safety, I thought. Fight, pay, charm. The options stayed with me. Which one, which one, my mind kept asking. "Charm," Popeye kept saying. "Charm."

Laughter breaks my concentration. Not my laughter. Someone else's. The old duffer and the stiff shirt. Well matched, I think, considering their unrelenting earnestness. Yet I find it difficult imagining them together, a lack of frisson makes it seem a rather pointless coupling. I wonder how they find it. OK at the moment, I think answering for them as I listen to their laughter. It is coming from the lower courtyard. Laughter and strange sounds, sounds I don't recognise. Another language, maybe one of the Indian languages. It is like patter, like a routine. It is rehearsed, sequential and they replay it. Once. Twice. The same words. Always breaking down when it comes to the stiff shirt who starts laughing, a touch of hysteria in his voice, his words quickening, finding new pace and rhythm and meaning, bringing on "Ahs" from the old duffer.

Intrigued, I stand up and look over the wall that separates the two courtyards. I can just see over it. The old duffer's room is to the right, the stiff shirt's is to the back of the courtyard. I have to stretch to see the old duffer's and then duck as the old duffer himself comes out of the stiff shirt's hut. He is smiling, shuffling, making his way to his own room. All his family sleep there. They crowd onto bunk beds amongst the old duffer's possessions. He seems to keep everything. Old radios, old doors, old shoes. They are visible on the bunk bed opposite the door. I shake my head thinking of the collection of cans and bowls on the top bunk. The old duffer moves inside. I think that is it, but, as I'm about to draw away and return to Meiggs, he reappears with a waistcoat in his hand, one like the islanders wear, but with two yellow bands down its sides. He's trying to sell it, I think. Like the bangles. Like the three kings and the hard sell. Bloody man. I move quickly, gathering my papers. I return to my room. Bloody old duffer. Bloody old duffer. I click my door shut. Lie low, keep quiet, he'll think I'm out. Bloody man. Bloody interfering man.

I fall onto the bed and snuggle up to Meiggs. I scramble through the pages. I think of his life, of how he made four fortunes - lumber in New York, real estate in San Francisco, engineering in Chile and railroads in Peru - and how each time he subsequently lost all he gained. In Peru he learnt of his loss on his death bed. From there there was no way back.

"Bloody God. I told him. I told him what I wanted. What to invest in. But would he listen? Like hell he would. You know what? I could have shown him how to *ponerse las botas* as the Spanish say. How to put on one's boots. How to make a killing. I could have gotten him out of some fixes. Huh! I was expert at that. You know in California I owed eight hundred thousand dollars. Eight hundred thousand dollars! That's a hell of a lot of dollars. I mean the interest per month was huge. So what did I do? I forged dollars, that's what. I mean that's what I had to do. I had to buy time. And time's like every god damn thing. It has its price. And because demand was high, the price was high."

"So what happened?" I ask.

"What happened? What happened was I got my commodity. I got time. Just enough to let me estimate the possibilities. You know what I mean?" He smiles. The broad smile, the icy smile, the calculated smile. It works on me.

"OK so you print dollars. You pay people off."

"And I'm back at home thinking up schemes and just wondering whether to stay or go. It came down to that. Jail or freedom. Why jail? What's the good of jail?" His psyche couldn't accommodate jail. Jail meant expiating his crime. He couldn't believe in that. Something told him it would do little good. That was his logic. It would focus and absolve many pressing issues. But so many things were left out. He didn't consider the way pain or prohibition could offer some sort of relief.

"Jail may have made you penitent, you know? It could have acted

126

as a salve," I suggest.

"A salve? What the fuck's a salve? What good could that have done me? I owed people money for christsake. They wanted paying."

And there it was, the old problem. The obsession. Nothing, in Meiggs mind, could substitute for money. That was the problem. He always believed he would pay them back. And to do that he had to be free. That was his logic. It made him believe that that was the best solution not only for him but also for his creditors. It was how they could benefit.

4

More disruption. A tap on the door. "Shit," I mutter when I see the door being pushed open. "Come in, won't you?" I add softly.

"Ah." The old duffer. The bloody old duffer with a smile on his face. Like wrapping paper around a present, I think. I want to reveal what's beneath. "Excuse. Sorry." He bows and stands by the door. "I .. I need say..."

I blow out, puffing my cheeks, catching my temper.

"This is waistcoat. It for-"

"I don't want it, understand? Do you understand?" I raise my voice. "I don't bloody want it."

"No?" The old duffer laughs. He tries to make little of my outburst, he tries to brush my reluctance away. It is as though he doesn't believe it. He laughs again.

"Look I don't want it. I can't carry it. I don't have room. So just sod off will you." I pause wondering why I have offered an explanation. Normally I just say yes or no. I don't offer reasons. They are mine. Private.

"No, you go wrong. This you."

"Me?"

"You."

"Listen I don't buy presents. Do you understand? I don't want it." I am seething now. "I no buy..." I break into some of the old duffer's speech patterns. "I no buy. You understand?"

"No?"

"I no want. OK?"

"You no buy. You have. For Christmas. For –"

"What is this? Appro?" Is this some kind of sophistication creeping in? I want to lighten the procedure. I want to ask if he takes American Express or Visa. But I think better of it. "Look just leave me alone. Just go, will you?" I jump off the bed and draw open the door.

"But you come. Christmas."

"OK, OK Christmas I come. But now you go. Listen, I'm tired, yes? You understand? I'd like you to go. I sleep, yes?"

"You sleep?"

"Yes."

"Now?"

"Yes."

"Oh." He smiles and begins to move out. "But Christmas, you come, yes?"

"Yes, yes. OK. Fine. Christmas, I come."

Bloody cheek. Bloody man. The old bloody duffer. I think about him all night. Giving me a Christmas present, trying to get me to buy it. "Who's the bloody salesman?" I ask myself. "He should be selling the bloody planes, not me. Old bloody duffer."

I laugh at that. There is something about it that seems audacious. I can admire it. I can curse him too. Like I do, last thing at night and first thing in the morning. So thick skinned, I think while having breakfast and reading through the deal the Brazilians want us to amend. "It's a standard contract," I whisper to myself, work taking over. "OK, OK, let's look at this again."

I can't believe how lenient I have been with the Brazilians. A bit like last night with the old bloody duffer. I wonder if I am losing my touch. I should have said no, we can't change. I should have called their bluff and seen whether they sprinted off to Boeing. I know now that I have to dupe them. I have to find something superficial. I have to find something that will lure them, something that will cost us little. "Easier said than done" I curse, again whispering to myself. I read through the clauses. "Nothing, nothing, nothing." The points come and go.

"So what do I do? What do I do?" Again to myself and Meiggs. Fight, pay, charm? Charm had failed. "Pay then," I mutter, thinking how Meiggs understood corruption, that he knew how and why and what it involved. He knew it worked too. He knew it cut corners, that you didn't have to bother with explanations, that it made life easy. He liked it. "Hey all you gotta do is assess how it is and go for it," I hear Meiggs say. "I mean it's kind of hard enough the market, if you let it be. But if you think about it, if you sort of tune in and get into it, well you can make it work for you, understand?" I nod. "I mean in my day everything was up for grabs. South America was, California was, New York was. So it was a case of working out how to exploit it. In South America it was infrastructure. Railroads. To develop you need trains. So that's what I did. I built the railroads. Mind you I had to get the contract. That was the difficult bit."

I turn the pages of the biography and read again how Meiggs allowed successive governments to sell themselves. I always wonder how that happened. Clandestine meetings come to mind. Dinners or lunches in pubs. That's easy to conjure. Popeye sitting there, holding court. The cry of, "I'll get it." The protests. The easy pickings that came to be expected. I smile when I reread that. I recognise that I use the same technique on customers and colleagues, that I build it in in exactly the way Popeye used to: in allowances, in commissions.

It is worth paying for. I know that. Popeye has taught me that. "Hey you've got to invest see," he'd say. "You've got to put something in to take something out." I'd see Popeye then running the show, setting up the meeting in his own way and in his own time. Do the research and be decisive, I'd think remembering his maxim. The groundwork would be character assessment, working out susceptibility and availability, though in Peru, at the time, everyone from the President down was available. It was the culture. So it was easy. "Hey come on. How much? This is a big contract for me. I'll pay. You know that. Course you do. So what's the problem?"

Popeye quickly came to know that every man in Peru had his price. His job was to work it out, to get it right. That was crucial. A wrong assessment would insult them. So it was 200,000 sols a year for some and 10,000 a year for others. And that was all built in to his estimates, inflating the figures, fattening them up almost to the point where they looked as though they were hiding something, which of course they were. "Twenty one on the books and rising. It's the only way. You show me an honest businessman here and I'll show you a bankrupt. That's how it is." I could sense him smiling, telling me secrets, how some were offered gratuities when they left office, sort of golden goodbyes that said thanks for choosing me, Henry Meiggs, the golden yankee. "And you know what? They all took the money. No-one refused. *Arrimar uno el ascua a su sardin.* They all drew the embers next to the sardines. That's human nature for you. They all looked after number one. And I can't say I blame them. But isn't it great? They get paid by me for giving me the contract. So it's benevolent old Honest Henry. That's me. Joe Cool eh? *José Suaves.* Forty thousand a mile, that's my price. And you know who's paying? I mean you know who's paying me and the President and the Minister of this and that? You know who? The Peruvian *peon* that's who. The fucked up guys who buy the government bonds they issue to pay for the railways. The peasants, that's who. Now ain't that a crime?"

5

The old duffer follows me after breakfast. He follows me to my room. Why isn't he checking out?, I think, turning to face him. He is carrying the waistcoat, the same yellow trimmed waistcoat. "You wear Christmas Day," he says again, placing it on the ledge. I think of Meiggs and the fire engine and the bell. I think of generosity and gifts, though the old duffer clearly can't afford to be generous. He is hardly in Meiggs' league. More like a *peon* buying a bond, I think, convincing myself the waistcoat is a gift, a Christmas present. There is no mention of money as the old duffer moves alongside the bed and stands by the window.

"My father's house," he says seriously, staring out towards the next compound. "He dead." He mimes a person sleeping by putting his hands together and gently laying the left side of his face on his horizontal hands. "Ah." The mime allows the coldness of the words to flourish. I somehow sense the old duffer likes his father dead. Perhaps it gives him more responsibility. "Oh my father. You father alive. I tell." He looks at me and smiles, a friendly smile, the first friendly smile. A new approach, I think, dismissing it. I sit up in the bed. "My father he live to one hundred and twenty."

I frown. A frown of disbelief, half questioning and half registering my amazement. The intrigue pulls me in. It almost tugs me into the conversation. No, my mind says, doubting what I am hearing. I blame it on the old duffer's inadequacy in a language he has picked up late. Something like numbers are doomed to be dealt with in a sloppy way. Seventy, he means, seventy, my mind tells me. I wait for a revision of the figure.

"One hundred and twenty," he repeats. "I have photos."

Photos, I think. What do they prove? I lock into the possibility as though something in a face or a pose can hold evidence like the rings on a section of a tree in dendrochronology or the numbers of carbon fourteen isotopes in radio carbon dating. It is such a strange thing to cite. A photo. Perhaps because it is new to the island, because it can click on a moment and be regarded as a repository of history, as a witness, as a testament.

"So old, so fit. He work to his death. He die in field. He so fit. He call me and I asleep. Like you," laughs the old duffer, giving me another of those new smiles. "Come, come, he say, don't waste minute. Ah..." The old duffer laughs again as something amongst all the memories amuses him. "And now I the old man."

I want to give up on this. I want to react as I had reacted before, to leave, to go to the *pueblo*. But Popeye intervenes. "Let it run," he says. "Let it run. There's always room for concern, remember? Fight, pay, charm. Concern's part of charm. You have to cultivate that, you have to learn when and how to use it." But why use it now? I think. "Because you want him out," is Popeye's answer. "How the hell do you propose to get rid of him? He's too old to fight. Hey, in any case, he doesn't understand you. Why the hell do you think he's back? Take the jacket. Smile. He'll go away." But he'll come back, answers my mind. "Yeh that's a possibility, yeh he may come back. You can't always get it right. But *tenir angel*. Be an angel. It's what the Spanish say. It means be charming."

"So how old me? You think?" The old duffer is prodding his chest now, pointing at himself.

131

"Go on. Charm him, charm him," urges Popeye. "Try it out. Go on. *Tenir angel. Tenir angel.*"

"Oh I guess..... Let's see." I give the old duffer a long look. I stare at his dry face, at his bright eyes, at his flat dark hair. He looks youthful. I exaggerate that. "Oh about forty," I say. "Perhaps forty two."

"Forty two! Oh you my friend." He turns and taps me warmly on the shoulder. "I am seventy."

"No." I genuinely don't believe it.

"Yes."

"But your children."

"They young. We marry late. It is the way. On Taquile. It is the way."

I mull over the ages of the children. I cannot believe he is seventy. He recognises that. He sees it in my eyes. An iciness. I seem to chill him, to bring back the reason for his presence.

"So," he says, moving away from the window to the door. "The waistcoat for you. For Christmas *fiesta*. You wear?"

I stare at the waistcoat all morning. "Bloody old duffer," I curse periodically expecting him to return for money. "Charm him," I shrug, cursing Meiggs too. "My father lived to one hundred and twenty," I say slowly, imitating the old duffer. A hundred and twenty. Here. In all this shit. Sure.

I shake my head. The contract with Varig is on my lap, some of its pages are spread out on the bed, pages I have gone through, pages that are now marked in biro with crossed out clauses and changed dates. "Prices," I say focusing my attention, but nothing seems to be overcoming the obstacles. Something clever, I think, looking up, something really clever. I remind myself how I am renowned for finding a way through. My boss says so. He always says, "Young", whenever things break down. I am the man. The man for the compromise, that's what he calls me. Normally that comes easily to me. I see it. I look at a page or a face and I see what is wanted. Yet, this time, nothing I can think of in the faces of the people from Varig or in the way they behaved when we were locked in a room suggests anything. I try to think back. I try to sense what was in their minds, what they wanted on price, what they wanted on the service deal. But nothing, absolutely nothing, comes to mind.

Popeye doesn't help. He just prattles on about where I went wrong in Chincheros and what I should have done and what I should do now. "You've got to get yourself out of it. You've got to take yourself away. You understand?. Get drunk. Get laid. Isn't that what you do normally? I mean back in Toulouse. That's what you do there, isn't it? Hey you've told me."

I do not listen. I don't listen because he is mistaking the routine for the unorthodox, the one-off. Drink and women are for Toulouse, for relaxation, for regeneration. They are necessary for a nose-to-nose confrontation with another working week. They are necessary for doing battle with the mundane. They help me survive. Because after all I'm a survivor. At least in work I am. Faces come, faces go, but I find enough in *Airbus Industrie* to hold onto. I think of my progress, of my promotions, of my last promotion. A name comes to me. Merle. Jean Claude Merle. I set it in context. My job. My present job. The job in sales. I had been working in planning. But it seemed like time I moved on and, whenever an opportunity arose, I sniffed around checking whether it would suit me. That meant going to my boss and asking who was on the shortlist.

"Merle and he'll get it," was the reply.

"Merle?"

"Yes he's alright Jean Claude. You don't think so. Well I'm surprised." My boss stared at me, taking off his glasses and laying them on the desk in front of me. He played with their arms, raising and lowering them. It was a sign of seriousness. "I know he's older than you and you think he's a little bit too conventional."

"Your word not mine."

"And he's a bit of a yes man."

"Your word not mine."

"But he sorted out Chester. I mean he went in there and –"

"Oh hell, come on, anyone could have done that."

"Really?"

"You know that. You know whoever went in there would have done the same thing. It was the obvious thing to do." I shrugged not willing to concede any ground or to take in my boss' proselytising.

"So you weren't impressed with the restructuring, with the reorganisation of the plant. I mean the way –"

"It was obvious, bloody obvious," I cut in again, maintaining my consistency. "In fact he should have cut further. You know that. He wouldn't have had to have gone back in if he'd cut it further. He held back."

"Cautious?"

"Conservative. That's what he is. He's safe. He's unspectacular. He won't let you down."

"Perhaps that's what we want."

"Well then you've got your man."

My boss was looking serious when I looked up. He was scribbling on a notepad. That was a habit. He did it in meetings, writing out questions to be asked and listing the gist of any points made. I wondered what was coming when the pencil was placed on a pad and he smiled. "OK," he said. "Who do we put on the short list? Any suggestions? All we've got is Merle. Desailles has applied."

"Desailles?" My tone conveyed derision.

"We need three names."

"Three," I mused.

"Any ideas?"

"How about Hugo Young, Hugo Young and Hugo Young? Any one of those will do. In fact any one of them will do the job well, a darn sight better than Jean Claude bloody Merle or Claude bloody Desailles. So what do you say?"

6

All that confidence. All that lovely confidence. I need it now. I know it is nearby. "You just need contact with people, with real people. That's all," says Popeye, confirming what I think. "You need the sort of contact you had with your boss."

"Hugo Young, Hugo Young, Hugo Young," I say to myself, laughing. But where is the potential for such contact? The stiff shirt? The old duffer? I can't contemplate long conversations with them. They're no-hopers. I have no respect for them. I can't contemplate wit or daring or anything remotely stimulating with them. Except, perhaps, through art, the stiff shirt's art. That intrigued me the first time I saw him. I smile, recalling my arrival, the way the stiff shirt stood out, the way he caught my eye. His dress alone was enough, his western dress, but it wasn't just that. It was his manner that drew me: the way he sprawled, the way he appropriated space, the way he laid out his paints by the arch near the reception area at the top of the cliff, the way he took over. It was his superiority that I liked. He looked superior, peering down through his glasses which he worked in a particular way. He played with them. Like a musical instrument. They slid down his nose. A fold of skin held and moved them up and down, focusing and refocusing as he transferred his gaze from the landscape to the canvas.

There was an energy about him, a purpose that told me he wasn't from the island. A strange thought, given that I'd just arrived and was more concerned with gathering my breath after the climb up the cliff side. As I got my breath back, the stiff shirt sat still. He didn't see the man with the registration book or the five sheep that walked towards me. He must have heard what I said. I asked the man with the registration book the Spanish for sheep. "*Abeja*," he said. "No goats?" I asked, "I mean *cabrito*? *Tiene cabrito*?" "Only sheep," said the man. I signed the book and walked on passed the stiff shirt. Again he didn't look up.

"He will when I ask him for a painting," I say to myself. I am sure of that.

"You want a memento? Of this place? You hate this place," remarks Popeye, finding a way back into my thoughts.

"No. I hate Chincheros. That's what I hate."

"Hey, come on, you hate Peru. That's what you hate. Remember what you said? You hate the roads, you hate the food, you hate the toilets, you hate the people, remember? You hate the people. So you leave him alone. Don't talk. Don't say a word. I mean is he of any use to you? That's the crucial thing. That's what it's all about....You ask yourself that."

Buying things usually cheers me up. It makes me realise money creates privilege, that it allows me to dispossess, to take something and have it for myself. I like that. I like the way it excludes and includes, the way it states where you are and how you are doing.

Getting on, it somehow says. I love it. I love exercising the privilege, going to shops, particularly exclusive shops like galleries, places where I have a track record, where the owner has assessed my status by what I have bought previously. It makes them smile more widely and invite me here and there, to go to the vaults or the attic and see what treasures are tucked away.

It also allows me to show off. In my flat in Toulouse I have big pipes running around the walls like scalelectrix lanes. They frame Stovepipe Woman, a fabricated metal sculpture, slightly *à la* Picasso but more late twentieth century with the metal painted gold and violet. I think of the way the piece points at one wall that is covered with a canvas. A Terry Nieell. My prize possession. All burgundy. Burgundy is Nieell's most expensive colour. His green is cheaper, his blue cheaper still.

I laugh at that. So silly, I think, the way you buy his paintings by colour and size. One colour on a canvas with a small ball of yellow, whatever the backing colour, in a corner. Mine is two foot long, the first one that is. Two foot by one. They are always by one. And one purchase gets you in. It puts you on a privileged list that means private view after private view. You need never buy again, though I did. A six foot Nieells. Burgundy again. It goes with the scalelectrix pipes and stovepipe woman. It separates them. It links them. It makes me friends too, friends of the people I meet at the galleries and of those who are above me at work. Always those above me. Always those who might feel obliged to offer an invitation to a meal or drinks in return for just a viewing of my Nieells.

That is networking. That's what I do at work, at lunch time, after work, in cafes, on trains. It is my leisure activity. It is my football, my cricket, my squash. And I have become good at it. Experience tells. I have come to know who to invite to what. I have come to know who gets on and who creates friction. Friction or frisson, I think, planning ahead, playing with names.

I look for mentors too, people who can pull me along, people who need others, who crave support and need someone to swear at and bounce ideas off. Support, I call it. It sounds like something out of the welfare state, but I use it. Like with Ken, my first section leader who worked on women with a charm that slipped out of a smile and slithered all over them in an unctuous, unappealing way. Lubricous, I called it, not really knowing the meaning of the word, but it seemed to fit. Ken was lubricous. The energy level of the word seemed right. Its wet eel sort of sound did too. Ken was a wriggler, a wheeler dealer. A man of the corridor. That was his habitat. That's where Ken delegated and promoted and asked his women out. I was his pal. I helped him out. I let him use my flat. He would pay me to go the cinema and eat at the best restaurant in town and all because one night when I was home I had reacted to a call from him that said he was in a lane outside town, to the south, up a track, in a field, in his car which would not move. Stuck, he said. Fine, I said, knowing there was something to be gained, that by going to his rescue I would score some points and have something in my own arsenal that could be precious, something I could hold onto and keep in reserve and use devastatingly at some later time.

Like memos, I think, my mind moving on from Ken and the new girl from reception who were waiting that night in Ken's wife's car for me to pull them out of the mud. And letters. I keep every memo and letter. I throw nothing away. I store them in boxes grading them according to how useful they may be in the future. "But you said on December 14, 1987..." I would pull out the memos and show how policy had changed, how promises had been broken, how procedures had been compromised; and I use them in a subtle way, going in early in the morning and confronting my adversaries and colleagues saying, "Peter, you know that memo..." or "Ken you know the note you sent me ... They are defences. They make me impregnable. Defend and attack. Fight, pay, charm. Strategy, I think, strategy, knowing I will do anything to move on and up, to earn more money.

Because money is crucial. I suppose it's what drew me to Meiggs. It was the one thing we had shared or, rather, hadn't shared. It was debt that drew us together. I always remind myself of that. I always reconsider it, thinking how debt was like a disease in Blenheim Avenue. It spread and became endemic as people wanted this and that. They had to borrow to get what they wanted. The never never, my mother called it. It sounded romantic. Like the end of the rainbow. Perhaps it was the romance that kept it

away from me. I had known it was there, at least I had my suspicions, but it rarely made itself apparent. And what I saw of it was
fleeting, like an acquaintance, like a neighbour saying hello and
goodbye, first thing in the morning and last thing at night. My parents were responsible for that. They kept me away from it.
Somehow they sterilised it and made it seem polite. So when a
man in uniform called one Monday and said, "Mrs. Young, you
want to pay off any of the arrears?", I was ushered into the back
garden and the windows were hastily shut and the back door
closed. The activity turned the strong man's voice into a whisper,
barely audible outside where I played. "But mum," I protested as
I was shown the back garden. "Mum!" I exclaimed, thinking that
I had heard the word 'arrears' before. On television. On the cricket
commentaries. West Indies versus England. It was always England
who were in arrears. "And England are one hundred and thirty six
runs in arrears." Arrears. In that context it didn't seem to have
much of a sting. It was unfortunate, not wanted. Like a cold or a
cough or a pimple. Yet the man in blue, the man in the uniform
who called, made it sound more like German measles, something
much more threatening.

"That's it," says Popeye. "Yeh, that's what it does. Hey listen to
me. That's what it does," he mocks himself. "It's what you do that's
important. What you do. I mean think of me."

So I do. A potted history. Henry Meiggs born 1811, died 1877,
married twice, seven children, three of whom die young. Nothing
remarkable there, I think, considering the details. It could have been
any nineteenth-century life, though I can't imagine it. I try to, but
it is all make-believe to me and the death of the children makes it
seem like a bad regime.

"Gee it was tough," sighs Popeye, trying to explain. "That's what
I'm saying. What you do is ignore it. You haven't got the money so
why even consider it? You let it go, you let it run. But if they kick
your arse and get clever, I mean if they call it in, well you're fucked.
So you have to pre-empt that. You have to get out. You run. I did. I
ran in New York. I ran in California. Would have done in Peru too if
God had let me. Fuckin' God."

"This nice. This good." The old duffer is with me. I am thinking and he is just standing there at my side. Now and then I take some time to watch him, wondering what he wants. "It's about the waist-coat," remarks Popeye, chasing away my thoughts of debt and the man who called on Monday. "Tell him what you think of it. Yeh, tell him. Tell him you don't like yellow. Tell him that you're allergic to it, that it reminds you of daffodils or some god damn awful thing. Tell him it's the colour of sick. That it's Japanese. Improvise. Make something up. Yeh. Mayonnaise is yellow."

"Is it?"

"Course it is. I guess we all have something yellow that we hate."

I keep my eyes down. The old duffer reaches across the bed and fingers my towel. A large arc takes his right hand through the surf on the pattern of the towel, across the sun and onto the blue island and the red tree. He stops under the tree. "So big," he says. "Why so big? Ah..." Something comes to him. "For me? Yes?" He indicates a divide. A finger points towards me suggesting I can keep the island and the tree, he will have the sun.

I protest. "Wait. Hold on," I say hurriedly.

He produces a scissors. "OK?" he asks, indicating what he is going to cut by drawing an imaginary line with the blade of the scissors down the middle of the towel.

"No," I say with a laugh. "Look, about the waistcoat."

"The waistcoat?"

"Yes."

"For me," says Sebastian, disregarding my diversion. Every muscle in his face appeals now. "Ah!" The familiar sound. The jauntiness, so well practised, seems to move easily into cliche. It grates then. I look away. "No," says Popeye. "Hey come on, you've tried that. It doesn't work. Take the scissors off him. Go on. Take it from him. Start again."

Fight, pay, charm, I think, still looking away. Charm, I think, wondering if I have the energy to indulge the old man. I think of his father, the way the other day Sebastian had stood by the window and looked out. It told me how he could open up, what was possible. "Oh come on," says Popeye. "Hey you can do it. The energy will come. That's always the problem. Finding the energy. But it comes, it always does. So come on. Yeh? Let's go for it."

But I can't sacrifice my towel.

"No?" says Sebastian, looking as though he has sensed a change, as though he can't quite believe it. Bewildered indignation follows. "Oh you have so much. I have nothing."

"You have a wife, you have this island, you have friends, you have two daughters and a son, you have a calf called Domingo, a cow called Antonia, you play the *charango*, you are in charge of culture on the island."

"Oh." Sebastian smiles. He listens to my list and nods. He recognises himself.

"That's nothing?"

"You have wife?"

"Me?" I laugh.

"No? But you have towel. All I ask is half towel. Half towel. For me. For Sebastian Marca Yucra." Again he uses his face to appeal. An impish look now. The face of an urchin not a seventy year old man. It shakes a little.

"But how will I wash?"

"You have towel. You half. There." He indicates the divide again. "No?" he asks, sensing my resolve. The engagement absorbs him. It seems to release an energy that he wants to retain. "OK, OK, when go, you send."

"What?" I try to appreciate what he is saying.

"When go."

"When I go, right."

"You send."

"When I'm back in France?"

"Ah." An appreciative nod follows. "Yes. You send?"

"Charm," Popeye is saying in my mind. "Charm. *Tenir angel. Tenir angel.*" A present from France, I think. Charm. OK, OK. A present from France from me. I can live with that. I mean the towel will have seen better days, so why not. "You sure it's just the towel?" asks Popeye. "I mean you're opening up. Be specific."

"The towel?"

"Yes. And trousers."

"What?" I object now.

"Just trousers. For when work."

"When work? When you're working. Right?"

"Black trousers."

"Not these?" I touch the fabric of my jeans. "Oh you mean my waterproofs."

"Yes. For me. For Sebastian Marca Yucra. Yes? For me in fields. Yes? Thank God for tourists," he shouts elatedly. "Thank God for tourists. Look! Look!" He runs out of the room.

"This working?" I ask myself. "Enjoy it," Popeye is saying in my mind. "You're doing OK. Just go with the flow. Hey lead him away." But I am not sure where I am supposed to lead him to and when the old duffer returns with a tape measure, I just laugh. I give in. Thirty inch waist, twenty six inside leg. Little boy's measurements.

I also laugh when he leaves. "Thirty, twenty six," I say. "Thirty, twenty six." I shake my head. I giggle and cough. "And he's seventy." I snigger again. Another shake of my head. "That's five or six hundred francs, I think. I mean for this quality, but then all he asked for was something black. I could get something cheaper."

Popeye tuts. "Cheaper? Five hundred francs, that's eighty dollars. It's worth every cent. Hey you know what? You're the man. He loves you. He fuckin' loves you. You've made him feel great. Full stop."

"Full stop?" I ask.

"Yeh, full fuckin' stop. You hold it there. You don't give another inch. That's what it's all about."

"I don't buy?"

"Like hell you do. You lose his address. You forget. You get a bit flaky. I don't know. You work it out. Do what you wanna do. Just don't buy no trousers."

It seems even funnier when Sebastian returns.

"Shit," says Popeye, sensing my vulnerability and the old duffer's over indulgence. "What the hell's he up to?"

I just smile, thinking how this is a coy Sebastian, diffident and bemused. Perhaps he can't believe what has gone on. Perhaps he is replaying it all in his mind, analysing the way the invader has been taken in, duped. Somehow it all says go back, push your luck. His final footstep in through the door is like dipping a toe in water. He searches for my reaction.

"You took your pen. I've got the paper," I say. "With your measurements."

"Ah."

Silence then. He nods and half turns, but pulls back. He nods again. "My *senora*," he says.

"Your *senora*?"

"Yes. She work in field too."

"So?"

"She work with me." A tilt of his head offers a humble look. It begs beseechingly. "She very nice. Like me."

"Like you?"

"Yes. With trousers, I dry."

"With waterproofs?"

"Yes, waterproofs."

"Proofs," I say trying to correct him.

"Waterpoofs for her?"

"OK."

"She has?" he gasps excitedly.

"Yes. You tell me her size."

"Here." He hands me a piece of paper with the measurements of his wife already written out and moves away, saying a long "Ah", the longest "Ah" I have heard.

"That's it," says Popeye. "Charm. Don't it work? Don't it fuckin' win them over? Oh yeh. Look at him, look at him." I watch him run up through the gateway between the courtyards. I hear him shout. "OK, game over," says Popeye.

"So?" I ask.

"So throw the paper away. You don't need no measurements, right? Sebastian's a happy man. That's what this's all about. He's happy. And you should be too. You were mean. As good as me. And *mi senora*," he laughs. "She very nice, like me. With trousers I dry." He stops and lets the laughter linger. He shakes his head. "Fuckin' Sebastian. He'll be waiting for his package and you'll be back in Toulouse, talking French and all that shit, reading your notebook and wondering what the hell are waterpoofs? Waterpoofs! What the hell!"

142

"Fuckin' Sebastian," I mumble, adopting Popeye speak. "I hate Peru. You hear?" I shout now. "I... hate... Peru." Loud and clear. Like before. Only there is an urgency now, a frustration because I am having to tolerate Sebastian's fawning. I wonder what will be next, what he will demand and what I will accept. "Sebastian," I say quietly to myself. My mind compiles a list. I hate his smile, I hate his smell, I hate his phoney sounding Spanish, I hate his teeth, his exuberance, his ahs, his ohs, his connivance, his plotting, his planning. As the list lengthens I think also how Sebastian's dreams seem particularly piteous. Towels and waterproofs. It disquiets me. I don't know why. It should amuse me. But all it does is make me want to shake some sense into Sebastian. I need to talk motivation, values, beliefs. I need to talk heroes. I wonder who Sebastian's hero is. I wonder whether he has one, whether it is God or a villager or some great *charango* player.

"So who was yours? I mean before me," asks Popeye.

I shake my head. I'm not sure. I suppose it would have been a footballer. After all I had always wanted to be a footballer. That was strange for a Welshman of my generation because at the time rugby players were the gods of Wales, yet rugby players were unpaid and played the game for the love of it. Football players were different. They were beginning to acquire power, to understand that if they were at the top of their game they could demand what they wanted. And rightly or wrongly, the good ones got what they asked for. That is power. Pure power. But I know too that it is the celebration of the person that I like, the adoration, the sense of being the property of the people, of always being available whether it be on the beach, in the high street, in Peru or in Britain.

"You haven't got close to that," laughs Popeye tuning into my thoughts.

"Oh I have, I nearly have. Once or twice. When I was young."

"Oh yeh?"

"When I was in primary school. And in secondary school." I am referring to my rugby playing days. I was quick. I played on the wing. I could swerve and find angles other players of my age couldn't imagine. I was intelligent too. So bright that I struck a deal with my father. Fifty pence a try. Twenty pence a conversion.

"So you went professional?" Meiggs could appreciate such an

143

attitude. He could applaud it.

"Of course."

"Hey what am I doing teaching you? You should be teaching me. Money, money, money. Yeh I like it. Hey that's the way son, that's the way. You're gonna be successful, real successful." He likes that word. He stretches the syllables and lets them pull his mouth into a smile, a big smile. It makes me realise Meiggs' confidence never falters. I know that, though I don't understand it. All those failures. I mean imagine fleeing from San Francisco, seeing a posse of creditors come after you and finding yourself thousands of miles away in a land with a strange language. To come through that requires an indomitable will and a colossal strength. "Hey you're talking my language," says Popeye, but, for once, I ignore him. This time his language is unfathomable to me. I can't empathise with it. I try. Broke, in exile, no friends, no family. It is so chilling. Yet it energised Meiggs. It made him take stock and fall back on the tried and tested ways that had worked. "You do this, you don't do that. You don't change what works. That's the bottom line. You hear? You stay disciplined. That's what it's all about. *No pierde los estribos*, as the Spanish say."

"What?"

"You don't lose the stirrups. You don't lose your nerve. You hang on in there."

Like a batsman, I think, a batsman waiting for the right ball; a batsman waiting for the ball that's too short, the one that sits up, waiting to be hit.

I see then. I understand. I understand that I am still waiting for the right ball. The stiff shirt doesn't offer it. He is outside when Sebastian leaves. He is reading. "What the hell's he up to?" says Popeye when I spot him. I know what he means, that the stiff shirt always seems to be in one of the courtyards washing or eating or talking. Up to now I had thought it was merely a coincidence but perhaps he was waiting to be engaged in conversation, in some sort of witty repartee that he likes and cannot locate on the island. Perhaps he imagines he can find it in me.

8

I think of Chincheros. I look straight ahead and think of Chincheros. It is hanging over me. Like a *faux pas*. Like a bad move at a meeting. Why did I go there? I recall making plans, plans to go to Pikillacta to see some *ruinas* of a pre-Inca culture, to go south down valley not up into the hills, to see the *ruinas* with their rich red walls that curve around contours, to sense the more open space, to smell the rich herbs and see the passenger jets turning north up valley towards Cuzco. Thinking of that almost works. It almost turns the events in the Church into something incidental, not major and overwhelming. But it can't quite manage it, it can't quite carry it off, because the fusion of the church and Chincheros and me and the squat little man, who now seems taller, clenches my mind. It holds it. And focuses it, focuses it on moments, like the second he approached me outside, the moment when he spoke, when the tone of his voice took me by surprise, the moment when I knew I had been complacent.

"I must insist. Now. Your film."

The voice. I knew it immediately. And I knew that my behaviour should have been enough to keep those words unarticulated. What had gone wrong? I looked him in the face, but the face issuing the words was unflinching. It gave little away.

"I can't let it go. You cannot get away with such things. I must ask."

He had followed me. He had left the church and the disarray and fended off the moans of the locals to catch up with me. I hadn't expected that. How could I be that important? Somehow the events inside the church seemed like a drama, a show put on to elevate his status, to impress the party he was accompanying and the locals. I was like a stooge, a stooge with a life of my own outside the church. And that's where I had moved to. The outside. I had expected him to stay inside, to stay with the disorganisation and try to sort it out.

"Why didn't you go?" asked Popeye. "Why didn't you listen to the Swiss guy? You underestimated him. That's stupid, real stupid. You never underestimate. You hear? Never underestimate. I've told you that. That's how you become complacent. That's how you get blown away. That's how you get incarcerated. Hey you stick closer to me in future. You hear? Stick like a fuckin' leech. Close to here, yeh?" Popeye pointed to his head.

"I should take you to the police. You see I have the power. I am a diplomat." The man reached inside his coat and flicked open a wallet. Some sort of identity card was displayed for a second. There wasn't sufficient time for me to verify the authenticity of the document. It was quickly put away, the man keeping his hand in his pocket.

"Look I'm sorry. I didn't see the sign. You see last week when I was here –"

"You were here last week?"

"Yes I was. And there was no sign."

"No sign? What are you saying? You saying you were here last week, that there was no sign? There is always a sign."

"Last week there was no sign. I asked the men on the gate and they said, fine."

"So last week you also took photos?"

"Yes."

"Your film. Now! I want it now."

"No." Another voice. A voice from behind me. The Swiss man's. He came into view and stood by my side. "Don't hand it over. Don't. He has no authority."

"He's a diplomat."

"Is he a policeman?"

"No."

"Then don't do anything. You don't have to."

"Your film." The man from the church kept his calm. An outstretched hand now waited to receive the film from my camera. Again the Swiss man intervened.

"He's something to do with the church. I can't work it out. All I know is the locals hate him. They're scared stiff of him."

"You cannot speak like that to me." The man from the church seemed a little shaken now. I sensed he wanted to say more, to straighten things out, to put the Swiss man in his place. "You cannot speak like that."

"You've said," replied the Swiss man. "But I wasn't talking to you. I was talking of you."

"I am taking him to the police."

"Now hold on." It was my turn to point out the injustice of the

146

reaction of the man in the church to the Swiss man's intervention. I didn't deserve it. I had complied or was about to comply. The man from the church had sensed that. It had quietened him down. It had made him feel I was ready to be corrected. And I sensed that would have satisfied him. "Look I didn't say anything. Look, look." I opened the back of my camera and pulled out the film. "Here have it. Take it."

"Oh that's stupid," said the Swiss man. "Don't give in. Don't let him have his way. He's just a bully."

"Your friend forgets where he is. This is Peru and we have means of making life unpleasant for you here."

"What are you saying?" I couldn't believe what I was hearing. Threats, I thought. I was being set up, set up for bribery or jail.

"You bastard," said the Swiss man.

"Right." The man from the church spoke with some menace. "I mean what I say. We have ways. We can plant drugs. We can frame murders. We're clever. And you have annoyed me. We will see what we can do. You come with me. I am a diplomat. I have the power. Look." Again he flicked open a wallet, revealing the official looking documentation that he had already shown me.

"You're French," accused the Swiss man.

"Yes I am French. So?"

"What?" I said trying to follow the conversation.

"He's French," said the Swiss man.

"French?" I couldn't comprehend what was going on. A French man? In Chincheros? A French man carrying out some sort of citizen's arrest. And I was the criminal.

"You come. Just you." The man from the church pointed at me and began to walk away. "We will find a policeman and you will admit to your crimes. You will tell him what you have done, that you have taken photographs in the church, that you have disregarded the sign and abused me. If you don't then perhaps we will find some drugs."

"Drugs?"

"Don't go," the Swiss man screamed over my words. I edged forwards. "They'll set you up. It's a scam. Can't you see? Don't be a fool. Don't do it." The Swiss man jumped in front of me and held my shoulders. He stopped me moving. He shook me. "Run!" he

147

bellowed, pushing me back the other way. "Run!"

"Hey," I objected, stopping and staring.

"He's right," said Popeye. "He's right. You're in one hell of a hole here. And when you're in a hole you don't dig it deeper, you get out. He's right. You better run."

"Now?"

"Yeh now. Run!"

part five

HUGO AND JOSE

1

I feel thwarted. The railway being closed for a fortnight. It being Christmas. The incident, the bloody incident. I couldn't have stayed in Puno and dealt with it. I know that. I knew it as soon as I saw Puno. I didn't like the look of it. I didn't like its intimacy: the way cars and people brushed by. It was as though my skin were chafing away as I shuffled through its streets. The guidebook didn't help either. Dangerous, it said.

By contrast the island seems agreeable. Popeye agrees. I wonder if he came here. I can't imagine it. He wasn't a holiday taker. No diversions for him, but it feels as though he is here now. He certainly spends a lot of time talking to me, which is just as well, because I need him, I need him to help me sort out what happened, to evaluate how the man from the church in Chincheros had outmanoeuvred me, how I had given in. I need him to tell me I had made the best of a bad situation.

"Come on then, what would you have done?" I'm always asking him.

"When?"

"You know when. When! When he said he'd go and find a policeman."

"Got me," shrugs Popeye, then he smiles. "Oh I guess I'd have done what you did, because you got it right. Hey you know what? Nowadays you get most things right. And you know why? Because you listen to me, that's why. And I'll tell you another thing. You can't stick with Chincheros all day. It won't do you any good. I mean that was a war not a battle, a fuckin' war. So take it one stage at a time. Allow yourself to get diverted. Hey get that painting. Strike a deal with the little shit shirt."

"Stiff shirt."

"Yeh. Now that's a challenge. Fight, pay, charm. Remember? And when you're not getting that sorted out, you can listen to me. Hey you know what I should be called? Nugget. That's what they should have called me. All this Popeye stuff. Nugget would have been better, because that's what you get from me. Nuggets.

Nuggets of pure gold. Twenty two carat stuff."

"One a day eh?"

"Hey don't sell me short. One a day," he mocks. "One a minute more like." He puffs out his chest to illustrate what he means. "Here's one. You ready? Right, here goes. Never work at flat rate."

"That's it, is it?"

"Yeh, but you've got to take it on. You've got to think about it. Why, you should be saying. Why?"

"OK. Why?"

"I'll tell you why. Because you need bonuses. Because it's the only way to get rich. You listen to what they want and make them believe it will take forever. Then you deliver it early and they'll love you. They'll say you're a genius."

I nod. And smile, smile because he makes me forget Chincheros. Instead I think how lots of people said Meiggs was a genius. He thrived on that. He loved compliments that began, "There's only one man for this job...." Such eulogies fell easily on him. The president even called him the first contractor of Peru. Others talked of the skill he had shown in mastering a Chilean workforce that was notoriously difficult. "I'd prefer to work with five hundred Chileans than a thousand Irish men," Meiggs said in response. He always said the right thing. He used his charm to the full. He used it practically, radiating it like rays from the sun. And it penetrated. It worked. It allowed him to treat the *peons* like the president. They liked that. They liked him. They wanted to know him, to talk with him, to say hello.

"That's how you've got to be," says Popeye, tuning in.

"Me?"

"With the shit shirt."

"The stiff shirt."

"Yeh with him. An' with the old duffer. Hey, but I'll tell you what, you don't need to work on him. You've got him. Fuckin' waterpoofs. Your magic has worked on him. Now work it on the stiff shirt. You're a natural. You know that? You'll be a name to drop. It's all they'll want to talk about. What you said. Why you said it. They'll love you."

Meiggs was certainly a name to drop, a big name. In Peru, in his day, he was the biggest name. Don Enrique Meiggs. After a year or so in the new world familiarity dropped the Meiggs. Don Enrique took over. Plain old Don Enrique. The boy next door. So familiar. It was as though he was initiating the sort of populism that South American politicians crave for. To Meiggs the populism was like a spell. It allowed him to get his way, to win contracts and build in clauses for early completion, clauses delivering a sliding scale of enhancements because the earlier the better, the earlier the quicker Peru would be propelled out of the Age of Guano. "Guano's bird-shit," Popeye tells me. "What a business. You know if I'd have arrived thirty years earlier I'd have bought up all the seagulls in South America and had HM printed on their wings. Shit for me my lovelies. What a business eh? Exporting shit. Ten thousand tons to the UK? You got it England. You fuckin' got it." I could hear Popeye laughing at that, a big booming laugh, sort of self deprecating. "Still it gave Peru the money to move on. I mean it turned shit into rail-roads. That's clever. Hey I suppose it means I'm a shit millionaire." He laughs again.

And listening, I recognise it as the sort of laugh I use when I think about globalisation. It is the sort of laugh I use after convinc-ing people that they should buy planes. "You need planes," I tell them. The Brazilians. The Mexicans. The Argentinians. The Chileans. "You need the best. You need to bring in managers and consultants and accountants and politicians. You need to impress. You need an image." That's the lure. It is like the railroad in Meiggs' day. Little has changed. The problems are still there. The dangers are too, yet the lessons of the past that should have been glaring are somehow obfuscated by ambition. We need it. Someone will get it. It has to be us. That's the call that signs the cheques and sends the money back to the First World, money that started in the First World, that cleverly circulates. As though it were on holiday, I always think, the momentum pushing me to say: "You need two." I'd work from timetables then, knowing the routes of the airlines and their needs and the long term benefits of servicing, the economies of scale that accrue. I'd know my bonuses too, the way commission soars. I understand that. I learnt it from Meiggs. "Make it seem like a lottery," he'd say. "Give the commitment and sort of guarantee it. Say yeh, I'll do it by such and such a date and for peace of mind I'll pay you a penalty, so much per month if I'm late. But what they don't know is Don Enrique ain't never late, he's always early. And that's because he manages for that. Get more people, get more machinery. Get them in at the slightest sign of trouble. Get those alarm bells fuckin' ringing. Because in the same way that there's a penalty, there has to be a bonus, a payment for being early, for giving excess earning potential. Understand? It's all about fairness." Popeye laughs at that. "Fairness," he scoffs. "Clever eh? Easy dates. That's what it's all about. Easy targets. You remember that. Make you millions I will. Millions."

★

After the army had chased Julia away from Chuschi it was the Deputy Director who told me where she was and what she was doing. It was just as well he kept me informed, because Julia never made contact. She never wrote. She could have and should have. She knew I cared, but she had moved on. I should have seen that, but I blamed the silence on her involvement and her need for cover. Cover, I thought, trying to reason against the strong case that existed for her keeping in touch. She owed so much, especially to my parents who explained her absence to the soldiers by concocting a story of her departure to Lima to begin a new life in Ate Vitarte, a shanty town. The soldiers accepted the story. After all from the accounts they had collected, they knew she had spoken out, that she had challenged Sendero. The governor, too, remembered her: the woman who had saved him. "Shame she's gone," said an army officer to my parents.

I learnt from that. I learnt Julia wasn't suspected. And rumour had it that no-one in the village had talked. Certainly none of the committee had. That was clear from the long drawn out interrogation of those held and the freedom one or two of the members maintained. Encouraged, I began to manage Julia's return. I spread the word that she, unlike the others who had fled, was not a suspect, that the performance in the village square had cleared her. She had saved the governor. But the returning Julia seemed more sombre, as though the experience had worn into her. Her jauntiness had gone. Her confidence was less brazen. She seemed shrunken, wizened.

"What did you do?" I asked, considering her time away.

"I found another unit. I worked with them." She told me how she had co-ordinated information on Aupachaka, an experimental farm that made cheeses. She studied who worked there and why, whether they were military or police. She calculated how many *cadres* would be needed to attack it and take it and what they should do with the cheeses and the animals. Give the cheese away, she decided. Free the animals.

"Yes I remember it," I said. "It made the news."

"It was a good target."

I nodded. I considered the opinion. It was a research station, a government station. It was a good target. And I remembered the dramatic way it was taken. I also remembered the press and their sense of alienation. They couldn't understand the attack. It seemed to be against the future. That was the way they put it. "Cutting out the vision," was one headline I recalled. It grated. It caused me concern. The obsession, I thought. Wealth, prosperity. What was wrong with the way things were? Chuschi survived. There was wealth there. All Sendero was doing was trying to make it wealthier, to direct wealth into worthy channels. Slight tinkering. That was all that was needed. Not new systems.

"Mind you it didn't all go according to plan," admitted Julia. She adopted a thoughtful pose. "The women kept getting in the way. They cried for the animals. They sobbed."

"But you said free the animals."

"I know. But it was too complicated. The *cadres* got excited. You know how it is. They started killing." She made it sound like starting up a car. "There was blood everywhere. Innocent blood. The women tried to stop them. Mind you, eighty cattle were dead by then."

"Eighty cattle," I gasped. I sensed outrage just below the surface, but it never arrived. Julia controlled herself.

"Oh people were killed too. It's war," Julia added seeing the look on my face. "Don't forget that," she warned. "It's kill or be killed. It's a culture. There's even a language," she added with a laugh.

"A language?"

"We waste them, we ice them. Come on you've heard it. It makes the word kill sound like a kiss on the nose."

"We?" I was a step behind, analysing Julia's choice of words.

"Sendero."

"Not you?"

"We."

I was appalled. I would not listen to talk of atrocities. I would not listen to blood and guts. Particularly from my sister, from Julia, little Julia. What had happened to her? How had it happened? This was the girl who, before leaving, had been at her best dealing with the tangential, with the corollaries that came along with the major trappings of life. Before she went away she could smile and laugh and corner them with a word or a scowl. She was so good at bringing minor crises to ground. More complex issues baffled her, numbed her even. *Vive la difference*, I thought, respecting it, realising it was that that had turned her into a loose cannon when she had been on Chuschi's committee. Her charm had let her get away with it. She would smile, turn as though she were dancing, coo. Some youthful touch would carry her through.

What had happened to that girl I knew? A sense of corruption overcame me. It numbed me. It left my mouth open and my eyes staring. Julia knew the look. She knew also that she needed to speak further, to clear herself if she could.

"I saw people killed. I mean I saw them shot down, slaughtered. It's not good." She shook her head slowly. The movement was somehow substantial. It was more than for effect, more than a consciously sombre guise. It was awkward and sad, but very real. And very lingering. It stayed with me. I cornered it. I interrogated it. It was what I wanted her to reveal. It was what I would recall in private moments, moments when we were separated and I would be wondering about her. Something told me there would be many such moments. That thought made me look up. "Who killed the people?" I asked. "Who were they? The people, I mean. The people who were killed. Why kill them? OK, OK," I slowed down. "Did you kill them?" There was disbelief in my voice. There was fear too. I could anticipate her answer, but I didn't want to hear it. I wanted some make-believe because, for all her admissions, for some reason, I doubted her proximity to violence. It was something I had kept her away from. There had been times in her childhood when animals had to be killed or accidents had drawn blood. On such occasions I had carried her into the house. And now that protection seemed in vain. All wasted, a voice in my head was telling me. All that protection. I couldn't allow its efficacy to be affected.

"We killed them. They killed us."

"They?"

"Oh come on you know how it is."

"No, no I don't. That's the trouble Julia. I don't know how it is. And I'm not sure I want to know how it is."

"OK, OK. We were no angels, but they were ten times worse than us."

"They? Who's they?" I must have sounded almost angry.

"The army. Who else? The guys we were fighting. The state, you know. They were the worst. They found us once. I mean my unit. They found us in a village," she said quite brightly, opening up. "I hid in a corn store. A soldier came to the door. He fired some shots in. One, two, three. Phew, phew, phew." The noise like wind eddying through a confined space, imitated the shots. She used a hand to indicate the bullets' path. They flew over her head. "They missed. We had a hiding place, a secret place under the corn. From there we could look out. I could see the soldier's eyes. Miserable eyes. They blinked. He shut the door." She nodded as if to say how lucky she had been. "I got up then. I moved out of the corn. I went to the door. There was a crack in it. A big crack. I could see through. And there he was, the soldier. The soldier with a young *cadre*. Tomos. He was seventeen. No older. *Terruco*, the soldier was saying. *Terruco*. Tomos kept still. He stared at the soldier. As though he were watching television." Julia stopped and thought. She laughed. A tickle of a laugh. It provided relief. "You know I expected him to applaud, to shout more, good, brilliant or nod some sort of acknowledgement. But he just looked at the soldier. And the soldier killed him. He killed him with a bayonet. He turned Tomos around and stuck it in his back. Then his lungs. Then his heart. And that was that. The soldier sat down and read a paper. He read a paper! He was so composed. It was as though it was his house, as though he had just come in from the fields." She broke away and took some time to think. "I mean it was like it was part of the day. Like getting up. Like having breakfast. How can anyone be like that? Can you tell me? Can any of your books tell me? Eh?"

I never heard her talk of her time away again. I didn't want to. Two years she was away. Two long years during which the Deputy Director would tell me she was well, working hard. Nothing more. No come up and see her. Or can we arrange a rendezvous? There was nothing like that. Not even a word or a letter. Just an occasional confirmation that she was alright, whatever that meant. It confused me. It made me wonder how Sendero, hell bent on social justice could forget about the importance of relationships, how its processes could depersonalise. Names. Numbers. Usefulness. What about friends and brothers? What about interaction? What about sisters?

It was when I was living in Puno that Julia reappeared. One day she was waiting for me outside my house. I came home from college and there she was. "Hello stranger," she shouted gleefully, pulling her body off her luggage and hugging me. "Julia," I said, doing a double take. Out of context I hadn't connected her with the slimmer, shorter haired, older version of my sister that confronted me. There were clues. Her elegance. Her bright eyes. The old teddy bear that she carried everywhere in her childhood was in her hands. She had come to consider it a lucky charm.

"You didn't know me."

"I did. Who else do I call Julia?"

"I don't know. Your lover?"

"My lover!" I laughed. Why was that ludicrous? Why was it acknowledged as ludicrous? It's just that she knows me, I told myself, that she understands how I value work, how it comes before everything. Lovers were not for me. Books were. Ideas were. Libraries and desks were. Lovers weren't. They were too whimsical, too carefree.

She lived with me then until my loose words in Lima. My fault. I knew that. I hated myself for it. I hated myself for allowing her to be endangered, to be stranded and left to face the backlash of my indiscretion. Those words. Those stupid words. I cursed the adrenaline of the moment and the way the drama had got to me, the way I had performed. Now that performance punished me. It went on and on in my mind, keeping me awake, its words finding the gravity they deserved. And my mind piled it on. Going analytical came easy to it. Piling on the guilt did too. "Can you love me?" I wrote in a letter. "Can you believe what I have done to you? I'm so sorry. I'm so very, very sorry."

★

There are tears. I hear them. I hate tears. They embarrass me. Even here. Even in the dark of the island. Tears are a sign of weakness, I tell myself. Tears signal a lack of control, a vulnerability. I hear the snorts of sobbing. The gulping control mechanism that tries to fend away feelings. It makes me feel uneasy. I want it to go away. Look at the ceiling, I think. That's what I normally do. Any embarrassment and I look away. I deny it. Like when my parents used to make love in Blenheim Avenue and I could hear them. Like when I leave a house after a party and it is time to kiss goodbye. Like when my mother's sloppy tenses came out in a parents' evening at school. "Focus on something, something blank and bland," I say to myself. That's always the answer. A coolness. A frostiness. But the sound remains. I move to the window. The night is still, so still. I listen again. The rhythm of sobbing. Its throaty sound moves across the courtyard. I listen hard. The old duffer, I think, turning my ear in the direction of his hut. The sound seems faint there, constrained, perhaps it is just reflecting back from across the courtyard. The stiff shirt. I listen again. I recognise its gentle tone and rhythm, the snorting like a percussion riding over it. I trace it several times. The stiff shirt, I think, wandering, the sound is everywhere now. It covers my image of the man. Like bruises, I think, picking up the biography of Meiggs. I will have to read. I will have to calm my mind before I can fall back into sleep.

I dream of Chincheros. "Why?" I ask Popeye.

"Hey listen you've got to deal with it. I mean you can't go on like this. Every night. Every fuckin' night. You let it go and it will climb all over you. That's what doubts are like. You seen a man who doubts? Wounded he is. It's like being shot in the leg, you hear? So you can't run. And you gotta be able to run. Man you gotta be able to run."

I nod. I understand. I think of Meiggs' last stand when Pardo, the Peruvian president, resigned and the government couldn't raise the money to further fund the railway that Meiggs was building inland from Lima. I think of the problems he faced building that railway. The disease amongst the workforce. The crime. The scandal over contracts. The violence. The inconvenience of the war that broke out between Peru and Chile, the way the Chilean workers were expelled, the way Meiggs protested and demanded them safe passage. "I came through," Popeye shrieks excitedly. "All that shit. I hate shit. Rules, regulations. That's shit. I hate that shit. I fight it. You get my drift? You gotta have big balls to do that. Big balls. You understand? Course you do. Talk good. Don't cry. That's what you gotta do."

"Cry? I haven't cried. I've never cried."

"But all these thoughts. You know what they're like? They're like tears, that's what they're like. And they ain't no use. You just got to stand up tall and take it. If you've gotten the energy, if you've gotten the courage. An' I think you have. Hey for christsakes I know you have. So you get back in there bobbin' an' weavin'. Bobbin' an' weavin', you understand? Keep movin', yeh?"

"Yes," I say.

"Good because there'll be others who'll try it on."

"Try it on?"

"That's what that gook in Chincheros was doing."

"Trying it on?"

"Oh yeh. He wasn't concerned about the state of the frescoes. God no. He was concerned about the state of his wallet. That's what he was concerned about. It was a scam."

"Chincheros was?"'

"Oh for christsakes of course it was. It was a scam. And I hate scams. Thank God I see them coming. I mean no little shit tried anything out on me and got away with it."

"So someone tried something then?"

"Oh yeh of course people tried things, but they didn't realise what they were up against. Oh no, they thought we'll out think him, but I was one thought ahead. Then it was oh we'll out punch him, and I knocked them out while they were thinking about it. I was a big, strong, bright fucker. And that's the choice."

"Choice?"

"Yeh, You gonna be yellow and pissing about for the rest of your

life? You know what you gotta do? You gotta stand up for yourself.
You gotta fight. That's what you've got to do. You gotta write that
letter. You got to tell it as it is. So see that woman when you get back
there. Yeh that woman in the tourists' complaints office in Cuzco.
Hey listen, believe me, there's nothing to it. You just go and see her.
Tell her the truth. The whole truth. Your name, address. The bits
you couldn't tell her before. She'll understand...... you listening?
You gonna do it? Or are you gonna give in and run away? So what's
it to be Hugo? You gonna be a man? You gonna be like me?"

2

When I wake the next day I give the day a name. I christen it the day
of the painting. "This is the day of the painting," I say as I sit and
stare out at the wall and the house across the lane and the rising bowl
of the island. "Go on," Popeye says, urging me on. "Go on. Fight,
pay charm. This is charm, remember? Let's see what you can do."

I see Dina approaching. Painting, memento. The strategy sinks
in. I have a project: to get the stiff shirt to paint me a scene, a view
of the island, a keepsake. Charm, I think, aware of the stiff shirt's
presence. I must talk to him, engage him, befriend him almost. I
smile. I stare at him. He has come for his breakfast, his usual breakfast, a coffee and a long look into the lane. He sits at the end of the
table and flicks some crumbs off its surface into his hand. He looks
for the small bin that is normally kept by the kitchen door. It is not
there. "Dina!" he cries, "Dina!"

"She's gone for eggs," I say.

The stiff shirt seems shocked. He turns quickly and looks my
way. A frown on his face tells me he cannot believe I have spoken.
"She was here. I think she's nipped out the back way." He gives me
a look that tells me he is unaware of there being a back way. "She
does that when people are eating. Well when I'm eating. I don't
know why."

"Look all I want is the bin. You seen it?"

I shake my head. I cannot believe what I am doing. I sense nothing in return. No surge of confidence. No warm self belief. It is just
a struggle. Should I go on?

The stiff shirt mopes about for a second or two, leaning into the kitchen, gazing in. Something prevents him from advancing. I do not understand. Just go in, I urge. But after a shake of his head he returns to his chair and replaces the crumbs on the table. A finger pushes the crumbs closer together. "Vegetable omelette," he says, looking up, taking in what I am eating. "It's very good. I have it for my lunch."

"The trouble is it's always very good. It's always a very good vegetable omelette." The charm is oozing now. It comes so easily, loosening up my face which seems suddenly concerned, alive to the stiff shirt's expressions and movements. "So what do you miss? Come on I know you're not from the island."

"You do?"

The stiff shirt suddenly sounds a little worried. I wonder why as I continue. "That's obvious. You don't dress the same. You don't look the same. And you wash. I've seen you wash."

"Oh the water, yes the water. The bowl."

"My shaving," I say, tapping into the stiff shirt's trail of thought.

"Yes, your shaving. That was very funny." He laughs a little and adjusts his glasses.

"So what do you miss? Come on."

The stiff shirt takes his time. I sense detail is important to him. He needs to be precise. I take in the look on his face which seems to be absorbed in a resourcefulness, a scheming that is looking for the audacious. Clever, I think. I expect something wonderful. "You know what," he says, still looking as though he is enjoying the exercise. "I mean more than anything I miss bread." Again he touches his glasses. "Not something most Peruvians enjoy, but I've taken to it. What I'm saying is it's the ordinary things I miss. It's not the wine or the caviar, it's the bread."

"Me too."

"Bread?"

"Baked beans."

"See? The simple things." He laughs, a short laugh. The response reveals a sophistication: I'm sure that an islander would probably have never heard of baked beans, yet they seem ordinary to him, as though he has lived off them. Perhaps he realises what he has given away, because his laugh is stunted, as though it were

162

offered begrudgingly.

"What else?" he asks.

And I am suddenly sidetracked, thinking of cravings, of what I miss most. Marmalade, bran flakes, lime pickle. The contenders parade in my mind, tempting my taste buds. I smile. Perhaps there is a pay off, I think. Perhaps there is a warmth, a buzz. Something.

"You're always reading," observes the stiff shirt, smiling. It makes me realise how serious he normally is. A frown is his natural expression. It is with him most of the time. "You never look up."

"I am now."

"Yes you are now. And I'm wondering why. Can I ask you about the words?"

"What they are?"

"Yes. What it is that's so absorbing? I mean the intrigue is that anything that so absorbs has a tremendous power. What I'm saying is, in a quiet way, it says so much."

This is what I am dreading, opening up, revealing myself. But I have to. This is the day of the painting, I remind myself. And that means I may have to tell the stiff shirt about Airbus Industrie and Varig and sales talk and the deal that we were brokering and Meiggs, about Honest Henry, Henry the awkward bastard, builder of railways and provider of anything the Peruvian *peons* would pay him for. "*Tenir angel,*" I hear Popeye say, "*tenir angel.*"

★

I couldn't get over it. It was so easy. He just let me in. No defences. I didn't have to find little lines of weakness. He capitulated. All of a sudden. Unexpectedly. He just looked up and conversed. Why? Perhaps he has been ill. Peruvian food, Peruvian weather. I think of everything that might have upset him. Or is it just some great love of paradox that he has? Will he return to silence tomorrow? It wouldn't surprise me if he did, but I tried my best to show him that I wanted conversation, that I wanted some sort of companionship. And I think he responded to that. I think it was that that made him show me his note book. He turned it towards me and left me staring at Puno, Arequipa, Lima and Huancayo. I read the names out loud.

"Puno, Arequipa, Lima, Huancayo."

"Any ideas?"

"Puno, Arequipa, Lima, Huancayo. Well they're Peruvian towns. Quite large Peruvian towns. Pairings perhaps. By geography. Lima and Huancayo in the north, the other two in the south. Or by size. Lima and Arequipa the largest and Puno and Huancayo? Well they're about the same size... Puno, Arequipa, Lima, Huancayo," I repeated, staring at the notepad, noting that Puno and Arequipa were linked by an arrow. Apart from that there was nothing unusual about the list. The arrow, I thought, returning to the idea about coupling towns. That sent me down a new trail.

"Give up?" he asked. "You want a clue?"

I did want clues, but I couldn't bring myself to ask for such luxuries. Then it came. Distance, space, intervening space. The arrow. It was something to do with the arrow. That was the clue. The big link. Arrows. Links. Yes links. Transport? Railways? Yes railways. The central railway. The southern railway. Got it. I stayed silent and smiled. And the Englishman smiled back. Good, I thought, considering the way I had handled it, that for once I hadn't been clever. Not even in my expressions. I had controlled what they were giving away. And the Englishman was talking to me, talking like an old friend, talking like someone who was communicative and generous. What's more he seemed urbane - urbane not shallow and temperamental and difficult, not as I imagined he would be.

"Give up?" he asked, playing with a piece of omelette on his fork. "Well?"

"Railways," he announced. "They're your railways. The termini. You know the beginnings, the ends."

"Lima and Huancaya," I said excitedly feigning discovery. "Yes, I have been on it. It goes through Jauja, the old capital...." I stopped the trail of words sensing I was about to open up and reveal too much. I smiled instead and felt happy, happy that I was controlling myself. I watched the Englishman wipe his hands in a handkerchief and tut as though in disbelief, as though surprised by my slowness. "I'll tell you about them," he promised. "But not today. I've one or two bits of business to see to today. Tomorrow perhaps?" I smiled and watched him gather together his papers and leave the chair and table. I tidied up after him, thinking of Hernando - I wanted to see

Hernando now, I desperately wanted to see him. "Any develop-ments, any happenings, any events," I imagined him saying. I could hardly wait.

Everything seemed lighter then. I sat in one of the plastic chairs and closed my eyes. I thought of Julia, Julia dancing. Julia at her happi-est. So light, so graceful. Julia, the Julia I treasured. Not the Julia of the committee and the talk of wasting people and icing people, but the dancing Julia. I recalled the dance steps that she learnt like lan-guage and perfected. She was so good. The best, I thought. The best in Chuschi. A celebrity. A star. A must for *fiestas* and weddings and birthdays and saints days. Everyone wanted Julia. "Is your sister free?..... Julia'll make it, won't she?....Isn't she good?...." The comments. The affection.

I sat back and pictured her moving slowly, her feet controlling angles, the angles that probed for emotions, exhilarating her face as the curves and the arcs combined. They told a story. They always told a story, using history, turning it into folklore. And Julia added to it. She drew on local events, qualifying them, commenting on them.

She loved that. She loved it from the age of six when she started dancing and through her teens when I took her to gatherings where she would make a mental note of steps and ask me what the stories meant. "Who are they?" she once asked sitting at the edge of the main square in Chuschi, almost at the spot where the ballot papers were later burnt. "Who are they? Do you understand?" She was looking at two dancers who were performing. They were both male.

"The village priest."

"He's not," she said sharply, realising it wasn't the man she met on Sundays.

"No, no, in the dance. He's a priest in the dance."

"Oh I see."

She loved that dance. More than any other it tore into her; she came to perform it easily, in a light way.

"So what's it about?" she inquired, losing patience with the man who was playing the priest.

"It's about a man who made people doubt."

"Doubt?"

165

"Yes. The man who ended blind faith."

I could see she didn't understand my words. The story would explain it. So I told her. I told her about the priest who some thirty years ago had shot into the market crowd, when drunk, after his birthday party. Somehow the dance portrayed that in a comic way. It blurred the boundary between the party and the slaughter and played on the way the priest had always been a source of light relief during the annual fertility rituals that informed the agricultural cycle.

"No wonder she was confused," I said to myself as I tried to recall the steps. I stood up and tried out the steps in the courtyard moving forward and then back, but mostly forward so that I went across the courtyard and through the gateway and down the steps into the lower space. I stopped outside the Englishman's door. So precious, I thought. Family, community, friends, the village. The warmth of such memories made Chuschi seem so important and so delicate. It crackled almost, crackled in my mind, like a radio signal, the communication coming and going, coming and going.

★

"No. Oh God no." The stiff shirt. I see him again through the open door. "Not again. Not now." I need to be left alone now. I had revealed enough. More than I had expected to. More than I had wanted to. But that's the nature of it, I think, realising that any project involves paying a price.

I moan as I watch the stiff shirt's shuffling movements, his feet attempting a rhythm, his head bowed, looking down at the shuffle and turns. Steps, I think, a dance. "Oh God no. Not now. Please. Go away. I don't want to see you again. Not now. Not so soon."

I take a step back and replay the earlier conversation with the stiff shirt. A chuckle to myself says impressive. Which my performance with the stiff shirt had been. I had run rings around him. "Yeh, you could say that," agrees Popeye. "Game, set and match I'd say. And I'm being objective. Yeh. Very impressive......So what have you learnt?" he adds, looking to scale down my successes.

"Learnt?"

"Yeh. What have you gained?"

"His trust?"

"Yeh, yeh. But what more do you know about him?"

"He's probably a painter. On holiday. A working holiday. Building up a portfolio to take home."

"Probably," says Popeye emphasising my speculation.

"Yes.... OK, OK it's not much."

"Fight, pay, charm boy. Fight, pay, charm. *Tenir angel*, as the Spanish say. *Tenir angel*."

Pay, a voice in my mind urges. Pay. Buy a painting, a memento. Something from Peru. Something after Chincheros. Something that says lesson learnt, chapter over. Something that says I have moved on and shown fortitude, that I have coped well with the stresses Popeye should have forewarned me of. Pay. Yes pay.

3

I wake with something over my head. It is like waking up in a dream, in a different place, a place with a web, with material spun around my face, material like a sac of skin. But I see yellow. A streak of yellow. And I know it is the waistcoat. The boring old waistcoat. It had been a cold night, the coldest yet. I can't remember sitting up and pulling the waistcoat off the edge of the bed and draping it over my face, but I must have. Now I yawn and push it away, letting my fingers run over its yellow edges. It feels so coarse. I shake my head. I can't imagine wearing it. I can't imagine going to the *fiesta*.

"Then don't go. And take the fuckin' thing back. You don't want it. You told him, but he's not listening to you. I mean he's all island, all fuckin' island. Island this, island that. He thinks it's great, so you should think it's great. Hey someone needs to take him to one side and tell him that life isn't always like that, that not everyone is interested in his shitty little island, that there are other places on earth that are just as good if not a hell of a lot better. I mean... well what the fuck do I mean? Hell, all in all, you know what? I'd prefer to be in Philadelphia. That's what I mean."

Not now. Not now. I curse Popeye. I want to tell him that I enjoyed talking to the stiff shirt, the bloody stiff shirt. It isn't so much the case that I like him. It is more the case that I just need him. I need people. I need a crowd. I need the buzz. I can't think of any other way of putting it, especially now, after the incident, after Chincheros and the church and the man, the bloody man. The bastard Frenchman. That was the Swiss man's word. "Bastard," I remember him saying it. And how, as he said it, I ran through the market, down the steps across a courtyard and into a road. It was downhill then, downhill and then a run along the flat passed houses and then a right and again downhill though down less of an incline to a line of buses.

Where was the diplomat? Where was he? "I want your name, your hotel in Cuzco. I want to see your passport...." He gave me no time to respond. "You follow me. We'll find the policeman and you must admit to your crimes. OK? If you don't we will find ways of making life unpleasant for you. You understand?" I think of nothing but the words and the way I stood with a group of tourists outside a bus, talking Chincheros and *ruinas*, the driver warming the engine up, my eyes every few seconds darting to my left up towards the corner, the way back to the square. "OK time to get going," my mind kept saying. It was trying to keep me from being complacent.

"*Vamos*," said Popeye, tuning into my thoughts. "You hear me? You go, the rest will follow. I mean most of the tourists on the bus are Italians. They need a bit of herding. So go on, get going."

"*Vamos!*" The driver this time. I led the way and we boarded the bus and left.

"Thank God," I sighed as we moved out of Chinceros. But it didn't end there. The incident stayed with me. It stayed with me on the bus, the mad bus with the Italians singing and the wine flowing, with me shivering as we stopped at checkpoints and were waved on. The seconds at those stops were like pins, pins sticking in me securing me to the moment, a moment the like of which I had never experienced before, a moment when I was out of control, free falling as though I had been pushed over a cliff, a high cliff. But I could see what was coming towards me. The diplomat. The man from the church. The man from Chincheros. The bastard French man. I could see him holding out his i.d. and all the authority of Peru lining up behind him, ambushing me at each checkpoint, his presence being announced by a shiver. It convinced me he would have phoned ahead with orders and a description of me. "You," the policeman would say as he roamed through the bus. "You, you, you," until the sound blasted in my mind. "You!" And I would throw up, my stomach heaving.

"Hey he's really got to you," Popeye declared. "He's really opened you up. I mean he's got you where he wants you. You'll have to leave, you know that? You'll have to go. All because of ol' Jupiter eyes."

"What?"

"You see his eyes? Didn't you notice them? Big baggy eyes. Big rings around them. You know I think he was as worried as you were. You heard of ruses? You heard of scams?"

"That wasn't a scam. He was a diplomat."

"Oh yeh and I'm the fuckin' Ayatollah."

Then we stopped. At the edge of Cuzco. Somewhere up on the rim of the bowl that marked the city's fringe. Horns were blaring, people were shouting. Spanish was flowing too quickly for me. Angry Spanish. Invective. "What's wrong?" I asked.

"Relax. It's the traffic. This is Cuzco." Only Popeye answered, feeding me what I wanted to hear. "Some schmuck's gone out of control. Someone *muy baracho*. Hey probably that diplomat friend of yours, that Frenchman."

Popeye laughed and I walked to the front of the bus.

"Too much wine," said an Italian. "The Englishman missed his beer, yeh?"

"You go on. I'll walk," I said to the driver.

"You'll be alright? Senor, the thieves. Everyone in Cuzco is an opportunist. Every tourist is an opportunity. You sure senor?"

"Yes. You go."

I ran out of the bus and down the hillside. I ran through backyards and down steps. I ran passed chickens and garbage. I ran along the railway line and down a narrow road. "Change hotels," I said to myself between breaths. I had worked out the Frenchman could get my hotel from the form I had filled in at the bus company's offices. "Change hotel, change clothes."

"Change clothes," laughed Popeye unimpressed. "Hey come on, get real. The game's over. You got away. You won. It was a ruse for chrissake. A ruse. That's all. Don't you see Hugo? You're safe now.

This is Cuzco."

I smiled lightly. I didn't feel safe.

"Go on then. Charm him. *Tenir angel, tenir angel.*" Popeye is taunt-ing me again, reminding me of the strategy I had chosen. "I mean he's an artist, right? So it's supply and demand, yeh? That's if you want a painting. Or do you just need someone to talk to? Someone to fuckin' talk to. Hey you've got me. I've just thought of that. Aren't I up to it? Don't answer that. Don't say a word. Let's just see what we've got, whether it makes sense. OK you're missing com-pany, missing the self confidence a good ol' conversation can give. I guess that makes sense. An' I guess you need someone who's your equal. An' that rules out me, because I'm so superior. OK, OK. I'll go away for a while. I'll leave you to it and we'll see what sort of shit you fall into. Yeh? That a good deal? What d'you say?"

I say nothing. I just consider how the congestion of thoughts is like a real weight applying pressure. I need to ease that. "Yeh," says Popeye. "That's right. Go on then, now's your chance. Here he comes. Go for it. *Tenir angel,* remember? *Tenir angel.*"

"Another omelette," remarks the stiff shirt, flicking the hair from his eyes as he sits down. "You have the pills? You know the nutri-ents, what do they call them in America? The multi vits, that's it. You have them?"

I wonder what you get from omelette, omelette, omelette? Or rather what it is that you don't get from omelette, omelette, omelette? The stiff shirt laughs. A long laugh, too long for what he has said. It must be tuned to his thoughts. "Mind you the diet here's quite healthy," he says. "A lack of fruit perhaps, but there's a lot of vegetables. They're lucky. And they have the lake, the fish."

His eyes begin to roam. They smile at me and then dart around the table to the kitchen door. He fumbles with a pocket then, a trouser pocket and stands up and feels in his back pocket. His wallet. He produces it and places it on the table. "Ah," he says, pulling out a ten sol note. "I thought I had left it on the bed. I don't know. Are you like that? I can't concentrate, not on small things, things like picking up money in the morning or turning off the kettle or locking the door. You know some mornings I have to go back and check the front door three times. Three times to see if I have locked it! My mind rolls on." He makes a motion with his hand. "It's a big problem," he shrugs.

A silence develops. He must wonder if I have returned to my previous mode, whether the conversation of yesterday was just an aberration.

He continues. "So what will you do today? Walk? Read? Sit in the sun?"

"You painting?" I ask.

"You know I paint?" He seems suddenly embarrassed. "You've seen me?"

"Up at the arch. When I arrived."

"Oh the arch. I go there sometimes...You know I am the worst painter in Puno. What am I saying? I am the worst painter in Peru." A smile flickers. "But I enjoy it. I enjoy it because I like art. Painting helps me understand the processes of art, the motivation of art."

★

I bit my lip. Why did I say that? Too clever, my mind was telling me. It warned me to take care. I pushed at my glasses and looked the Englishman's way.

"Well anyway I need a present. Something to take home. A memento, you know to remind me of here."

"Taquile?" I prompted.

"Yes....... I like landscapes. Do you do landscapes?"

"Do landscapes? I paint people," I uttered. Do landscapes indeed. A voice in my mind sounded appalled.

"People?" The Englishman nodded and tried to smile, to warm up and give me some support. Perhaps he sensed I needed the encouragement. "People. Yes, people," he said thoughtfully.

"But I'll paint you a landscape if you like. Mind you it may not be a very good landscape. I mean technically. But I'll try."

"You will?"

"If that's what you want, then yes, I will."

★

I always respond well to signs of flexibility. It reminds me of Meiggs always saying yes and then considering the pitfalls. Grab it and see was Meiggs' philosophy. He would return it quietly if it couldn't be done. I remember the strategy, adding, "I'll pay," when I realise the need to return the kindness. "How much will a landscape cost? I mean what do you normally charge for a portrait? Just so I've got an idea."

★

Money. Always money. The elevation of it so quickly in the conversation annoyed me. I avoided the temptation to say no, it's a gift, something from Peru, something for you. I realised I had to go along with the Englishman, that I couldn't afford to disaffect him, that any mildly complaining tone may seem churlish. Not that I would drift into that. I had a too highly developed sense of dignity to argue or complain. Though the Englishman intrigued me. What was he doing here? Why was he withdrawn? And why did he want to indulge me, to buy one of my paintings?

"Can I see some of your work?" he asked.

"Of course."

"And they're of peasants?"

"People," I said rather curtly.

"Yes I mean people."

I let the moment linger. What a change in the Englishman. The man who was unable to find one word of thanks was now so compliant. Dense, difficult, I thought, trying to unravel the motivation. Or perhaps he was just settling in, getting used to the island and the characters it threw up. That made his behaviour seem almost acceptable. Particularly because he was British. I had encountered British reserve at conferences. I knew it well. The coolness. The distance. I knew that once it crumbled a warmness lurked. It was in him. I convinced myself I was just beginning to feel it.

★

Silence. The stiff shirt's abstraction shuts me up. "Say something, fuckin' say something," urges Popeye. He is like a director now, prompting my lines. "Hey what's gotten into you? This is supposed to be a charm offensive. You don't go all coy in a charm offensive.

172

You effuse. You get excited. You know what excitement is?"

A cough from the stiff shirt breaks the silence. "Can I ask you something?" he says, speaking quickly. "Just one thing. You can tell me to mind my own business if you like. I mean I'll understand."

I nod. I brace myself then. I begin to think I have opened myself up too much, that I shouldn't have even considered letting the stiff shirt in. "OK," I say.

"OK?"

"Yes. Go on. Ask away."

The stiff shirt shakes his head. He looks down as he starts to speak. "I just want to know why you're here."

"Why I'm here?" I sound reflective. The gentle probing strikes me hard. You mind your own business, a voice in my mind says. Just go away. Leave me alone. You hear? I don't want to tell you, you hear? Understand? I make a face. I feel I am being ridiculed and why? Taquile hadn't featured in my plans. Circumstances had contrived to bring me here. Circumstances. And I am supposed to be recuperating. Not taking flak, not answering whatever questions come into the stiff shirt's mind.

"*Tenir angel*," says Popeye, orchestrating the strategy. "Fight, pay, charm, remember? You've chosen charm so generalise. Just generalise. Make it vague."

"Well..." I say, playing for time. "I guess it's... How can I put this? It's hero worship. That's it. We all have heroes." I rub a hand on my hair and smile. "You have a hero?" I ask. "Mine is Meiggs."

"Marx?" said the stiff shirt having difficulty with the quick pronunciation. "Hey he's mine too. So you believe in the dialectic?"

I accept the confusion as though it is contagious. I arch my brow, opening my eyes widely. And I laugh. I laugh loudly and suddenly and wonderfully. "Marx? You think...."

"Yes Marx. You believe in the destruction of capitalism?" The stiff shirt somehow ignores my mirth.

"The destruction of capitalism?"

"Yes."

Again I laugh. The sound signals the end of the intrigue. It seems unfair to draw the stiff shirt on. I have already learnt so much. I laugh at the way his philosophy and beliefs have been inadvertently exposed. "Mm I think you've got the wrong man."

"Karl Marx," says the stiff shirt, proudly, boldly.

"Honest Henry," I say. "Honest Henry Meiggs."

"Not Marx?"

"Meiggs," I say, shaking my head. We laugh together then. The stiff shirt slowly, almost deliberately, considering how he should have sensed the distance between our thoughts; I more brutishly, enjoying the misunderstanding to the full. The laughter pushes me back against the chair. I tilt it up against the wall. The strength of the laughter tells me how much better I am, that my energy level is increasing. I am beginning to cope with all the ordinary things again. "Oh dear..." I splutter. The sound makes it clear that I would never support the dialectic. Preposterous it is saying, rising in volume and pitch, coming to a crescendo before spluttering back to life once or twice as it peters out. My turn for questions now. "Why peasants?" I ask.

The stiff shirt sighs. He seems to dislike talking about his interest in art. "Why peasants? Oh I don't know. I mean how do you choose the subject? I suppose the subject is the whole point. You know what you are really asking? You are really asking, why art? And what I'm saying is if you understand that you understand the peasants." He adjusts his glasses with a turn of his nose. It leaves a strange look on his face, a look of disapproval as though he has discovered something he dislikes, something he abhors. The look takes my mind off his cleverness which assaults me. What does he mean? It must be straightforward. His gaze says so. That overly used frown, the almost permanent stare somehow topped up with a glint in his eyes. What does he mean? I turn over what he has said. There is nothing there. No explanation. Why peasants? Why art? I struggle. I wonder whether it is a function of my Spanish, my good Spanish, my European Spanish. I need accuracy now. I need concentration. I stare at the stiff shirt. I feel a frown come over my face. A pondering. It tells the stiff shirt more words are needed, that more explanation has to be forthcoming.

Once more he fingers his glasses. "I mean it has to be about people. It has to be about the way we live, the way we are."

"The human condition?"

"Yes, yes. It is about problems. All art is. All good art. It is an expression of the problems. It may hint at solutions, but it can't be too specific. It only expresses conditions. It exaggerates them. It tells a story about them. Not the causes or the solutions. Just the condition. That's what art is good at. It gets inside."

"Inside?"

"Inside ideology."

"Ah."

"Inside what people believe. It gets into human life. Art brings it out."

Again I struggle. I take a deep breath and sit up. I stare moodily at the stiff shirt. He whistles quietly to himself. A daft tune. It makes me sense any lack of communication frustrates him. His mind seems to search for more words, for clearer words. "Look. I paint. I paint faces. The blood, the sweat. The disappointments, the struggles. They are the conclusions."

"Of life?"

"Yes. Of life. What else? Of society. Of the system."

I nod. Something has been unravelled. But I need more. I wonder how I should move the conversation on.

"Listen," he says more softly. "I am from a place called Chuschi. It's a small town in the hills...."

★

Was that in the story? That admission. Jorge, I thought, recalling his words. Was I supposed to be from Chuschi? Be vague. Hold back. Think before you speak. But he is from Europe. And he doesn't talk to anyone else on the island. Apart from Sebastian, that is. And he's just plain rude to him. And I need to make what I mean about art clear. And Chuschi is where my interest in art began, where it came from.

"Is that significant?" asked the Englishman, breaking in.

"Where you come from? Of course it is. I mean if you deny where you come from you are denying who you are. It is your genes, your culture. You are little else. You are denying everything. You are trying to reconceive or transplant yourself... Look what I'm saying is, where would you be without your past? Can you deny it, eh? Do you deny it?"

"Deny it?"

"Some people deny it. I'm not sure why. Perhaps it's because they come from somewhere like Peru and Peru is third world and poorly developed, a dull old ex colony. Is it that? Or is it because we're nearly all peasants? Poor people in a poor country. That's not sexy, eh? That's not chic, so we deny it. But where do we go then? How can we go anywhere? I mean you have to know where you have come from to know where you are going. And that's what I find in art. And that's why I paint peasants because the land is in them. I bring it out. I bring out the battles. The battles with landowners, with the Church, with the soil." I smiled. Suddenly I was enjoying myself. I sensed I had regained the initiative. "What it is, I think, is an allusion to reality. Just a touch of it. Nothing more. It can be no more. But it is enough."

The Englishman nodded. He didn't seem inclined to contribute which was just as well because I wanted the conversation to continue quickly. I wanted to exacerbate my pleasure, to heighten it, to draw more words and explanations. If I lost it now and then to passion and sentiment well so be it, but I needed to encourage the Englishman. He'd pick it up then. He'd get the issues. I was sure of that.

★

"You're the man, hey Hugo, you're the man......." I hear Popeye praising me. I have to get in there. I have to make my point while it is clear in my mind. All that talk of culture and society and being blessed by upbringing. I have not been blessed. I have been hampered, held back, restrained and constrained. Only now am I leaving it behind, leaving it in Wales, in Blenheim Avenue. "But it's not just that," I say quite boldly to the stiff shirt.

"That?"

"Your home and upbringing. You're a Marxist, yes? Isn't that influential?" I see a slight look of doubt on the stiff shirt's face. It draws me on. "Suppose I'm a reactionary. Say we paint the same peasant. Would we come up with the same feel to the picture? Well?" It is my turn to smile. I enjoy it immensely. I enjoy winning. I enjoy seeking confrontations as long as the other person backs down or sucks up. I gain a little vanity from that. It isn't an attractive trait. Vampire like, some think, sensing I draw energy from it. "Well?" I press the point. Come on, a voice in my mind says. Come on you stiff shirt. I've spoken to you, well and truly spoken. Now it's your turn. So come on.

"There is such a thing as detachment."

"Not if you're a Marxist there isn't....." I stop myself. I try to find a diversion, to pull away from any emphasis on strictness.

"OK."

"OK?"

"I'll show you my paintings tomorrow."

"Right," I purr. The tone says I would like that.

"You have time? How long are you staying?"

"A week or so. I have to be in Cuzco January 3rd for a flight back to La Paz."

"La Paz," says the stiff shirt in a thoughtful way, as though it holds some great significance.

5

"La Paz! He's going to La Paz! Now that is a development. You see it's just as well I ask, eh José?" Hernando seemed to suspect a parallel text was lurking in my mind. He tried to stir its presence, but I just nodded. "That's good José, that's good. That's where Julia is, eh? So he can see her, talk to her."

"Yes, yes he could." I must have seemed less than enthusiastic. Quickly I tried to recall what I had said about Julia. Julia my wife. Julia who had left me. Julia who had walked out. I recalled the story Jorge had drilled into me. The dispute, the way of life, the culture of teaching and its expectations, the story I had told Hernando, the way I had placed her in La Paz. That was the only truth. And now that was married to the Englishman's reality. The reality of a plane ticket into La Paz, of an overland trip to Titicaca into Peru and Puno. Soon he would return to La Paz, retracing his steps before flying back to Brazil. Brazil where his business is, where his colleague is devising strategies for renewed negotiations.

But first La Paz. The thought lodged in my mind. It made me envious, the envy coming from the way the Englishman could be close to Julia, from the way he may pass her in the street or sit in a cafe where she may be working, the way he could just bump into her. Just bump into her. That sounded so ordinary. Julia. La Paz. The Englishman. A meeting on the street. But there was a flaw. I sensed it. I understood what it was, that Julia and La Paz couldn't mix with the Englishman. They couldn't make contact. They couldn't cohabit the same space. They weren't compatible. At least not with the feisty, difficult man who had displayed such a level of ignorance, with the man who couldn't be tolerant.

"So what's he like?" Hernando asked the inevitable question.

"He's fine," I lied.

"Fine?"

"Yes."

"Fine!" exclaimed Hernando. "And what does that mean? If he's so nice, why was he silent? What was all that about, eh José? Why didn't he talk to you? And why was he rude to Sebastian?"

"He was ill. The altitude." I dismissed the questions.

"So if he's so fine, go on, ask him."

"Ask him?"

"Yes. It's perfect, eh José? He can go. It's easy for him....." Hernando thought deeply. I imagined him checking the prospects and playing over what could happen and how it would help me. "So you'll ask him, eh José?" There was no reply. "You should. Hey you a gambling man José? Why don't we have a wager? Just a little one. Yes, let's have a wager." Hernando must have seen my reaction. The touch of contempt. "A wager? Come on José, why not? Look ten sols. Ten sols says he'll do it. He'll see Julia for you. What do you think José?"

I laughed.

"Listen. I know he will. He likes you. All the talk of painting and him liking Peru and wanting a painting."

"He never mentioned liking Peru."

"OK, OK, but the painting José. That's good for you. Hey you could stay and paint. Have a study here. You thought of that José?"

"A studio," I mused, forgetting myself and correcting Hernando, but my attempt at correction was disregarded or overlooked.

"You could do little paintings of me. You know. Hernando on the jetty. Hernando on his boat. Hernando in the lake. Hernando laughing. Hernando sleeping. Hey that's easy José. What a life!"

But I wasn't listening. I was back with the words about bets and getting the Englishman to look up Julia. Perhaps Hernando was right. The Englishman must like Peru. Why else would he be here? Then I remembered Meiggs, the Englishman's hero. I had forgotten to pursue the name and inquire about the significance of the man. But it was a strong association. It had to be. The dreams of youth. The wealth of experience. 'Hero' encapsulates all of that. It is a source of inspiration, holding an awe that no school subject could compete with. It is out on its own.

So what about me? I wasn't aware of any such influence. So who is my hero? Who, who, who? Philosophers began to parade before me. Artists too. And one or two writers. But I found myself returning to the philosophers. Always the philosophers. Marx, Althusser, Gramsci. I finally settled on Gramsci. Gramsci, a thinker, a Marxist, an Italian. I thought of his life and times, of Italy in 1929 when Gramsci's powers were at a peak and the Italian Socialist Party held one hundred and fifty six out of five hundred and eight parliamentary seats; I thought of the hopes and expectations, how the Third International was formed out of zeal and endeavour. I smiled at that. Zeal and endeavour. Where was that now? Where had it gone?

"See. You think so too," Hernando broke the silence. He had been watching me, seeing the consideration develop and move, warming my face. The topic of consideration and its nature was beyond him: he had presumed: it had to be the Englishman, what he could do, how he could do it, how I would benefit.

I smiled. Briefly I stayed with Gramsci, thinking how he had influenced not controlled, how he had questioned, enjoying a pre-science and a fallibility. He was versatile too - his cultural writings equally gratified me - and his concern with the international rather than the national always attracted outsiders like myself. So I smiled through the words directed my way.

"It makes sense José."

"What does?"

"The Englishman. Getting the Englishman to see Julia." Hernando nearly spelt out the words. "I mean why's she in La Paz? La Paz!"

"I told you," I said quite sharply. "She left me. Went there."

"To a friend's?"

"Yes." I made it seem so simple.

"But you want her back, yes? I can tell José," Hernando smiled broadly in a knowing way. "I can tell. And the Englishman can be a go-between."

"A go-between," I laughed. The sound almost shouted down Hernando; telling him not to be so ridiculous. But he disregarded it. He just shrugged and continued. "You ask him eh José? Ten sols he says yes."

I smiled again. It seemed like the normal response now. It interrupted Hernando, cutting his flow, slowing him down, settling him. It probably made him believe the point he was impressing upon me.

"We have a bet, yes José?"

A nervousness crept into my features. The realisation of what I was committing myself to had struck me. I couldn't do it. I knew I couldn't gather myself and find the face to ask the Englishman a favour. I hardly knew the Englishman. What cheek, I thought. But I still went ahead, thinking of what I should ask. Find Julia. Question her. Give her a message. It was all much too dangerous for the both of them.

"It makes sense José."

"Yes, yes it does." I smiled, pushing my glasses up my nose towards my eyes. The movement settled me.

"So what will you do?"

"It's just, well......."

"Well what José?"

"I hardly know him."

"But that makes it easier."

"Easier?"

"Yes. Easier to take if he says no."

"You think he'll say no?"

"Of course he won't say no. Hey come on, I've got ten sols on it, ten sols that he says yes, eh José. Ten sols. You mark my words José. He won't say no."

★

I stare at Meiggs. I stare at his fair hair and blue eyes, the sharp eyes. The same effect, the usual effect. The eyes dominating, overwhelming, charming.

"You'd have loved it," I say, imagining how he would have coped with the conversation, with my introduction to the stiff shirt. I recall the moment. The shock. The shock of the silence being broken. The stiff shirt didn't know what to make of it, though he settled into it, albeit with a degree of disbelief, a suspension of judgement perhaps as he waited for my new found sociability to dissolve. But it stayed. It lingered and threatened to change the way he viewed me. Plain. Quiet. Quiet in a simple way, not a troubling way, not a disturbing way. But suddenly all that is chased away and I am loquacious, enjoying words, enjoying the challenge of describing and explaining, enjoying the selection and the emphasis. So different from my performance up to that point. Not a word, I think, wanting to laugh, enjoying the mystique it all creates.

"So what does he do?" asks Popeye. "You found out yet? I mean you told him all about me. He's a teacher, yeh? I bet you he's a teacher." His tone holds little respect. Such an easy route, it says. Safe, predictable, it says, making it seem all teachers sink into society without making a wave. Ineffectual, it says. "Not like me eh? No sir. No way. Hey get real."

Real? I wonder what he means. I want to engage that, but, as if on cue, the stiff shirt appears. He comes through the gate from the lower courtyard and smiles. "Meiggs?" he asks, seeing the papers in front of me. I nod thinking we should be discussing art and prices and which part of the island I want on canvas. Instead he seems to want to clear up the confusion over Meiggs and Marx. There is something fussy about his nature. It is like the way he plays with his glasses, the way he wipes the chair and the table down before he sits and the way he looks toward the kitchen door anticipating the appearance of the old duffer's daughter. Everything has to be in the correct position I think. Meiggs and Marx aren't. They irritate him.

★

Money, fortunes, wealth. I heard about it all. Meiggs was a capitalist, a real capitalist, a mega capitalist. He was the epitome of a capitalist, the acme of a capitalist. I heard about his timber business in New York state and of his drift west with the forty-niners and how in California he built homes and made a fortune out of real estate. It was a good story. It was entertaining, suspenseful. But I craved some depth. I wanted to ask: what about ideas? And in particular what about the idea that it's sick making money out of land? Shrewd perhaps, but certainly sick. All I could do was stop and stare, but the little interludes I manufactured seemed to provide lulls that the Englishman felt a need to fill. He thought I was interested, not bored or angry. Couldn't he see I found it all abhorrent? Property, class, advantage. Couldn't he sense the antagonism I felt towards such a route of advancement? I tried to make it clear. I tried to create a chill. I gave him a look, a long long look. I went, "Ah" and questioned him and bit my lip until my mind ached. And he went on revealing, analysing, making me think only of what was going on, how bits of a man's life were being presented. Just bits. The crucial bits. The deals. The scams. Nothing about his wife and children and interests, nothing about whether he was religious or benevolent, no mention of philosophy or belief. Nothing substantial. Just the trimmings. But what about the omissions? They were important too. They must have been. They must have been necessary to any explanation of the way Meiggs had given up the riches of a developing California. I cursed the Englishman's cool articulation. I wanted the gaps filled in.

"So when did he come to Peru?" I asked.

"The 1860s. After California...." The Englishman paused. He seemed to have difficulty sequencing dates and events. It was as if his mind scrambled them, drawing out what he deemed important and ordering it using criteria that had nothing to do with chronology. "Went to Chile first. Then Peru."

"Why Peru? Why did he leave Chile? Why not Argentina or Brazil?"

"Opportunity, I suppose." The look in the Englishman's eyes said more. It explained so much. It glowed. Scams, charm, it said. All the things I've got, it said. All the things I'm using on you, it said. All about getting ahead, about getting one over on people. On me, I thought. "And he had to get out?"

"Out?"

"I mean leave. He had to leave California......" I shook my head. The movement signalled something more than distaste or disapproval, perhaps I was hoping to convey revulsion, perhaps I was calling for more analysis of the life that was being revealed. I could do no more than that. I couldn't argue against it. I knew the Englishman would dismiss anything I said. Unless I gained his respect. But I wasn't sure how I could do that. "And you admire him?" I asked in an amazed tone, for a moment forgetting myself.

★

"And you admire him? Get that. Hey what sort of question's that? You know what? You've got a prize gook here. Get the fuckin' painting and run. Get the hell out of here. Otherwise he'll be following you everywhere. *Estar hasta en la sopa,* as the Spanish say."

"Meaning?"

"Oh come on. He'll even be in your soup. Meaning there'll be no getting away from him. So you get the painting and run. And the quicker the better. All this shit. Hey you know what? You'll have another Chincheros on your hands if you don't watch it. I mean this jerk is up to something. I can sense it. Believe me I know when a jerk is up to something. Hey come on. You're too soft, you hear? You've gotta shape up Hugo baby."

But I am enjoying it. The buzz. The talk. The battle. I wait for another question. It comes almost immediately. "So you work for yourself?"

I wonder where the question has come from, what has initiated it. Oh yes, Meiggs, I think, Meiggs the entrepreneur, a man by himself working on hunches, taking gambles.

"You work for yourself?" the stiff shirt repeats.

"For myself? No, no I work for Airbus Industrie. They make planes. You know?"

I see him nodding. "I've flown in one," he admits.

"If Airbus does well, I do well. It's a close relationship. And it works. Means we get on. I'm a salesman. Second sales. Below Helmut, the smooth-talking German. You ever met a smooth-talking German? No you wouldn't have. Helmut's the only smooth-talking German in the world. He's unique."

★

183

He laughed. He laughed at his own words. They seemed to surprise him. They didn't surprise me. I just listened, trying to appreciate, trying to comprehend. But it was beyond my experience. Smooth-talking Germans? Second sales? Another world.

"I tell you one taste of this and you're away," he said, shifting from the specific to the general, to capitalism.

"Is that true for everyone?"

"Oh yes, yes of course it is. For everyone. That is for everyone who tries. Not everyone tries. I mean you've got to be adventurous and ambitious."

"Not able?"

"Yes, to succeed. To succeed you have to be able."

"And what about the others? What about the ones who don't try? And what about the ones who try and fail?"

"Oh come on it's you or someone else."

"You believe that?"

"Of course. It is."

"So it's selfishness."

"Oh it's something much stronger than that....."

I couldn't take in what he was saying. I couldn't comprehend the image he was building. I couldn't visualise it. I didn't want to. I couldn't allow myself to, because it was worse than I imagined it could have possibly been. It really was. There had been so few things in life that had revealed themselves to be worse, but capitalism was succeeding, at least the Englishman's version of it was. What was this aggressive selfishness that he was advocating? What did it mean? Trusting no one, working for yourself, staying ahead of the game. But what is the game? What does this mature form of capitalism really look like? And how is it sustained? It made me think of society. The bits I like. The warmth of people. The way they hug. The way they touch. The way they smile. Their devotion. Their loyalty. Their care. Then I returned to the Englishman and what he was saying. "So you just do things for yourself?" I said qualifying what I was taking in.

"All the time," the Englishman answered confidently. "I do things for what I can get out of a situation."

"So you wouldn't do something for me?"

"Not normally. I may do here, now, because this is different. It's not my normal day to day life." The Englishman laughed. "It's not as easy as that."

"You're making it easy for me are you?"

"You're intrigued," observed the Englishman.

"It interests me. It makes me wonder what you see, what you're doing here with me."

"Oh that's easy. I'm enjoying myself. Believe me. I'm not apologising if that's being selfish. Enjoyment is selfish."

I left then. I couldn't believe what the Englishman was saying. He was saying I was his plaything, that I was there for his gratification. And he wouldn't do anything for me. He admitted that. He said so. Unless there was something in it for him.

6

"So who's this Meiggs?"

"He's a capitalist. He's the Englishman's hero."

"Hero?" The expression on Hernando's face said that he couldn't comprehend what was being said, that the islanders had no scope for hero worship, that their lives were too simple, too unambitious.

"It happens."

"Happens? Worshipping someone? I mean that's what you make it sound like José. You make it sound as though the Englishman's life is all mapped out by this Meiggs character, whoever he is."

"He wouldn't see it like that." I baulked at Hernando's interpretation. "I mean it's not a case of.... You see he is free to make decisions. It's the underlying philosophy that is set for him, the guidelines. Meiggs provides that..." I stopped. I wasn't happy with the words.

"So? Do you think these guidelines can accommodate Julia? I mean a visit to Julia. You think José?"

I shrugged. I did not know. I could not know. Although instinct told me no. It seemed unlikely.

"Oh you must not give up José."

"I mustn't?" I struggled to follow Hernando's line of thought.

"No, no. There's still a chance that he'll agree to the scheme."

"You mean he'll see Julia."

"Yes. There's always a chance."

I understood what he was saying, but I wasn't sure how to continue.

"You'll learn José. You'll understand what makes him tick."

"Oh I know what makes him tick."

"You can't. Not yet. You've got to give it time José. Time."

"Why?" I stared deeply at Hernando. I demanded an explanation. "I mean I believe in principles too. It is the only way in life. And I know now what is at the base of all he says and does."

Hernando raised his eyebrows in disbelief.

"No, no I do. I believe that. I firmly believe it. You would too. I mean this man is..... Well he's like nobody I've ever met. He is direct, forthright. He cannot charm. He's not tolerant."

"But you've got to tolerate him José. Isn't that right?"

I nodded. Of course it is right. I have to. I have agreed to. I was involved with the Englishman. I was painting him a landscape. But that was as far as it would go. I knew that all he had said had changed my attitude towards him, that I would no longer hold back. Now I would show him what I was made of. Now I would show him what I could do.

"I'll get another tea. This omelette." The Englishman shook his head. "You can take my mind off it."

"Me?"

"Yes you."

I smiled. I knew the Englishman didn't dish out compliments. I also knew that there was a degree of manipulation in what was being offered. Instinct told me that. The Englishman had told me too. I recalled our previous conversation.

"You got things to do?" The Englishman looked disappointed.

"I've something to show you," I said, cheering up my tone. The change coincided with a reassuring smile. I fumbled in my jacket pocket and pulled out a piece of folded paper. The Englishman tried to look over its edge as I opened it out. A quick nod, an excited nod. He's enjoying this, I thought as he moved towards the paper.

He watched it being spread out on the table.

"Is this one of yours?"

"One of mine," I managed to say with only a touch of exaspera-tion. "One of mine? No, no. I use this in one of my courses."

"Courses?"

"I teach."

"You teach?" Something about the tone of the words told me the revelation wasn't unexpected.

"You know it?" I asked, referring to the image on the paper, the image of a city, a European city, a British city.

"Know it?"

"The place. The city."

"Must be London," said the Englishman, taking another look.

"I guess it's changed," I said quickly.

"No it's London," he said adamantly. "Somewhere hilly. Hamp-stead Heath?.... So what's all this about?" He seemed to like unravelling complexities and seeing order. Where did this fit in?, I imagined him thinking.

"So what do you think?" I asked, referring to the painting.

"It's a landscape."

"So you like it?"

"Yes, yes I do."

"Is this what you want me to paint? I mean this sort of thing."

"Yes...." He looked at the painting again. "Yes that would do." Then he hesitated. Perhaps he sensed a touch of derision in my voice.

"And this is a landscape?"

"Yes.... It's a hill overlooking a town." The Englishman's eyes were fixed on the painting. "...It's a landscape." The Englishman stopped and looked once again. He seemed unsure, as though his words were unsatisfactory. Clumsy perhaps. Or understated. It was as though some point had penetrated them and was shaking them up, making him try to move them around or hold them up.

"You see it as a landscape?" he asked.

"Mm...." I wasn't ready to comment fully.

"Hey, you're the artist."

"Well I think there's a bit more to it than that." I leant across. I took in the detail. Meticulous, sharp, annotated. Technical adjectives

187

came to mind. Straightforward, I thought, though it was easy for me. I saw it in colour. Like the original. Red brick. Cream stone. Mundane. Quaint. Timid. Those were the adjectives that followed the visualisation. I knew there was nothing in the solid landscape of the painting that really impressed. Concentrate it, I thought, sharpen it, steepen it, shorten it. Even that didn't help. I pulled a face.

"You don't like it," said the Englishman, seeing the expression. "Come on. You don't, do you? Why?" He looked at it again. He liked it. I could tell that. He liked its contours, the cut of the land like a familiar suit. It made him feel at home.

"Too tame."

"The landscape?"

"There's nothing dangerous. Nothing terrifying. You look at this island. You look at Peru. The land is like a creature. A wild creature. Sometimes it's terrifying." I laughed. The sound shocked the Englishman. It seemed out of place, out of step with the words. He couldn't accommodate it. "But that's not why I showed it to you. I mean we respond intuitively. You like the softness? It is familiar. It's your territory. You should know it, you're associated with it. I'm not. So perhaps I notice it more. I see what's there. It's different to me. You see? I'd be the same with the Andes, with a village in a valley."

"You were going to say something else," suggested the Englishman, noticing how the conversation excited me. He sensed I needed such talk, that I had been deprived of it for some time. He must have wondered why.

"No, not really."

"Not really," he scoffed.

"Well.... Well I was just going to say that we live in one place. That we're stuck with it."

"Stuck with it." The Englishman shook his head. The words didn't quite match his expectations. "No ... There's something else. You were going to say something else. Something in relation to my question."

"Your question?" I said excitedly, surprised by the Englishman's sudden show of sensitivity.

"About landscape. It must have been about landscape."

"Oh landscape. You know who painted this? Turner. One of your greatest painters. And it's Leeds. You know Leeds?" I waited for a shake of his head. "Oh well what I'm really asking when I look at this painting is: what challenges, what really challenges? You see this is the point. You have to get inside." I paused, searching for some recognition, giving it a little time as though it should be familiar and immediate. "This is an industrial painting," I emphasised. "A human painting. It is about people. They are the dynamism. The rest of it is dull. You see? The rest of it says nothing. But the people, well they work. They really work."

The Englishman looked at the piece of paper again. He had missed the people. He took in the careful detail of activity, the detail that drew in dress and expression. The physical environment came in too. A sunny morning, he must have thought, breezy. He could see that by the shadows and the trailing hair and the clothes that were drying. It was an outdoor sort of day. There were people picking mushrooms. There were labourers building walls. Milkmen were coming up the hill after the morning delivery to the town.

"You see?" I said, urging a continuation of the analysis. The Englishman smiled. He nodded. I wondered if he identified the conflict and the sense of novelty. The condition, I thought. The sense of society being reorganised and people finding their way, the sense of some of them still clinging to nature, still gathering mushrooms and growing crops. The condition, I thought. The sense that the countryside had moved to the city.

"I see," he said, trying to take it in.

★

"A daft, militant, waste of space," says Popeye chiming in. "Listen to him. A real ol' scum bag. And you've spooked him, you know that? You've fuckin' spooked him. You know what you did? You know what you did that made him suspicious? You told the truth. That's what you did. Crime of crimes. You told the fuckin' truth."

Of course Popeye is right. The one thing I am always plain about is capitalism. And it had come up in the previous conversation. It had come up in the context of Popeye.

"So he goes all arty-farty on you. I mean he has to. It's the only way he can get on top. You see that? I mean do I have to spell it out? You know what's goin' on here? And you know why? Because you said you're selfish. Because you said you wouldn't do him a favour.

I mean for fuck's sake. What the hell were you thinking of? You should have been agreeing with him. I mean gee where was the angel? Where was the fuckin' angel?....."

But the stiff shirt and I continue to talk. We walk and talk. And I enjoy it. I actually enjoy it. I try to pull away from it, to laugh at myself, to question why I am putting up with all the words. Because of a painting? A memento? No it's more than that. It is company. It is the buzz of association. It fulfils a need in my make up for contact. So I listen again. I listen to the stiff shirt.

★

"I like the idea of work. That is so strong in the painting. You see?" I gave him time to snatch a quick glance. "It builds the city. It changes lives. It controls. It still does. I guess what I'm saying is I like its power...." I waited for a response. I was enjoying myself now, deploying my cleverness, outmanoeuvring, not giving the Englishman a chance to express all the nonsense of individualism and capitalism. I was in charge now. I waited.

"Right," he said awkwardly, the look on his face telling me it was a form of power he could not recognise. He certainly had never before considered it. His curiosity told me that. Confusion, I thought, deciphering it. I shook my head thinking that the Englishman's principles constrained his interpretation of power. I wondered how to articulate the power I believed I had. "I have some power," I declared rather flatly.

"You do?"

"Yes. Education has power. So I have it vicariously. Do you see?" Again I waited for a response. I had expected my words to be provocative, but the Englishman just smiled, a slight smile as though what I had said was insignificant. "Althusser, a French Marxist, said the school is so quiet..........."

I was enjoying this now. The Englishman was too. I could tell that. I could tell by his face, by the way it beamed at answers and questions. Perhaps his strictures were different, perhaps he couldn't

190

engage the material in the way I could, but I was willing to allow for that: our societies are different; the people in them are different; the Englishman and I are different. I know that. Yet we were communicating. OK in a limited way. It would be disingenuous to suggest otherwise. But the limitations were acceptable to us both and, in a way, they focused the Englishman's attention.

"You see," I said continuing. "The key thing is the state has always identified so strongly with the Church. All its attention was taken there, its long disrespect for education left education vulnerable to, well to infiltration. You understand? What I'm saying is groups could find a way in."

"Revolutionaries?"

"Yes."

"You," said the Englishman following the gist of my point.

"Yes," I agreed rather hesitantly, thinking over Sendero's pedagogical roots, how it claimed university faculties, how it developed in the sixties and the seventies out of a defence of free education which a military government had tried to cut. I knew now that was a crucial battle, that many undervalued it, thinking it just another protest. At one level it was, but it was also making the point that people need instruction. The State realised that too. It needed a free hand, but it didn't get it. And because it didn't get it, Sendero advanced, claiming Ayacucho, claiming Puno, applying Lenin's concept of a vanguard party whereby intellectuals took a lead in transmitting ideas.

"You know what I don't get?" The Englishman broke up my thoughts. He sounded serious. "Why you're here? I mean you're an outsider –"

"I've explained that."

"No. No I don't think you have. I mean I believe you're from Chuschi or whatever it's called and that you have a wife..." The Englishman shook his head. "But you're not from here," he added in a way that made it seem the gaps in his knowledge were being stated. "You're an academic and you teach philosophy and art. I can see that. But why are you here? I'll always ask myself that."

"Because a cousin of mine...."

"No. It's not just that. There's something else. I know there is."

I smiled at the vigour of the words and thought how astute the

Englishman could be. A little concentration and his mind was almost dangerous. "Right," I said slowly. "I'm here because...."

And I told him. I told him everything, everything that there is to be investigated, namely why I was on the island, everything about the lecture in Lima, that I had left the text and been persecuted, that the civil guard and the police were waiting for me on my return to Puno, that I had been smuggled to the island. And he just listened. He just sat still and listened. He didn't flinch. He didn't play with his food or talk about Meiggs. He just listened.

And it was like the lecture at La Contute again. Something got to me. Some sense of power. It was what I had tried to relate to the Englishman. Standing there, commanding, being the cynosure. I could captivate. I could sweep people along with whatever ideas I wanted to promulgate. That was such a privilege. And I abused it. I always abused it. Whether it was a first year seminar or a talk in Lima, I always showed what I could do, what I knew. I couldn't hold back. It was the same with the Englishman. I got carried away; I said too much. I gave things away. Except Julia. I didn't mention her. Somehow she didn't need to come into the explanation. Somehow she didn't seem part of it. Besides I didn't want to jeopardise any hopes I had of convincing the Englishman he should try to look her up in La Paz. I would still try to do that when the time was right, when the opportunity arose.

"When the time is right!" I laughed, turning over on the bed. "Another cop out. Like not killing. Like being a sympathiser. Like getting Julia to do my dirty work, getting her to be a voice on the committee. Julia," I shook my head. "Jorge," I cursed. I wondered why I had believed his promise of an address and access. Where was the contact he had promised? How long would I have to wait on the island for some news? How would he contact me? To him I was a liability now. "He'll want me to stay here," I said as though I had stumbled on a revelation. What use was I to him? The logic backed it up. A couple more days, I promised myself. A few more days. If I heard nothing by then I would became proactive, I would go to Puno. Hernando would take me. I convinced myself of that. "If Jorge won't come to me, then......... then I'll go to him," I said, turning over again on the bed.

7

I can admire the stiff shirt. I can admire his passion, his commit-ment. But I can't associate with his cause. It just doesn't make sense. The collective. The control. The condemnation of education. Of the church. To take those away would atrophy society. And for what? To put new institutions in their place. And what institutions? I wondered what would fill the vacuum. It seemed to me all sorts of evils could invade. So no. I would keep the system. I would be happy with it.

"Yeh, long live the individual," says Popeye joining in. "Long live you, long live me. Especially me. And shall I tell you why? Because we can make it. All those no-hopers. People like the stiff shirt. I mean he's kind of reassuring."

"Yes. You're right. He is."

"Of course he is. I mean we're in control. We can choose to pull away at any time. Hey why don't you do that? I mean why don't you just leave him to his painting? You've learnt enough."

"I suppose I have."

"I mean you know he's a pinko. What more do you need to know? I mean that's enough. So why go on?"

Because I am enjoying it. I am enjoying the words and the thoughts and the interaction. I am enjoying the way he thinks and the way he goes on, on about art, on about the Church and educa-tion and the state and the way Peru is and the way he thinks it ought to be. The way he confirms what I believe is right. The man from Chincheros, the stiff shirt – force, threat or tact – nothing can shift me. Nothing. I like the security that comes from that.

★

"Sorry. I was thinking." I apologised to the Englishman. He had walked passed me and taken his normal seat at the plastic table. It was his agitation, tapping a knife on the table while he waited for his omelette, that had stirred me from my thoughts. I smiled. I was pleased with myself, with the superiority my cleverness gave me. I applied it immediately. "What Marxists would call diversionary institutions." In my mind I made a face at the jargon.

"Thinking?" laughed the Englishman.

"Escapism," I said. "Like that." I pointed at the biography of Meiggs that was on the table.

"Like travel," suggested the Englishman. "Or art."

"Sort of."

"Pretend worlds."

I nodded. The Englishman had got it exactly right. It was pretend. It was fantasy. It was entertainment. Nothing else. Me, him, art, Julia. It all helped to take one's mind off things, to cover what was really going on in society, to cover the disappearances and under employment, to cover the poverty, the malnutrition: the gloom that pervaded Peru.

"So what do you do for entertainment?" I asked.

"What do I do?" A touch of exasperation showed I had missed the obvious. "I spend money."

"Yes of course. You buy paintings."

"And cars. And flats. And women. And trips to Peru. Money tells you where you are, what you can do. Can do is important."

I shook my head. I had never thought of money as a toy. It was always too serious for me.

"We have a game." The Englishman laughed now. The longest laugh he had offered me, a laugh that emphasised the idiosyncrasy of what he was about to relate. I knew immediately I wouldn't understand it. I knew immediately that it would bother me. "Some lunch times we go to a bar. Or after work, after a long day. A group of us. And when we get there we decide what's going to happen. I mean we decide whether we should drink champagne and what we should eat, you know how much food we should order, what we should have? All that's declared."

"And this is a game?"

"Yes. We turn our pockets out. We see how much cash we're carrying. The person with the least cash pays for the evening or the lunch or whatever it is."

"The person with the least?"

"Yes."

"The poorest?"

"No."

"But you said –"

"The person with the least cash isn't necessarily the poorest. These are all well-paid guys."

"So?"

The Englishman laughed. He didn't attempt to explain. He just sat and grinned and tapped his knife again on the table. "So what about you?" he countered. "What do you do for entertainment? I mean apart from paint."

"Apart from paint? Oh I talk –"

"To the fisherman?"

"Hernando? Yes. And you," I said warmly with a smile. "I write too."

"You write? What? Books, poems?"

"Letters. I write to Julia. I let her know where I am, what I am doing."

"And she writes back?"

"No."

The Englishman was struggling now. There was something about the depth of bonding that touched him, yet he seemed to want to sense a wholeness, a reciprocation. My words had let him down.

"I can't send my letters," I explained. "I don't know where she is. Well actually I know she's in La Paz."

"La Paz," repeated the Englishman.

"I'll find her. My letters always find her. You see sometimes it doesn't matter. I mean she may not see the words. She may never see them, but I feel as though I'm talking through things with her."

"It makes you feel close."

I hadn't expected the Englishman to understand what I had meant. I expected him to be as lost as I was over the money game, but he seemed to be following my words. I wondered how much he could appreciate, whether he could appreciate how words on paper could replace conversation, how they tied ideas down, paring them to the bone. I liked that aspect of them.

I watched the Englishman raise his eyebrows. Surprise, disbelief, a lack of comprehension. He seemed to be letting the idea go. I began to lick an envelope, sealing it down. He watched me pick up a pen and write "Julia". There was a flourish about my writing, an elegant curl adorned the tall letters. It was easy on the eye. "You have it," I said. "You may's well. You can throw it away. Deliver it if you want to. While you're in La Paz. Search her out. You could find her, I'm sure of that."

8

"I've done it."

"You've done it? Hey what is this, eh José? All the excitement. You got something for me, something we like receiving and discussing? Who did you get it off? Sebastian got another guest, a new arrival?"

"No, no," I said excitedly, looking around for somewhere to sit down. We were half way to the beach, half way from Sebastian's, past the *ruinas* if you took the western path and the *pueblo* if you took the looping eastern path. We were where the paths met. "Let's go over here. Let's sit down."

"But I haven't the time. I'm meeting someone."

"One minute. Just one minute. I need to tell you."

"Over here?" asked Hernando beginning to leave the path and walk towards some standing stones that fringed a home made volleyball court. Some boys were practising, cheering good shots, dismissing poor efforts. I looked forward, beyond the boys, at the school, at the dusty football pitch with the rickety looking goal posts, at the eucalyptus-like trees that flanked the pitch, at the blue painted metal double gates and the blue framed windows of the building, at the rusting tin roof, then back along the walkway that was marked by two lines of stones all the way to the school building.

"Now what is it, eh José? Is it news? Is it a happening or a development? Or an event? Is it an event José? Should I guess?" Hernando began his games. He was smiling again, smiling broadly and searching for a reaction in my face. "OK, you think I will not get it. Right," he said a little too seriously. It meant he would try. "It is something to do with Sebastian. With the *fiesta*. With what he wants you to do. Am I right? No, I am not right. Not Sebastian." Again he interpreted the slight changes in my expression. "So nothing to do with the *fiesta*. OK, OK. It's Jorge. He's turned up. He's written you a letter, yes?"

"No." I knew now he was playing with me. That this was his way. I cut him short. "It's the Englishman."

"He's gone?"

"No."

"But you're smiling. Then he's made you happy. Now what has he done to make you happy? He's paid for his painting, eh José? He's paid for the canvas."

"No. I've given him a letter."

"A letter?"

"Your wager."

"My wager?"

"Our wager."

"Oh our wager. Yes, yes."

I stared at Hernando. I waited for a reaction, a positive reaction, a reaction that would praise me for at last moving forward, for using the canvas and the confidence of the Englishman. It was a long time coming.

"You have a photo?" Hernando finally asked.

"A photo. A photo of what?" I asked quite aggressively.

Hernando was revelling in this. He cast a furtive look my way to see how I was taking it and then looked away to check the location of the radio that had begun to blast out some sentimental tune. In a mentholated voice he sang along.

"Hernando!"

He shook his shoulders and moved with the smoochy rhythm, smiling and pouting, enjoying the way he could veil his intentions and make me squirm. To him, it was like handling a fish on a line.

"You know what I'm on about. Don't pretend."

"I'm not," he said breaking away from the song. "I'm not. I'm waiting for an answer. I know you cannot have given the Englishman an address. You do not know an address."

"Not yet."

"Right. So you have given him a letter, yes José? A letter with Julia's name on the envelope. So where does he start? How does he find her?"

"I don't know. It's up to him. He's clever. He's a problem solver."

"Finding a girl in La Paz! What sort of problem's that? Eh José? You have to help him. You have to help him all you can."

I saw what he was saying then. And without knowing it, he was right. I could help. I could help because Julia was distinctive. Even to the untrained eye, she was distinctive. She was thin, sinewy even. She had long limbs. She looked rhythmic, even in photographs she

managed that. She had an ease about her, a harmony. The Englishman would see that.

★

Writing letters. I laugh at the thought. Such communication is
anathema to me. Why bother? What do you say? So little truth, I
think, false admissions probably, false everything I would imagine,
making up life to make it seem more interesting. Besides, to whom
could I write? Helmut? My boss? You see, work first. Not a thought
of my mother or father. Well, perhaps my mother. I had sent her a
postcard and perhaps I would have phoned and said, "Merry
Christmas," if there had been a phone.

But writing? It is like living in the past, like going over events that
are done and dusted, that can't be influenced. Why do that? It is the
present that is imperative. It is the present that has to be worked on.
Like my conversations with the stiff shirt. I recognise how they are
rewarding me, the way they are satisfying me and filling time, the
way they are confirming my beliefs. I chuckle at the views of the
stiff shirt. All that nonsense about Sendero. All that nonsense about
community. And all that shit about entertainment.

"Diversionary institutions," says Popeye.

"Cinemas, cars, houses, drink, even work."

"Work," echoes Popeye. "I mean how the hell can work be a
diversionary institution. It is the institution, the institution," he
emphasises. "You hear me? It's what it's all about. It's where you
are. That's what work is."

"The one thing it isn't is writing letters."

"Oh yeh, you got that thing? Where the fuck is it?"

"The letter?" I reach up to the windowsill and locate the envelope."

"Let's see. To Julia, eh? Julia."

"Nice name."

"Nice name," mocks Popeye. "You won't have time for any nonsense like that. Finding Julia," he tuts." Hey rip it up. Go on. Rip
the thing up. You hear?"

The next morning when we meet, Christmas Eve morning, we talk
Gramsci. Or rather the stiff shirt talks Gramsci. I talk markets, I talk

198

freedom. We disagree. He bores me. He bores me with jargon. Diversionary institutions become instrumental reason. I just stay with the truth, with the way it is. "Some lead, some follow. That's how it is." I say, not mentioning to the stiff shirt that I've ripped up the letter, that it is in the bag of rubbish that I'm planning to leave in my room when I depart for Puno.

★

He was all Hobbesian, talking of individuals and dictators; and I was brilliant. For the first time I was brilliant. I actually spoke as I had planned. I found the words and checked my mind. I didn't rush ahead. I just talked Gramsci all through breakfast, all through the Englishman saying it seemed anachronistic. "Look at the west," he kept saying. "The market is working." I called that what it is: a hegemonic belief. "A what?" said the Englishman. "A belief taken for granted." It was the sort of thing I wanted people to challenge. "That's why teachers are important." I suggested. "They have to become persuaders."

I liked such optimism. I didn't mention the Frankfurt School and their pessimism, their belief in the dominance of the structures of the state and the idea that media gave capitalism a mental domination. I could have mentioned it. Perhaps I should have. But I didn't want to. Instead I kept it in my mind. I imagined it working. Adverts pushing success, saying, "Go on, you can do it" and "Greed is good" and "Go for it". It was formulating a moral authority. It was overwhelming. Besides I had the Englishman voicing such things. He was adequate. Why should I help him?

"It's global," he was saying.

We were out now, outside of the compound, down in the *pueblo*, watching smiling boys in their white shirts and waistcoats and their red hats, pom poms dangling and moving as they spoke. The sun streamed in between the buildings. It lit the cracks in the wall that separated the *pueblo* from the vista of a snow topped Bolivia.

"It's here," the Englishman stressed. "Working away now. On you. On the boys. On Peru. It's the only way. It sorts out the good from the bad."

"Bad? Oh come on. Bad is a harsh word."

"You know what I mean." The Englishman waited for some

199

reaction. It didn't come. I continued to stare at the wall, at the strange pink effect of sunlight on the stone. It was like a stain, like a whitewash, only thrown on, dripping here and there. "I mean some people like to dominate," qualified the Englishman. "Others like to be told what to do."

I nodded. "Instrumental reason," I said.

"What?"

"Oh nothing." Instrumental reason, I thought, linking the Englishman's words with the Frankfurt School. The issue of domination again. They had made such a big thing of it. People on people, the system on people, I remembered their view: being passive; people accepting things.

"That's how it is," continued the Englishman. "Some lead, some follow."

"And you and I lead," I suggested, laughing lightly at the Englishman's indignant look. "Why us?"

"Who said us?" he laughed. "I mean me. I lead."

"Oh and I follow, is that it?

"In terms of the First World and the Third World it is."

"But as individuals?"

The Englishman drew breath. Something seemed to change. Something seemed to say comprehend. "Yes in our own countries we may lead," he suggested.

"So why us?" The question returned.

"Talent."

"That's it is it?"

"And strength. You have to be strong. Firm."

The Englishman's belief in meritocracy had little place in Peru. I wondered if the Englishman realised that, if he had heard of the Peruvian oligarchy, of the small group of families which had dom-inated Peru since the arrival of the Spanish. Four hundred years of domination. Four hundred years of accumulating wealth. It was almost like a caste system. It was hideous. I wanted to explain it, to refer to it as an ogre, as a dinosaur. I wanted to mock it, but I couldn't. Softly, softly, I thought. Be gentle. Be clever. Outwit him. Just outwit him. That was all I was interested in now. Scoring points. Winning.

9

The painting for the Englishman came on quickly. To me it began to look like a swarthy face, like something I knew. Like a gasp. Or a puzzled look. It seemed to be almost human whenever I looked at it, which was only at the end of sessions when I'd sit back and compose myself and think how easy it is to be drawn like the Englishman had been into consumerism, to be pulled into a web of needing, needing to have and to hold and to discard and to update. "Easy," I'd say, listening to the wild lap of waves. "Once started, that's it, you're committed," Like art, I thought, noting the strange parallel.

I sat back and viewed the painting. It wasn't like painting Hernando and finding all his expressions and activities. This wasn't like that at all. This was so superficial - the hill, the steps, the bundles of herbs, the women climbing with their packs, the children playing. This was selective, leaving out the row of toilets that were built for the tourists and now stank and the single shed that was an office and never seemed used. And I knew what that meant. It meant I was compromising, selling the art short. Cooking it up, I called it. It was all about selection. And in this case, it was all about leaving out the modern, but in the one view that Hugo liked ("..how about the quayside?" he had said when I asked which landscape he'd favour), there were cardboard boxes and dead fish and a half sunk boat. Horrible things, things much worse than a cut or a bruise or a wrinkle. Normally I would just move on and find somewhere more sympathetic. But in this instance I couldn't. So I searched for something I liked. The idea of arrivals and departures came to me. "But is it anecdotal?" I asked, trying to point to a feature of my art. He didn't understand.

My art. Sounds so important, doesn't it? My art. Perhaps I'm learning from the Englishman. Perhaps some sort of secretion or conduction – some strange physical process – is affecting me through our contact. Perhaps I'm coming to be like him. I gasped at that. How could I be like him? History dismissed any connection. Chuschi dismissed it. Ayacucho dismissed it. Sendero dismissed it. And, most of all, my work dismissed it.

"José!" Hernando made me jump. I hadn't noticed his approach.

" I can't stop. Look at these nets. Good as new. Mended by Hernando, by the best net fixer on Taquile, eh José? The man with the needle, that's me. And you are the man with the paintbrush, eh José?"

"The landscape," I said, explaining what he was viewing.

"The painting for the Englishman? Oh it's good." He stood back and viewed it, craning his neck to appreciate what was in the landscape and what had been left out. "Very good. Hey José these would sell. You could set up by here, wait for the tourists and sell them their first sight of Taquile. That's brilliant," he said in an appreciative tone. "But I've got to get on. I'll see you later, yes?"

"Any news," I shouted as he began to walk away. I knew the boat from Puno would have arrived by now and that Hernando would have found someone to talk to and cadge a paper off.

"Any happenings? Any events?" added a laughing Hernando.

"No I mean news. Newspaper news."

"Subsidies are coming off." He continued to walk towards the place where his boat was moored. "That's the rumour in Puno. Roberto told me. Huge price increases on the way. The IMF have ordered the government. So the poor get poorer, eh José. Can you get that on your canvas? Can you do that?"

★

"Ah."

The old duffer. I know from the sound, from its ridiculous softness. The whispering Sebastian. I dread the conversation that will follow. "Keep your eyes shut," urges Popeye. "Just act dead, act as though you've been poleaxed."

"Thank God for tourists," the old duffer says, laughing now. He stands by the door for a second and then advances. I can hear his movements. I can smell him too.

I can't do this. I can't just lie here and wait for him to move away. He'll touch me, shake me. "*Buenos tardes*," I say, pretending to wake up.

"*Tardes*," repeats the old duffer. "Oh. You tired? I go. I no stay."

"OK," I say smiling at his words. The offer seems too good to be true. "You come tonight?"

"Tonight? It's Christmas Eve. It's December twenty-four."

"Yes. You come? Tonight we praise."

"You praise? The *fiesta's* tonight?"

"No. *Fiesta* tomorrow. Tonight praise. We go bed five." The words are accompanied by elaborate movements and mimes, mimes of sleep in this instance. He folds his arms and rocks himself gently. "Oh...." The sound has a little tremble of anticipation.

"You go to bed at five?" I say, offering the old duffer a thoughtful look.

"Yes, yes. Five. Then we...." Another mime. A repeat of the sleep, but longer as though the old duffer has been paralysed in the position. One twitching eye moves him on.

"You sleep right through?"

"Through? Through? What is through?"

"You sleep until Christmas Day?"

"No, no, no." The word rattles off and a frustrated look comes over him. "No. We up..."

"You get up?"

"Yes. We up at eleven."

"In the night?"

"Yes." He is more relaxed now, smiling. He reflects for a few seconds, considering his next words. "You come to kitchen?" he asks.

"Now?"

"No. At eleven."

"Tonight?"

"Yes, yes." These are big yeses. They tell me he has broken through, that he has made himself understood. He smiles. A smug smile. It seems to be everlasting but breaks down into the dreamy anxiety that associates with his struggle for coherence. The next word, I think, recognising the look. "We eat and then go to Church. Rebecca, Dina, *mi senora*, Alejandro, my brothers. We all go. And you?"

"Me?"

"Yes. I like." More smiles. "And José. He come. Good singing. Christmas singing –"

"Carols?"

"Yes." He laughs now. A sign it is all over. A dull snort calms him and he fixes his eyes on me.

Fight, pay, charm, I think. Fight, pay, charm. I wonder what to say.

I check it with the stiff shirt. I meet him in the upper courtyard. He is staring at a canvas. "Hi," he says looking up. He has a brush in his mouth and is playing with some paint with one of his fingers, smudging it, moving it, rolling it. Like a piece of clay, I think, surprised by the physicality of the process. "It's coming on now," he says happily. "Yes, I think I've got it. I've blocked in all I want. The sea, the hills. I'm getting to know them. I'm getting to know them well........ They are the faces I am working with now. I'm just beginning to get a feel for them. That's when it works."

"Good," I say, trying to offer something more than just the mild enthusiasm that I feel.

"You like it?"

Another big effort. I have to give it time, I have to make it seem I am interested, that I actually like what is being presented, that I am not indifferent to it. "Yes, yes I do," I enthuse. A warm sound in my voice holds up the sentiment. It makes it believable.

"Good, good. That helps. You off somewhere?"

"Just a stroll."

"The family are in bed. No food tonight. No vegetable omelettes. It's quite a relief," whispers the stiff shirt.

"I hadn't thought of that."

"What?"

"No food."

"You know then?"

"About Sebastian and family? Oh yes. He came and told me."

"And invited you?"

"Oh yes."

"And? Are you going?"

"Are you?"

"I think so. It will be quite an experience."

"Good."

"That means you're coming too, does it?" The stiff shirt's smile fades as he looks up at me. "You OK?" he asks with some depth of concern.

I wonder what prompts that. It makes me check my demeanour. A loose look. A transparent word. "I'm tired," I admit. "Don't know why. Too much sleep, I think. I've just been lying down listening to the radio."

"All day? No Meiggs?"

"Meiggs? Oh he's been quiet today. Thank God." I smile.

"And what's been on?"

"On? Oh I forget. I couldn't concentrate properly." I am lost. This is small talk. I always fail to engage small talk. *Tenir angel, tenir angel,* a voice in my mind says, urging me to make an effort. "Oh I remember now. Something about the IMF."

"Our failing economy." The stiff shirt puts down his brush and stares into the canvas. He shakes his head. "The IMF," he says disparagingly. "That's what it comes to. You see? The IMF! They say our problem is that we borrow and we squander, that we don't generate wealth, that we spend too much, that we don't control inflation, but what we need is reinvestment. That's what we need." He stops for a second and wipes away a little paint before looking up again and mixing a darker blue. "I mean the oligarchy are untouched. They're the problem. They make the wealth and reinvest it in the United States. It doesn't stay in Peru. It doesn't help those who are dominated."

I nod. I want to argue. I sense an affinity with the oligarchy. They make money. I make money. I would behave like them. I would reinvest Peruvian profits in the United States. It makes sense.

"Our government should stop the leakages," says the stiff shirt quite snappily. I can tell I have touched a nerve, though the irritation isn't sufficient to draw him from his painting. "There. That's right," he remarks holding back his head and looking into a corner of the canvas.

"So you'll be there?"

"Tonight? Oh yes, I think so. Won't you?"

I don't want to go. I don't like Christmas and I don't like the thought of spending the first few minutes of it with the whispering old duffer and the inquiring stiff shirt. I mean, don't get me wrong, the stiff shirt has served a purpose and I have enjoyed the buzz of talking politics no matter how ridiculous his arguments. But Christmas is something different. I prefer a quiet Christmas, quiet and drunk or with a woman. But here there is no woman and no drink and no food. And I am starving. It seems everyone apart from the boys who are setting up some sort of public address system in the pueblo have gone to bed early.

So I stay on the bed. There seems no point in moving. For a while I read a page or two of Meiggs' biography, then I doze and the next thing I know is a knock on my door. The stiff shirt. The stiff shirt whispering, "It's time. It's eleven. Are you awake?"

"I'm going to sleep through. Make apologies for me."

"You sure?" The stiff shirt sounds disappointed.

"Look I'm out of it. I'm knackered. I'll see you tomorrow. Tell the old... tell Sebastian, tell him that. Apologise for me, will you? Say sorry."

"Sure, I'll tell him. If you change your mind you know where we are."

★

It was extraordinary. Out of silence came a cacophony of radios on different stations and firecrackers and discordant hums and crashes from the public address system. I sat in the upper court-yard and waited for Sebastian to wake up. Eleven o'clock, five past eleven, ten past eleven. The intensity of the noise increasing by the minute.

At eleven minutes past Sebastian began to add to the intensity. He came through the gateway into the upper courtyard fussing and saying, "No, no, I am late." Several times he tutted, moving from the kitchen to the restaurant area and down into the living quarters where I could hear him call to Dina and Rebecca and his son, Alejandro. "Our guests are up and we are late."

"No Hugo?" he asked the third time he appeared.

"He's too tired. He said he'd see you tomorrow."

"In the *fiesta*?"

"Yes."

"Actually I'm here. Is that OK?" With the words, the English-man appeared. He came through the gateway to the upper courtyard with one hand back over his shoulder scratching at an itch inside his shirt. He looked ruffled. Like an unmade bed, I thought as I watched him struggling to tuck his shirt into his trousers. He brushed back his hair, then felt his face and blew into his fingers. All he managed to say was, "It's cold." We sat together then. The Englishman looking miserable, unmoved by the sound of firecrackers and the movement of people in the lane, the steady stream of people processing with candles. "Christmas," he yawned, a weariness in his voice.

"You don't like it?"

"God no. You?"

"I like it. It's sort of heritage. You know? My father used to read the Bible for five hours on Christmas morning. Then we'd go for a walk. Then there'd be church."

"Church," scoffed the Englishman. He didn't seem inclined to mention his Christmas programme.

"So what do you dislike about it?"

"Oh the whole thing, you know."

I smiled at his evasion, secretly admiring his composure. I tried again. "You don't talk about your family."

"What do you want to know?"

I shrugged. From the kitchen, a radio started. A lovely female voice, from warmer climes, from a beach somewhere or a hot city overlaying the beat of another station that hid the fullness of Sebastian's orders that seemed to be getting more and more strained. He was a quarter of an hour behind schedule. How could he make it up? I understood the tension. It was in his voice. The tone of authority crept in. It always did. The authoritarian ritual, I thought, considering the way it would infiltrate proceedings, how it was suddenly with him when he came out into the courtyard to see us.

He sighed and put his hands up. "Oh... Now we are ready," he said.

We followed him into the kitchen. The stove was hidden around a corner that was sectioned off by a raffia partition, but we appreciated its heat and the Englishman's hands appeared out of his trouser pockets. "That's better" he said, rubbing them together as Sebastian gestured to us to take our places at the table. I observed that this was a much finer table than the one in the courtyard that the guests were expected to use. This had the look of a driftwood top, somehow gnarled from a period in water, rough, as though small creatures had nibbled into it. I admired it and stared at the line of candles on the table's top that flanked the radio. Across from us Rebecca was shivering.

"Rebecca is *frio*," said the Englishman, suddenly finding the common touch. It made me smile.

"Yes," said the little girl. She played with the dial of the radio as Sebastian brought in some bread, some special bread that merited a long "Ah" as he placed it on the table. He stood back and clapped. "Special bread," he said.

"Special bread?" repeated a puzzled Englishman.

"It's bread with sultanas and fruit in it," I explained. "For Rebecca?" I asked offering the little girl a piece. She seemed eager to accept it, but Sebastian intervened, holding up a finger.

"For all friends," he said, beginning a speech. "I wish health for New Year. Joy for Christmas. *Feliz Navidad.*"

"*Feliz Navidad,*" we repeated.

"And prosperous new year for 1990. For all friends here. At the house of Sebastian Marca Yucra. For Hugo. For José....."

★

The old duffer doesn't know when to stop. He goes on and on. His broken Spanish provides openings that let in the stiff shirt who sips his *cafe con leche* and says thank you and yes and *bueno*. It is mostly *bueno*. "This milk Antonia's" brings a *bueno*, as does "This milk one hour old", as does "This milk sweet, this milk special milk". Some gasps follow when Sebastian mentions that Antonio's calf Domingo is not so good and that earlier he had to take the calf to bed with him for five hours to keep it warm. Popeye intervenes then. He can't resist. "Now I've heard it all. I mean what the hell are you doing up at this time listening to this old duffer telling you about his Christmas Eve in bed with a calf? I mean what the hell is all that about? You know what? You know what you should have said? OK fine, that's what you should have said. All that at the house of Sebastian Marca Yucra stuff, all that shit. So fuckin' what? A mud hut with a candle and a cup of warm untreated milk that will probably give you the shits for years, that's what. What sort of scumbag serves that up? Hey what sort of Christmas is this? That guy needs to shape up. You tell him from me. He needs to shape up. In a big way." Popeye is livid. He goes on as much as the old duffer. "You should have been sleeping, you know that? I mean I've heard some speeches, but that one. Jesus!"

I half agree, though I stay silent, letting the stiff shirt over enthuse and send warm smiles my way. "Thank you. Thank you," he says. But the bread is stale and the coffee is sickly sweet, so sweet that I have to purge my face muscles to prevent a grimace.

"That's where you went wrong," Popeye cackles. "You should have said Yuk, this is shit man, shit. You should have said, get this, that all you've eaten at the house of Sebastian Marca Yucra has been shit. They need a bit of truth these guys if they're gonna shape up. All these fuckin' *buenos* and *buenissimos*. Fuck that."

We go to the *pueblo*. Sebastian doesn't come. He decides to wait for his brother. A tradition we presume when we get to the main square and see large groups of people arriving. They are quiet, but a generator is humming and firecrackers are breaking up its sound as though it is shorting and sparking. A carol from the church becomes clearer as we draw nearer.

The sound is wonderful. A few bass voices seem restrained and special, their isolation picking them out at the bottom of the range. A swirl of contrasting treble overlaps as the female voices come in. They are extraordinary. High and very nasal, their close tones are only broken by a baby crying and a delicate stringed instrument that provides introductions to pieces. It is rehearsed. I sense that when the songs almost break down and are clawed back by a directing voice. The other voices hang on the one sound. I try to pick it out.

"Come inside," says the stiff shirt.

"No, no I'll stay. I won't be here long. You go on. I'm tired."

"You sure?"

I watch him move in amongst the men who are sitting in the pews. They are separate from the women who sit at the front of the Church squatting on the floor. Even more peculiar than the segregation is the way the congregation changes. There is little discretion about the change-over: men climb over pews; women barge by, but the sound stays large and intriguing. Again it is the female voices that I focus on. They are so different, so unconventional. I listen closely, wishing now that I had followed the stiff shirt inside, that I had moved closer to the source.

I move to the door. That is closer. I know when to do it, when to anticipate an invasion and a retreat. It happens at the end of the carol when the stringed instrument plays through a link. The last hallelujah of the Hallelujah Chorus and I am in the space by the door that had been vacated half a second earlier by a young man carrying a ghetto blaster. More boys push past. They hurry through as though they know they are to feature in the next carol. I wait, leaning against the door, seeing legs and feet now, legs and feet dangling from the small balcony that is at the back of the church. I can see the ladder leading up to it on my left. A boy stands on its rungs and clings to a rail spectating. He smiles and I look away into the blue paint of the door and then up, above the door, to a fading red cross on the whitewashed wall.

"Hey you shouldn't be here. You know that?" Popeye is railing in my mind. "I mean what the fuck have you got to do with this? That's always a good question to ask, you hear? What have I got to do with this? It sort of sorts you out, tells you if you've done a shit-head thing. And you know what? You've gone and done a shithead thing, so get the hell out of here? You hear me?"

But I stay. "Gloria, gloria hallelujah," chant the men. The women sing the verses. "Gloria, gloria hallelujah!" A tune for Popeye, I think, wanting to join in. I am enjoying it. I really am enjoying it. "The Hallelujah Chorus" quickly turns into "The Battle Hymn of the Republic". Where is the logic? I laugh and shake myself. I feel so relaxed. I feel so open, so vulnerable because I am taking it in for its own sake. I just want to absorb it, to allow myself to remember it forever. So I stay there, hidden by the darkness, hanging onto every note as a scratchy "Silent Night" is reprised. "All is calm, all is bright," I sing, forgetting myself.

part six

HUGO

1

"Strangers can change your life, you know that? Hey now you do, yeh. Now you fuckin' do. That Frenchman eh? That consul."

I am used to outbursts from Popeye. They come frequently, involuntarily. They show what is going on in his mind. The vitriol somehow fills his face, weighing down his jowls, pulling at his eyes.

"A stranger did me once, you know that? Is that in the book? I bet it is. Everything's in that book. So you'll know he well and truly did me." He checks that I am listening. "Mind you, what is a stranger? I mean what would you say if I said to you who's the president of your company? I mean he's the man. And I bet you don't know him, eh? But if I said to you, what the hell's he like? Now that would be different. You'd respond. Sure as hell you would. Yeh? Because you know of him. Now there's a difference."

I enjoy the conversation or the discourse or whatever it is that Popeye provides. It is like a swim on a warm day, a swim after a long session on the phone or drafting a contract or talking delivery times. I hate talking delivery times. Scribble, scribble, phone, phone. I know the order. First name terms with people I haven't met, people my mind has faces for. It is always a disappointment when they walk in looking lean when they should be fat, or plain when they should be cute.

And now I am thinking of strangers. Strangers changing lives.

"How? I mean how do they change lives?"

"Strangers? Hey just think. They're the guys who make the laws. Politicians, civil servants, teachers, planners, people who write articles in papers. People who make laws about how to bring up your kids. You know. One hundred and one reasons why you shouldn't let your kids out after six. After six! I mean, come on."

"So who changed your life?"

"Who?"

"Which stranger?"

"Oh hell." Popeye laughs now, heartily, almost uncontrollably, a spluttering laugh. It recognises the usual suspects. "Which stranger?"

he mutters. "I don't know. I mean Christ there's a hell of a lot of candidates, but if I was pressed and you're pressing me yeh?"

I nod.

"Well I guess I'd sort of have to say Napoleon."

"Napoleon?" This is marvellous. The ludicrous always appeals. It is like trying to sell planes to countries that can't afford them or countries that don't need them. You have to make up your own logic and believe in it. That is crucial, the unfaltering belief. No matter how half baked, no matter how much it lacks credibility, you have to believe in it. Like this banter with Popeye, this discussion of strangers that has progressed towards a conclusion, bringing in Napoleon.

"Not *the* Napoleon mind."

"No?"

"Oh no he was around before my time. This Napoleon is Napoleon the Fourth. You got that? So we're not talking Bonaparte. No sir, this is some descendant, some little shit who decided to float French bonds at the same time as we were floating Peruvian bonds to pay for the railroads, I mean pay me for the railroads." He pauses and allows a wry smile to come over his face. It suits him. A moment of reflection, I think. "Yeh, you know we didn't stand a chance. I mean France against Peru. Shit. Peruvian railways against the Franco-Prussian war. I mean what would you prefer to invest in? Peruvian trains or dead Germans? See? We weren't even in the ball game. No sir."

"So all the spare capital went to France."

"That's it. You got it. Shit creek for me. I mean they couldn't pay me. They couldn't raise the money. Not even with me beavering away."

"Beavering away?"

"Yeh. I was spreading the word. All over Europe I was spreading it. Every meaningful finance house. I told them the bonds were great value, that they'd get a great return, that they needed to get in early because they'd go like hot cakes."

"And did they?"

"Did they! Course they didn't. Hot cakes, huh. Stale buns they turned out to be. Stale buns. Fuckin' Napoleon."

I have time for such considerations because the train to Cuzco is late. I am in Puno, at the railway station, in a grim waiting room. It has a dark, wet look, as though wet feet are permanently passing through it. Strange strips of mahogany cover the walls reflecting the darkness, intensifying it. I sit facing the grilled service windows, all closed now, their closure indicated by drawn lace curtains. "*Esta prohibido el transporte de mercanderia de contrabando*" says a sign above the grilles. "Rules," I curse. Have to, have to, have to. I turn away and look towards the left of the grilles. More notices. All the information you need to know. The *horario*. The *tarifas*. "*Quanto? Quanto?*" a man is shouting, staring over heads, trying to read the prices that are illuminated in a ray from the poor strip lighting. The women around him, snuggling babies, seem so much calmer, as though they are more used to interiors. The men seem edgy, moving more and talking; they seem out of place, nervous. "*Hola* mister..." A conversation. I move away, smiling, away from my seat and over to the main door, the big orange double door that opens onto the platform. It is shut now. I stand facing another sign. "*Ingreso solamente del pasajero con su boleto y documentes personales.*" And another warning: "*Solo treinte kilos de equipaje de mano.*" Only thirty kilos of hand luggage. More rules. I hate rules. I hate this place. Have to, have to, have to.

A woman disturbs me. She calls my name, a woman in a red hat and red suit under a black coat, a uniformed woman who makes everyone stand up and stop talking. "OK," she says," you can go, out onto the platform. The train is there, Through the doors." She indicates that I should turn the handle and progress onto the platform. I smile and move, stepping outside and finding myself alongside the engine. "Chicani, Expresso Cuidad Blanco," I read the name on the driver's door and look beyond the train to the next track and an isolated freight truck that is full of pink rock and at a man running down the track towards the freight truck, a railway worker carrying a hammer and nails.

I see everything then. I hadn't expected to, but my brain starts telling me, "Meiggs was here. Right here. Where you are now." Oh yeh? I need proof.

"Sir, this way." Another uniformed woman tries to direct me. I don't respond. A Frenchman who comes through the double doors as she speaks mistakenly thinks her words are aimed at him. He moves with her; she doesn't object. I gaze to my left, beyond the waiting room to the wall that separates the station from the outside pavement and road, at its yellow colour and the band of orange at its base. Orange and yellow, the railway's corporate colours. They are everywhere, shading the metal roof that covers the platform and the roof's strange stanchions. Some proof, some proof, my mind says, sweeping my gaze away to the right across the tracks towards the water tower and the sidings and the fleet of lorries with their engines running and their drivers huddled together in a group, smoking and talking. "Some proof," I whisper.

I cannot find it. In desperation my gaze settles on the station-master's house. It seems quaint, rustic. It is the sort of structure you'd expect to find at the end of a platform on some remote rural English line. I like its small garden and the bell outside the main door, a huge brass bell with a rope tied to the wall, a rope with a big loop. A small man in a uniform appears as if on cue and pulls the rope once. Security men arrive, responding to the signal, men in a brown uniform with "*Securidad integral*" embossed on their jumpers, in yellow, in capitals. Two peals. Three peals. And I look away. Four peals. And I look back. And I see it, there, near the orange bin and the one large shrub and the small orange and yellow painted pots on the window sill, there, left of the window, above the door, there in large numbers over the door. One, eight, seven, four. Eighteen seventy four. The proof. "That's it," I shout.

"Hey you're improving, you know that? Yeh 1874. I was here. Where you are now. January 1st, 1874. The first train into Puno. Puno's mayor was to my left and some representative of the gov-ernment was to my right. And I was there in the middle, just where I should have been. Don Enrique, first contractor of Peru. Right there, right in the middle. You're the man, that was saying, you're the man. And over there, against that yellow wall was the band of the naval ship *Callao*. They played "For those in peril on the sea" over and over and fuckin' over. "For those in peril on the sea." Popeye tries to sing it. "Well I guess it was all they knew, sea shanties and hymns, naval hymns. For a railroad. I ask you."

"You enjoy it?"

216

"Oh yeh. Did I enjoy it? Christ it was such hard work. I guess it's a sort of culmination. I mean we started on January 29th. 1870. Took six years."

"Six years?"

"Yeh before the trains ran regularly. We had problems," he smiles knowingly and takes a moment to gather his thoughts. "Hey you know what? For some reason the beginning always has more celebrations than the end. I mean at Arequipa, where we started the line, we had all the usual shit. The silver shovel. You always have that. The ornamental silver shovel and the hewn bit of stone. Marble, I think. Should have been sillar. You know sillar? It's a volcanic stone. All of Arequipa's built of sillar. So they go out and cut a bit of marble. Shitheads!"

"So you dig with the shovel?" I try to picture the opening ceremony. The silver shovel and Popeye become the equivalent of a celebrity cracking a bottle of champagne against a hull or someone pulling open curtains to display a memorial plaque.

"Did I dig with the shovel? With a silver shovel? Hell no. They inscribe the thing. You know the date, who was there, who the contractor was, namely me, Honest Henry, the first contractor of Peru."

"So who was there?"

"Me. I told you."

"Who else?"

"Hey who else matters?"

"I'd like to know."

"You'd like to know," mocks Popeye. "Oh you know. All the usual hangers on. The government representative." Popeye smiles. "Hey and you know who that was on this line? Juan Francisco Balta, that's who."

"Who?"

"Balta. The brother of the president, that's who. Talk about cronies. At the time he was the Secretary of State for War and the Navy. And the other main man, yeh the other main man, the region's sort of mayor, was also called Balta. Talk about fuckin' patronage. Another brother. So that was it. Balta to my left and Balta to my right and I'm left to do all the work, holding a silver shovel and talking all the shit. Christ I was good at it."

"You were?"

"Oh yeh. Had to be. Let's see.... Yeh.... Got it.... Prophecy, optimism, that was my formula. Gee I love formulas. Gets you there, don't you think? Right to the core. I made railroads sexy, you know that? I made them Christian too. I always said they were the spirit of Christianity, that they spread opportunities, that they were all about fraternity. Yeh. Oh I was good. They loved me, you know that? They fuckin' loved me."

2

I feel confident then. On the train it is Hugo Young, Hugo Young, Hugo Young. Just as it should be. The anxiety is replaced by a certainty. A belief in my cause. I suddenly can convince myself that my oppressor, the Frenchman, had got me because I was tired and because he had tricked me, because he had ambushed and outmanoeuvred me. It was his stage. The church, Chincheros. It was his geography and the people around him were his audience. He played to them. I couldn't win. I was his stooge. I hadn't seen that. I had just stayed on the stage, duped by the occasion, shocked and shaken because I had to deal with something I hadn't legislated for. That happens so infrequently. And it was made all the more difficult because I was in Peru, travelling alone. It wasn't like being in an office. It couldn't be solved by calling people together and talking things through or writing a memo or going to a section leader. This was a church, a church in the mountains, a church with views of white topped peaks. It was new to me. Like the exercise in school, the exercise all those years ago on working out how to build a railway in Peru, the exercise when I had opted for strange tunnels disappearing everywhere, strange tunnels going for mile after mile through the hills.

"There's only one short tunnel, you know that?" asks Popeye interrupting my thoughts. "One short tunnel between here and Arequipa. Ah they weren't necessary. You know the highest embankment's only one hundred and forty one foot and the deepest cutting's one hundred and twenty seven foot. That's all. I mean gee that's peanuts. That's nothing at all. It's all gentle slopes and treeless plateaus. It was a cinch."

"And what about Cuzco?"

"Cuzco? What do you mean Cuzco?" The question seems to stop Popeye. He tries to hide away. I leave him for a second. I look up, across the faces of fellow passengers in Inka class, across the plastic tables on metal stands, passed the reclining khaki seats and down at the khaki carpets and up again at the video screens at the front and back of the carriages. Quite chic, I think, knowing Peru can't quite carry it off. Knew it, I think when I go to the front of the carriage to use the toilet. It is locked.

"You have to have a key," says a young American who is smoking and looking out of the window. "Ask one of the girls."

I nod, my eyes catching the graffiti on the toilet door. "The killers" it says, in English, in scratches, menacing scratches that cut through the orange livery. I sigh. I, too, look out of the window, at the bare earth, at the tufts of grass, at the compounds, at the thatched huts, at the furrows and the water hollows, at the drainage ditches and embankments, at the paths, at the river cutting into the plain, at a girl pulling a smaller girl by her ponytails.

"You English?"

I nod.

"Thought so," responds the American.

It is all he says, though we stay side by side in the corridor all the way to Juliaca, thirty miles from Puno. We stay together as the train pulls its way into the town through a market. The window we share is like a frame. It separates the market stalls, displaying them to us individually. A stall of spades. A stall of bicycle wheels. A stall of wing mirrors. A stall of ropes. A stall of nuts and bolts.

Then the station. The station full of policemen in white polo necked shirts and baseball caps with their rank on the cap and their names above their breast pocket on their shirts. Black gloves, black boots, white truncheons. I stare at a decorative rope that swirls across a shoulder and fixes into a pocket. A black whistle dangles out of another pocket.

"What a country," remarks the American. "I mean look at it. I've seen some shit, but this beats it all, beats it all."

219

The American smiles and walks away. "OK, OK," I whisper, calling Popeye. "What's wrong with Cuzco?" There is no reply. "I'm waiting." I stare out, into a compound on the platform where people are penned like animals while they wait to board a train.

"You still looking," laughs Popeye. "Hey that's good."

"I want proof."

"An' that's not so good."

"What do you mean?"

"I mean you've lost faith. That's not so good."

"I just want to know about you, about the railway, about Cuzco. It's why I'm here."

"Why you're here? Really? Well listen, it's a long story."

"I've got all day. It's a long journey."

"Sure. Two hundred and ten miles. Two hundred and ten miles across the *puna* from Juliaca to La Raya, a climb from twelve thousand three hundred feet to fourteen thousand feet, then all the way down to Cuzco. It was so easy I never finished it."

"Never finished it?"

"Built it to Marangani. Yeh I did that. That's about one hundred and thirty miles. I did that. But then I got ill."

"Oh shit."

"Yeh you've guessed. Let's just say I didn't quite make it to Cuzco, yeh? Let's just leave it at that, OK?"

3

Stepping foot inside the complaints' office isn't easy. I expected it to be. Because I felt so calm after seeing the date on the station-master's house and imagining Popeye on the platform with the naval band and the dignitaries. I felt so at ease. It seemed like it was going to be Hugo Young, Hugo Young, Hugo Young all over again. But it isn't: a semblance of doubt remains. I consider what the woman in the office will think, how she will behave, what she will ask, what she will tell me. All the questions about my visit, the vital questions come to me as I sit on an iron chair in the Plaza de Armas outside the office. Calm yourself, take it easy, a voice says. Not Popeye. My own voice, my own voice like an echo, emphasising, repeating. Take your time, stay calm, it says.

So I do what the train journey has taught me. I observe. I gain patience. I let things come and go. I allow myself to be distracted. And out of that I notice how busy people in Cuzco are. They are always carrying something: a newspaper, a letter, something that looks like a phone card, a small purse, sun-glasses, a hat, a cardigan that trails in the wind like Spanish moss on a desert floor. Even the shoeshine boy carries a box, a battered black box that unfolds and opens quickly and releases tins of polish and a chamois. I stare at the boy's brown and red striped football shirt, at his black cap with "Boys' Town" embroidered on it, at the tag with an image of a soldier on the left thigh of his jeans. A smiling boy.

"You go ahead," I say, responding to his intimation that he would like to polish my shoes.

What! I have never said yes before. I have never acknowledged a shoe shine boy before. But now it seems right. I should look my best. Casual, but smart. My blue cotton shirt and my Levi jeans are fine, but my shoes are dirty, dust covered after the journey.

"You go Macchu Picchu?" asks the boy, beginning his normal routine.

"Yes." I smile again.

"Good... Macchu Picchu good." He proceeds to run through a list of attractions. "And later San Blas, yes?"

"San Blas?"

"The church. Very fine mister. Very fine."

"Yes."

"You read mister. You read?"

I nod accepting the paper that he carries in his box. Smears of black and brown polish underline words and headlines. I unfold it realising it would serve a purpose, that it would close down the conversation, that it would absorb me and let me think, plan, devise, but only for a few minutes. I emphasise that. A few minutes.

And in those minutes I think of the night when I walked into town after the incident at Chincheros. This is the square I had retreated to, the square that welcomed me after I had left the bus up on the rim and had run through the suburbs. It feels different now. There is a lightness rather than a honed anger, the cut of thoughts that said, "Change hotel, change appearance, leave

Cuzco." has gone. It is warm now. I lie back into the scene. "This is normal," I say, feeling the shoe shine boy tapping the toe of my shoe.

"Next one mister."

The same woman greets me. The woman with the wild hair, the mature woman with the broad smile, the nice woman. "Oh hello," she says, recognising me. Her face makes the necessary adjustment. She smiles. "Yes, you said you'd be back didn't you? I remember now. You're flying out of La Paz. To London."

I do not correct her. I smile thinking of the way her training has programmed her to find appropriate words and expressions. English, English, her mind would have been saying, her smile clicking in, her effusion toned down, a slice of seriousness like a twist of lemon in a drink working its way through the look. Distressed she would be thinking, coming to conclusions about my manner on my previous visit. Difficult, anxious, volatile. The adjectives would flow.

"I want to add my name and address to my statement," I say interrupting my mind. "I want to make sure it goes further."

"I'll get it," she says quite positively. She half smiles and walks over to a filing cabinet. "Meiggs wasn't it?"

"That's the name I gave. Yes. Donald Henry Meiggs."

"Now where have I filed it? Sometimes I forget," she explains. "You see in Peru we use both family names, so you may be under Henry or Meiggs. In Peru the last two names are last names. I guess Henry is one of your first names?"

I nod and wonder when she will move things on.

"So you want to add your name and address to your statement?"

"Yes," I say quite sternly.

"Your address in France?"

"Yes. Did I tell you I live in France?" I am surprised by that. It doesn't seem to fit my character or the situation.

"You gave it away. Something you said." She stops thumbing her way through files and stands up. "Oh you said you'd report him when you got back home to France."

"Did I? That's unlike me."

"Perhaps you were just thinking aloud. Now where is it? You

know I think it's out. Yes, it's out. I saw it yesterday. I remember now. " She moves away from the filing cabinet towards her desk and sits down. "No," she says. She reverses in her chair, sliding it expertly to a point where she can turn and see the desk of her superior.

"OK, OK. Fine." The words are followed by sighs. "Should have got further with this. Let's see what he's done. Right," the woman in the office adds reading through the file. "Ramon's written a letter, but it hasn't gone out yet. I wonder why." Again she reverses in her chair and examines her superior's desk. It seems to yield little. "I think there may have been another complaint. I'm certain that's it. I didn't deal with it. One minute," she says, standing up and moving further back into the office. Tuts and moans precede her movement into a back room.

I look around. I feel relaxed now. A weight has been lifted. I take in the room and particularly the exhibition space that is sectioned off by a rope that runs from the woman's desk, fencing off an area that is only open during the day. I recall what had been on when I first came into the office, an art show called "Fifty years of Cuzco culture". That has been succeeded by a photographic exhibition. My eyes follow the shots of the mountain Ausengate at sunset and sunrise and during the winter and summer and the human shots of Cuzco life – Church processions and protests, brick making and tea picking and a *corrida*. The photos are brown and old looking and the exhibition seems to be shouting, "stability", saying that little has changed. I stare at a photograph of a football team. There, I think, something different: the players in a line, not in rows, one line, the tallest player on the left and the shortest on the right all with their hands on their hips not folded. I think of the symmetry most modern photographs of teams strive for with a large centre half providing the pinnacle.

"Right," the woman says returning, moving towards me. She seems uncomfortable.

"So what's being done?" I ask.

"The director's dealing with it."

"I'm sure he is. What I want to know is how is he dealing with it?"

"I can't say."

"I want to know. When's he in?"

She gives me a quick look, a look that says she prefers my previous dispassion to the new combative me, a look that in extending itself says my defiance isn't attractive, that it is disturbing. I try to temper the touch of aggression that bites with my words. *Tenir angel*, a voice in my mind says. *Tenir angel*.

"I'm sorry. I'm just interested. It's just that I'm quite strong and this man got to me and if he got to me then I worry what he may do to other people."

"And that's it, is it? You sure?" The woman seems thoughtful. "You know you didn't seem interested before."

"You say there's been another complaint."

"It's unsubstantiated."

"What do you mean?"

"I mean the other person was like you."

"Like me?"

"He refused to give his name."

"He was afraid. There's nothing wrong in that. If you'd have witnessed that man you'd understand."

"Perhaps." The woman reaches across and picks up a pen. She scans the statement before pressing down the top of the biro to push out the ball point. She moves her hand and points to an empty section on the form. I see the word address and, beneath it, the hand written word 'unknown'. "You see nobody gives names. And people go. We can't trace them. We can't find witnesses, except for the locals."

"They're scared too."

"Perhaps."

"Look are you saying this is pointless?"

"No." She pulls a face. She looks disappointed with my conclusion. "No I'm not saying that."

"What you mean is you can't say that."

"No."

"Hugo Vaughan Young. That's my real name. My address in Toulouse is..."

And she writes, slowly and clearly, listening closely to the sounds, stopping once to go back and check the spelling of Vaughan and *maison*. I check the letters, correcting her, and take the biro from her to sign my name at the bottom of the page.

"I'd like a letter," I say as I am reading through the statement.

"A letter?"

"Telling me what you've done. What action you've taken and what the outcome is."

"Fine."

"I'll get it?"

"You'll get it."

"And perhaps I'll call in. Just before I go. I'll see your superior. Can I do that?"

"Of course. Now, if you'll excuse me." She gathers up the papers and slides back towards her boss' desk. "Oh and enjoy your stay," she adds turning back my way. "We are taking your complaint seriously." There is an assurance in her voice. It says trust me, believe in me. It says things will be done.

I do enjoy my stay. I phone Francine, my secretary in Toulouse, daily and she tells me what is going on and that, with regards to the Brazilian deal, there are few developments. "Don't try and change your flight," she says adamantly. "There's no point. The ball is in their court now. They'll have to make the first move and Helmut reckons their main man is ill. So fly back to Brazil on the flight you've booked. You're safe till then."

So I stay on in Cuzco. I even think about going to see the Frenchman, the man from Chincheros, of telling him where I work and what I've been doing, that the president of the company and the local prefect in Toulouse will be talking to the Foreign Office, that I will get the company lawyer involved, that I will name and shame. I sound like a reporter from the gutter press. I even write the story, imagining headline after headline. I borrow some like "Gotcha!" and imagine others like "Our man in Scamland." I laugh at that.

"Hey that's funny," Popeye chimes encouragingly. "Oh yeh. You get him. I mean if you decide to get someone, you get them. Understand? Be vindictive, that's what I say, be thoroughly vindictive. That's what I should have done in 1877. That fuckin' coup."

"Coup?"

"Yeh. Balta lost. Balta the president that is. He lost the election and he should have gone, but he was slow and the army got itchy.

They thought he wasn't going to go, that he was staying, hanging on. Mind you they didn't want Pardo, the guy who won. I didn't want him either. In fact I can't think of one person who wanted Pardo, so how did he get in? I mean who the hell voted for him?" Popeye shakes his head. He is recognising missed opportunities, realising how he should have acted. "I mean Balta was a friend. He was on my books, but he had to give up. He had no choice. And I told him so. So he did."

"So what was the problem?" I try to follow Popeye's reasoning, to link him with the spark of the conversation: the need to be vindictive. Too often, Popeye allows the fascination of the events that went on around him – in this case the ministrations of the politicians – to draw him away from the point he is making.

"The army wanted him to stay, so Guitterez intervened."

"Guiterrez?"

"The Minister of War."

"Right."

"Of course he had put his brother in charge of the army."

"Another Guiterrez?"

"Yeh. And it was the brother who grabbed Balta."

I nod. I can see the attraction of such detail. It verges on farce. The patronage mixing in names and intrigue and complicating loyalties, the density of the relationships drawing Popeye's attention. Who cares, I think, listening to Popeye.

"An' Guiterrez –"

"The head of the army."

"Yeh that Guiterrez. He thinks, hey I like this, yeh this is OK. He suddenly wants to be the head man. So he decides well I've got one of the fuckers, what's the harm in getting the other."

"The other?"

"Pardo, the guy who won, the other presidential candidate." Popeye smiles, a fluctuating smile that reacts to the demands of the tale and the pleasure he derives from its telling.

"So he gets Pardo?"

"Oh Pardo's sharp. He gets wind of what's going on and hides in the Brazilian Embassy. When they go to get him there, he slips out and hides in the botanical gardens."

"And they get him there?"

"Hell no. He blacks up. He goes nigger and floats out to sea in a fishing boat. Only the navy, still loyal to Balta, picks him up. You with me?" asks Popeye, enjoying the moment. "Of course Guiterrez, the army's Guiterrez, has lost the plot by this time. His brother –"

"The Minister of War?"

"Yeh. He's been lynched by the mob in Lima. He's dead, So Guiterrez, the army man, starts calling himself the Supreme Chief and wonders around the Royal Palace in some sort of trance mumbling, "I have been called, I have been called." Well I mean it was plain to see he'd gone ga-ga and in one of his mad moments he wandered into the room where he was holding Balta and shot him eleven times in the head."

"So Guiterrez became president?"

"Oh hell no," Popeye laughs. "You see what I'm saying? You see what I mean about being vindictive?" Popeye pauses. He wants me to go on and predict the outcome of the tale. "I mean all this entrapment. Nobody's getting away with anything."

"So?"

"So the people were pissed off. I mean the ex-president of Peru was dead and the president elect was out in a fishing boat. And Guiterrez was playing God. Fuck that, they thought."

"They killed him?"

"Oh yeh, they chased him from the palace. I mean he could feel his men getting tetchy. He could sort them out but he couldn't flee the mob. They caught up with him in a chemist's shop, found him in a bathtub. The Supreme Chief of the Republic was hiding in a bathtub, a fuckin' bathtub! So they shot him there and then. Some say he drowned in his own blood. But I think the old rumour mill was a bit fanciful there. Still, that's being vindictive don't you think?"

"I want something done."

"We are investigating."

"Listen. I....WANT....SOMETHING....DONE."

"And I'm sayin –"

"I know what you're saying. But do you understand what I'm saying? Listen. I'm a representative of Airbus Industrie. Do you understand? Do you know what that means?" I decide to exaggerate.

"I am the chief sales negotiator of Airbus Industrie. You got that?"

The man's stiff, almost permanent smile falters.

"You got that?"

A nervous movement of his cheek tests the smile and it collapses. The man grips the paper containing my statement more tightly. Through the gap under his desk I see his knees pumping. "Mr. Young we're taking appropriate action believe me."

"What sitting here?"

"I'm assessing."

"But there's nothing to assess."

"Mr. Young there have been other complaints."

"But that man is corrupt, you understand? I'm telling you that. And I'm telling you he has to be sorted out. Have you spoken to him?"

"That's not in order."

"Not in order?"

"Not yet. It's not the way we do things."

"The way you do things! I'm not interested in the way you do things. I'm telling you what to do. I want him taken in. I want him threatened, abused. I want him out of his job, out of Cuzco, out of Peru."

"Mr. Young I do not have the power."

"Then who has?" I shake my head and brush a hand across my face. I keep control. My face is warm and bright; my voice is light again. "So are you saying I should go to the police?"

"No."

"Then do something."

"Mr. Young I am doing something. I am following our normal procedures. I am piecing together a picture of what is going on."

"I've told you what is going on." I shake my head and look down at the floor. I am fed up now. The man has had his chance. "Listen I want him in here this afternoon. You hear me? I want to sit in the square and see him walk into this office. I want you to tell him complaints have been made against him and that he's being investigated. I want you to tell him who has made the complaint. He'll work out the rest. You hear? Do you hear?"

"I can't do that."

"You can and you will."

"Mr Young...." The smile returns to the man's face, but it is more vague and minimal now. It looks as though it is slightly withdrawn, waiting for some sense of relief to edge it back through the man's skin.

"Listen I want something done. I want him here. I want him cautioned. I want him to sweat. Like he made me sweat. I want him to know that I'm going to get him. That there's no doubt about that. You hear?" There is no response. "Do you hear? I'm going to nail him."

"Mr Young...." The man laughs. A nervous laugh. It is a last resort, an attempt to break down the anger, to warm me, to charm me. I recognise it.

"You don't get me do you? Listen. I have a strong sense of grudge. I nail my enemies. That man is an enemy. And if you don't shake yourself you could end up being an enemy of mine too. I wouldn't advise that. You understand?"

"Mr. Young are you threatening me?"

"Of course I'm threatening you. Now for the last time." I pause. I calm myself. "I fly to La Paz late this afternoon. At one thirty I will be in the main square and I expect to see that guy over there, the Frenchman, the bloody Frenchman, walk into this office smiling and come out shaking. You hear me? I want that done."

It is a fine afternoon. I sit in the square, leaning back, closing my eyes, letting the sun warm my face. I look across occasionally to check the time and the view of the cathedral. At one thirty the man from Chincheros appears. He marches out of the cathedral, down the steps and, skipping across the road, cuts a corner. He stops to talk to a military man who is nodding and shouting. "Yes, yes..... I'll see you," I hear the man from Chincheros say. He smiles with a warmth that I cannot associate him with. He smiles and smiles and shakes his head. He reaches the door of the complaints' office and walks in.

5

La Paz is so different. So calm. So safe. At breakfast on my first morning back at Hotel Milton, the hotel I used during my previous stay in the city, I am surrounded by government workers. They fill the hotel from Monday to Friday. *"Eres muy grande,"* they keep saying, trying to avoid sitting by me. When I was here previously it was a running joke: who will be last down?; who will have to sit by the *muy grande* European? I grapple with a huge mug of milky chocolate and the bread rolls that are served with some sort of caramel spread. I have a plate. The Bolivians use the table.

"So South American," I think, staring out, enjoying the view that confronts me. I find it endlessly entertaining. A dental surgery is across the road. I read its sign quickly. *"Alto velocidad,"* it boasts. High speed. And *"Attencion permanento"*. Permanent treatment. That slogan alone would take any pain away. I stretch to look down at the pavement to see if any toothless people are emerging into the La Paz sunshine. Next window along is a doctor's practice. Doctora Elizabeth, I read. *Ginecologa y obstetra.* The words are made up of strips of blue tape. They fill the panes of glass and spread across rusting window frames. Across the smaller top windows, again in blue, is the name of the practice. Willy's. "Willy's!" I laugh out loud. The Bolivians sharing my table laugh with me. They like the sound. The man next to me, reading a morning paper, smiles politely. My eyes smile back and then pull away, across the paper, reading the headline, *"Brasil siempre sera Brasil."* Football, I think. Brazil will always be Brazil. But I am back viewing the next window, the window adjacent to the gynaecologist's; a lawyer. Santa Rosa, *abrogado de los casos impossible.* Saint Rosa, lawyer of the impossible cases. I laugh again. But this time the Bolivians do not join me. Their buses have arrived. The buses that take them to wherever it is they are heading. "Ah". Moans follow. Moans and curses.

"You want?" asks the man who has been reading. He indicates that he is willing to leave me his paper.

"Yes, OK. Thanks, thanks," I say responding effusively.

"We go today," he adds. "Tomorrow is a public holiday. *Alasita.* There," he says pointing to the paper. Happy *Alasita* says the headline on the paper.

"Alasita?"

"You have *fiestas*?" I ask Popeye.

"Oh yeh we had *fiestas*. Lots of them. I loved *fiestas*. You know me. But nothing called *Alasita*. Not in Peru."

"Well this is Bolivia."

"Guess it is."

"You have contacts in Bolivia?"

"Bolivia?" There is doubt in the tone. I let him contemplate and look up at the man alongside me who is falling forwards as he sleeps. "Gee this is great," remarks Popeye, presumably referring to La Paz's main square with the church of San Francisco and its fawn stone and red tiles that are catching the sun. It is warm. A dog sprawls out at our feet and a number of Bolivians find comfortable angles on the sculptures at the top of the square. They fatten the sculptures and seem to emerge from the stone whenever they wake up and move away.

"Bolivia?" muses Popeye.

"You like it here?"

"Yeh I can live with it. I mean it's sort of strange, but Latin America's strange. Wherever you go, wherever you look. It's something about scale. Everything's too big or too small. Nothing goes."

I turn around and look at the sculptures, at the oversized head of Bolivar, the nation's founder, and the more abstract looking indian sculptures that seem too small. I nod. He's right. Popeye's right. Everything is awkward. The good intention of creating a meeting place where there would be conversations and fountains and pigeons is alienated by Bolivar's big head and the clumsy arrangement of cultures in sculptural form. Tiahuanaco and Spanish grate rather than cohere.

"And they even throw in the contemporary," laughs Popeye, gazing at the billboard that dominates the back of the square. A large blue and white advert splashes colour like big balloons above the sculptures. *Elimina las manchas*, I read working my way up the advert. Then the brand name. Omo. Gone, I think, disappeared from the west. "So this is where it's been hiding," I add, realising that more Middle English names like "Comfort" and "Drift" had taken over. Omo, I laugh, turning back, moving slowly and gazing at a sleeping man and then at a man writing a letter and then at a child in the lap of one of the sculptures and finally at a young girl having her photo taken as she rests against Bolivar's huge chin.

"I employed Bolivians," remarks Popeye, reminiscing. "Hey and I supplied them with rifles, you know that? Did I tell you that?"

"Rifles?"

"Yeh. Rifles."

"But you built railways."

"I supplied railroads."

"Same thing."

"I supplied anything. Railways, rifles. You name it, I got it."

"Rifles?" I make it all sound shady and not the sort of trade any self respecting businessman would get involved with. Ethical trading my look says. Popeye dismisses it.

"Yes. Oh shit, I remember now." He smiles, his jowls moving as his face lightens. Easy, I think. The charm oozing. The charm proliferating. "Yeh, that president they had. What was he called?"

"On your books was he?"

"What the hell was he called? Shit. I guess it will come to me. Melgareto, that's it. Or something like it. Hell of a name. Let's call him Mel."

"You were paying the president of Bolivia."

"He was a man of influence. I've told you. Fight, pay, charm. You buy influence. You need influence. At least you normally do."

I sense a problem. "So what was the trouble?" I ask.

Popeye sniggers. "The trouble? The trouble was Mel was drinking away the money I sent him. I was paying him to get drunk. I was destabilising the whole region without knowing it. I mean sometimes ol' Mel would be drunk for a month. Well you can guess the rest. I mean the guy was issuing scary edicts and declarations. I mean he was declaring war on anything that moved. Still he was alright about the rifle contract. But the Peruvians weren't."

"They weren't?"

"Hell no. They called it contraband. They were threatening to seize the damn things."

"So more bribes?"

"Yeh more bribes."

"And they worked?"

"Oh yeh. Mel could have his rifles. But Mel lost the fuckin' plot. I mean one day he got slewed and sent his troops into Peru. Hell of a mess. They got as far as Puno and killed some indians and took some cattle and two indian women. I mean what the hell."

"So no more arms for Mel?"

"Hell no. The Peruvians seized them. Mind you they paid me for

232

them. They compensated me. I made damn sure of that."

"The Peruvians paid you?"

"Oh yeh. And I gave the money to Mel."

I am astonished. I can't get over the subterfuge, the plot and sub plot, the way Popeye's mind works on a series of planes. Level one, level two, level three, I think, wondering how it all manages to come together.

"I didn't tell him."

"Mel?"

"Yeh I kept it quiet. Just said the rifles couldn't get through. He was happy with that."

"So why give him the money?" I still can't fathom that and Popeye knows it. A quaint combination of nods and smiles and shakes and shrugs says smarten up. I try to think, to think quickly, to comprehend. "I should know," I state decisively.

"Yeh. Yeh you should. You're the man remember? The rising star. That's you."

I nod. But nothing comes. I can't understand. I can't think of one possible reason.

"You got the broader picture?" he asks slowly. "You haven't asked about that."

"So what's that?"

"It's contracts. What else? It's what was up for grabs at the time. It's railroads, it's mineral resources. It's irrigation. It's shipping. It's money. What's a few rifles, eh?"

"Contraband," I say quite smartly.

"Yeh," laughs a surprised Popeye. "You're right. Hey, that's good. Contraband. Yeh."

I put Meiggs away then. I have bought him a bag, a black linen bag with a zip. I need that. I need its control. I need to feel alone. That is the only way I will be tested. I need to know that I am confident again, back to normal, that Meiggs isn't diverting me away from the whispers and gazes, from any pandemonium that is going on around me. I want the full picture now. And I want to be sure of my place in it.

So I step out, out of the open square, passed the plaque saying,

"*Sesquicentro de la fundacion de La Paz,* 16 June 1975", out past the children sliding down the soft stone of the sculptures, through the Plaza Murrillo with the bronze bust of the President who gave his name to the square and was frog-marched from the Presidential Palace and lynched for courting favour with too many cliques. "*No soy enemigo de los ricos, pero soy uno amigo de los pobres,*" I say aloud, stopping to read the words below the portrait. "No enemy of the rich, but a friend of the poor. No wonder," I add, considering the president's fate as I walk on, making a mental note of places to return to. I zigzag. I walk back down into the valley and the main avenue and return up the other side of the hill. Down, along and up, that is my rhythm. Down, along, up.

And I am going up when it happens, up near the old indian market where they sell lucky charms. "The witches' market," someone is calling it as I pass by a stall of llama foetuses that are in baskets, the head and neck of the foetuses are lifted upwards. The pose makes them look calm and contented. Like sleeping babies. I almost expect them to shake themselves and jump out of the basket and move away across the array of sacks that surround them. I look at the sacks, white sacks, their tops peeled back and neatly tucked into the sides to show what is available. Something like all bran, something like tiny white packages, something like walnuts. Behind the sacks a stack of home made shelves, on one shelf some cards held together by an elastic band, on another a paper box, like a large matchbox with a number seven written in black and the word "*poderes*" scrawled under the number.

"*Poderes,*" I say to myself. I leave the market and turn a corner. "*Poderes?*" I move uphill. A man brushes by me. A running man. He drops a package and turns right at the next corner. He disappears. It happens so quickly. I don't have time to call, so I bend down to pick up the package, but I am beaten to it by another man who must have been walking just behind me. He swoops and scampers after the man who has fled. I watch the second man turn the corner in pursuit.

Ten seconds later he returns, smiling broadly. "That poor man. He go. He just go." He holds up his hands to indicate he has done all he could to catch the man. "You see?" he repeats, shaking his head. "Oh it's too bad. You get a look at him?"

234

I stare at the man who is holding the package. He is tall for a Bolivian. Five foot nine perhaps with a sharp smile and bright, twinkly eyes. He looks clever, alert. He rubs his chin and, for good measure, shakes his head again.

"So what will you do? Take it to the police?"

"The package? Yes, of course. And they will keep it."

"Is that what happens?"

"All the time. Hey this is Bolivia. They take, they grab. Well their wages are so poor. I do not blame them. But there. Shall we see what they are getting?"

"You mean open it?"

The man shrugs. "OK. Let's have a look. There could be an address in it. We could return it." He opens the envelope which is sealed. "Hey, hey, hey."

There is a wad of notes. A mix of dollars and bolivianos. Big notes. Twenty dollar bills. Used and dog eared. There is no address.

"There must be... there must be..." The Bolivian starts to count the notes but there are too many so he estimates the value, getting excited, extremely excited. "Look we could... Hey what do you say? You and me. A happy new year for us, eh? We'll count it out and split it, yeh? You in?"

I'm not sure how to respond. I stand still and stare at the money.

"Poor devil. I mean losing this. Just after Christmas too. I mean what can we do?" The Bolivian lays it on thick. I step back and look at him and see the perspiration on his face. That isn't just through effort. Adrenaline then? He laughs and coughs. "Well?" he says, engaging me again. Why me?, I think. Why me? What about the other people who are around? The people in the shops, the people on the pavement, the people in vehicles. There are plenty of people who would have seen the package fall out of the man's pocket. Plenty. And why didn't the second man just take off, why didn't he keep going when he started the pursuit? I had reacted slowly. He had seen that. He could have fled. I would have. I would have wanted it all for myself. So why come back and draw it out? It doesn't make sense.

"OK let's split the notes," I suggest. "Down the middle."

"Here?"

"You just take what you think is half. Give the rest to me."

"We can't do it here.'"

"I don't mind if I get less than you."

"No."

"It really doesn't bother me."

He ignores me. He starts to count the notes and then hesitates. "We'll go up here. I know a place. A quiet place."

I am suspicious. Something says leave it. Run. Get it right. This time get it right. Remember Chincheros? Remember what the Swiss man said: go, leave the scene. He had been right. Go, go, go. Yes, that's it. Yes. I start to run and feel a sense of well being, a sense of getting things right, of using experience, of avoiding temptation, of seeing through it and judging and evaluating and comparing, of being scientific. I had made a decision. I am dominating. The other man is running too, in the opposite direction. He begins as though a sudden movement is not new to him, as though he expects the movement to bring a punch or a grab.

"You nailed him. You fuckin' nailed him." Popeye is saying. "Good for you. Yeh good for you."

But it isn't clear cut. That's the problem. Not like Chincheros. There was no ambiguity about that. It was clear there that the Frenchman was hell bent on putting me away or extorting money out of me. I knew that. Everyone else knew it too. Popeye knew it. The Swiss man knew it. They knew it straight away, before what was happening became clear to me. They had got it right.

This scam was more subtle. I convince myself of that, but what frustrates me is the way in which I left the scene with nothing but suspicions. I have no proof. No proof to show I was in danger, no proof to show it was a scam. That's so disappointing. Have I interpreted events correctly? I am sure I have, but that isn't sufficient to make me feel that I have managed the situation well. "They were accomplices," I start to tell myself, over and over. "The running man, the finding man were accomplices." There were others too, up the alleyway, waiting for me, I convince myself of that.

"You did well," says Popeye acting as a diversion, mulling over events. "Yeh, you did OK. Nice job."

"You sure?" I somehow sense the praise isn't quite as full as I had anticipated, that Popeye is holding back. "Yeh, I mean given what you've gone through."

"What I've gone through! What do you mean?"

"I mean some people would have lost confidence. They wouldn't have coped with what happened out there. I've seen them. Oh yeh. Big men. Big, big men."

"So how would you have handled it?"

"Me? I guess I'd have handled it fairly much the same as you."

"Come on."

"Yeh much the same." He pauses and runs through the events. "Except I'd have got the money. I'd have reacted more quickly. I mean you were dreaming."

"I was thinking."

"Hey but this was money, a lot of money. That comes first. That cuts in. This was serious money. Money you should have got your hands on."

"How? Come on, tell me how."

"Well you could have just grabbed it."

"You think?" I shake my head. I am shocked that Popeye has been drawn in this far, that he hasn't seen through the situation. "You don't see it, do you? OK, my hypothesis is that those guys were accomplices –"

"They probably were."

"Right so they're working that corner, luring Europeans into alleyways and thieving their money. I don't know how they do that, whether they use force, but I'm sure that's what's going on, yeh?"

"OK, I'll buy that. Yeh."

"So what about the money in the wad?"

"What about it?"

"Would they risk it?"

"Oh..." Popeye has it. The tone of his exclamation says that he sees the full story, that they wouldn't risk a wad of real cash in case they lost it, in case in some way they were outwitted and the person they were trying to inveigle into going into the alley made off with it. It wasn't worth that. "Counterfeits, yeh. Hey you're right. You're goddamn right."

"So you agree?"

"Yeh, yeh. My way of seeing it: you'd be sitting here counting your counterfeits, thinking you were a thousand dollars richer. Yeh

I buy it. So it wasn't real money."

"But I can't prove it."

Later in the hotel bar I am aware of a European voice. A northern European voice. A Dane talking English. A Dane talking to a girl, an English girl. I listen.

"........ And this one guy comes running from my back and drops a little package of money......."

I keep calm. I listen harder. I forgot that if they were working the corner they would try it time after time, that the results of the ruse would vary. I sip on my coffee and turn my head slightly so I can hear the European more clearly.

"And he just disappears around a corner. And another *Boliviano* guy grabs it and he runs after the first guy, then he realises he can't catch up with him and he turns to me and says, "*Vital, vital.*" *Vital* means let's split it. Do you want to split it?" The voice is excited now. It is sensing the drama, capturing the moment, making it all sound convincing. "And I go, yeh, yeh let's split it. Yes of course. Cause I could see there were loads of dollars and everything. So I said yeh, let's do it. And the guy stops and looks around and says it's too dangerous to split it in the street, so he notices this alleyway and we go down it. We end up in a very obscure place."

"Oh dear and you went?" A gasping, soft, thin English voice enters the conversation momentarily.

"Yeh. He seemed OK. So we went down this alley and he sat at a bench and he was about to part the money when this other guy, an older fatter guy came up to me and said, I've seen you two *chicos* pick up my friend's money. And I thought we were like going to say no and that we were going to run and disappear again, but the *Boliviano* who found the money started offering the fat guy his own money. He took out his own personal wallet."

Another gasp from the girl. "So when did you get worried?" she asks.

"I got worried when he asked me to give my money. At first I thought I was just going to show the fat guy that I didn't have the envelope, but then the tall guy said, it's OK, just give him your money. I just couldn't understand what was going on."

238

"So what did you do?" The English girl seems to enjoy this now. She is carried along by the narrative.

"I did nothing. I just watched."

"So what happened next?"

"Another guy arrived. He called the fat guy over and that gave the tall *Boliviano* a chance to whisper to me. I said to him, what are you doing and he said that if we give the fat *chico* our money we'll get away then we can split the big wad."

"Did you have much money?"

"On me? Yeh, I'd just been to the bank. I had cashed a hundred dollars. A fortune for a *Boliviano*."

"So did you give him any money?"

"My money? No. Something happened. There was something about the *Boliviano* with the wad and the fat guy. Facially they were so alike. They were father and son or brothers. I could see that. They had the same gestures, the same speech patterns."

"So did you run?"

"No, no I just told them. I told them I knew what was going on, that they would run away once they had my wallet."

"Brave."

"I didn't think about it."

"So what did they do?"

"They just walked away." He sighs, softly, contemplatively. A nervous sigh, a sigh coming out of relief. "Hey listen, it wasn't brave. I know what *Bolivianos* are like. I've been here some time. I worked in Potosi. There is a Danish restaurant there. The man who runs it said to me that *Boliviano*s never, never do anything to hurt you, they prefer to walk away and not get the money than hurt you. And he's right. I've learnt that. Mind you these guys didn't need violence. They were good at it. Without the language, without a cool head, I'd have handed over the money."

So would I, I think, smug now, cradling the coffee cup. I feel as warm as the coffee. I feel back on form, content with myself.

"Hugo Young, Hugo Young, Hugo Young," says Popeye excitedly and, as always, he is right. I am confident again.

Meiggs stays in my bag for *Alasita*. I call the office early and they fax me through details of Varig's considerations. It is vague. I look and think and consider. It doesn't make sense, but there is a date for a meeting. Four days time. "Perfect,"I say to Gunther on the phone.

"You got the figures?" he asks.

"The price?"

"And the service package?"

"Yes, yes. We've softened."

"A little. More post-service support, less frills on the plane."

"Thrills?"

"Frills Hugo. F for Fritz. Frills."

"More Spartan you mean?"

"It will look East German, but there. You get what you pay for."

"Gunther you sound like a whore."

"I feel like a whore. I am still in this bloody bedroom."

"You'll be at the airport?"

"On Thursday? Yes, yes I will be at the airport. For once I will be pleased to see you."

After the phone call I head for the places the man in the hotel foyer has told me about. "The best places for *Alasita*.....". To the Plaza Murrillo first, the square with the Presidential Palace and the parliamentary buildings and the Cathedral, the square now full of stalls. And I am confident and calm, taking my time, easing by people, chatting and smiling.

Feria alasita, I think, my mind casting more than a glance at the word. *Alasita*. I divide it, reconstruct it, try to recognise its derivation, its structure, perhaps its transformation. Work with the syllables, I decide. Al. As. It. A. Nothing. No semblance of sense or insight. *Quechua* or *Aymara*, I decide, trying to find a way out. And I am disappointed, as though I expect to come away with an insight into what is on view.

Counterfeit money is on view. Monopoly money. Scam money, I think, picturing the tall Bolivian and the Dane. It is everywhere. Wads of it. Stacks of notes bundled together by elastic bands. Dollars mainly. Dollars with a white wrap, stacked imaginatively as though they are cans of baked beans or packets of washing powder in a supermarket. They come in all sizes. Some are the exact size of dollars; others are the size of small mats. Those - the ones of the larger size – act as table cloths or drapes. And here and there, between the dollars, are credit cards, gold and yellow visa cards with the horizontal stripes, Mastercard with its circles. And passports. United States passports mainly. And models of cars and houses. Frank Lloyd Wright houses with Lamborghinis. And models of farms with animals and crops. And pillowcases that look like life belts, filled with goodies. And between the credit cards and the currency and the models of cows and llamas, are strange looking dolls, male dolls, with white faces and Hollywood teeth, all smiling and fat with hats and waistcoats, all looking as though life has been good to them. "*Ekeko,*" the woman stallholder keeps saying. She has been following my gaze.

"*Ekeko?*" I say pointing to one of the model men.

"Si. *Ekeko,*" she replies.

"*Ekeko,*" I say, taking the name with me across the square to the cathedral. "*Ekeko, Ekeko.*" It is like a celebration of consumerism. A celebration of aspiration, I think, correcting myself. So strange. I have always thought the people of South America are supposed to be content, that the spiritual makes up for their poverty, that they are satisfied with much less than I would be. But this shows something different. They are all buying counterfeit dollars and counterfeit credit cards and counterfeit airline tickets. They're just like me, I think, shaking my head as I reach the top of the cathedral steps. Parallel to the door and in front of me are a line of men kneeling. Their knees are on the top step, their legs and feet are below. They are in jackets and hats with old newspapers laid out in front of them upon which are old saucepans and prima stoves. They each have a bottle of paraffin and a box of matches and a plastic bucket. They each have a ladle too. Why a ladle?, I wonder, transfixed by the scene.

I see it then. I see its use. A man passes a coin to one of the kneeling men, who smiles and picks up a ladle which is put into the saucepan. It scoops up something that is giving off steam. Molten metal. Lead probably I decide, watching the man who has paid the money pick up a dessert spoon and extract some of the molten metal from the ladle. He throws it quickly into a red plastic bucket that is half full of water. One sizzle and the metal solidifies into an extravagant shape. The kneeling man ladles out the metal onto a plate. Its shards look like a flat fish. The kneeling man grasps it and starts talking to his client. Fortune telling, I think, reaching into my pocket for money.

"You will have a safe journey home," says the man interpreting my metal's shape. It looks like a staircase, jagged and crooked and sharp. So different from the previous client's. "But a difficult week lies ahead."

"A difficult week?"

"Yes," says the man, turning the metal over. "Yes there will be some problems, but you are used to dealing with problems. You talk your way around them."

"I negotiate," I say, prompting the man.

"There are problems," he reiterates, "but you will get through them. You will remain calm and easy."

"Easy?" What does he mean? I shake myself. I am taking it all too seriously. Everyone else is taking it seriously too: a crowd has gathered, as much as a crowd could gather on the top step of the cathedral; men hold their hands in their pockets and stretch to listen in; women are open mouthed, their stare fixed on the hands of the man who is prodding my honeycombed piece of metal, turning it over gently, tossing it like a pancake. "I see some children and a big move."

"A big move," I say, revealing to him that I am not at all interested in children.

"I see a young woman, not a child. A young woman in a large house. She is all in white. A uniform perhaps?"

"And the move?"

"You change jobs, I think. But not next year. The year after perhaps. You change countries too."

I enjoy it. I enjoy the theatre of it, the quality of it. I enjoy the spiritual and the commercial, the way they are fused or used, the way they are mixed and savoured. I see that in the faces around me, the faces that are hanging on every word and gesture. They know the nuances. They know whether I believe or am just treating it all

242

as one great ruse. I smile. I smile at the old kneeling man and he smiles back. The old and the new, I think, the global and the local. "This woman in the uniform she is there, very strongly there," he warns. "I do not like her. She is strong, stronger than she looks. She is more dangerous than she looks."

"OK, OK," I say. "And thanks." I hand over my money and nod my head in a warm appreciation. "You are very good. I'll recommend you." He smiles shyly and half shrugs as if to say it isn't a case of being good, it is just a case of delivering a gift, of using it wisely, profitably.

"Bye," I say waving and weaving my way down the cathedral steps. I cross the road which is full of people now, a mix of civil servants in dark overcoats with briefcases under their arms and students with books and old men and women who laugh and talk. There are traders too, traders feeding off the crowd. Chocolate sellers. Toothpaste sellers. "Sir, sir," one of them shouts. "Photo, photo." I smile and shake my head. I stare at his box camera on a tripod, one side of the camera is masked over with red cardboard, a backing for photos that have worked well and are now a showcase for his skills. A man is sitting on the fold up chair four feet in front of the camera, posing, a red curtain is draped on a small ladder behind him, his arms straight down his side look limp and lifeless, emphasising his unease. I laugh thinking that he looks as though he is preparing to face a firing squad, as though he has giving up all hope of being reprieved.

"Popeye would love all this," I say to myself. All this misuse of time, all this mooching around. "That's why you're number one," I can hear him saying. "It means you can do this. As long as you've got a good man working while you're lazing around. Someone like my brother John." I know Popeye's words now. I know the way he would respond. I know too he would have appreciated the way I am willing to sacrifice time to get to know the people. That is so important. You have to know the people. Popeye recognises that. He knows exactly what to expect from whoever worked for him whether they be Irish, Italian, Peruvian, Chilean or Chinese. He understands people.

I think about that all the way down to the valley and all the way south to the main park where the majority of the *Alasita* Fair is housed. There, a giant *Ekeko* greets me, a twelve foot *Ekeko* that stands under a banner that is draped across the road between two trees. "*Alasita*s 1990" says the banner. Around the giant doll children are on their father's necks reaching out to shove fake dollar notes into the pockets of *Ekeko* or into one of the many jugs or boxes that have been draped over him. Alongside the jugs and boxes are huge German sausages and bottles of wine and coca cola and boxes of detergent and models of cars and washing machines and houses, huge houses, ranch like houses. I realise then that *Ekeko* is holding people's dreams, supporting them with strength and smiles. It is saying this is how you should be.

"Go on," shouts a man from behind me. "Give to *Ekeko*."

"Me?" I try to turn around and face the man, but there is pressure from all sides.

"Yes you. Give to *Ekeko* and *Ekeko* will give back. Whatever you want. You'll see. Go on."

The people around me laugh and nod and urge me on.

"OK, real *bolivianos*," I say, putting a note into the same brown and white ceramic pot that moments earlier had received the little girl's offering. "Yes?"

"Good, good."

I back away. I wave and nod. "*Feliz Alasita*," I shout, moving to my left, into a crowd that is watching a display on a stage.

And then I am shocked. What I see stops me. It holds my breath. It suspends the festivities. I look away. I look back. "Yes, yes," I say, recognising the woman on the stage. I know her. The stiff shirt's wife. "Julia," I say. It is as though she has come out of the photo he gave me. Her clothes look the same and I could freeze her movements to leave her in the graceful pose of the half swivelled hip with the half raised leg, the pose of the photo. She kicks out of that and twists and turns and swirls naturally and gracefully in front of me. I turn away. "Find a distraction, a distraction," I repeat. Got it. A road cleaning crew. I absorb their bright red uniforms. I take in details: the yellow pockets and yellow belts, the company name boldly splattered across their chests. Starco. I read the company name over and over. Starco, Starco, Starco. It can't be her. It can't be Julia. Starco, Starco, Starco, Starco. Not in a city of this size. I can't just bump into her. I am making assumptions. A girl on a stage. It could be anyone. I would believe that any girl on the stage dancing with grace and elegance would have been her.

"Starco, Starco, Starco,"I mumble looking at the cleaning crew again. This time at the man with the big bin on a trolley and the man next to him with a broom, the brooms also have the company colours, red handles with yellow heads, red handles to match the red hats on the workers' heads. Only the sacks in which they are depositing rubbish are uncoordinated. They are white, brilliant white, the cleanest white I have seen in South America. Starco, Starco, Starco.

But it doesn't work. My eyes return to the stage and the performance. It's her, it is her. Julia. She is dancing with another woman now, a strange dance. The crowd love it. They respond with laughter and cries. It is a pantomime like dance. An Oh-no-she-isn't, Oh-yes-she-is sort of dance. The responses purl down the valley-side, enthusing me. I clap. I cheer. And there is more. A slow dance. A classical dance. Julia filling the stage, every limb managing a perfection, showing a hesitancy or a joy, a range that enraptures the crowd who know what will happen next and where the movements all lead.

The stiff shirt, I think. The bloody stiff shirt. I think of the painting, of his kindness, of his naïvety, of the way he would worry and fret and misread, the way he would trust. Little hope of fulfilment, I think, imagining how his life will turn out, the way he will be used, how his faith will let him down, how it will be tested by all sorts of people, how they will use his good nature. So trusting, I think. And I remember the promise. The deal he had tried to strike: no payment for the painting, instead a favour. A letter. A letter to Julia. He had asked me to deliver it. "Deliver it if you want. While you're in La Paz. Search her out. You could find her, I'm sure of that." I recall his words. I recall him handing me the letter, the letter I had binned on my departure from the island.

Julia begins another dance. I clear my mind and watch her. I enjoy her. My eyes stay on her as she dances with another woman. It is a quick dance, a comic dance made up of insults. The audience loves it. They laugh. Julia laughs. I laugh. More insults. And thoughts too of the fact the stiff shirt hasn't sent on her address, that if anyone has been involved in betrayal it is the stiff shirt. "I'll send you an address, yes?" I remember his exact words. So where is it? Why hasn't it arrived? I curse him and watch Julia twist and turn and sit down and stand up and pout.

Following Julia is easy. She runs up a bank at the end of her dance, the bank of grass that is filled with spectators. I watch her go. I wonder if I should call out, if I should make any form of contact. "Excuse me," I say to the people by my side as I begin to move after her. "Sorry.... sorry," I say threading my way through the crowd. Perhaps I should call after her. I know she will be more agile than I am, that the thin air will take its toll, as might the slippery bank. "*Perdon, perdon,*" I keep repeating as I move and people tuck in their feet or move their children. I smile too, all the time keeping an eye on her. She is at the top of the bank now. I will lose her. Quicker, quicker, I tell myself. I watch her climb up and over a wall and wipe herself down as she stands on the top walkway. It is forty or so yards to the road now. Forty yards and, if a taxi or a lift is waiting, she will be away. "Shit!" I curse, slightly tumbling. "Shit!" again when I see she isn't there. "Shit!" once more when I reach the road and I cannot see her.

I smooth down my clothes and flick some mud off my knee. What have I been doing? Why am I chasing? Because I want to, that is the truth. I want to. Because there is little else to do. It is a bit of excitement, a bit of intrigue. It is what I want. I want Julia. "OK, OK, let's get back to the hotel." I try to be rational. I try to pull myself together. "Let's pack, let's get ready to go home. Well at least back to Brazil."

I start to walk along the road. There seems little point in return-ing to the crowd and all the strangeness of *Alasita*. I'm not in the mood for that now. Home, I think. A drink in the hotel cafe with the Dane perhaps. We could swop notes. I could get all smug and supe-rior and let him realise that I hadn't fallen for the scam. "I'll show him," I say to myself. Then I see her. I see Julia. In a taxi, a taxi that sweeps passed me. "Right, right," I spy another taxi, a waiting taxi. I run towards it. "You follow," I say quickly to the taxi driver. "Follow!"

"Follow?"

"The taxi in front."

"Jorge."

"Jorge?"

"The driver. The driver of the taxi in front. You want me to follow Jorge?"

"Yes, yes I want you to follow Jorge." I get in and sit in the back of the taxi. The driver touches the ignition and we're away.

"We won't do it."

"We won't do what?" I ask.

"Stay with Jorge. He's too quick and the traffic in La Paz is too chaotic. And there are too many traffic lights."

"Of course we'll keep up with him. Just concentrate."

"You English?"

"I said just concentrate."

"You're English," says the driver. A smile sweeps across his face. He sniggers and drives quite quickly away. "You like La Paz?"

I do not reply. I sit forward resting my arms on the seat adjacent to the driver. I stare ahead at Jorge and the outline of Julia's head in the back seat.

"You like Bolivian girls? I can get you a girl. You like?"

"I said just concentrate."

"Very cheap and very special." He looks up into the mirror and smiles, a cheap smile, a knowing smile, a smile that recognises my masculinity and its needs. The smile lingers, searching out any weakness that my expression conveys. "You like Latin girls? They are sensual. They are passionate. You English do not know the meaning of passionate, eh? But you can find out. Some of the girls I know will be willing to show you. What do you say? Eh?"

"I say keep your eyes on the cab in front. If you lose him..."

He loses Jorge at the first big roundabout, the special round-about near the National Stadium that has a sunken inner area that is filled by artifacts from the Tiahuanaco culture. The driver starts to tell me about the roundabout and the culture and how the arti-facts came to be sited there. When we go around a second time and he is still talking sculpture I know he has failed.

"You've lost them," I snarl.

"It doesn't matter. It really doesn't matter," the taxi driver says softly, reassuringly.

"What do you mean, it doesn't matter? Of course it bloody matters. It matters to me. It matters a hell of a lot to me."

"We were being stupid. Why should we chase Jorge across half of the city? We'll just wait for him. He'll be back after his fare, because this is where the crowds are today. It's *Alasita* remember? The *Feria*. That's where you'll get fares. It's where Jorge picked up the girl you're interested in."

"Julia," I say somehow thinking the conversation would benefit from some personalisation.

"Julia, yes. He'll come back for another Julia. And what he'll get is you. He can take you to where she got out. You'll just have to hope it's where she lives."

Where she lives. The words stay with me while we wait. The driver sits in the car listening to the radio, smoking. I sit on a wall. I want Julia, I tell myself. I need her. I need the challenge. And I have the excuse: my association with the stiff shirt, the bloody stiff shirt. Her husband.

"Here he comes," shouts the driver, beeping his horn and waving to the approaching taxi. It draws up alongside the taxi I had used. A frenetic conversation follows. It is accompanied by several smiles and a long period of shrugging and arm waving that ends in a salvo of *si, si*, yes, yes. I am called over.

"OK, he'll take you," says my taxi driver. "He says he is certain where he dropped the girl is where she lives. It is a big house south of the city ten minutes away. Ten minutes Jorge?" he checks with the other taxi driver who has stayed in his seat, staring out in turn at me and the taxi driver.

"You take me?" I inquire smiling his way. "I am a friend of hers."

The driver replies in Aymara. My taxi driver translates. "He says he doesn't care who you are as long as you pay."

"How much?"

"The going rate. He won't do you," says my driver.

"He'd better not. Tell him I'm only paying half the fare."

"What?"

"Tell him what I said."

"But who's paying the rest?"

"You are."

"Me?" The taxi driver stares at me, then laughs. "Hey that's funny."

"That's fair," I say getting into the car. "After all you caused me to hire a second taxi."

"That's funny," he repeats.

"I'm not laughing," I shout through the window as we drive away.

We travel south, staying deep in the valley. The heavily eroded landscape that is loved by tour guides is to our right, as is the zoo. Three miles out of La Paz the taxi stops. I look out at the avenue of white walls and manicured gardens that are half hidden behind severe looking metal fences.

"This it?" I ask.

"Yes, yes. She asked me to pull over sixty, perhaps seventy yards down the road. She said thank you and paid me and said that normally taxis pull up around the back. There's some sort of service lane there that taxis use. The residents prefer it."

"You see her enter a house?"

"I saw her walk up the steps."

"But not go in."

"She was getting out her keys. I saw her fumbling in her pockets. I saw a key."

"But not go in?" I repeat impatiently.

"Not actually go in."

"What number?"

"Forty six. I saw that. I saw it clearly. They've got it marked on the wall. Big metal numbers. You'll see it. You can't miss it."

"We'll see," I say gathering my things together. "You'll stay here and wait? You'll take me back?"

"OK," agrees a reluctant Jorge.

"So you saw her?"

"Yes."

"You just followed her?"

"Yes." I sigh. I am getting impatient now. I can't see the relevance of Popeye's interrogation. I have done nothing wrong. There is no reason for it.

"So you're telling me you just took off and chased her. What the hell's got into you? I mean that sounds dangerous, mighty dangerous. I mean do you know why you did it? It's sex, isn't it? Oh Jesus Hugo there's much easier ways of getting women. For chrissakes listen to me. Listen to this one piece of advice, will you? Don't ever be satisfied with instinct. You got that. Because it ain't good enough. You got to have solid ground to stand on. Hey you gotta know what you're doing and why you're doing it. You gotta understand. You hear me?"

I can't begin to understand the nature of Popeye's concern. He is with me now, in a coffee shop. It is the first he has learnt of my afternoon.

"I mean, Christ, you're in South America, you know that? This isn't downtown Swansea or whatever you call it. This isn't sad old Wales. There's all sorts of shit out there, you know that? All sorts of shit just waiting for you. So you don't just go off following some stranger. You're crazy. You know that? Fuckin' crazy."

"I saw her."

"And you followed her. That's flaky, real flaky. A girl. A Peruvian girl that you don't know."

"I sort of know her." I want to object now. I make that clear in the scowl my voice adopts. There is reason. There is a need, a desire – call it what you will: I know what I am doing.

"You sort of know her," mocks Popeye. "Hey I sort of know thousands of people, but I don't go off chasing them."

"I had nothing else to do."

"So you chase a stranger?"

"She isn't a stranger."

"What do you mean she isn't a stranger? Hey come on you've never met her. You've never set eyes on her before."

"She's the stiff shirt's wife."

"So."

I take out a note. A letter. It had been waiting for me when I returned to my hotel. The stiff shirt. The stiff shirt on cue. No name. Just an envelope addressed to me with the frank, "Puno, Peru" on it. The date stamp is smudged. And inside is a postcard and on the card is a handwritten address. It is where I had been, Julia's home.

"Hey what is it with you? A sniff of a girl and you're off. You've got a weakness. You know that?"

"A weakness?"

"Yeh. A weakness. A big fuckin' weakness."

part seven

JOSE

1

I had planned my Christmas Day conversation with the Englishman. I wanted to tell him about Pisarro, Camille Pisarro the artist. I wanted to draw his interest by relating that Camille Pisarro and Henry Meiggs were contemporaries in South America. I'd play on that, imagining that they had met and tolerated each other just as the Englishman and I had: perhaps Pisarro would have offered to draw Meiggs a peasant or a landscape and Meiggs, using his influence as a great benefactor, would have pressed his preference for landscapes.

There seemed a certain stability in that, as though an equilibrium is in place, an equilibrium making our responses, the Englishman's and mine, seem predictable, an equilibrium suggesting that the caveats and coolness of our relationship were not our doing but were more institutional, cultural. I found that appealing. It made excuses for the Englishman, which he needed because he had travestied my painting. He had accepted it and said fine, thank you, and that was it. He didn't even look at it. He was too busy, too absorbed in preparing for something or the other. A walk, he said, a Christmas morning walk, something he referred to as a tradition. But why didn't he take a moment to ask about perspective or colour or just who my favourite painter is? Particularly that. He could have asked that. He should have needed to know where the painting was coming from. What made you paint this? What were you trying to do? Such questions would unravel the painting, because all paintings need to be unravelled: they are parcelled up in style and colour. I wondered if he knew that. I doubted it because the Englishman didn't ask anything. He just said fine for a second time and left the painting on his bed. A sideways glance checked the carrier bag and my attempt at gift-wrapping it and a salvo of nervous, unnecessary words asked me to name a price. I refused, but that didn't change anything: he still asked no further questions; he just smiled as I told him I had also put some photos of Julia in the carrier bag so he would recognise her if he decided to deliver the letter I had given him for her in La Paz.

I couldn't bring myself to return the smile. To me the transaction seemed incomplete. I still expected him to pull himself together, to shrug and laugh and apologise and stop what he was doing by asking me to name the greatest artist ever or to pass comment on contemporary art. Who's your favourite? Pisarro I'd say explaining that what I liked was the way Pissaro drew people. That was so important to me. Drawing people. Pisarro did it beautifully. He used crisp, clear lines. His drawings were unstuffy, succinct. He picked out features and his honesty exposed the plight of poverty. He drew and drew. Washer women, beggars, water carriers. The drawings were always anecdotal, fixing the subjects quickly with a vitality that moved him on to the next glance or laugh or tear. Such voracity. I knew I couldn't match it. I always got too involved with the subject. That was it. I felt the misery. I understood the scandal of it. I knew where it came from, who was responsible for it. And I wanted to change it.

I arrived early for the *fiesta*. I wanted to give the Englishman another chance. He would have had all morning to consider the inadequacy of his response. "Fine." I couldn't get over it – the detachment, the coolness. He'll be all over me now, I thought, opening the door of my hut and moving into the courtyard, but only Sebastian was there, Sebastian sitting on the steps that led up to the plastic table. He was polishing a belt.

"Look," he said without looking up.

I looked closely at the belt, at its embroidered patterns and motifs. I wondered what deliberate structures lay behind the patterns. Fields, birds, stars, I thought, absorbing the detail. "It's very splendid. Rather beautiful," I finally said.

"Beautiful," said Sebastian, sounding rather displeased. It didn't seem to be a question of beauty. "You understand?" he asked, searching for a clarification of my thoughts. "You understand what is beauty? You understand the symbol? You see?" He shook his head. It was a vigorous shake. It suggested some essential significance had been missed and needed to be located and considered. It told me it was to do with the island. Something to do with the motifs on the belt. Fields, birds, stars. I ran them through my mind. The essence of the island, I thought.

"The land," said Sebastian supporting my thoughts. "You see?" He looked for confirmation. "We believe the land and spirits."

"You believe the land and spirits?" I couldn't quite make out what he was saying.

"Yes, they linked."

"Ah."

Sebastian sighed and sat down on the steps that led to the upper courtyard. "We observe. We observe stars, birds, the lake. They tell us."

"What? What do they tell you?" I recognised the gentle touch of the old man, the manipulation he so enjoyed, the way his voice barely rose above a whisper.

"Ah." The expression of glee, of joy. He shook his shoulders. He smiled. "Everything. They tell everything. When plant, when harvest."

"Like the duck? I mean the night time duck. That did the same sort of thing, didn't it? It is like a sign."

"Yes, yes." More joy. More enthusiasm. "Like the duck. There, you know." Sebastian laughed, though the brevity of the sound told me the duck wasn't overly significant, that it didn't top the chart of things to be observed. "*Chaska* is the most important."

"*Chaska*?" I was in danger of mixing *chaska* up with *chuspa*. *Chuspa* is a belt, *chaska* is...

"*Chaska* is star. When *chaska* close to moon, it important." Sebastian emphasised the words for effect. I waited for a corollary, for some other great swathe of knowledge that something or the other provided by its mere presence or mood. I was surprised when Sebastian began to offer a qualification of the star's significance. It was delivered in a reverential tone. "*Chaska* gives warning. When it near moon and no air –"

"No air?"

"You know..." Sebastian gestured with his hand fanning his face.

"Oh wind," I suggested.

"Yes. When near moon and no wind," he emphasised, "you no walk in fields."

"Never?" I gasped, giving the old man a chance to lighten up.

"Never," stressed Sebastian. He was enjoying himself now. I could tell. I could read the glint in his eyes and the jabbing nod of his head. "Same if there is a ...."He waved his arm about as he tried to find the word. "Oh..." Yet another variation. This time a low sound, a sound that suggested he was struggling with vocabulary. A lightening of his eyes said he had found what was necessary. "A small star on top-"

"Above it," I suggested. "Above *chaska*?"

"Yes above it. At three or four in morning."

"Three or four a.m.," I repeated, making it sound as though I couldn't take in the degree of detail. "Really?" I said.

"Yes. It no good." Sebastian smiled. His cheeky smile. His broad, fun loving smile. "But today is very good, yes? Today we eat and drink and play. Ah," he said appreciatively as the belt began to shine. "Today is good, yes?"

Neither Hernando nor the Englishman made it to the *fiesta*. At the time I missed them both but I thought little of their absence until the following day when I heard Hernando knocking on the door of my hut. His was a distinctive knock. He tapped on the clasp. Two touches and one louder thump. The thumps soon outnumbered by calls. "José! José!" I wondered what was coming. "José!" Another call. It was time to respond. It was time to call him in and calm him down.

"José, you're in," he said quickly when I opened the door. "A good Christmas, eh José? I saw Sebastian," he said, explaining the source of his knowledge.

"You didn't make it," I remarked, sounding a little disappointed. I returned to the bed; Hernando opted for the ledge. He crossed his legs and rocked back against the wall. I smiled. We knew our places now. We knew the order of our conversations too. I held back; Hernando advanced.

"Hey José, guess what? A happening," he announced. "And you, you don't know. I can tell that. I can tell it by your face. And by your silence. You haven't heard, have you José?"

"Heard?" He gave me a moment, a moment I could have filled in any way. I should have talked about the *fiesta*, of Sebastian's *charango* playing, of my attempt to duet with him on the pan-pipes, of the food we ate and the *chica* we drank, of the way we stopped at some point to listen to the Archbishop of Lima on the radio. But I didn't say a word. I stayed silent. That was my answer and his prompt.

"I thought so."

"What?" I pushed up my glasses and smoothed my chin. I felt prepared then, prepared for whatever was to follow.

"No-one knows. Sebastian doesn't know. Not that he'd care. Mind you he might miss the money. That's all he worries about."

"What?" I stepped in. I needed clarity. I knew what was happening, that the excitement of the situation was getting the better of Hernando, scrambling the events. It was as though he didn't know quite where to start. "Right. Now what's going on? What's it all about, this happening?" I urged.

Hernando took a breath. "I have been on the Puno run," he said excitedly. "Roberto is ill."

"Again?"

"It's Christmas. He is young. He drinks too much. So I go to Puno. But when I go to get my boat the jetty is full of people. My boat is full too. There are *gringos* on the roof and on the deck. The boat is creaking with *gringos*. So I organise a second boat. And some of the *gringos* moan and I moan back. It is as it always is, eh José?" He searched for a smile from me, for a sign of reassurance. It is issued easily and quickly and is pulled back with an even greater eagerness. Even so, it has little effect: the happening Hernando was trying to relate must have been irresistible; Hernando would not be diverted. "So there are arguments about who will go where, who will change boats. And there is a big party of Israelis, noisy Israelis. They will not separate, so it is complicated and I have to be the United Nations. You there, I say. And the first boat goes. I wave them good bye and leave a message with Javier, the harbour boy."

"And the happening?" I sense Hernando needs a prompt. I fear long winded details about the condition of the sky and the sea, about how he felt and what he was thinking.

"Right, yes the happening. Well I start the engine and untie the ropes."

"Blue skies?" I joked.

"Yes, blue skies." He did not laugh. He looked through me. "I checked the engine. It was fine. So I start. I cast off and the boat glides away. And I am happy eh José? Out on the lake I am always

259

happy. And two Germans play cards and an Italian tries to interview me on his tape recorder. I tell him yarns. All sorts of yarns. I yack and yack. It is a normal trip, eh José? And then I see him."

"Him? Who? Who do you see?"

"I see him at the front of the boat, under cover. He is reading, ignoring everyone, keeping himself to himself, so I wedge the tiller and go over to him."

"Who's him?"

"The Englishman. The Englishman has gone José. He's in Puno."

I should have told Hernando there and then that he had lost his bet, that Hugo wasn't inclined to search out Julia in La Paz. I knew that as soon as Hernando accused the Englishman of ignoring him during the passage to Puno. "I said hello, José. I said hello. How are you?, I said. Are you leaving? And he just looked up and smiled. He didn't say a word. A smile is all he offered. A brief smile. That was it. And when we got to Puno and I was helping people off the boat, he didn't even say goodbye or thank you. He said nothing." Hernando's humiliation was clear. I felt sorry for him. He had miscalculated. He should have realised that characters nearly always revert to type, that he and the Englishman had acted as they normally would. The open and the devious. But where was the charm, the mysterious charm? Where had it gone? I summoned reasons for the Englishman's character changes and mood swings. I had imagined he had been ill or lonely or overwhelmed. Had I got it wrong? So badly wrong.

"Oh come on José," said Hernando graciously when I voiced concern about my judgement. "You just don't know. One day he's fine, another day he's miserable. José there are lots of people like that. He was a fish out of water. And he knew it. So don't say you got it wrong. Hey I tell you what José, I bet I'll still win my wager. I mean that. I bet you the Englishman will make an effort to see Julia."

2

Over the next few days I enjoyed our efforts to chase the Englishman away, to clear him from our minds. Hernando called it
chewing over the bones. He said he liked the way chewing always
released some small succulence. I agreed. Even in the Englishman's
case there were flavours to be savoured. The taste of loyalty, for
instance. His loyalty to Honest Henry Meiggs. Meiggs the capitalist. Meiggs with the sneering mouth and the glacial eyes. I
remembered the photograph of him and some of the stories and
the way he affected the Englishman. It was like a transfusion, the
spirit and ideas being passed on and somehow refined and delicately mixed by the experiences of the Englishman.

I had tried to explain to Hernando the power of Meiggs over the
Englishman. He couldn't comprehend. He suggested Meiggs was
like a good footballer or politician. I nodded, though I didn't fully
understand his point. Instead I remembered being a student and
the influence of Arnez, my tutor. That was the nearest I had come
to having a Meiggs in my life. I was impressionable and Arnez was
clever. He had a way with words; he said the right thing; he always
said the right thing.

"The Englishman was just looking for something to fill time,"
remarked Hernando, cutting through my thoughts. "I mean you
have time on your hands if you travel, eh José? There's no routine."

"So?"

"So Meiggs was just a good book. That's all José, a story to fill
the Englishman's days."

Arnez stayed with me after Hernando left. Arnez. My mind recalled
his influence and charisma. So much about him came back to me
quickly which was a sign of his importance. A sharp man with
quick wit and a huge amount of humour. And such a dapper figure.
He wore a blazer with a handkerchief in his top pocket, a perfectly
pressed and spotlessly clean handkerchief. He said all his salary
went on clothes and I believed him: he was immaculate. "Believe in
the best," he enthused. "Find the right woman, the right philosopher, the right God. And the right jacket. Always settle with one.

The best. Understand?" The emphasis made it all seem final, as though the revelation would dispel any yearning for anything else, anything different. "So I have Mao. I have one philosophy. I have one lecture. You may think you're hearing different words, but there's only one idea. One lecture, one quote. Understand? That's all you'll get from me. In three years that's all you'll get. It will be like being on bread and water. Every day, over and over, the same diet. Mao, Mao, Mao."

That was the message in his first lecture. I remember leaving the lecture theatre; I recall the conversation that went on, the assessment.

"Bloody nutter."

"Arnez? You think?"

"God yes. So predatory. That look."

I pulled the face: grim, determined, drilled, fixed, contemplative.

"That's it. Yes. God, if we've got him for three years."

"Great," I said, relaxing my expression. "I enjoyed it."

"You mean it?"

"It's what we need. Someone to get us thinking. Everyone has just come in and said this is what so and so said about this and that. Nobody else asked what we think. He'll be good for us," I said, laughing at the glum expressions on the faces that met my words. "He will. He's an end product. It's what we'll be."

"But what about balance? He's forgotten about alternatives."

"No he hasn't forgotten them. He's rejected them. He knows they're there." I spoke quite strongly now, emphasising how my fellow students needed to listen more carefully. "He'll talk about all the other philosophers, but in the context of Mao, why they can't come close to Mao, why they're inadequate. I look forward to that. It's a good way of investigating them. Anyhow who are you going to study for the first assignment?"

"What will I read? Mao."

"See?"

"What?"

I laughed. I shook my head and thought how my words highlighted the manipulation, the way our first assignment which was to read and criticise the work of a major philosopher or political figure was going to be geared towards Arnez's point of view. Mao. That's whom I would read too. That's whom most of my contemporaries would read. And it was all because of Arnez's performance, because of his choice of words, because of his strange slant, because of his charisma.

"Another Hernando delivery, eh José? José!" Hernando was calling from the courtyard. His light voice. His joy. It moved me from the bed and a siesta. I must have looked weary when I pushed open the door. He was standing there, waiting and smiling, his characteristic effusion urging me to accept what he was holding in his hand. An envelope. "For you," he said warmly. "Hernando's special deliveries. It came on the morning boat."

"Today?"

"Yes today. Roberto was handed it by a nervous man, quite a large man."

"Handed it?"

"Yes you know José. Like this." Hernando enjoyed pushing his hand towards mine, imitating the procedure. He laughed, ridicule pervading his role play. "Take it José. It's what you've been waiting for."

What I've been waiting for? What I've....? It came to me then. The nervous man. The quite large, nervous man. Jorge. The communication. At last word of Julia, of what was going on in La Paz, of her new life. Yes, my mind exclaimed, sensing the thrill of knowing that some shape was being given to events. "Thanks," I muttered, accepting the letter.

"Hey slow," urged Hernando viewing my attempt to open the letter quickly. My finger slid under the flap of the envelope, but the seam split and the envelope almost broke in two. I drew out the letter.

"There's an address," I uttered.

"Good."

"And news."

"She's well?"

"Working as a maid. In south La Paz, wealthy La Paz..."

Hernando tried to look over the top of the paper. He seemed to expect more, some precise confirmation, something more personal and evocative, something that would almost take me there and place me at her side and so comprehend what she was doing and how she was. "So? Is she enjoying it? Does she miss Puno and the lake and the fish and the winds and you? You, José, does she miss you? Is there a note from her? I just thought it would be reassuring. I mean for you. You know what I mean José?"

Of course he was right. I should have expected some lines from Julia. Some domestic chit chat. Some local gossip. Some discussion of dancing that would have indicated her state of mind. I looked inside the broken envelope, flipping over the letter, checking. There was nothing more, nothing but Jorge's few words which were tantalising and inadequate. "She's fine," he said. "Living at the address below and working as a maid. We'll arrange a visit soon. OK?" OK! No it wasn't OK. It was shoddy and insulting and undervalued the relationship Julia and I enjoyed. It made me believe no such plan for a visit was in place. So perhaps I should take over, perhaps I should plan it, perhaps Hernando would help me. He could organise a boat to Bolivia. He would be pleased to do that. I was sure. Perhaps I should go today? Why wait?

" So you'll send on the address?" asked Hernando, assessing what we had gained from Jorge's communication.

"What?" I asked still allowing my mind the freedom to assess what action I should take.

"To the Englishman. You promised José, you promised. You said he'd given you his La Paz address and that you'd inform him of Julia's address once you knew. That's what you said José."

I smiled. "You still want to win your bet?"

"Too right I do. And I will. I've always said I will. Haven't I José? Haven't I?"

I sent on the address. I wrote a short note telling Hugo that Sebastian couldn't wait for his parcel from France and that I had missed our confused chatter about Meiggs and Marx and that I was still on the island, but hoping to move on soon – perhaps within a week or two but certainly within a month. I went on to say that I wasn't sure where I would settle, but that I would call into La Paz to see Julia.

I entered into role play then, knowing that, in the same way that Jorge had drilled Julia's fantasy relationship with me into the tale of why I was on the island, so Julia would have been rehearsed too: she would be from a broken home or an orphanage somewhere in the Bolivian mountains; she would have no close relations or would have a father and mother who couldn't care; she would be a tragic figure demanding the sympathy of any policemen who dared to call for her papers. Yet I knew also that within the household where she was resident and working, she may have been allowed to keep her identity. I reminded myself that it was a safe house, that the residents were sympathisers, that there was no need for cover in such a house. In such a house she may have been called Julia, Julia from Chuschi, Julia with a brother José. I hoped that she was. I prayed that she was. I sensed she needed to be, that she needed a background that went beyond the teddy bear she had had since a child, that went beyond memories and scars.

I wondered what the Englishman would make of it, almost believing for a moment that he would take the time to visit her, that he would be fascinated, drawn in by what I had told him of Julia and my words in Lima and the hatred of the regime. But then I paused and held back and checked myself. Which Hugo is this?, I asked. Which version of the Englishman am I talking about? Because the Englishman could be self centred, indifferent and absorbed in nothing but self-gratification. He could be a devotee of nothing but his own importance. He could totally lack compassion and have no sense of altruism. I knew that he would do what he wanted in La Paz, though I couldn't imagine what that would be. I didn't know him well enough to imagine his days and how he would fill them, but I did know that the letter he would receive in five or six days time from me would probably mean little to him. He would probably laugh at it and think it sad and be pleased at his efforts to inveigle me. But then I doubted that he would think any of that. He would probably just crumple it up and throw it away.

"So you've sent it, eh José? He's got the address."

"Of course."

"Oh he's such a good friend José. He likes you. Really likes you. Like me, eh José? He's just like me. Next time you write you tell him what he missed on Christmas Day. Your duet with Sebastian. The dancing, the singing, the jokes."

"You weren't there." I laughed.

"Ah but I know José, I know....."

The pause that followed was unusual: pauses were not a feature of our conversations; we normally talked and talked. But, then, this conversation was different in that it didn't come out of anything in our vicinity, out of the flight of a thrush or the smell of the lake, neither did it come from a piece of news in one of Hernando's newspapers. For once the source of our chatter was more abstruse. It was Hugo, the enigmatic Englishman.

"Is he in La Paz now José?"

"He gets to La Paz in five, six days time, on the twenty fifth or sixth. Flies out on the twenty eighth. Doesn't give him much time."

"Oh he'll get to know his way around," remarked Hernando. "You'll see.... So how will we know who has won the bet? I mean we may not know." Hernando made it sound quite unsatisfactory. "At least not until you see Julia. Then you will tell me, eh José. That is how it will be, yes José?"

"Yes," I said convincingly.

3

A week passed, maybe a little more than a week. The routine of the island dug in, bedding me down with Sebastian and Quechua lessons and with Hernando and his papers. And between those activities, when I was by myself, I thought of Arnez and Castro and Julia and the Englishman, particularly the Englishman. I had him blending with the mountains, talking to Meiggs about rivets and buffers and gradients and money, particularly money. I would also wonder where he was and what he was doing and whether the postal services of Peru and Bolivia had combined to deliver my note and whether he had acted upon it.

Hernando wondered too. He would always ask, the question slotting in, finding a place after the now statutory inquiry about news, developments, happenings and events.

"I've worked it out and it must be soon José. I mean time is moving on and he only had a few days to act, so now's the time. You know that José?"

I smiled and nodded. I knew that. I knew it so well. I knew it like a birthday. The date lodged in my mind. The date Hugo departed for Brazil. I reminded Hernando. "He flies today."

"So if the letter has arrived and worked, he will have visited Julia, eh José? And I will be ten sols better off. Do you want to pay up now José?" His confidence was strong and vibrant. It seemed difficult to dislodge or undermine it. "He has acted José, you know that? I can sense it. I really can."

I moved up on the bed. We were in my hut. It was a hot day and I had the door and the window open. The avenue of air encouraged a throughput of breeze. I breathed out and found a more comfortable position. "I hope you're right," I muttered, settling again.

"José I am sure. I saw you together. I saw the mutual respect."

"Really?" I smiled. "We'll see," I said diffidently. "Now why are you here?"

"You mean what have I got?" Hernando beamed. "A paper. Look!" Hernando, who was sitting in his normal place on the ledge in front of the bed, reached down to a bag he had brought with him. "*El Commercio*. Look José. That Italian had it. Did I tell you about him? Arrived yesterday. You remember?"

I nodded, remembering Hernando's report the previous day on arrivals and departures.

"I saw him this morning down by the school. I asked him and he gave me this. One day old. That's all José. Yesterday's." Hernando waved the paper in front of me. I saw its headline. Electioneering. Something about a new party emerging and gaining some support. He threw me the paper.

"There's a new party that's doing well."

"In place of Izquierda?" asked Hernando eagerly.

I scanned the paper. I looked for policies, for decrees and promises, anything that would intimate the party's position. "Centre right," I suggested, "but then again." I read that the new party was against the austerity measures that the International Monetary Fund was promoting.

"Does it have a name?" Hernando shuffled uneasily.

"Seems to be called Cambio Ninety. It's led by an agricultural engineer of Japanese extraction."

"What? He's got no chance," decreed Hernando.

It was then I saw it. At the bottom of page two, sandwiched between stories of arms smuggling in Colombia and of trouble at a carnival in Brazil. Taxi driver killed was the headline. The story told of a taxi being riddled with bullets in the wealthy southern sector of La Paz. It said the passenger survived but had head injuries and was said to be comfortable at a private hospital nearby. It was then the story really hit me. I read it silently. "The passenger, a British subject working for Airbus Industrie, was due to fly out to Brazil tomorrow. Police chief Cabreto said he would ensure that further details of the shooting would be announced at a press conference early tomorrow."

"A British subject....Airbus Industrie...." I considered the words making sure I had got them sorted in my mind before I read them out loud. My concentration seemed to disarm Hernando. He fidgeted, seemingly shaken by my quietness.

"The Englishman?" questioned Hernando, his face blank and disturbed, taking in the details, assembling pictures. "No," he uttered understanding the sense of the stream of words.

"It's unbelievable," I said speaking slowly. "Head injuries. South La Paz. A taxi riddled with bullets. He's worse than they're saying."

"You think?

"Don't you? He won't survive."

"Oh José we don't know," objected Hernando. He sensed I hadn't fully taken in the words, that I was chasing after them trying to tune into their rhythms, picking out key stresses and signs. "José you can't tell from that. We'll have to find out."

"How?" I asked suddenly, sensing that Hernando might be right, that the guile of journalism was unfathomable to me. What was the slant of the story?, I asked myself. Perhaps they're trying to make it graver than it is, employing a contagion that makes the grimness seem so clear. The surrounding stories from Colombia, Paraguay and Brazil managed that: so many events, so many ghastly events, so much tragedy.

"How?" mused Hernando. "Easy. I'll have to go. That's it. I'll find out." He moved off the ledge.

"Go? What do you mean go?"

"I'll go back with Roberto, back to Puno. I'll get a paper. I'll get two papers. Today's and first thing tomorrow I'll get tomorrow's paper."

"But what about me? What can I do?" There was a sense of panic in my voice. My mind still hadn't freed me. The message remained the same.

"You? What can you do? You 'll have to wait, wait until this time tomorrow. One day José. You'll be OK."

With each reading of the story, the more I came to mistrust the words. A shooting, a death, a foreign national injured. It was enough for a paragraph, but little more, so why did it merit an appearance on a second day? What else was there to say?

The protraction seemed to kill off Hugo. I convinced myself that in the interim he had died. I jolted back on my bed and cried and replayed conversations picking on moments when I seemed to break through and something sank in, something that suggested we could get on, that friendship beckoned. And it had seemed to. I hadn't been deluding myself. It wasn't all about finishing the painting and him moving on. I believed that. Yet that was academic. The Englishman had gone. He had joined Castro, my teacher, and Michael, the doctor, and Tomos, the young *cadre*. My mind gave them all a last breath. Each was significant. And they helped me as I thought of them, reminding me of what death meant, of how they had affected me. Of course Castro dominated. He was the greatest influence. Educating me. And introducing me to art: the art of the church in Chuschi. That had fascinated me. I had felt the presence of beauty, man-made beauty, created by man in adoration. And it had been adored, really adored. By me. And by Castro, whispering over my shoulder, saying, "You may be an artist. An artist. Someone who produces art."

He made it sound like being a baker or a steelworker, a manufacturer. I had thought it was all about processes but as soon as I walked into the church I knew of the complications: the inspirations. It was like setting foot in another country. The paintings were like a new sun streaming down. They shone in my eyes. And I squinted, looking hard, taking it all in before settling my gaze on the south facing wall. I liked that best. I particularly liked the plaster which was flaking, leaving all the colour of old paint peeping through like covered over graffiti. Other days, other ways, I had thought.

"Hey if you like Chuschi you should go to Ayacucho" suggested Castro. "And San Blas. You should go there. San Blas's in Cuzco."

"Cuzco," I purred. I had heard so much of Cuzco. Cuzco, the navel of the earth. Cuzco, the capital where Manco Capac held court and the Spanish were victorious in 1534. I knew it all. Castro had been thorough. But San Blas? I hadn't heard of San Blas.

"There's a magnificent pulpit." Castro smiled, a huge rolling smile that could collapse like a wave and spread itself. "It is supported by carvings of all the great heathens. The traitors of the Catholic Church. Martin Luther, Henry the Eighth of England."

"Henry of England," I said with relish. We had moved such a distance. I couldn't work it out.

"They're all there. And at the top is a skull."

"A carved skull?"

"No. A real skull. The artist's skull. What praise eh? And what a sacrifice. To be part of your own sculpture."

"He wanted that? I mean to be part of it."

Castro laughed. He cleared his throat, pulling a face that made his eyes seem piercing as though he were enduring pain. "No. I'm joking. I shouldn't do that."

"But...." I stuttered. I was intrigued. I wanted to know. "So what's his skull doing on top? I mean where's the rest of his body?" Something about the light in the church gave Castro's face a sheen of a look. It emphasised an expression which told me I should have guessed what had happened.

"The Spanish killed him," he said bluntly.

"Why? Didn't they like his work?"

"They loved his work."

"So why did they kill him?"

"They thought he might copy it. They wanted it to be unique so to be sure, just as he was about to finish it, probably the very day he was applying the finishing touches, they killed him."

Hernando came straight to Sebastian's compound when he returned. I was standing on the top step that led up to the path waiting for him. I should have been having lunch, but I couldn't eat. I had looked at a vegetable omelette on a plastic plate, but it had seemed too much like a sulking face. I had cut off a corner, taken one mouthful and had given it up.

Hernando was breathless when he arrived. He had tried to run the last twenty yards. "I have them José. I have the papers. Yesterday's and today's. Come on, come on," he said, urging me to follow him to the table. He laid out the papers. "Do we want to know José? Do we really want to know? I mean we could pretend he's gone, I mean gone back to Europe. We could pretend he's well."

"But he's not well. We know he's not well." I spoke over the nonsense. "He's injured, badly injured. We need to find out." I breathed in deeply. "Look what I'm saying is you can't sweep what you don't like away. It's real. The car. The bullets. The dead driver. That's how it is."

"OK José. OK. Go on then." There was a touch of resignation in Hernando's voice. It was saying goodbye, registering the grief of a death that was unexpected. "Let's get it over with."

I picked up the first paper. I scanned page one and page two and then three and four before returning to page two. I found an index. Foreign news page seven it said. But there was nothing there. "Nothing in the foreign news," I told Hernando.

"Nothing about the police statement? There must be José, there must be. Try that bit where you found it yesterday."

There it was. There it was. Englishman stable, said the headline. "He's OK," I said excitedly.

"The Englishman?"

"Hugo's stable."

"I knew it. I told you José. I told you."

"He's no longer in danger," I continued to reveal more and more detail. "Police Chief Cabreto suspects robbery is the motive."

"Robbery?"

"He's warning visitors to take care. And it says...." I stopped suddenly. Something struck me. Some little detail, something struck a chord.

"Yes José?"

"He says not to venture to remote parts of the city."

"Remote parts? He was in a suburb. Remote parts," laughed Hernando.

It was the address that had shaken me. I kept quiet about it. I didn't want to worry Hernando or allow him to link what he knew with the scene of the crime. An alleyway off Avenida Arce. I read the report again. Avenida Arce, a main thoroughfare, it said. An artery of the southern, wealthy suburbs. Avenida Arce. It was the address Jorge had given me. It was where Julia was living.

Was it coincidence? How could it be? What were the odds? I should have asked Hernando, I should have told him that he had won his bet. But I couldn't believe that. Was my assessment that far out? Or had the Englishman really taken to the island and me? Perhaps he had. Yes, perhaps he had.

I walked and walked, moving around the island thinking of nothing but Hugo and the accident in the road where Julia is living. Where Julia is living, I'd repeat over and over. Coincidence? It had to be. It is a main road, but why would the Englishman be in the southern suburbs. Passing through? Visiting some wealthy friend? Visiting an exile perhaps? I didn't know. How could I know? I could only speculate. But the connection seemed so strong. He must have been looking for her, searching for her. My letter must have arrived. It must have told him where she was. And he must have stayed at Hotel Milton. He must have kept his word.

So he was robbed going out to see her. That made sense. The dangers of South America crowding in unexpectedly, the dangers striking at a most inopportune moment for him and me. I should go and see him. I should turn up and talk and smile because he had been willing to help me. Would that be dangerous? What about Julia? She could help, but would she know? If he was on his way to see her when the robbery occurred, she wouldn't know anything of him. But what if he had called, what if he had seen her and they had spoken and laughed and he had charmed her?

I shrugged. There were so many possibilities. I had hoarded all the papers Hernando had handed on to me. I picked them up at random. The reporting attracted me now. I used it to corroborate all my doubts about what had happened to Hugo. I read back through stories Hernando and I had picked at, the rarefied worlds that drew pictures in our minds. The power of that was so incisive. It pitched into my mind and fixed images. In particular I recalled the agriculture minister drinking his soup, the way Hernando had decorated the restaurant and found the chef disappointed and the way the next day the misreporting had scrambled that and reconstructed the murder scene in the open air with a crowd of well-wishers straining to say hello and welcome the minister at the very time that a bullet floated above them and sank into the minister's skull.

We could believe so much, I thought, again considering Julia and Hugo and their proximity when Hugo ended up slumped in a car that was riddled with bullets. There was so much opportunity for speculation and misinterpretation there. It was a reporter's paradise or hell. I wasn't sure which. I shook my head and turned to another paper, but something about another story, about the terrorist shooting of the government minister in Puno, drew me back. The date. The date of that killing. December 8th. The day after my talk in Lima. I hadn't made the link before, but I seemed to have an instinct now for connections. December 8th, my mind repeated. I was triumphant then knowing I couldn't have been implicated, so there was nothing of substance in the link. I was away, out of it. I couldn't have been suspected. I would have been if I had been in Puno on the day of the killing. I knew that. It made sense. But I was in Lima so it was left to all the other Sendero sympathisers to shake and shudder and wonder if they would be suspected. Sympathisers like Jorge. Yet he hadn't been threatened. At least he hadn't mentioned being interrogated or visited.

But why hadn't he mentioned the killing? I closed my eyes. I had to concentrate now, but Jorge and the railway station and the walk via the video centre to the port seemed so distant. It seemed part of another world. And I was outside of it. Like a newspaper report or a television play, it was something I had viewed not experienced, something I had been engrossed in. Like a good book. It was in that sort of sphere. It kept me trying to recall whether Jorge had mentioned the killing. I was sure the first I heard of it was when Hernando had presented me with a paper to read. Yet, at times, Jorge's words were like whispers and I had been numb, some emotional pull dragging me away. All that talk of invasion, intrusion. I didn't understand. Perhaps he had mentioned it then. Perhaps he had slipped it in and left it to develop in its own way and in its own time.

Or perhaps it was outside of his remit, nothing to do with Sendero, but all down to a renegade, a disillusioned something or the other. A farmer, perhaps? Or a local politician. A man with a grudge. A deranged man. A long list of possibilities began to roll in. Yet they didn't mean much because I knew the usual suspects would be considered. That meant Sendero, that meant Jorge, that meant Julia. Julia! I had forgotten Julia. It couldn't have been her. Not Julia. Besides Jorge would know if the call at my house was related to the killing. He would have told me. He would have said they suspected Julia. He would have explained it away and left me free and alone in Puno with my doubts and worries. That's what he would have done. Isn't it?

It had to be the talk. It had to. There was something in it that was too critical, too condemning; something I should have written out, something Jorge should have seen. "You can't say that." I knew his words; and his frown, the shift in his eyes that displayed surprise. He said it frequently and I overreacted, swiping at the script with a pen, saying, "OK...What if I say..." I'd modify it. I'd never omit. I'd just adapt, fine tuning the tone, softening the sarcasm or intensifying the wit. I'd be persistent, keeping on and on until Jorge would nod nervously.

So what was it? Something in the content, something farcical, something macabre, something that would bring disapproval and impel intervention. But what? I ran through it. The start. The core. The content. It was about levels. The local and the national. The diversity of power. The prevailing idea was that Sendero was invading localities, taking over villages and shanty towns and imposing new laws and orders through committees that sanctioned punishment beatings and trials. It was disciplining society and the government acquiesced knowing it could always hold Sendero at that level, that it could punish it if it wanted to and drive it out when necessary. I suppose I was suggesting a new status quo. But what was controversial in that? I couldn't find anything. It was direct and true. How could it have condemned me?

Perhaps it was time to see Jorge. He could help. He could eliminate distractions and provide some explanations and confirmations. I needed clarification. I needed the truth. My talk or the killing in Puno? I moved from one to the other recalling moments in my talk and then conversations with Hernando. It had to be the talk. It had to. But why hadn't Jorge mentioned the killing? It was so fresh, so crucial. Why hadn't it placed itself adjacent to the discussion of a crack down? Hernando would have made the link. "Sendero," I remembered the way he apportioned blame as I read the story from the paper. "Sendero". And I had run through the squads, the method of execution. The assassination squad. The distraction squad. The observation squad. And the tidying-up squad. I had left them out at the time. The tidying-up squad. Omission by design? Perhaps? The tidying-up squad that swept in, like a cat crossing a garden, after the shot had broken the silence, after the blood had soiled the scene. How could I have forgotten that squad? Perhaps because normally it comprised one person, more often that not a woman. A woman. Something about that shocked me. A woman. I knew why, I knew that Sendero chose women for that role because of the idea of equality. A positive discrimination. An overemphasis to try to suggest balance. It meant some of the hardest, most savage people in Sendero were women.

5

The following day I headed for Puno. Hernando was shocked when he saw me. He was talking to Javier, standing outside the concrete hut that seemed to have placed itself on the jetty.

"Hey José, you off? Where you going?" Hernando seemed concerned, alarmed by the way it looked as though I was attempting to match the secrecy of Hugo's departure. "A day away, eh José?" Something tempered his tone. Perhaps my lack of baggage. My intention was just to see Jorge, to see him and return to the island. I needed some explanations. Ten minutes with Jorge would satisfy me.

"That's it," I said, "a day away."

"Hey José you know what you're doing? If you want a day out come with me out onto the lake. You could paint." Hernando shook his head, emphasising the option. "Ah perhaps next time, eh José. When I've got a paper."

"Tomorrow," I suggested.

"Yes. Hey the forecast is good. The lake will be flat. It will be beautiful. You know what I mean José?"'

It sounded so persuasive. I watched him move away. He seemed satisfied with my manner and conversation. He sensed no danger. He knew I would return. A wave said so. An extravagant wave. It said OK have fun, enjoy your trip. It said see you tomorrow.

Jorge lived four hundred yards from the railway station in Puno, up a slight rise, near a school on the road that continued on, out of town, past the prison on its way to Juliaca. I knew the road well. I had taken it every Tuesday on my way to my outreach course. I had passed Jorge's house each time and always glanced its way. The curtains shut. The paint fading. It was such a contrast to the fine housing nearer to the station, the houses guarded by soldiers, flying Peruvian flags with a Mercedes car on the driveway and a pet llama on the grassed gardens. The local administrators lived there. The judges and council leaders and army chiefs. Jorge brought Sendero to them. He boasted that he was on first name terms with most of them, that he would see them at his local *panederia* and *farmacia*.

I knocked his door softly and stepped back. I wasn't sure what I would say, whether I would stay calm and clear or feel trapped and hurt and lose my cool in some rearguard wildness. I waited and waited and tapped on the door again. I heard movement. I saw a shape through the glass coming towards me.

"José!" The gasp revealed a high level of surprise. It was followed by a sweep of a look that took in the pavement and the road and the traffic. It identified pedestrians. "Come in, come in."

I walked into a long room. A Christian nativity scene, a leftover from Christmas was still in the window. Books partitioned it off, sectioning it from the sofa that faced a television that was on with its sound turned down. Beyond the sofa a round table was made untidy by cups of coffee, used cups with drip marks down their sides and sprinkles of sugar around their bases.

"Tea? Coffee?" Jorge asked. I wondered why the obvious question hadn't followed, why Jorge made it seem that I called regularly. I took in his smile. It surprised me. It disturbed me.

"No. No coffee. I need to talk. I need some answers."

"Answers? About Julia? I sent a note. Last week, I sent a note. I said I would. Soon we'll arrange a visit."

I nodded. "But what about the killing? Why didn't you mention the killing?" I didn't hold back. I wanted this over with. "Why?" I repeated. "I mean all that consideration about crack downs and timing and my role in it. My role in it! Come on."

I watched Jorge scratch his head. He forced a smile. "Killing?" he asked slowly.

"The assassination of the government minister. Remember? On the day after my lecture in Lima. A couple of days before my return. It was that they were sniffing about after, wasn't it? They wanted the killer."

Jorge laughed. "No, it wasn't us. They know that. That's why I didn't mention it. It was nothing to do with us and they knew it. I mean they know everything. They know as much as we do." He slipped off his shoe and played with it, his toe picking it up and putting it down. "It was nothing to do with us. And you know that. You know we wouldn't have allowed all the photographs, all the eye witnesses. You know that José." Another laugh, a snigger. "You must think we're losing our touch. The assassination of the government minister," he scoffed.

"I don't for one minute think that," I said trying to offer a sense of reassurance. I wanted to lure a false sense of security.

"It was someone with a grudge. One person. Not Sendero."

"Not ex-Sendero? Someone who has got used to killing. Someone discarded. Someone who wants to fight on, who wants to prove a point."

"No." He shook his head.

"You sure? You sure it wasn't somebody currying favour."

"Killing people!" Jorge swept his hand through his hair. "You don't curry favour by killing someone."

"Someone you want out of the way?"

"José you need to view us more positively."

"What about somebody who just feels excluded. Someone who wants to fight, but is no longer wanted."

"Speculation. Oh come on José. That's speculation."

"Perhaps." I sighed. I felt frustrated. It seemed that I was getting nowhere, that Jorge's evasion was accomplished and that I was too indirect, too peripheral. I needed to fix on something, to be specific. "So it wasn't Julia?"

"Julia!"

"Why not?"

He laughed, an unlikely lingering laugh, a mocking laugh. Its sound crunched into me. It emphasised the outrage; it ridiculed. And, with my confidence crashing, I fidgeted. That seemed to incite him to continue. He shook his head. He sniggered. It seemed he didn't need to say anything.

"When was she last active?" I asked.

"Julia? Three years ago."

"You don't use her?"

"No. No we don't."

I shook my head. I didn't believe him. I couldn't believe him because that would have meant returning to another analysis of my speech. I knew every nuance of that now. I had dissected it and put it back together and even reformulated sections that hadn't worked well and had bothered me in spare moments during the crossing and back on the island when I was alone in my hut. The speech hadn't offended. I was sure of that, as sure as I could be.

"Listen, don't think about it," urged Jorge. "It wasn't us. OK? It was some madman. It's one of those things."

"One of those things," I scoffed.

"You know."

"OK. So we don't know."

"Right," said Jorge putting great emphasis on the word. It told me the conversation had nowhere else to go. It was stranded, stuck in a groove. Politeness would follow, but I wasn't ready for that. I hadn't come all the way from Taquile to be tackled by politeness, by cups of tea and talk of college politics. There was more in my armoury, more trickery and devices and cravings. I took a breath and wondered what to draw on. The Englishman, I thought, the Englishman. The Englishman in La Paz. I didn't know how Jorge would react to that. I couldn't predict what he knew of the car that was riddled with bullets and the dead driver and the hospitalised

Englishman.

"Of course there's been another killing." I waited for the reaction. I had to look carefully, scrutinising every flinch, every fold of skin, every roll of an eye. I knew Jorge occasionally gave himself away, that he was prone to lapses. I took in the look he gave me, the long look that culminated in a small laugh. It was nervous like a tic.

"What killing?" he managed to say. I said nothing. "You scan papers José. You look for things. You ascribe blame. You say Sendero, Sendero, Sendero. But listen, you're so far away, you don't know. Understand? You can never really know enough and your instincts are not your strongest point. They've never been a strong point of yours. You know that." He wiped his nose, pinching his nostrils and sniffing. The flourish ended with a shake of his head.

"There was a man on the island."

"Look José I really haven't the time."

"No, no. This is important."

"A man?"

"Yes, an Englishman." I saw it then. A touch of shock. Electric. A shiver. As though the connection is cold. Like ice. I didn't imagine it. I couldn't have imagined it. It was there, in his face, glowing, illuminating. It was as though it had escaped, not been jettisoned or discarded. It was involuntary. I had caught him, shocked him. His frown, the shift in his eyes told me something. Something I was offering was new to him. New and significant. New and shocking. It built on his knowledge. It attached itself to what he knew. "The Englishman was on the run. Like me. Look, what I'm saying is we got on."

"Oh no," bayed Jorge. He knew what was coming. "So you spoke to him. You told him about Lima and the speech and why you were on the island."

"He was safe."

"How do you know? How do you know? You should never open up. You know that."

"And I told him about Julia. Julia, my wife, remember?" I reminded Jorge of the story he had drilled into me. I just let it slip that she was in La Paz. And he said he was going to La Paz. So I painted a picture for him and he said he'd go and see Julia. I suppose we did a deal. He said he'd just see her and say hello and say that he'd seen

279

me, that I was OK and thinking of her."

"But we do that. You know we do. We keep her informed."

"Yeh, yeh. Like you keep me informed."

"José it's been a few weeks, a difficult few weeks." His face told me he couldn't comprehend such criticism. He shook his head and blew one breath up and over his face. He peeled off his pullover, rolling down the sleeves of his shirt before doing up the buttons on the cuffs.

"Then I see it in *El Commercio* that the Englishman, my friend, has been in a car crash in La Paz. It looks bleak. The driver is dead; the Englishman is badly injured, head injuries."

"I'm sorry."

"Oh I could take that. But then I read that the car had crashed into a wall on Avenida Arce, the road which according to the letter you kindly sent, is where Julia is living. So what is that? Don't tell me, you're going to say it's a coincidence."

"It must be."

"I thought that. But I'm not sure any more."

Jorge was slow in responding. He cast a glance my way that suggested he couldn't match my dreaming, that his bog-standard academic life couldn't match long days on an island where there was time to draw up tales and work them towards a suitable end. "OK, so you think Julia shot the driver, yes?" His laugh made it sound quite preposterous.

"It's as good as any other explanation I can come up with."

"Why? Why should she do it?"

"No idea. I've absolutely no idea. And I guess we'll never know."

"Never know?"

"Well she'll deny it. Wouldn't you?"

"And the Englishman? He may have an idea."

"Traumatic amnesia. He can't remember a thing. At least that's what the papers have been saying."

"Well.....really?....." The two words Jorge proclaimed made his relief clear. I smiled. It was there. I saw it. I felt it. He controlled it quickly, shaking his head, saying, "José, it's just coincidence. Believe me. I'd tell you if I knew anything about this. It's coincidence. I can assure you. It's just coincidence."

I walked away from Jorge's slowly. I didn't think of what he had said. I didn't analyse or mark his performance out of ten, though it did seem like a performance and the walk away down the hill, past the railway station and the market and the stadium was like a back-stage. It had an emptiness. I filled it with thoughts of Castro, Castro and San Blas. There was something appropriate about that. The art perhaps? Or the twist in the storyline. I remembered it so clearly. I pictured it. Me drawing, recreating shapes. The petals. The cracks and patches in the plaster on the wall of the church. The window over the door. The inlaid patterns in the wood of the door. The metal cross, the altar. I investigated it all. I understood it all. How the shapes worked, how they worked symbolically, practically.

"Can I see?" asked Castro when he found me in a dark corner of the church.

"It's raw. It's still," I said as he stared at the petals. "It's lacking the texture."

"Texture? You know some words. For a young boy you know some words."

"You taught them to me."

"Then you must stick with them and learn how to understand them. It will help your art."

I smiled. His words seemed like a new anthem. If only others thought like he did, if only others had the opportunities I had been granted. If only.... The dimensions of dreams and curses span away.

"You'll be a good artist," I heard him say. "Soon you will paint your own petals. That can't be bad, eh?"

"When?" I asked.

"When you've learnt. When you've got your own view. It will come. I can see that." He looked again at the drawing. "You know I used to draw. I used to paint too. I'm not sure I was any good. I thought I was. But I suppose we always think we're better than we are." Again he shrugged. He made it seem as though he thought his view inconsequential. "You should paint people," he said bluntly.

"People?" I directed the question as much to myself as Castro. I hadn't thought of people. There was more depth there. Like the layers beneath petals. The veins, the age, I thought, viewing his face.

"People hide things," he said. "And they give things away. Take me. There, you see?" He sensed my attention. "You see how it works.

I tell you about things, but not everything. I hold things back."

"Like what?" I asked.

"Like..." He paused to think. "Well like the skull at the Church in San Blas."

"The sculptor's skull," I said.

" I've told you one thing."

"The Spanish killing him to make the pulpit unique?"

"Yes. The Spanish. That's one story. But there is another."

"Another?"

"Yes. Another version. Another tale I suppose. A tale that says the artist fell while working on the final touches of the sculpture, that the flourish and joy of the last stroke of his chisel pulled him off balance and he fell from the gantry to the floor. He killed himself." Castro's hand waved down. It emphasised the fall. "As easy as that," he said slowly. "You judge," he added, walking away. "You work out what you want to believe, because that's what it often comes down to. Interpretations José, interpretations."

part eight

JOSE AND HUGO

1

I had never seen a hospital like it. Small rooms with carpets and flowers and easy chairs and prints on the wall. A Picasso in the Englishman's room, a late Picasso with dancing dryads and a Greek God-like figure playing a flute. Nineteen, two, fifty-six, I read, seizing the date and categorising the stage of Picasso's work. And below the print a coffee table and a kettle with cups and a saucer filled with sachets of coffee and sugar and dried milk. A potted plant sat alongside the sachets. A geranium.

I drew the room.

Then I leant forward and touched the clean sheet. It was so white. Not a mark on it. Not even a crease. A perfect white. The white an angel's wing would be. And on it lay the Englishman. It made him seem part of the perfection. It made me want to touch him. He seemed so beautiful. Lying there. The blond hair brushed back. The sunburnt face. It made me want to cradle him, to rock him, to communicate as best I could that there is support, that there is care, that there is understanding.

I drew the Englishman. I drew him well. I understood where the look on his face had come from, why it was vague, doubting, etched with concern, pain, bewilderment. I had a sense of what was lurking inside his mind. I sensed the thoughts and questions that built the geometry of the expression. And while I sketched I felt like a thief or a spy. Like a suspect being interviewed by the police. I was unsettled, nervous and looking around as though there were eyes on me, made up eyes, the eyes of the state perhaps or something much stronger, something like the eyes of my father's religion. They were hunting me, closing in so that I focused only on survival, on saying hello and planning my escape when I should have been confessing, when I should have been telling the Englishman what I had led him to. Instead, I looked over the bed and gazed out through the long window and thought only of hospitals, this hospital, this private hospital and the state hospitals in Cangallo and Puno, the hospitals I had previous experience of. A nose bleed and a broken finger. I thought of my reasons for having been to the hospitals. And to see Julia when she had cut her hand and some infection had pumped it up like a tyre. She had needed antibiotics then. The doctor had come to see me saying there were no antibiotics available in the hospital and that I would have to buy them outside from the vendors who operated at the roadside, that I had to depend on the black market to make her well.

"You're the friend from Peru?"

A doctor. A man in a white coat. He moved towards me and smiled as he began to do the things doctors do. He picked up the notes that were clipped to the end of the bed. I smiled; he nodded, shining a torch into Hugo's eyes. Hugo. I use the name. Hugo. No longer the Englishman. Now he is Hugo. For the sake of intimacy, of humanity. Hugo.

"He may well wake soon. The deep sleep is characteristic of the condition. He may remember you. He may not."

"His condition, is it serious?"

The doctor seemed to wonder how to respond. I could tell there were a number of manners available to him, all of which he had rehearsed thoroughly. He smiled and considered what he should say, then a small look, little more than a glance seemed to signify that he had made a decision. "Oh he is suffering from post traumatic amnesia."

"So there is no major damage?"

"Damage?" The doctor gave me a questioning look. It threatened sarcasm, but withdrew. "It depends on how you assess damage." Another look, a warmer look told me he had sensed the depth of my concern and approved of it. "He'll probably have difficulty accessing the accident or indeed details of what had happened in the hour or so prior to the accident."

"So we may never know?"

"Never know?"

"How it happened. The accident."

"The car he was in was shot at, haven't you heard?" The doctor seemed astounded. He must have wondered if I had just stepped off a plane, avoiding newspapers. Then tasks took over again. He filled in something on the notes. "He'll improve everyday," he said while writing. "There'll be symptomatic signs of recovery..... Little things....You know.... Like a baby taking a first step." He clicked the top of his pen and replaced it in the top pocket of his white coat. "And you may find him strange," he added, walking towards the door.

"Strange? What do you mean strange?"

"Well he'll probably comprehend all you say and he'll speak as much as he can. I mean that will be unaffected, but he may find articulation difficult. Most do. Some talk nonsense for weeks. Maybe months." Another smile followed as he opened the door and walked away leaving me alone again with Hugo.

★

I am putting together a picture. This is no doctor. This figure opposite me. The figure that sits and locks itself into a position and stares. Sometimes it seems as though it has moved away. It is almost out of sight, sitting there across the room, not contributing, just linking arms with the stillness. But it worries me. Something about it is disturbing. Perhaps the stillness itself. I wonder what is going on, whether it is thinking or staring or waiting. What is its purpose? What is it doing?

I listen. There is a sound. A slight sound. Like the gnashing of teeth, an eating sound. Or is it the rustling of clothes, the friction of sweater on shirt as an arm itches or a neck tilts? There is a smell too. Oranges. Juicy oranges. Winter oranges. The sweetest oranges. But the smell is too strong. It is too sweet, too artificial, too concentrated. Like squash. Like marmalade. And behind it the sound, the constant small sound. The essential sound. I begin to detest it. Go away, a voice in my mind says. Leave me alone.

I sleep.

And it is there when I wake up, though it is fainter and the rhythm is different. Something is breaking it up, some interference. Some competition. Some other function. Tears. I hear them. And I know them. I know them like a pet's bark. I know them like a friend's affectation. I just know them. But they go with dancing not stillness, with a hummed tune and the tap of shoes. They go with the sound of water. Or of a stove being primed. Or of the thud of digging in a field. They go with the lake. With the island. With the stiff shirt. The bloody stiff shirt.

"OK he's gone."

"What do you mean he's gone?"

"Your friend from Peru. You know. The guy who painted you a picture and put you in hospital. Your friend. Shit shirt."

"Stiff shirt."

"Yeh. He's got big balls that guy. I'll give him that. I mean he's even coming back tomorrow. Hey you've got to tell him. You've got to put him right."

"He's been here?"

"You know he's been here. You know what? You're playing on this, aren't you? All this amnesia shit."

"Traumatic amnesia."

"Yeh, yeh. Just don't try your tricks on me OK? I mean I'm no Peruvian shithead. I'm pure American me. Made in the U.S. of A." Popeye pauses and grins, examining me up and down. "Oh shit look at you. I mean what the hell were you thinking of? Dumping yourself in all this shit. Chincheros and now Avenida Arce. So where next eh? I mean are you accident prone or what? You know what your trouble is? You don't recognise your enemies. That's what."

"My enemies?"

"Yeh. Hey none of this would have happened if you had just spotted who was dangerous. I mean you've got to assess. You can't just take everything at face value. And that's what you do. You believe any ol' shit. An' you know what happens then? People run rings around you, that's what. Listen you got to reveal. You got to uncover. You got to see. Really see."

"What? What have I got to see?"

"Motives, that's what. What people are hiding away. What they're really after."

"Motives!" I laugh. This is ridiculous. I normally respect Popeye's zest; I normally admire his insight. But this is too much. He is saying I'm being manipulated. Me! I am the manipulator. Can't he see that? Can't he remember how I charmed the stiff shirt, how he was taken in?

"You see I knew my enemies."

288

"We've been through this."

"We have?"

"Napoleon."

"Napoleon! Hell no. Hey, see? You don't listen. That's your trouble. You assume. You presume. But you don't tune in."

I'm too tired and too confused. I let him go on. I listen to his point. I know he had problems too, but how he dealt with the difficulties that confronted him is known only from hearsay and tittle tattle and the long stories that wind themselves around the myth of the man. Whether he fretted or cried, whether he came down hard or just swept his problems away isn't clear. What is clear is the way he hid himself behind a line of bureaucrats and officials, some of whom were aggressive manipulators like his brother John.

"Listen, you know what your trouble is."

"You've just told me."

"No. I'm generalising now. Generalising, OK?" He waits for me to respond. "Your trouble is you want to be a big boy when you're still in short pants. And that makes you look kind of silly. What you gotta do is shake it up a little first. You know what I mean? You've gotta change things, get things done. Then you get the protection, you know the boys who deflect the shit this way and that. Boys like brother John. With him around I stayed so squeaky fuckin' clean. So you've got a way to go yet. Fight, pay, charm, remember? Fight, pay, charm."

I remember. But it doesn't always help. I remembered in Chincheros, but the difficulty is deciding. Fight, pay, charm. Fight, pay, charm. It isn't obvious. So choosing becomes the key. Being able to choose is crucial. Popeye never mentions that. He makes it sound so easy. Think of shit is all he says, meaning think of how you act to sort things out. Learn from experience, his voice is saying, learn from your mistakes.

"So if it wasn't Napoleon, who was it?"

"My enemy? Oh that's easy. I mean there were a lot of opponents but you cope with them. You just outwit them. But enemies? Well one springs to mind, Davila."

"Davila?"

"Don Tomos Emilia Davila," Popeye says very precisely. He pulls a face as thought the name leaves a nasty taste on the tongue.

"So who was he?"

"Exactly," laughs Popeye. "Who was he?" His tone emphasises the level of historical significance accorded to Davila. "He was a nobody. That's who he was. But he thought he was somebody. So I had to sort that out. I had to put him in his place."

"What did he do?"

"Have I told you about the Moquegua line? No? well it's a small railroad. I built it in 1872."

I had read that Moquegua was different from anything Meiggs had previously encountered. Small not large. Coastal not upland. Rich land not poor land.

"Davila owned a big chunk of the land in the area. He didn't want the railroad crossing his land, so he thought he'd sabotage it."

"Sabotage it?"

"Yeh. Oh he was clever. I'll give him that."

"In what way?"

"Well he did what I'd have done. He infiltrated my organisation. He took a job with me. Now that's smart."

"He spied on you?"

"Yeh. He dug up all sorts of dirt. The next thing I knew he was writing in the papers saying I'd defrauded the state of two million sols. Damn cheek. It was at least four! So what did I think? Derail it, that's what. Let the state move in. Attack me, attack the state. That's the beauty of it see? Because I've got it, I've fuckin' got it. I mean it's sort of lying out in front of me. Like a dog, a big ol' dog showing me its tummy and I'm tickling it. And if I stop tickling, it wonders what the hell's happening. So the state snaps back saying what a good boy I am. Salt of the earth that boy Meiggs, ol' Don Enrique, salt of the fuckin' earth. An I guess that was OK for a while. I mean it worked, but that Davila he kept coming back, he kept writing in the papers. So I had to stop him once and for all. I had to sort him out. You do that if a guy doesn't get the message. You hit him hard. Just once. On the chin. Smack on the fuckin' chin. And that meant a backhander."

"You bought him off."

"Davila? You think I....Oh hell no. I wouldn't give him money. Davila!" Popeye laughs. "Hey come on, I've got standards.... You don't get it do you? Fight, pay, charm," he emphasises. "Let's spell it out for you. Davila, he's the baddie, you know the shithead who's after me, he approaches the judiciary with all this shit about me defrauding the state. Nice job *Senor* Davila, eh? But whether a case of defrauding the state goes to court is determined by.... wait for it... the president, yeh the fuckin' president."

"Oh I get it."

"So did Mr. President," gloats Popeye. "A big bag full of it. Fight, pay, charm, eh? So for some reason, Mr President decided not to act. He just sort of sat on it. He smothered it. He killed it off. Killed ol' Davila off too. Sort of stonewalled him away. Oh there were a few more newspaper articles, but they were old news, back on the inside, out of harm's way. He couldn't hurt me there. He kept trying. I admired that. Hey you know I think I even sent him a Christmas card that year, just to say no hard feelings *Senor* Davila. Just to show him who was boss. I like sending Christmas cards to gooks. Makes you feel sort of warm inside, you know what I mean?"

"I don't want to see you, you understand?"

"Hugo I have come a long way. I am concerned. I read about you in the paper. I needed to come, to check you are OK."

"And now you've seen me and I'm fine. So now you can go."

The stiff shirt shakes his head. "No you're not OK. Not yet. You will be. But you must see. You must see that I had to come..... Look what I'm saying is you can't trust newspapers. They say what they want to say and when they want to say it."

"And what I'm saying is I want you to go. Understand?" I am blunt. I am clear. I will take in no defence. There is no negotiation. My mind is composed, steady.

"But you need a friend."

"That's as maybe."

"Someone you can talk to. Someone who considers you, who wants to help. You'll be lost here, don't you see? You must see. Hugo, I want to help."

No pleading will draw me; no manipulation will work when my mind is set, as it is. Exclude him, that's what Popeye was intimating. All that talk of enemies, of recognising enemies. Don Tomos Emilio

Davila, I think. Don Tomos Emilio Davila. "Listen you can go voluntarily or I can press this button. That alerts the staff. I will ask them to call for security. They will remove you. With force, if necessary." The statement is piercing. It hurts. It makes it clear just how far I am prepared to go. I watch him shake his head. The movement is slow and considered. He cannot comprehend. He is shocked. That is clear. I like that. I like to know I can still surprise him. I can surprise myself too. But there is one concern that I have. I move to quash it. "And don't blame this on my hospitalisation," I say with some authority.

"Your hospitalisation?"

"My illness. This is me. Rational old me. It's got nothing to do with any trauma."

"Traumatic amnesia. Loss of memory. Loss of articulation."

"You know all about it?"

"I've been reading up."

"Then you'll know there's no loss of reason." I sigh. I let him know I am impatient. I also want to prove my rationality. That gives me a brief. "You know I've covered for you."

"What?"

"I've put the police off. I've stopped them asking questions about your appearance here."

"The police?"

"What did you expect? I mean you arrive here immediately after I've been involved in a murder incident. You arrive. A Peruvian. My only friend."

"So what have you said?" asks the stiff shirt. He seems quite shaken as though he hasn't considered the implications of his arrival in La Paz.

"Who's he? That's what they asked. Wouldn't you? I mean if you were the police."

"I suppose."

"I mean you were hot headed. Slipping into Bolivia, turning up here....."

The stiff shirt takes his time responding. I imagine the analysis, quick thoughts rolling through his mind. He would be thinking of the police and the border and his fellow sympathisers and terrorists, how there are so many potential hazards and pitfalls. I wonder if he knows his enemy. I recall Popeye's words. "Don Tomos Emilio Davila. Leaves a nasty taste on the tongue boy. A real nasty taste."

"What do you mean slipping into Bolivia?"

"You entered illegally. You must have."

"Why should I do that? I am not suspected."

He is convincing. I wonder what has changed. "But all that time on the island. You were hiding."

"Mistakenly." He smiles and opens his hands as though he is dismissing something. "I called at Puno on the way through. I saw a guy called Jorge, a friend. He told me it was a mistake."

"But your speech."

"The door-to-door search in Puno was nothing to do with my speech."

"Door to door?"

"Yes. They called at a number of homes. I am free Hugo. I am free."

I do not know how to react. I wonder what the revelation tells me, what it really tells me, but the gaps in my knowledge caused by the amnesia frustrate me. I know I cannot think clearly, that I am not the force I should be.

"I think you should go now." My hand hovers over the call button. I will press it. I will. And the stiff shirt senses it: he retreats quickly.

2

Julia sang to me. She clutched her old teddy bear and used the tune provided by a radio to back her through a song. The shrill voice. The child's voice. The rhythm pulsing through her hands bouncing the teddy bear on her knees. Her pretty knees. And those shapely legs, long for a Peruvian woman with ankles that angle in and draw eyes to the muscular tone, the perfection. Her loveliness seemed to strike me more than ever, that and the comfort of familiarity, of the bonds family brings. They were things I had missed, really missed.

"Great," I said when she finished. I hugged her. The embrace made her smile. She felt the familial warmth too. It made me wonder how I could curtail it and turn on the peace with the weight of inquiry. Perhaps I wouldn't or couldn't. I certainly felt disinclined to disturb the lightness of the moment.

"It's so good to see you."

"And you." I was always clumsy with expressions of emotion.

"You been OK? Still reading those books?" She laughed behind a sprinkle of tears, light tears, tears that seemed to blend with the words and smiles and explain them. "I would take your books, remember?"

"And read them."

"Take in your paraphrasing more like. I didn't understand them."

"You didn't understand the jargon."

"And you didn't like the jargon."

"Right."

We smiled again and held hands and she cried and I stared into her face as though I were scrutinising a document searching for a blemish or a word that was too light or too severe, a word that stood out when it should have gone unnoticed. Nothing. I believed the tears. This was joy. This was softness.

I nodded. "Nice room," I volunteered. She had taken me to her room, a small room, a single bed and a chair and a television. The room was painted white. Perhaps it was that that made me think that it was like Hugo's hospital room. All it needed was a coffee machine and flowers. Geraniums.

"Hey don't we have friends in high places," remarked Julia. A lightness returned.

"Don't we?" I said uneasily, taking in the wealth, the comfort, the pleasure it gave. It seemed a little reticent in her room, but I had seen its glories in the hall and the stairs. I had felt the lush pile of the carpets. "You look good. I mean well. You look well." Again my words were clumsy.

"I'm fine.... Hey how's mum? How's dad? How's Chuschi?"

I shrugged.

"Oh shit. Shit, shit, shit," she exclaimed, realising that I, too, had been inconvenienced, that I too hadn't escaped the crackdown. It made her seem self centred, too focused to understand the wider dislocations and unrest, the way others had been implicated and suspected of something. Anything, I thought, considering how it had been, the way the authorities threatened a brutality that could only be resisted by lying low in safe houses or fleeing to mountains or forests or islands.

"Were you shocked? When you had to get away? I mean I was in school. I got a call and someone said there was a car waiting. I knew what that meant."

"A call?" I knew this was the equivalent of Jorge in the railway station, but I wanted to hear more. I wanted details. It was the only way I would understand. I had to construct the widest possible picture of what had gone on. Details, I smiled. It was the same with books. I had a thirst for detail. If I read a novel, I would want details. I would want to feel that I was there, that I was part of the action.

"Yes. The deputy head came to my room. You know him? Tall man, moustache, a scar on his cheek. Anyway he's one of us. And I knew what would happen when he told me, that I'd come here."

"You did?"

"Oh yes. I know the escape routes. I knew I'd come here. I was so annoyed."

"Annoyed?" I almost gasped at her choice of words. Was she accusing me? Was she saying you fool, how could you do it? The speech at La Contute began to roll again in my mind. I stopped it. It was clear. The speech was fine. I almost gritted my teeth. It wasn't the speech.

"I was annoyed with the killing, the assassination. I mean it was so unprofessional, so hazardous."

"A madman?"

"Oh God yes."

It was then I began to retreat. She's so professional, I thought, impressed, knowing I couldn't ask her directly not after all she had said. But I could ask about Hugo, because I was sure she wouldn't be aware of his link with me, that as long as Jorge hadn't sent a message, she would be shocked by our connection. I built myself up to tell her. I had to keep my eyes on her. I had to watch her face. It would flinch. I knew that. Something would convey the shock.

"So why did you come here? I mean you're not a great traveller. Apart from conferences that is."

"I go to Chuschi twice a year."

"Exactly."

"I get travel sick. I hate buses, I hate planes. And you know what? I hate boats too. That's one thing I've discovered in the last couple of weeks." I paused. She had offered me the perfect question; this was the way in.

"So?"

"Oh a friend of mine got hurt," I said quite casually.

"Here? In La Paz?"

"A car accident. Actually not far from here. Just around the corner."

"Really?" She didn't trust my words. I could tell that. Her tone conveyed it. She must have wondered where they were leading her. Perhaps she sensed a ruse. "Come on. You've just come to see me."

"It's partially that."

"You mean it's mainly that."

"OK it's mainly that." I smiled admiring the manipulation, the sparkle of her words, their lure. I normally moved towards them, but now I had to draw away. I could sense that she hadn't worked it out yet, that she hadn't connected the man in the alley with me. I could see it in her eyes. There was still wonder there. Not shock. Not distaste. I had to make it plain now. I had to move the wonder on and change the emphasis. "This is daft," I remarked resuming. "I mean I make a friend on the island."

"Just the one," giggled Julia. She knew of my liking for staying in and reading, for engaging words rather than people. She knew how difficult I found dealing with people.

"Well some of us find it difficult. We're not all like you."

"So who was this friend?"

"This is a good friend. You know responsible, caring."

"A male friend?"

"Yes a male friend."

She looked disappointed.

"He's marvellous." I was almost dramatising my loss, my words drawing sadness in their tone, a reverential tone. "He was involved in an accident. A robbery. The driver of his taxi was killed."

"Oh God!" She made the connection. The shock was clear, but it seemed momentary. It didn't linger long enough for me to get to grips with it. Somehow the control returned. "The killing. The killing in the lane. Oh God I heard about it."

"The lane?"

"The service lane. It happened just behind the house. There's a service lane. For tradesmen. For rubbish. For parking in the garages."

"You heard about it?"

"The robbery? Yes, the police called. And it was in the paper. A taxi, wasn't it? The driver was killed. It's worried the whole neighbourhood. Rocio says criminals are bound to their territory, that geography is important to them. That's why we worry."

I sat still. I suppose I should have asked who Rocio is, but I let the opportunity slip away. So calm, so clear, I thought. Nothing seemed to be forfeited or lost. She actually made it seem that the outrage had affected her, that it had touched her life. All that Rocio stuff. Yet I sensed a slight detachment too. It was in her body language, in her lack of movement. Normally she used her body so well, so expressively, but it seemed listless now. Uninvolved. Unresponsive. I drew on that. I wondered why. Why no gestures? Why no mimes and shrugs? Why did she seem so stiff and difficult?

*

"What do you mean you sent him away? Oh Jesus, hey listen, I need to talk to you. I need to talk to you now before you're left with nothing but bleak hospital afternoons and me. What the hell are you playing at? Eh?"

Popeye. I am used to such outbursts, to the pleasure he derives from my misdemeanours and misadventures. But I am at a loss here. What have I done? I breathe in and look at the white walls and the thriving geranium and at the biography of Meiggs that is on the bed. I open it. To page forty eight. To page sixty four. To my favourite pages.

"Hey!" blasts Popeye. "You listening? Because you need to. Boy do you need to. Is it me? Don't I make myself clear? Don't I make myself understood?"

I am puzzled. I look hard at the words wondering what it is that draws me, why I do not move on to another challenge. There must be someone else. There must be another interesting life to investigate.

"You see you don't respond. I mean just say what you think.... Come on get off of the silence. Hey say something for chrissake."

I still struggle to seize the point. What is he on about? I can tell he is upset, but he cannot just come out with whatever it is that is bothering him. That's not his style. What he wants is for me to discover it, to reveal it as it moves amongst his words and expressions. It's there. I know it's there. It's in those glacial eyes.

"You've sent the shit shirt away you dumbhead."

"That's it, is it? You said to. You bloody said to."

"What do you mean I said to? I say plenty of things, plenty of sensible things, things that you should use to build your life. But what the hell do you do? You screw up. You screw up big."

I stay puzzled. I have followed his words as though they are instructions, guidelines perhaps. I recall them. I check them. Know your enemies, my mind says naming the stiff shirt and applauding the speed of my action. "I did it," I claim.

"Oh yeh you did it alright. You sure as hell did it."

"I identified my enemy."

"Like hell you did."

"I did," I insisted.

"Well then I guess you need to go back to square one and start again. Only this time remember to think, remember to store away all your malign attitudes and just think. You'll see then. No?" He notices the furrows on my face, the frail look that suggests I still do not understand. "OK, OK." He recognises the need to come to my aid. "Look, that shit shirt, I mean for chrissakes, is he the enemy?"

Is he the enemy? Of course he's the enemy. Popeye said so. Didn't he? I try to recall all he said and highlight it. I want to announce it, but it is vague. I decide to let him face it.

"Jesus, he's come all the way from Tranquilee. All the way from that fuckin' island. I mean he's concerned, real concerned."

"But you said..."

"What? What did I say? All I said was that he was your friend, that he painted you a picture. Which he did, yeh? And that he'd put you in hospital. And indirectly he did that too. That's all I said. No way did I say that he was your enemy."

But if it isn't the stiff shirt, then who is it? There is no one else. Not that there has to be anyone. It could just have been bad luck, a sort of being in the wrong place at the wrong time experience. If it wasn't that then I'm stuck because there is no-one else, no-one else that is apart from.... Julia. My mind booms the name. Julia. But the stiff shirt would have known what she was like. He wouldn't have sent me to see her knowing of the danger. I mean they're husband and wife. Isn't that enough? He would have known. Or would he? Modern marriage, independence, I reason. So I try out Julia as the enemy. And I realise the danger, that I know nothing of her, nothing at all. Apart from her beauty and her dancing. How would I get to know her, to understand her? "Understand your enemy," I say to myself, over and over. I come to see that I could grasp an understanding of Julia only through the stiff shirt and I have sent him away. What have I done?, I ask myself. What on earth have I done?

★

"...You know once when I flew to Florida a man from Petro Peru sat by me. He said he liked the plane, that it reminded him of home. I didn't know what he meant. So a few weeks later when I was in Lima I looked him up. Home was Miraflores. Posh Peru. Posh Lima. There were big walls around his house and barbed wire and a guard in a turret and a servant on the driveway dusting down his Mercedes and he was out the back in a courtyard sitting by a swimming pool, watching a video. Just like the plane, he said. And I understood it then. He liked being inside. That's what he meant. He liked being contained. It was safe, secure. Look, what I'm saying is that's the future. That's capitalism's end game. Guns and turrets and videos...."

I talked and talked. About me, about Peru, about capitalism. Hugo slept. He lay still on his bed, the white sheet wrapped around his body up to his chin. I was used to that. It was how he was much of the time. The doctor said it would be. And I had taken to talking through problems with him. Normally that meant Peru's problems, though sometimes I became more personal. Perhaps I said too much then. But it seemed safe, controlled. "And then there's Julia," I'd say, opening up. "My Julia. I am so responsible. I let her go. I let her taste adventure. But she is so nice. She is still so nice. That is her heart. Not this." I cried. The tears were so welcome. They seemed to be breaking my worries up, dispersing them. "I got you wrong. I got her wrong. Perhaps I get everything wrong. Perhaps I'll never know. Never really know. I should. I mean the truth is there. It's in her. Not in her words. They are decoys. I know that.

But it's in her beliefs and perceptions. It's given away in looks. And I should be able to see it. After all she is my sister. I should know her." I shook my head. The relationship seemed so multi-faceted as I spoke, as I teased out reason. "It seems so unbelievable. I mean a girl in a maid's uniform, a girl clutching a teddy bear, singing a song. That teddy bear." Again I shook my head. "She takes it everywhere. It went with her when she went out to play when she was a kid. It goes to school with her. It lives in her teaching bag. And when she gets home it sits on her desk. She's so soft, so sweet....."

★

Thank God he came back. I knew he wouldn't stop visiting, that he would have found some excuse to explain away my anger. My illness probably. The drugs or the trauma. Something covering my reason. He probably thought that I would fall asleep and forget all about my words telling him to go. And now he returns and thinks I am asleep and talks and talks. And he almost says that she did it. He thinks she did it. I can tell. He does. I'm sure.

And she's his sister. His sister! Not his wife. So he lies too. Yet I sense I can disregard that. It carries a sense of insignificance. Sister, wife? She is Julia. My enemy Julia. She shows me how a simple little wife or sister can become hard nosed and dangerous. Julia is moving like that, finding the grace of dance one minute and losing all its poise and measure behind the blast of a gun the next. And I can't follow it. Neither can the stiff shirt. He rambles on about a taxi driver and a government minister. About someone called Jorge. And he talks of death and victims while I almost blush with the recognition that there is a motive beyond robbery, that the suggestion of it being nothing more than bad luck is being swept away. Instead I am a target. I do not understand that. I am Hugo Young. No-one else. Do I look like anybody else? Do I look threatening? It is daft, plainly daft, though he tells me that Julia, my enemy, is nervous and rattled and isolated. Her judgement is flawed by the circumstances. She is vulnerable.

He also talks of coincidences. He mumbles that word a lot. Coincidences. Can I believe it was a coincidence? It could have been. After all I hadn't seen Julia. Not in the alleyway. I know that now.

So much has returned. The shots. The cry from the driver. I can remember that. But I don't think I saw the gunman. Which means it could have been her. But how did she know the car was there? Again I think over the events. I can recall calling at the house, leaving the taxi in the lane, being told I'm sorry there's no-one of that name here, the terse reply, the door opening and closing, the maid smiling, me knocking on the door again, shouting "Damn you!" as I walked away. But I didn't see the gunman. I'm sure of that. Because I can recall the alley too. The back entrances to the houses. So perhaps she could have hidden in one of those doorways or behind some of the garbage that was accumulating. It must have been collection day. I remember the bags, the containers. They were everywhere. There was a dog scavenging. And someone chased it off. Yes, somebody chased it off. So there was somebody there......

The stiff shirt goes away and returns. Again he talks and talks. And I am focused now. I want to learn about his visit to Julia. I want revelations. But he goes on again about the past and the future and I smell his gum, thinking how he doesn't bother to remove it now. It is as if, to him, I'm not really here, as though I no longer demand a sense of respect. Rather I am something remote, something that doesn't cling or interfere, something that allows him to hold my hand and call me a beautiful boy. He starts on that again.

"You searched her out. How could I have doubted you? Shit! Shit!" he exclaims. "How could I have got you so wrong?"

Again he embarrasses me. I open my eyes and gaze towards him before allowing the look to fade away. He has his head in his hands.

"She says you didn't call."

Lies. Damn lies. She is lying.

"And I don't know what to believe. I just don't know what to believe. She hides the truth. Understand?..... Look what I'm saying is I have been hurt before. There are things that go on in Julia's life that I cannot tap into. There are things that I don't want to know about, things that would frighten me. Yet she can be so nice. I mean when she saw me in the doorway of the house in Avenida Arce she laughed and smiled and took me to her room and sang to me. She sat there singing and crying. And she asked about Chuschi and our parents. She was so concerned. So how can that person, that warm considerate person do all these awful things? Because it must have been her. She must have been on the photo. They must have recognised her...."

Photo? What photo? Come on. But he is quiet. His head down on his hands. He sits still. What is he thinking? What on earth is he thinking? I need to know.

3

I wash myself in the mornings now. I take off my pyjama top and fill the sink full of water. The water gurgles occasionally. The pipes play, vibrating, drawing nurses who seek the source of the sound.

"I'm OK. Thank you." I have to say.

"If you –"

"If I need anything? Sure, I'll call." I smile. The nurse backs away and I wash, wetting my lank blond hair, which I rub with a towel quickly. I will not let it dry flat. I shave too. And I plan. I have it now. My plan. What I am to do. How I will deal with my enemy and sort out the stiff shirt, how I will put him right.

Popeye laughs.

"So what's so funny?"

"You're gonna get her, aren't you? That's what this is about. Hugo Young, Hugo Young, Hugo Young, yeh? It's like that fuckin' Frenchman, the man from Chincheros. It's like that all over again."

"What are you saying?"

"She's replaced him."

"Know your enemy," I respond, considering how Popeye seems rather cool over the issue. I expect more of him. I expect support. The lack of enthusiasm surprises me.

"You've nailed him and now you're gonna nail her. Hey you're like an assassin. You know that? Boy if she knew what she was up against. *Andar pisandro huevos* as they say in Spain. She's walking on eggs. That's what she's doing. Shit who'd be her? I mean she's on the run. In La Paz. And you turn up. On the doorstep. I mean what the fuck is she supposed to think. A stranger on her doorstep. No explanation. Just an "Oh hello I'm from Puno, I'm a friend of your husband's". And because she's clever she knows she's not married. So what the hell is goin' on? No wonder she shot at you. Hey you got off lightly."

"OK." I dismiss the intervention.

"And you know what that means, that OK? It means, oh Popeye I take your point, but I'm still gonna nail her, because nobody tries it on with Hugo Young. So what you gonna do now? You got any idea? You got a plan?"

"Of course I've got a plan. Don't you know? I'm going to get the stiff shirt to turn in Julia."

"You're gonna what? No way!" laughs Popeye. "You'll never be able to do that. The stiff shirt turn in his sister? No way."

"I'm going to get the stiff shirt to turn in Julia."

"That's it, is it? The end game. The big plan."

★

I needed a plan. I knew that. I sat in the corridor that led to Hugo's room. I stared at the floor, at the black and white tiles, at the scuff marks on the leather. Then up at the wall. At a painting. A print. An abstract, de Kooning-like, late de Kooning. It was conciliatory, calming. It made me tap my feet on the red carpet that surrounded the chair. It made me close my eyes.

"Hey how are you?..." "You're late...." "He's much better today..."

The observations and comments of passing nurses broke into the conversation with Julia that was replaying in my mind. The nurses always smiled. They always moved quite coltishly. I observed them. I wished I could see Julia as clearly. My mind played tricks. Values, beliefs, opinions weighed in and distorted my image of her. "Shit!" I stifled a curse and a grunt and got up and moved along the corridor towards room H3, Hugo's room. He was standing up looking out of the window when I opened the door.

"Hey isn't it a great day?"

The enthusiasm shook me. He stayed by the window, his head craning a little, looking up and then dropping down. "Not much of a view. I mean the suburbs. The road, the houses, you know, but it's bright, so bright. When I got up there was snow on that roof over there."

"It snowed overnight," I remarked. "It's that time of year. Seventy degrees in the sun, but cold enough for snow overnight. I like the climate here."

"Oh so do I, so do I," he agreed. "And you know what?" He turned now. I saw his hair had been combed and brushed down. It looked as though it had been cut. "I'm remembering more and more. It's all coming back. They're astonished, the doctors. They think it's down to you."

"Me?"

"They think you've triggered the recall. And I think they may be right. I mean as soon as I saw you I remembered the letter."

"The letter I sent with the address?"

"Yes. I remembered the Hotel Milton. The foyer. I opened the letter and thought yes, I'll go. I'll go and see her. I didn't think twice about it. I went straight away. I got a taxi. The driver was called Jorge."

"And the crash? You remember the crash?"

He nodded.

"The attack?"

"Sort of. I mean what I saw of it. Actually what I heard of it. The sounds seemed more important. It was the sounds that told me something was wrong."

"So you remember calling at the house?"

Hugo paused. He sat down on the bed. "I don't know," he said, his voice hushed and concerned. "Yes. Yes I think I do. Yes the house. Some woman answered."

"Julia?"

"I don't think so. No. Some other woman. Another maid. I asked for Julia. The maid who answered said there's no-one of that name here. She turned me away. But I insisted. I said I know Julia Norville Perez is here. I said the taxi driver who brought me here knows she lives here. Should I go and get him?, I said. He's mistaken, she said. As cool as that."

"And the car? The shots?"

Hugo gave me a dark look. I was asking a lot. I was pushing him back into the scene. He seemed to take his time as though he were stepping slowly and surely around the alleyway and the car and the shots. "I remember the alley," he confessed. "And I remember getting into the taxi. I was thinking. I was absorbed in something else.

Can't remember what. Perhaps it was the dog."

"What dog?"

"A scavenging dog. It was rubbish day. There were bags everywhere."

"Did you see anyone?"

"Someone shooed the dog. A girl. A little way down the lane."

"A girl?"

"A woman. She was in uniform. A maid's uniform, you know?"

"Would you recognise Julia in a uniform? I mean dancing, yes. You've seen photos of her dancing. But as a maid? Are you sure you'd recognise her?"

The question penetrated. Hugo raised an eyebrow, shrugged and smiled. Then he looked away, out through the window, at the sun, at the sky. "Can't say for certain. I mean this girl was fiddling with rubbish, putting out bags. I don't think it was Julia. No I didn't get excited and think it's Julia. No I dismissed her. I paid no attention to her. It wasn't Julia."

"You sure?"

"It wasn't Julia."

"Do you remember anything about her? Absolutely anything. About her dress. About her face. About the way she moved. Did she speak?" I sounded a little desperate now. I needed to eliminate her, to find something in her appearance or behaviour that indicated it wasn't Julia.

"Dark shoes," said Hugo. "A sort of house coat over a blouse and skirt. Dark hair. A watch, yes a watch. She looked at her wrist, at the time."

"Good," I said encouraging him. But there was nothing there. Julia had dark hair. She also had a watch. But so did most of the maids in southern La Paz. Few had been eliminated by Hugo's words.

"You remember a lot about this girl."

"I suppose I do. It's because we waited there. I mean we didn't move. I made him wait because I couldn't decide what to do. Should I go back and knock the door again? I couldn't decide whether I had done enough."

"Oh I think you had," I said encouragingly.

Hugo shrugged. "I don't know. I still don't know. Anyhow we sat there in the alley. I watched the girl come out of the doorway and move a bag. Then she stood there. She mooched around. She was forty yards away. No more. But she didn't look up. She didn't look our way. Isn't that strange?" It seemed as though the peculiarity of the observation had just come to him. "She should have looked, shouldn't she? I mean if you put your rubbish out every week and this one week a taxi is just sitting there, you'd look. I'm sure you would. I know I would. But she just got on with her job. And I thought nothing of it. I looked away. And the next thing, you know the next thing I knew was that the engine had started and we were moving away."

There was something remarkable there. I tried to discern it. "And you hadn't said anything?"

"About going? No. The driver just took it upon himself. I tried to stop him. I reached forward and said, hey just a minute. But I never finished my words. There were shots. The metal of the car was singing. The driver's hands came off the wheel. I ducked down."

"Anything else?" I realised that I was none the wiser, that all the possibilities still existed. "Anything? Anything about the girl's behaviour."

"You think the girl fired the shots?"

"She was there. Nobody's come forward. I mean why hasn't she? What's she hiding?"

A lightness came over the Englishman's face. He had recalled something. I sensed it.

"Well.... actually there is something," he chuckled. "But I don't know whether it's worth mentioning. It's silly. It's really silly."

"Come on."

"Well the only other thing I remember........ I didn't see a gun. It didn't cross my mind to look for a gun..... I mean this is so strange. She turned around and was in profile. And I saw it in her right hand. A teddy bear. She put it down alongside her. That's strange isn't it. I must be imagining it, don't you think? It must be the amnesia. The doctor said it would play tricks."

I have to see her now. I have to be blunt, forthright. I have to confront her with what I know. With my doubts. My fears. But why didn't he recognise her? How could he have looked away, convincing himself that it wasn't her? When it was. Julia. I knew it. She would make a good assassin. She would treat it like a dance, as something to learn, as something to polish and perfect. She would have thought it through, building in the possibilities of this and that and drawing up contingencies, which mainly involved getting closer and closer and firing more and more shots.

But on this occasion it hadn't come to that. Four or five shots and the car hit the bags of rubbish and rubbed along a wall. Four or five shots and the driver had a hole in his head and there was blood spurting everywhere. Hugo would have felt it in his hair as he leant forward. He may have thought it was his own blood as it stuck to him and trickled down his face. Get out, get out, he would have thought when the car smashed into a barrier. "Out," he would have said after the car had overturned.

★

I stand by the window. I am watching the sky and the hospital entrance and the ornamental shrubs and the birds and the dust. I am watching everything. I am fidgeting and fussing, rearranging things in my mind, disciplining myself to follow my scheme, to stick to it. I assess how it is going. I sit down on the edge of the bed. Again I smile.

"Someone's happy," remarks Popeye."What's up with you? Gee I hate guys who can't find words."

I laugh.

"See? Gee that sucks. I mean you ask a simple question and what do you get in return?"

"Sorry."

"Oh don't mind me. Hey are you gonna be civil and let me in on the funny."

"I'm just thinking over my conversation with the stiff shirt. And don't say shit shirt."

"I'll say what I like. Shit shirt. There. OK? Shit shirt."

"Oh come on."

"What's wrong with that? There's nothing wrong with that because that's how I see him. I mean shirt and flannels and jacket. No style. No idea about how to look. Because looking is important. It says so much. And when it comes to him he just hasn't got it. I look at him and what do I say? Shit, that's what I say."

I wonder how to react. I fall back onto the bed.

"You see?" asks Popeye, not used to my behaving so freely, so openly. "Hey you listening to me? What's wrong with you?"

"Me? I'm fine. I'm just thinking."

"Thinking?"

"Yes. I'm wondering how far to take it."

"You take it all the way," Popeye says quite assertively. "No half measures, eh?"

"He's seeing her tonight."

"Who is?"

I give him a long look. I wonder if his mind is elsewhere, back in his own century, back with Davila or Balta or his brother John. Who is. The words roll over in my mind. Who is. They make me see the obvious sometimes flits around him. Or he avoids it. Or he is playing with me, coaxing out more detail than necessary, details that aid decisions about what to do and how and when to do it.

"The stiff shirt is seeing Julia tonight. Well this afternoon, later this afternoon."

"He's told you?"

"Yes. He came back late last night. Said he'd phoned her, that he needs to see her. He's meeting her at "Vinnie's" at four thirty. Is she in for a surprise."

"Hey you know what? You're like that guy who picked up that wad and chased after the guy who dropped it, the guy in La Paz, you know the guy who came back and offered you those counterfeit dollars, you know that?"

"A con man? No."

"Hey, why not? This is a scam, yeh. You're getting enjoyment out of tricking this guy. He's gonna turn in his sister for chrissake. That's a hell of a thing to do."

"His sister nearly killed me."

"OK." Popeye seems to concede that there is a degree of provocation. "So what happens next? You feed him more nonsense. You tell him that you remember Julia?"

"There won't be any need for that. He knows that." I smile. Popeye has tried to invoke a sense of guilt and shame and sympathy. But it hasn't worked. I feel in control. Hugo Young, Hugo Young, Hugo Young. I know the stiff shirt's image of his sister has been tilted, that the reality of killing, of unnecessary deaths and an attempt to kill me has worked its way through his mind. He would despise that. He would always have despised it. I had done nothing to change that. What I had done was confirm that his sister was perpetrating such crimes, that his sister was dangerous and untrustworthy, that his sister had lied, that she had kidded him along and played on her image of being creative and lovely and essentially nice. That image had nestled in his mind for too long. Now it had gone.

5

"It's only me."

"Only me. Who's me? That brother of mine? How are you?"

"Fine I'm just checking you're OK."

"Why shouldn't I be? Where you speaking from?"

She always asked that. She was always worried that I would speak from my hotel and that the phone would be tapped.

"Where am I? Let's see?" I turned and stared at the street sellers, at the traffic. "I don't know exactly. The town hall's a hundred yards away and the law courts are just up the road. I guess I'm half way between them. I'm in one of those communications places. I think they're mainly for travellers, you know? Listen I could send you a fax if you prefer. They're right up to date here."

"You don't change."

"What do you mean?" I said a little harshly.

"You know."

You know what? Neither do you. You are a killer. You are a liar. You are a manipulator. You are a shit, a total shit.

"You there? You're thinking aren't you?" added Julia in such a way that indicated she was used to my pauses for thought. "Look I'll see you later."

"That's why I'm ringing."

"You can't make it?"

"No, no I'm just checking you remember the time."

"And the place?"

"What?"

"The time and the place. What you need for a meeting."

"And?"

"Vinnie's. Four thirty."

"Can we make it quarter to five? I've promised the Englishman I'd call in and see him this afternoon. It's a fair walk from the hospital."

"How is he?"

"Hugo? Oh much the same. Still sleepy. Still confused."

"Quarter to five then." She ended the conversation.

Replacing the receiver I went over what my mind had considered. That was much more important than the spoken words. All they managed was to offer me the opportunity of giving Julia one last chance to explain herself. A place and a time. What was needed for a meeting. It was what was needed for an ambush too. Or an assassination. I could set her up. If I wanted to. If I thought she deserved it.

I was confused when I went into the hospital. I had to sit in the corridor again, the corridor with the tiles and the de Kooning, the tiles as wild as the painting with their scratch marks and scuff marks. "You don't change." The phone call's phrase recurring, together with my mind's response. "You know what? Neither do you." But perhaps I should change. Perhaps I should reveal her to the world. Perhaps I should strip away the dance steps and let the gun shots ring out.

When I walked into Hugo's room, he was standing by the window.

"You're in time," he announced.

"Time?"

"Yes. It's three isn't it?"

"It's three."

"Well come here." He beckoned me to his side. "Now watch this." I looked at his eyes, at his smiling eyes and followed his gaze towards the garden beyond the hospital's entrance. "You see this is what you pay good money for. This is what Airbus Industrie and the French government are handing over francs for."

I looked out. The garden was lush. Palms and ferns intermingled. There was a perfect balance and use of space. It was so well planned.

"It's on its way," promised the Englishman. He held up his wrist so he could view the garden and the time. "This is special," he said synchronising the final word with a spurt of water that flew upwards out of a hidden nozzle. A spray of water silvered the scene as other nozzles joined in. "Isn't it brilliant?"

"Very impressive."

"Twice a day."

"Another one later?"

"No earlier. At about half past eleven." His eyes stayed on the shooting water. "I didn't expect you," he remarked. "Oh look at that." One of the nozzles began shooting water at intervals.

"Thought I'd call in on the way. What does this cost?"

"A fortune. An absolute fortune..... On the way?"

"I'm seeing Julia."

"Oh yes, I forgot. I meant to look for that note you gave me to give to her, you know the one you gave me on the island. Thought it would finally be delivered. But I couldn't find it. Shame. Still it will turn up. I'm sure of that."

I looked at Hugo squarely. He seemed so innocent, so unaware of what he had told me. A teddy bear.

"You OK?" asked Hugo.

"I'm fine, I'm really fine," I answered slowly.

I had my plan. I lived for two hours with it. I liked to place it, to put it in the context of the restaurant where we were to meet and eat. "Vinnie's". It was Jewish. The menu was printed in Hebrew on one side and in English on the other, though I doubted the need for a menu because it always seemed full of regulars. Everyone seemed to know each other. There were so many hugs and embraces that on my first visit by the end of the starter I felt alienated. I had been about to leave when my eyes caught sight of the chocolate cake. It was more like a trifle than a cake. It was a slithering thin layer of delight. It was wonderful. I skipped the main course and tasted it and smiled looking away from the people towards some drawings on the wall. A waiter told me they were self portraits of customers. Dates told of when they had been eating the chocolate cake.

"We whitewash it two or three times a year," the waiter had commented bringing me a second slice of chocolate cake. "You know people come back here five years later and they want to see their drawing. They think it will still be here." He pulled a face that emphasised their stupidity. "So before we whitewash it now we take a photo. They are happy if they can see a photo."

The restaurant was perfect for a meeting. Or an assassination. Or an ambush. It was up a flight of steps on the first floor of a corner building. There were two entrances: one on a main road and one on a side road. The entrance from the main road had a phone booth, a dark cupboard of a booth around a twist in a dead-end corridor. And above it, on the first floor, the restaurant itself comprised three rooms. It was open plan but two of the areas were small and intimate with just two or three tables. And reconnaissance had told me that at four thirty Vinnie's was quiet. A lull between lunch and dinner.

Julia was there when I arrived. I was surprised at that. She wasn't renowned for punctuality. She was usually late, so late that normally when she appeared I would have to count to ten and smile and remind myself that she is my sister and that I love her and that love requires tolerance and understanding. Besides I understood her lateness. I knew she checked things over, that she would look into faces and buildings and get a feel for an area. Perhaps now, her new life allowed her to feel safe and secure. In a way she was no longer Julia Norville Perez, teacher and revolutionary. She was free of that. Liberated.

"Let's go round the front."

"What?" She was sitting in the main room. A Jewish woman, who had followed me up the stairs, was walking passed her towards an adjacent table.

"I like the window seat," I explained.

"You like looking out?"

"Yes. Sometimes it's better than looking in."

"You're crazy. You know that? My crazy brother."

"And I have to phone. There's a clock in the other room. I have to phone at five."

"Phone?"

"The hospital. I've got to confirm that I've got the pills. Hey you remember when I had to buy you pills. For your hand."

"He's still in a coma?" Julia disregarded the nostalgia.

"The Englishman? He's conscious now and again, but he drifts away." I shrug. "What I'm saying is there's very little improvement. So they're experimenting. And there's one drug the doctors haven't got. I've got it now. I pulled my hand out of my pocket and revealed a packet of pills. They were white pills, aspirins, though to Julia they were the pills the doctors had requested. "It's four forty eight now. We've twelve minutes."

As the minutes passed I became resigned to losing Julia. Losing her? Yes, it was like that. It was a religious feeling almost. Like a loss of faith. Like the exclusion Julia and I came to feel when we were little, when our father talked God and we would kick each other under the table.

I placed Julia by the window and told her to sit round so that she could see out. I ordered the chocolate cake and coffees, an espresso for me and a milky coffee for her. "It's the only place in La Paz you can get an espresso," I remarked.

"God you're choosy," remarked Julia. "You and your espresso. All we need now is a bit of Brahms. You still like Brahms?"

"Yes." I wondered what else to add.

"And that big brass sound. That thumping sound. What was that?"

I frowned. She had never before discussed my musical tastes. Big brass sound? Thumping? I ran through the possibilities thinking how she was right: I loved brass, heavy, strong sonorous brass. Bruckner's ninth. Shostakovitch. Most of Shostakovitch. And Leos Janacek. Taras Bulba. And the Sinfonietta. That was it. The Sinfonietta. I hummed the opening.

"Yes." Julia recognised it. "Even I came to like that," she admitted. I hadn't known that.

We talked then. We talked about Chuschi and in hushed tones about Sendero and the way it was functioning. That allowed me again to ask about the shooting. "You've not heard anything?"

"About the shooting? No. No one has. We're all afraid. We go out in pairs now. I go out with Rocio."

"On the street?"

"On the street. In the alley."

"The alley behind the house?"

"Yes."

"You go there often?"

"The alley?" she laughed. "Why should I go there? Oh sometimes I put out the rubbish. Sometimes I have to check the car, clean it out. Apart from that no. Oh sometimes there are deliveries."

"How many staff are there in your house?"

"What? What is this?"

"I just want to know. I'm interested. I thought perhaps one of them may have seen something."

"Nobody saw anything. We saw nothing. We heard nothing. OK?"

"Oh it's just the police keep asking about Avenida Arce. They can't work out why he was in the alleyway."

"Is he gay? Some people say gays use the alleyway. No-one's ever seen anyone there, but you know it's the sort of place they use."

"He's not gay."

"How do you know?"

I shrugged. "And nobody called at your house? I mean just before he was shot at?"

"Nobody. The police asked us that when they called."

"You told them?"

"Yes. We told them. The people in the other houses did too apparently."

"The other houses?"

"The police called at all the houses."

"I'd better make that call."

I said it so purposefully. Yet going down the steps to the small booth I felt so alone. I was losing so much. I was losing a child, a child in my mind, a child always laughing and playing and talking, a cheeky beautiful child.

I leant back against the wood of the booth. I reminisced. I

thought of the mornings when my father took Julia and me with him up the hill to see the sunrise. I was like a second in command then. It was I who walked with Julia, who told her stories, who humoured her when she slowed down and moaned with tiredness. It was I who occupied her when we reached the summit and waited for the sunrise. I would make her do her *k'intus* which involved bundling together coca leaves. The bundles were needed for religious ceremonies. It was I who discarded the broken leaves. It was I who discarded the folded leaves. It was I who reminded her that the shiny sides of leaves had to be touching each other. "Twinkle on twinkle," she'd say. That was how she'd remember it. And "cloudy on cloudy" for the dull sides. And when the sun rose and its rays touched us on our foreheads it was I who told her that we give praise to the sun and for the sun. To and for. The old and the new. The indian and the Catholic. It was always me. Never my mother. Never my father. Always me. Always José. So I am the one who has to pick up the phone. I am the one who has to stop her killing.

I dialled the police station's number. A voice answered. I shook. I rubbed the bridge of my nose. I took the receiver away from my face. I looked at it. I stared at the mouthpiece. I heard the "Hello, hello," that the policeman was uttering. I was breathing heavily, champing my teeth. I was biting hard like an animal in pain.

I put the phone down.

I slid to the floor in the booth. Music was coming from the cafe. A bass sound was coming through the floorboards. I recognised the rhythm. I hummed the melody. I had hummed it before. Recently. On the island. In the courtyards. I recalled the steps. The steps I had missed. The steps I had got wrong. They drew me to my feet. They drew me to the stairs.

Julia had moved back into the main room of the cafe. She was dancing. I watched the slow push of her feet, the slouch of a shoulder, the swing of the other shoulder. The movements gathered momentum. They were tied to the music and the waiters responded, pushing back chairs, sliding tables, creating space for Julia to move into. I watched her as closely as they did. I saw the intricacies that I had missed. She was moving forwards. Her back was to me. But as she began to turn, something intervened. Why are you watching?, a voice in my mind asked. What are you doing?

I pulled away. I couldn't make eye contact with her. Something had changed. Respect, I thought. The mutual respect that had nourished our relationship had gone. Now there was distaste. She could dance and kill. I couldn't accommodate that. So I backed away. I turned and moved slowly down the stairs. I could hear the waiters laughing and shouting encouragement and clapping. Julia was entertaining, being lovely, doing what she was best at. And I could not look. That hurt. It made me bustle by two policemen who were talking by the entrance to the cafe. "Sorry, sorry," I said waving an apology. I imagined they were considering a broken down lorry that was blocking the road. Its front wheels had sunk into the mud. A crowd had gathered. I stared at the back of the lorry at a red plastic bag that was fixed to its tail and was acting as a hazard warning signal.

Suddenly I cried. I cried and cried, the noise of police sirens covering my sobbing.

part nine

JOSE AND HUGO

1

"You back. Ah...... Thank God for tourists...... Thank God for tourists....." Sebastian was more animated than ever. He fussed, moving about in front of me, trying to take my suitcase and then pointing at a chair. He ran to the kitchen, brought me a bottle of coca cola and panicked. He had forgotten a glass. "Oh..." he buzzed. His warmth reassured me; I had been right to return to the island; I had been right to think it was the obvious place to go, that it was where I had friends, where I could sit and relax and think over my behaviour which had made me feel depressed and distraught. While he was searching for a glass, I thought over the way I had slipped away from Vinnie's and had returned to my hotel and packed and headed for the bus station. I had left without saying goodbye to the Englishman. I regretted that.

"I know you come. I know you come." Sebastian said excitedly rushing towards me with the glass. He was trying to explain his presence in the upper courtyard when I arrived. I had looked over the wall and there he had been, standing by the plastic table and chairs. "You walk..." Sebastian strutted and pointed at his feet. His heels hit the ground.

"I walk like that?"

"Yes."

"I don't."

"Yes, yes...." He attempted the movement again.. It was a heavy walk, exaggerated with his heels clipping, making a noise. He broke into a laugh and gripped my hand. "Ah... Good, good..... *Alimpunjay tata.*"

"*Alimpunjay tata. Pacharem cama.*"

Sebastian seemed delighted. He smiled and smiled. "You want tea? Yertil?.... I get Dina. Dina!.... Thank God for tourists....."

I watched him chase away. I liked all that. The exuberance. The warmth. It allowed me to relax. I sat down at the plastic table, pushing my suitcase to my side. I took a deep breath. I sighed. It was a shame I hadn't been able to meet Julia here; the environment would have helped us to get on. It may even have reformed Julia. Nobody could think of guns and blood here. Nobody.

I became edgy then. I tidied up a cup and saucer that some visitor had left on the table. But that wasn't enough. I wanted to investigate everything. My hut. The Englishman's hut. Sebastian's hut. The kitchen. The field. The animal pens. For some reason I crossed through the courtyards and went there first. I stared in at Domingo. I sat on a wall by her pen.

"*Hola!*" I waved at Alejandro who was working in the field. He raised his digging stick in the air. Even the quiet Alejandro who gave little away seemed pleased to see me. It made me smile. "And how are you?" I said, turning back towards Domingo. "You better?" Domingo the pretty fawn coloured calf was curled up in the shade. "Rebecca is *frio*," I added remembering Hugo's words on Christmas Eve when we were being told about Domingo's illness. "It's because we've drunk her milk," I recalled him saying on the way to the pueblo. "Hugo," I said, shaking my head, wondering how he was, whether his amnesia was clearing.

"José!.... José!" The cry was from the main path. It woke me up. I knew who it was immediately. I recognised the tone and the level of excitement. I recognised the footsteps too, the scampering. I heard doors opening and closing. I heard the familiar tap on wood and the accompanying cries that grew louder and louder. "Ah," Hernando sighed as he turned the corner and saw me lying on the wall. "How are you? How are you? Are you OK José? How did it go? Did I win the wager? Eh José, eh? Hey you look fine," he added before I had a chance to react. "Good, good. Now any news? Any happenings? Any developments? Any events? How is the Englishman?"

"He's fine. He'll make a full recovery."

"A full recovery. Oh I'm so pleased José. Hey are you sleepy?" He sensed a stifled yawn as I drew my legs off the wall and moved them towards the ground. I shook my head.

"So he was fine when you left him, eh José? And did you sort out the mystery?"

"What mystery?"

"Whether he saw her? I mean could he remember?"

"No, no he's still suffering from the amnesia. He can't remember anything about the week or so prior to the incident."

"Oh dear. So we don't know. Oh well...." Hernando seemed to deal with the disappointment philosophically. He shook his shoulders and nodded. I smiled. I wanted to move things on, to move away from my lies. "And Julia? I mean she'd know, wouldn't she José?"

"She was away."

"Away?"

"I didn't see her. She was on holiday."

"Oh José. I'm sorry. Anyhow the Englishman."

"He's had a rough time."

"But he remembered you, eh José?"

"Yes he did. The doctors were pleased at that. I think they thought it may jog his memory."

"But it didn't?"

"No. It had little effect. It just made him talk about the island, about his times here."

Hernando folded his arms and fell back against the wall. He took in all I had said, formulating new possibilities. "Hey I've got something to show you José. You wait. You wait." He pushed himself away from the wall and began to move away in the direction of the courtyards. "One minute, one minute..."

"How did you know I was back?" I asked.

"How did I know? Hey José this is Taquile. There are no secrets here. You should know that. Word gets round, eh? And when I heard about your return...." He raised his voice as he disappeared through the gate that led into the courtyard. "....when I was told you are here I went to my hut to get something, something that I was given yesterday. Only yesterday.... It's here somewhere.... I left it in my bag. Ah."

He returned, his fingers grasping a newspaper. "There's a photo I want you to see. Page four, page four."

"A photo?" I was intrigued. I accepted the newspaper.

"Yes you'll see. A big photo."

"Julia!" I gasped. "How did you know?"

"The photo you gave to the Englishman. You showed it to me. I remember. I remember faces, eh José. It's all the travelling back and fore, all the boat journeys. I remember faces. I saw that face and I thought Julia. I thought that's Julia."

And it was. I scanned it, every inch of it. And I couldn't believe what accompanied it, the story related that Julia Norville Perez had been taken prisoner in La Paz and that the police had checked the bullets that killed Peruvian minister of state Enrique Valquez and the taxi driver who was killed in southern La Paz and that they had concluded that the bullets came from the same weapon, a weapon found in Julia's possession. In her possession! Does that mean she carried it round with her? Like her teddy bear, I thought. Does that mean she had it in "Vinnie's", that she had it while I was talking to her, while she danced? Oh God.

"Come on José," urged Hernando, demanding words.

"It's a bit of a shock seeing Julia."

"OK, OK."

I read on about the other unsolved terrorist attacks that were being investigated, how the Peruvian army and police were liaising with the Bolivian authorities and about the foreign national who was involved in the incident in southern La Paz, how he was due to fly back to Europe tomorrow.

"José?"

"It's err...." I stalled. I wondered what to say."It's about a festival. She was the star."

"Oh she's a pretty girl."

"Yes she is. I mean when she dances she is. She won all the prizes....." I read on about the police operation and the arrest. The account suggested that Julia was arrested at Vinnie's. "What!" I exclaimed.

"There is something wrong?"

"No, no. It's the prize. It's a big prize."

"More than is on our wager?" laughed Hernando. "Eh José?"

"Yes..." I smiled and read on about the police reacting to a tip off. A tip off from.... "No...."

"What José?"

A tip off from me, from Miss Norville Perez's brother as the report puts it. Her brother who has been missing since giving a talk in Lima on December eight.

"What is it José?"

322

"I think I'm tired. It's a long trip La Paz to here."

"Hey I don't think, do I? Look I'll come back. I'll let you rest and I'll return. What do you think, tomorrow José?"

I kept the paper. I returned to the upper courtyard and the plastic table and chairs and I drank a cup of Yertil. "Police received a call from Mr Perez at four forty nine p.m......" I read the story out loud. "That cannot be. I was with Julia at four forty nine. I rang at five o'clock." Somehow I had convinced myself that my call had been traced, that the police knew it was me, that my heavy breaths and long tears had been enough to identify me and that in some wonderful way they had put two and two together. The powers of detection, I thought, widening the realms of possibility. "But no.... What am I saying? I know I didn't talk to the police. I tried but I couldn't do it. I mean I should have. I should have turned her in. I should have."

My mind raced ahead, remembering that we should have met at four thirty, that I had phoned her to ask if we could meet up slightly later, at four forty five. The change in time allowed me to visit Hugo on my way to see her. She had agreed. I remembered her agreeing; she was impatient on the phone.

"So what are they saying? What are they saying?" I sat back. I took a long sip of tea. I saw it then. I saw that they were saying what should have been the truth. I should have split on her. I should have turned her in. But I hadn't. It wasn't me.

"She'll know that," I said out loud. "She'll work out the times. She'll know I was with her when that phone call was made. She'll get word to them......" Them was Sendero. I knew I was in trouble if they read reports like this, that they would come after me, that they would find me, that they would interrogate me, that they may not believe me, that they could kill me. I needed to get away.

★

2

"So what do you think?"

"What do I think? Oh boy."

I am showing Popeye the newspaper. The report on Julia's capture emphasises that I have won the wager, that I have succeeded in turning the stiff shirt against Julia.

"That's amazing. It's exactly as you said, yeh?"

"Yes it is," I say proudly.

"It sure is. Hey how, how did you do it? Shit that man, ol' stiff shirt, the one thing that was clear about him was that he was loyal. God was he loyal. He loved his sister. He respected her, yeh he respected flesh and blood, family. You could see that. So how the hell...."

"Split loyalties."

"Eh?"

"Split loyalties." I sit on the bed. I am packing for a taxi ride to the airport and a flight with Aerolineas Argentina to Buenos Aires before an onward flight to Paris via Madrid. I have been relieved of the Varig negotiations: Gunter is going to deal with them on his own.

"You saying he chose you?"

"Me? God no. He chose non-violence. That's what he chose. He chose to stop some of the killing."

Popeye looks perplexed. He reconsiders what I have said. He recoils at the news, shaking his head. "So he turned her in. Gee that's a hell of a thing to do. Can you believe it?"

"What do you mean?" I tap the paper. "He did it. It says so here...." I place the last pair of socks that had been stored in a bedside cabinet in my case. I close the case.

"So where is he? Where the hell is he? I mean the guy will need help. You know that? He'll need some counselling."

"You think?"

"Oh God yes. The last thing he'll want is to be alone. He's turned his sister in for chrissake, his own fuckin' sister. Jesus! And it's not just that."

"It isn't?" I click the clasps of the case shut and turn the combination lock.

"God no. Listen, he's a dead man. She'll have friends. She's a terrorist isn't she? Don't you see? He'll be looking over his shoulder wondering where the hell they are. And one day they'll be there. You mark my words."

"Another wager?" I ask, emphasising my superiority. The words cut into Popeye. He looks startled, surprised perhaps by my coolness and control.

"Hey that's good. That's funny. Real funny. Yeh."

"Funny?"

"Yeh. You're so quick now. I mean back there."

"Back where?"

"Chincheros."

"Where?"

"You know. The Frenchman, the man in Chincheros, the man in the church, the fuckin' church....."

I ignore Popeye.

"Where you ran, when you got on the bus and you shit yourself." He laughs. "You fuckin' shit yourself. You know? Yeh course you do, but you've come through."

"I've what?"

"Come through."

"Yes I have." I pick up the case. I look around. I check nothing is left. No clothes. No paper. No pens. No documents relating to the Varig deal. I check the bed. I look under the bed. I check the cabinet and the table with the kettle and the sachets and the plant. Nothing. "OK," I say.

"We going?"

"Ah the newspaper. You finished with it?"

"Guess so. What a story. Hey what do I owe you? I mean gee a bet is a bet. There's got to be something on it. Hell that's what it's all about. So how much did we say? Eh?"

I begin to walk towards the door.

"Hey come on, how much?" repeats Popeye.

"You owe me nothing," I say opening the door.

"Hey where you going? Hugo? Hugo!"

The corridor is longer than I imagined. My shoes squeak on the floor tiles which are black and white and worn. They would only be found in a hospital. Like the plain cream walls.

I reach a desk. A woman is speaking quickly. She is on the phone. As I pass, the light provided by a nearby window emphasises her smile. She waves. I nod. The phone clicks as she replaces the receiver. I am beyond her, but her voice follows me.

"Bye mister .... mister err? ....." She forgets my name.

I do not look back. I stride forward. "Hugo Young, Hugo Young, Hugo Young," I say.

ACKNOWLEDGMENTS

I am indebted to Watt Stewart's 1946 biography *Henry Meiggs, Yankee Pizarro*. I am also indebted to the following authors and books: *Shining Path of Peru*, edited by David Scott Palmer; *Peru: Time of Fear*, by Deborah Poole and Gerardo Rénique; *Peru under Garcia: An Opportunity Lost*, by John Crabtree; *The Peru Reader*, edited by Orin Starn, Carlos Ivan Degregori and Robin Kirk.

I am grateful to the Arts Council of Wales for their award of a Writer's Bursary, to Helen Sinclair for her close reading of the early drafts of the book, to Carmin Azurin, Third Secretary in the Peruvian Diplomatic Service for her advice regarding sourcing materials, and, above all, to the Peruvian people for their hospitality during my extended visits in 1984 and 1997.